THE COMPLETE CASES
OF MR. MADDOX, VOLUME 2

T. T. FLYNN

THE COMPLETE CASES OF
MR.

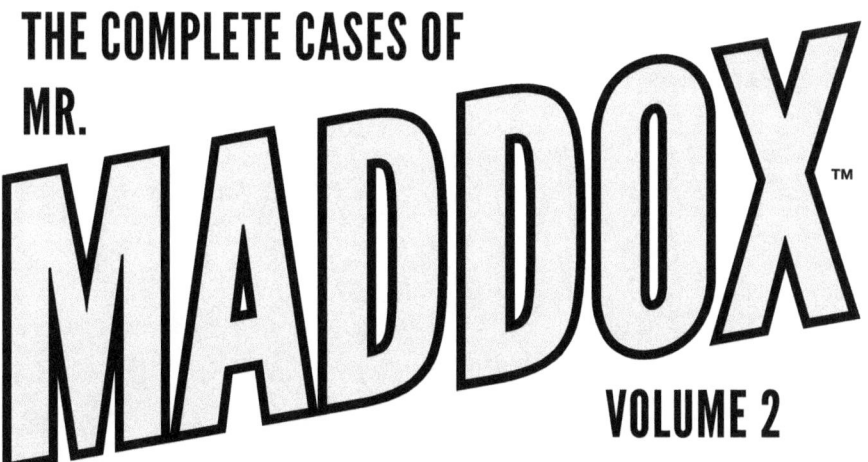

MADDOX™

VOLUME 2

T.T. FLYNN

ILLUSTRATIONS BY

JOHN FLEMING GOULD

ALTUS PRESS

BOSTON • 2015

TABLE OF CONTENTS

KENTUCKY KICKBACK

IT WAS DERBY WEEK AND THE LID WAS OFF LOUISVILLE TILL AMERICA'S GREATEST TURF CLASSIC HAD BEEN RUN AT CHURCHILL DOWNS. GAMBLERS, TOUTS, CON-MEN—THE DREGS AND BLUE-BLOODS OF THE SPORTING FRATERNITY HAD DESCENDED ON THE CITY—AND MR. MADDOX. THAT BLAND BUDDHA OF THE BANGTAIL CIRCUIT HAD DESCENDED TOO. BUT HE LOST HIS KICK EVEN BEFORE HE HAD TO HOCK HIS FAMOUS DIAMOND AND THE NIGHT HE COVERED A BET FOR A ONE-EARED MAN IN THE MORGUE HE KNEW HE WAS SLATED FOR TROUBLE. TROUBLE HE COULDN'T COPE WITH TILL THE WRONG HORSE WON THE DERBY AND THE RIGHT GIRL LOST IT IN A SWEEPSTAKES GARRISON FINISH.

CHAPTER ONE

OLD-MAN MONEY ON A SAW-DOWN HORSE

THE DAWN over Churchill Downs turned from gray to scarlet-and-gold as a voice at the grandstand rail spoke with unconscious excitement. "Danny Moore's taking the wraps off El Conde!"

A score of binoculars were trained on the same sight. Two score stop-watches clicked at the same instant. Silence fell over the top-coated and sweatered railbirds standing singly and in groups at the edge of the track. Glasses and keen eyes followed the black horse and rider sweeping along the backstretch.

And just then the rim of the golden sun burst up in the eastern sky. East of the bright gay flowers and deep greensward of the infield. East of the old green-and-white stables huddled in serried ranks beyond the backstretch where El Conde was making his run. Another spring morning at Churchill Downs. Another spring day of Derby Week.

The Kentucky Derby!

And on the stretch-turn El Conde streaked through a shaft of golden sunrise in an effortless rush that eased off abruptly.

A gaunt, hook-nosed little man excitedly shoved a weathered hat back on his head and caught the arm of the man beside him. Face working, long nose twitching, he thrust out an old stopwatch.

"Look, Maddox! One-twelve-three for six furlongs! And breezing! He coulda done two seconds better and still made the Derby route! Man O' War was only a plater! I seen it when the Conde was a yearling! 'Don't sell a Derby winner!' I begged Cap'n Jim's girl. An' wha'd she do? Wha'd she do?"

"What did she do, Sully?" Mr. Maddox repeated. "She sold to

Gloria Gerryman. And Gloria Gerryman boasts that she's already bet eighty grand that she's got a Derby winner."

Mr. Maddox glanced down at the expensive stop-watch cupped in his own big hand.

"One-thirteen even, Sully. You're so hipped on that black nag you're edging on the time."

"I've clocked 'em since I was in short pants!" Sully retorted heatedly. "If somebody's two-fifths off, it's you, Maddox! Maybe you've got reasons! You bookies oughta be worried about the dough you musta laid against the Conde! Serve you right if he cleaned you!"

Men near enough to hear the exchange were smiling.

One called out: "You'll have long white whiskers, Sully, when you see Joe Maddox cleaned!"

"Yah?" Sully snorted. "I've seen him cleaned! In twenty-eight I seen him so busted at Belmont he couldn't cover a double-buck from Avenue A. He'd lost that chunk of ice there on his finger an' peddled the hock-check on his benny. If they can take him once, they can take him again. An' maybe the Conde's the one that'll do it."

HEAD and shoulders Mr. Maddox towered above the gaunt and shabby Sully, who'd been Tim Sullivan to his mother and plain Sully to a host of turf followers from Bay Meadows to Saratoga and points between.

And when you looked at the vast and prosperous bulk of Mr. Maddox, and gauged the great white diamond on his left hand, you could doubt that so much assurance and prosperity had ever hocked an overcoat, been without an expensive diamond or a fat bankroll.

You could be ready to join Mr. Maddox in a resentful sneer and a sharp retort to Sully's slander.

But a grin was on Mr. Maddox's broad bland face. A chuckle shook Mr. Maddox's vast girth as he instinctively touched the great gem on his finger and nodded.

"It was tough that year, Sully. I lost forty pounds from not eating and looked like I'd been tailored by a tent-maker. How much are you betting on El Conde, Sully?"

"Huh?"

"How much?"

Sully looked embarrassed. His long nose twitched. He spat, grunted, started to turn away. Mr. Maddox put a hand on his arm and chuckled again.

"How much on El Conde, Sully?"

Sully shook off the hand and managed to look irritated, defiant and sheepish at the same time. "I'll handle my dough an' you handle yours, Maddox!"

"Two to one you're talking El Conde and laying cash on Jeanne's Hope, that oat-bucket of Jeanne Cavanaugh's," Mr. Maddox offered.

"So what?" Sully snapped defiantly. "So what, Maddox? Is it my dough or ain't it? I got a right to back Jeanne's horse if I like him!"

"You've got a right to jump off the New Albany bridge if you like it," Mr. Maddox chuckled.

One of the listeners laughed. "Sully'll get his money back faster by jumping off the bridge. Jeanne's Hope hasn't got a chance."

"Yah?" said Sully. "Yah?" and stamped away muttering to himself.

Mr. Maddox pocketed the stop-watch and looked after the gaunt little figure with an understanding smile.

"Sully knows a horse," Mr. Maddox said. "He's tossing away his money just because Jeanne Cavanaugh has got a horse entered and he can't bear to bet against her."

"Damn fool!"

"Just Sully," said Mr. Maddox.

El Conde had drifted past the hawk-eyed railbirds before the grandstand. The big black horse was breathing easily and worrying the bit that held him back. A great horse. Chances were he'd take the Derby. And that would be another feather in Gloria Gerryman's fabulous cap. Another tribute to the Gerryman millions that seemed bent on buying in a few years what others had taken generations to acquire.

Oil money came fast, spent easy. The Gerryman stable of thoroughbreds and great breeding-farm in the Kentucky Bluegrass, the Gerryman yacht, the Gerryman villa at Palm Beach, the Gerryman Long Island estate, the Gerryman private plane, the Gerryman oil interests, had all been a matter of money.

And like a jewel topping a fabulously constructed crown was Gloria Gerryman herself. The rotogravure, gossip and society columns filled in the picture....

Breathing deeply of the cool crisp dawn, Mr. Maddox walked back under the grandstand to the clubhouse entrance. This was the best part of the day, these early mornings when only the railbirds and stable hands were out to watch the morning workouts. In these early hours the turf belonged to those who loved it.

A SCATTERING of automobiles were on the parking-space before the clubhouse entrance. More were arriving. By breakfast time there'd be still more. The eyes of the world were on Louisville, here by the broad Ohio. Visitors already were swarming over the town.

Uncounted thousands more were starting the annual trek toward the Bluegrass classic of the turf. By tomorrow night, just before the Derby, they'd be sleeping in shifts, and overflowing into the parks.

"Mist' Joe!"

Mr. Maddox paused at the door of his big blue sedan, stared inquiringly, and then nodded recognition of the monkey-like little Negro who had slipped furtively around the back of the car and jerked off his cap in a bobbing, grinning greeting.

"Hello, Chimp. So you made another Derby? What's on your mind?"

"Chimp" was short for chimpanzee—and there was a resemblance, even to the hunched way Chimp moved and the long arms and big hands that almost touched his knees. Chimp was so ugly you hardly noticed he had only one ear.

"Sho' made hit heah again, Mist' Joe," Chimp chortled, fumbling inside his ragged greasy coat.

"Need a couple of dollars to eat on!" Mr. Maddox guessed, reaching for his billfold.

"Naw, suh, thankee, suh. I'se been workin' eround de stables. Plenty greens an' fat meat for ol' Chimp dis spring. I'se got feenancial trouble, suh."

Chimp drew a clenched fist from under his coat and looked warily around. "You still makin' book on de Big Race, Mist' Joe?"

Mr. Maddox put back his billfold and chuckled. "As usual, Chimp. Want to make a bet?"

"I ain't got white man's money," Chimp mumbled, looking around again.

"Seeing as it's you," said Mr. Maddox solemnly, "I'll lay you from a quarter up. Track odds or how'll you have it?"

"White folks odds de folkses gitten eround de Brown Hotel corner," Chimp decided. "How dat pay me on dat saw-down lil Jeanne's Hope?"

"Jeanne's Hope?" said Mr. Maddox, lifting his eyebrows. "Have you been working for the Cavanaughs too, Chimp?"

"Naw, suh."

"Just got a soft spot for old Cap'n Jim and the horses Miss Jeanne and her brother own, I suppose?"

"Naw, suh," Chimp mumbled uneasily. "Never knowed de Cap'n, suh. Never done no work for dat family. Dat lil saw-down horse jus' my style, suh. An' does I win, I wants de winnin' money, suh. White folks style. You de payinest man I knews, Mist' Joe. You ain't hold out no winnin's on of Chimp."

"That's right, Chimp. You'll get your money if you win." Mr. Maddox frowned thoughtfully, cleared his throat, and decided: "I'll lay you twenty to one."

"Thankee, suh. An' please, suh, you won't say nothin' 'bout of Chimp bettin' he own money on dat Jeanne's hope? Jus' don't say nothin' is you asked?"

"Not a word," agreed Mr. Maddox solemnly.

Chimp looked furtively around again, then opened his sooty fist and disclosed a wad of grimy, much-folded bills. Twenty-dollar bills.

"Hit's two hunr'd an' fawty dollars, Mist' Joe. I bets de whole on de nose. Jeanne's Hope—an' I gits twenty to one."

"Wait a minute," said Mr. Maddox sternly as he leafed through the money. "Where'd you get all this, Chimp? Does it belong to you?"

"Yes, suh. I knowed you believe me, Mist' Joe. Hit's de dice some. But mostly hit's jes' ole Chimp savin' back er doller now an' then. Takes me long time to hold back so much, Mist' Joe. I been waitin' fer de jack-pot time to git me old-man money for when I gits old. Dis de time an' dat's de jack-pot money."

Mr. Maddox eyed the ugly little black man sharply, and then nodded. "All right, Chimp, I believe you. You're on Jeanne's Hope to win, two hundred and forty at twenty to one. And if it's your old-man money, I hope you make it. Forty-eight hundred and your money back if you win. That'll keep you in hog jowls and turnip greens for a long time if you stay out of crap games."

" 'Deed hit will, suh," Chimp cackled—and broke off suddenly with a contortion of his money-like face that might have meant anything. "Lawdy God, I done talk too long! I knowed hit!"

Mr. Maddox stared in amazement as Chimp vanished around the back of the automobile.

MR. MADDOX was putting the money in his billfold when an automobile horn blared peremptorily. Mr. Maddox looked, recognized the big cream-colored sedan rolling into the parking space. He'd seen the car back at the stables two days before, seen it disgorge its owner the evening before at the Hollister House on Broadway, where Mr. Maddox was staying.

O'Toole owned the car. Honest John O'Toole, the well known betting commissioner, race-horse owner and big-time gambler. Slim Pasternik was driving the O'Toole car as usual and was alone.

Behind the wheel of his car Mr. Maddox lighted a cigarette and dallied a moment before leaving, watching the big sedan.

And a thoughtful frown came on Mr. Maddox's forehead as Chimp shambled to the side of O'Toole's car.

"Now what," Mr. Maddox muttered as he drove off, "do you make of that? Is O'Toole or Pasternik trying a fast one with that nigger? Trying, maybe, to put me behind the eight-ball?"

A small two-hundred-and-forty-dollar bet seemed to refute the suspicion. And Chimp had always been an honest colored man. His story had sounded straight. His grimy much-handled money backed up the story.

But Honest John O'Toole being what he was, Mr. Maddox carried a lingering suspicion over to Third Street, and downtown to the hotel and breakfast.

THESE days before Derby Day were busy. Churchill Downs was a mutuel track and bookies were not wanted in the city. Hourly now, horse money was flooding in on trains, automobiles and airplanes.

Men and women were arriving who knew Joe Maddox of old, at other tracks, in other cities about the country. And it was good business to be seen where the race fans were gathering. At the better hotels and restaurants, along Broadway, out at the track and stables.

And while Mr. Maddox moved in the public eye, his man Oscar stayed in the hotel suite taking bets and quoting odds over the telephone—on the Derby. This one week of each year, Mr. Maddox laid only against Derby money.

At lunch they met in the hotel suite over sandwiches while Oscar brought the betting-sheets up to date.

"Got to cut the odds again on El Conde," Oscar warned. "He's getting a play. If it keeps coming in and he takes the Derby, we'll be out on a limb."

"My guess is he'll take it," said Mr. Maddox. "He worked like a black ghost this morning."

"Yeah," said Oscar. "It's all over town. What's the matter with the dope who's training the Gerryman Stable? Why don't he cover up a little if he's got a good thing? Why let every tout on the rail know all about it?"

"The Gerryman girl should worry about the odds," guessed Mr. Maddox. "She's got her money bet, I hear. She's out to win a Derby—and if half what I've read and heard is right, the more publicity the better. She's a headline hog. A horse that wins that race is as good as a murder in the family when it comes to publicity."

Oscar's thin shrewd face puckered in distaste.

"A lot of crummy people are cluttering up the tracks these days. You could peel 'em down to their last bank account and wouldn't find anything a horse would go for."

Mr. Maddox laughed. "Styles change, Oscar. When I was a yearling, the Gerryman type bought diamonds and pearls for the yokels to read about. Now horses rate bigger headlines and show up better in the roto and society sections."

"And sometimes you can't tell which is the horse," Oscar groused. "There's a few regular folks left anyway. We got a grand and another five hundred on Jeanne's Hope this morning. That Cavanaugh horse. Old Cap'n Jim Cavanaugh's Stable. I heard his daughter and son took over after he died."

Mr. Maddox's bland, Buddha-like face grew thoughtful as he nodded.

"Jeanne and Jerry Cavanaugh. They were youngsters the last time I saw them." Mr. Maddox suddenly chuckled. "Cap'n Jim had Jerry over a knee in front of the tackroom door, whaling the dust out of his pants and cussing him. And Jeanne was standing by wringing her hands." Thoughtful again, Mr. Maddox asked: "Who's betting on Jeanne's Hope?"

"Harley Smith bet the grand. Girl called Norlene Bell telephoned and then brought the five hundred up. Said she'd bet with you in New York, and when she heard you were in town she looked you up. Said when her boy friend got in, she'd have some more to be covered."

"I don't remember her," Mr. Maddox said. "Don't give her any credit. Smith's good for a grand—even if he is as crooked a louse as ever cluttered up Chicago. Here's two hundred and forty more on Jeanne's Hope. The name is Chimp."

"Initials?" said Oscar, writing on his sheets.

"Just Chimp," said Mr. Maddox, smiling as he stood up. "Watch the Jeanne's Hope money. I'm interested in who likes that horse."

"Something doing?" Oscar asked alertly.

"I don't know," said Mr. Maddox. "But just in case there is, I want to know. I'll call you from the track. Kopper King might cop that third race and we'll make some easy money."

Oscar grunted disgustedly. "Those four horses you ship around the country wouldn't win a race if they were running together in a four-horse maiden race. Why you waste dough on four cheap platers and get the ha-ha for running them now and then is too much for me, Joe. They ain't race horses. They're walking glue pots stuffed with oats an' too lazy to waddle."

"I've got Gerryman blood," Mr. Maddox chuckled. "If Kopper King wins the third, I'll get a headline."

The door closed on Oscar's derisive: "If Kopper King *finishes* you'll deserve a headline."

CHAPTER TWO

LITTLE MISS MILLIONS

THE THIRD race that afternoon was a ten-horse race. Kopper King dashed under the wire ninth by a nose. Mr. Maddox was not too cast down as he went to a telephone booth to call Oscar. Kopper King had beaten one horse at least.

"Another grand on Jeanne's Hope," Oscar reported. "Fellow named Starky."

"Don't know him."

"He brought cash up, so it's all right, Joe. Says he knows friends of yours. And here's a hot one. That punk, Stiffy, telephoned and said a dame named Cavanaugh wanted to see you."

"Jeanne Cavanaugh?"

"I should know," said Oscar. "Stiffy said she'd been crying. Said he told her you'd probably be around the barn some time this afternoon."

"I'm on my way over there now," Mr. Maddox decided.

Stiffy was the seventeen-year-old exercise boy for the Maddox Stable. He'd come in on a horse van and stayed on the payroll because all the gossip of the stables rolled out in Stiffy's endless stream of talk—and because Joe Maddox was soft-hearted.

Now, talking to his employer, Stiffy's big Adam's apple jumped in his thin neck and his pale-blue eyes blinked rapidly as he nodded jerkily.

"That's her all right. I knowed her before she tol' me her name. Got that runty little Jeanne's Hope that's entered in the Derby an' a couple platers that nobody'll ever claim offen her. Kinda pretty too. I hear that wise-crackin' guy on the other sida Stable Five made a pass at her an' got his face slapped. She shore looked like hell too when she come askin' where you was. Kinda sniffin' back up in her nose like a stable bitch that's lost a pup. I ast her what was—"

"Stiffy!" said Mr. Maddox sternly. "My lady friends don't sound like dogs, don't look like hell, and it's none of your blasted business what they want. I told you what'd happen next time you started swearing near me!"

"My God, I fergot!" Stiffy gulped, and ducked as an open-hand clout knocked him rolling.

Choking, Stiffy scrambled up. His raw-boned young face was agonized. Tears filled his eyes.

"Too bad, but I'll learn you," said Mr. Maddox gruffly. "Here's a dollar. Cut out that crying."

Stiffy grabbed the dollar and dived toward the nearest stall, gasping: "Ain't cryin'! S-swallered my chawin'!"

Mr. Maddox was smiling as he headed toward the barn which held Jeanne Cavanaugh's horses. The hard-boiled little Stiffys of today would make the veteran haltermen of tomorrow—because they loved horses and horse racing. Because their life was the long pungent stable lines, picturesque stable hands, wise little jockeys and handlers, and the hard gamble of breeding, buying, training, racing sleek thoroughbreds.

There was plenty of activity at the Cavanaugh barn. Horses that had raced were being walked out and cooled off under blankets. Last touches of expert attention were being given to horses that would race later in the afternoon. Owners, friends, visitors, jockey agents, track officials were moving about. The drumming rush of horses in the fourth race pounded past on the nearby track.

Mr. Maddox saw Jeanne Cavanaugh before she saw him. She was walking nervously back and forth before the stalls.

Baled hay was piled there, clean straw scattered underfoot, leather tack and a metal feed basket hung on pegs. Jeanne wore slacks, a light jacket sweater. A gay silk handkerchief was tied around her forehead

and blonde hair. She seemed oblivious of her surroundings, and probably was unaware that the square set of her shoulders was very like
the wiry carriage of old Cap'n Jim Cavanaugh.

"Hello, Jeanny," Mr. Maddox said.

She gave him a blank look and then a forced smile. "It's Mr. Maddox,
isn't it?"

"I hear you were asking for me."

"Was I?" she said vaguely. "It—it was nothing. I didn't mean to
bring you clear over here."

HER EYES were red, although she'd effectively used a mirror and
vanity. Her forced smile was almost good enough to seem natural. If
Mr. Maddox had been in a hurry, if the memory of Honest John
O'Toole and black Chimp hadn't lingered in the back of his mind,
he might have smiled it off with a few bantering words and gone
away. Instead Mr. Maddox walked over and sat down on a bale of hay.

"Some little girls do get mighty pretty when they grow up," he
observed. "Where's Jerry?"

The simple question took the forced smile off Jeanne's face. If her
look wasn't frightened, questioning, Joe Maddox had lost his astute
perception.

"Jerry? Did—did you want to see Jerry for any particular reason?"

Mr. Maddox chuckled as he reached for cigarettes and matches.
"I wonder how much Jerry's changed, too. Bet you can't guess how I
remember him."

"No," said Jeanne, standing there with her hands in the sweater
pockets and the fixed welcoming smile more frozen every moment.

"The Cap'n was whaling him over a knee and you were taking it
harder than Jerry was."

"I—I think I remember," Jeanne said. "Wasn't it at Latonia?"

Mr. Maddox nodded. "Is Jerry as good with horses as his father
was?"

"Jerry," said Jeanne in a stifled voice, "doesn't like horses very well.
He—he's been working at a bank here in Louisville. I've managed
the farm and stable for both of us."

"Sit down, Jeanny," said Mr. Maddox, moving over on the hay bale.
"You must have the Cap'n's eye for a horse. Got a Derby entry, I hear.
I want to look him over while I'm here."

Jeanne sat down and stared at her toes. "Would you like to buy Jeanne's Hope, Mr. Maddox?"

"Before or after the Derby?"

"Now."

"It'd have to be now if he stands any chance of winning," Mr. Maddox said genially. "Derby winners come high. Too high for old Joe Maddox."

"I mean *now*," said Jeanne in a flat dull voice. She was still staring at her toes. "Twenty thousand cash—and I'll tell you what we've kept hidden. Jeanne's Hope is faster than anyone thinks. He stands a good chance of winning."

"Then twenty grand is robbing you," said Mr. Maddox. "Look at the Derby purse. Seventy-five thousand this year."

"You mean you don't believe me. You don't want to buy him."

"I can't," said Mr. Maddox regretfully. "I'm using all my money making a book. Anyway, I can't use a twenty-grand horse or a Derby winner. I'm a bookie and never have tried to be much of anything else."

"I thought so," said Jeanne in the same stony voice. "I've tried to sell him to everyone who might have the money. I've offered to run him against a stop-watch to prove how fast he is. Everyone thinks there's something wrong because I'm offering him just before the Derby."

"*Mmmmm*, I suppose so. Can't blame them, Jeanny. He might break the track record and still be a dog who'd quit when the heat went on in the stretch."

"I don't blame anyone," said Jeanne without looking up. "If I can't get twenty thousand from you, I can't. I'm sorry you had the walk over here for nothing."

Mr. Maddox quietly asked: "What's the trouble, kid?"

Jeanne swallowed. Her small hands were clenched. She looked like she was fighting tears. Her voice had a dry huskiness as she shook her head.

"No trouble. Please forget it. And don't bet on Jeanne's Hope. He probably isn't as fast as I thought he was. I—I might change my mind and scratch him."

Mr. Maddox protested: "That'd be a crime if he's as good as you think he is."

"He is."

"Funny, Cap'n Jim's stable turning out two horses good enough to rate the Derby," Mr. Maddox mused, watching Jeanne's profile. "Kind of slipped up when you sold El Conde, didn't you?"

JEANNE'S cheek muscles bunched. "I knew how good he was. But I had to have money and Gloria Gerryman was willing to spend it. The Gerrymans bought Green Acres, the Harmsworth breeding-farm, near us, you know. Or don't you?"

"Everyone in the game knew when Sam Harmsworth got rid of his father's horses and breeding-farm. Too bad young Sam didn't have the liking for a thoroughbred his father had. He didn't need the Gerryman money."

"The papers said New York business was taking all his interest," Jeanne said dully. "Anyway, the Gerrymans bought the place. And bought El Conde. And according to the papers, she's after Sam himself now."

"So?" said Mr. Maddox. "Well, why not? Sam Harmsworth has family and social position. That's all the Gerryman sideshow needs now, isn't it?"

"I suppose so," Jeanne agreed. "If Sam's fool enough to fall for it."

"Maybe Gloria Gerryman would buy Jeanne's Hope," Mr. Maddox suggested thoughtfully. "Have you tried her?"

"Tried her?" said Jeanne—and suddenly her small fists were beating her knees. "That—that cat! *Oh*—"

Jeanne's voice broke. Snatching out a handkerchief she ran into the next stall, which was empty.

Mr. Maddox lumbered to his feet in astonishment, shook his head, scowled, and went to the stall door. Jeanne's shoulders shook as she stood with her back to the doorway.

"What is it, kid?" Mr. Maddox asked gruffly.

"Go away!" Jeanne all but wailed without looking around.

Mr. Maddox entered the stall and stood behind her. "Listen, Jeanny, I'm only old Joe Maddox, the bookie. Maybe there's nothing I can do. But I won't make it any worse and I might be able to help."

"Go away!"

Mr. Maddox shook his head helplessly, cleared his throat, swore inaudibly and stood his ground.

Cap'n Jim probably would have known what to do. Or her brother,

Jerry. Or any man who had reared a daughter. But a hard-boiled old bachelor like Joe Maddox could only flounder helplessly.

"I'll stay here until I get some sense out of all this," Mr. Maddox decided grimly.

"Go away, please!"

Mr. Maddox retreated to the doorway and bulked there with a helplessness alien to his usual vast assurance.

Jeanne wiped her nose. Her slim straight shoulders still shook. But she made no sound. Mr. Maddox swore again to himself. Jeanne was crying all right. Deep down inside she was crying, and there didn't seem to be anything to do about it.

Mention of selling Jeanne's Hope to Gloria Gerryman had set this off. But why? Nothing wrong about the suggestion. Jeanne herself had sold El Conde to the Gerrymans.

Perhaps, Mr. Maddox decided, it was too much to have to sell a horse like El Conde and then sit by and see what a great horse he'd become.

Funny though about Jeanne and her brother having to sell El Conde. Cap'n Jim Cavanaugh had seemed well-fixed. Nice string of horses, nice Bluegrass farm for his mares and yearlings. But you couldn't tell. A stable could be on top one year in the racing game and scraping bottom the next.

And there still was this matter of selling Jeanne's Hope. Only something near to desperation would drive a girl like Jeanne Cavanaugh out peddling a Derby entry the second day before the big race.

"Why don't Jerry get out and do it?" Mr. Maddox asked himself. And then had to admit that maybe Jerry Cavanaugh had done it, was trying even now.

LAUGHTER, voices, sounded outside the barn, to the right of the doorway. A feminine voice said loudly: "So this is the horse Gloria might have bought instead of El Conde? Gloria darling, how *terrific* you were to pick El Conde!"

Jeanne stiffened.

Mr. Maddox looked out the doorway as a man commented: "He's too small. Not enough leg for the Derby. How about it, Sam?"

It was a gay group, seven or eight, in front of the second stall over. One of the young men was patting the brown muzzle of the horse inside.

Mr. Maddox whistled softly, and then the tall young man patting the horse looked around, saw him and called: "Is the owner around?"

"Just a moment," Mr. Maddox replied, and turned into the stall. "They're asking for you, kid—and if I didn't see it, I wouldn't believe it. Honest John O'Toole's out there with a Club House bunch. I think one is Sam Harmsworth. And even money says the brunette in the middle is Gloria Gerryman."

Jeanne was already opening a vanity and starting to dab at her eyes and cheeks. Her reply was bitter. "I could expect her to do this."

And then, astonishingly, Jeanne was smiling as she went out.

Mr. Maddox paused outside the doorway and watched the tall young man smile broadly as he stepped to meet her.

"Hello, Jeanne!"

"I'm afraid...."

He was disappointed. "I'm Sam Harmsworth."

"Oh! Of course! How are you, Sam?"

Mr. Maddox handicapped Sam Harmsworth with a look and found him passable. Tall, rangy, with clean lines, a likable smile. Nice voice, too, when he introduced the others.

"You know Gloria, don't you? And this is Miss Anderson, Mrs. Lloyd, and Tony Lloyd, Mr. Sanders, Mr. Conwell and—er—Mr. O'Toole."

Mr. Maddox was watching O'Toole—Honest John O'Toole—who looked like a bluff, hearty Irishman, immaculately dressed, including Homburg, gloves and cane.

And O'Toole was watching Mr. Maddox. In a moment O'Toole stepped around the others and came to the empty stall.

"Hello, Maddox. I didn't expect to meet you here. Friend of Miss Cavanaugh's?"

"Hello, shyster," Mr. Maddox said with scant ceremony. "How'd you deal yourself a spread of suckers like this?"

O'Toole reddened and his mouth shut with a snap. "Going to be nasty, are you, you slob!"

"Louses like you bring it out in me," said Mr. Maddox, enjoying himself. "Which pocket are you getting set to pick?"

"Some day," said O'Toole, keeping his temper with difficulty, "I'm going to take a crack at you. I don't like you, Maddox."

"Thanks for the compliment," accepted Mr. Maddox blandly. "I'll have to be asleep or looking the other way when you get nerve enough to take the crack, shyster. Tell Slim Pasternik that too. Tell him you both smell like skunk to me. All smell and nothing else."

That harmless remark produced an effect. Honest John O'Toole stood scowling, and then his forced smile was white-lipped with strain.

"I'll tell Slim," he said, and turned on his heel and rejoined the others.

The Anderson girl had a sharp, catty face and the high-pitched voice that Mr. Maddox had heard first. She was saying: "Miss Cavanaugh, do you *really* think your horse is as good as Gloria's El Conde?"

Jeanne laughed. "Does Miss Gerryman think so?"

"Heavens, *no!* But Gloria's betting-commissioner, Mr. O'Toole here, says he's worried about the chance your horse has to beat El Conde."

MR. MADDOX, still beside the stall door a few steps away, almost grunted aloud. So O'Toole had been handling the flood of Gerryman money on El Conde. And keeping it quiet, too. Not even Joe Maddox had suspected.

You might know O'Toole would finagle himself into such a spot. But O'Toole worrying about Gloria Gerryman's losing a race? Mr. Maddox smiled sardonically. You could bet that O'Toole had already made sure of his cut. And you could "if" the bet that O'Toole didn't give a sour mutuel ticket what happened otherwise.

O'Toole's deprecating smile and almost humble reply to the Anderson woman brought another sardonic quirk to Mr. Maddox's mouth.

"A good horse always has a chance, Miss Anderson. Naturally I try to overlook nothing that will help Miss Gerryman."

Mr. Maddox had been sizing up Gloria Gerryman. Even prejudice had to admit she was an eyeful. Dressed like a certified check. Dark hair and make-up as near perfection as care and money could attain. She hadn't been bad-looking at the start. Experts had gone on from there.

That was it, Mr. Maddox decided. She'd been modeled in smart beauty salons for the daily parade. And looked it. And the hard pouting line of her mouth hadn't been changed.

Take Jeanne Cavanaugh now, in her slacks, old sweater, silk handkerchief carelessly around her blonde hair. Jeanne was like someone's casual kid sister. You might admire the Gerryman. Jeanne caught at your liking.

And now Jeanne was smiling as she remarked: "We never know what a horse will do until he's finished the race."

"Jeanne had an eye like her father for a horse," Sam Harmsworth remembered genially. "Better look out, Gloria. O'Toole may know what he's talking about."

"O'Toole is an idiot," Gloria said sharply. "Now that he's bet my money—and enough of it, heaven knows—he pretends to be worried. I don't believe him. The only thing that will beat El Conde is a trick. There are so many dishonest people around race tracks. Isn't that so, Miss Cavanaugh? Thieves, swindlers, and such people."

From where he was standing, Mr. Maddox could catch the quick bunching of Jeanne's cheek muscles. Jeanne's left hand clenched tightly and then relaxed. But she was still smiling when she replied.

"Race tracks have cheats and frauds about as often as other places. Most of us don't admire them any more than—than Sam would."

Sam Harmsworth laughed. "Which isn't much, Jeanne. Let's look at your horse—and then I'll duck from these folks and we'll talk old times." He grinned broadly. "I didn't tell them, but the reason I suggested walking over here to see your horse was to see you. It's been a long time since we used to race bareback on the road back of your farm."

Gloria Gerryman spoke sharply. "Sam, you were going to watch my horse run in the sixth race!"

"So I was," Sam said carelessly. "I'll see him run some other race, darling. You always have a horse running somewhere. I can't always meet Jeanne and talk about old times on the farm."

"You can see your farm at the house party tonight. After all, *I* own it now."

"You don't own what Jeanne and I have to talk about," Sam chuckled. "Now let's see your horse, Jeanne. Tony, here, says he's small for the Derby."

Jeanne was pale, but still smiling as she turned back to Mr. Maddox. "Do you mind?"

"I'll see you later," Mr. Maddox said genially. "I just remembered an appointment myself."

Mr. Maddox had no appointment, but questions baited him as he walked back to the barn where his horses were stabled. "That Gerryman cat took a dirty dig at Jeanne with that crack about thieves or I'm a liar," he muttered. "And if Jeanne didn't get back at her, I'm another liar. Bad blood there! And Jeanne's in trouble and needs twenty grand fast! And where does O'Toole come in? He's slick and he's crooked. And if he ain't got an extra ace, I'm a liar three times."

Stiffy was leading the blanketed and placid Kopper King in circles before the barn.

"Know a one-eared nigger called Chimp?" Mr. Maddox asked.

"Nope," said Stiffy warily. "Uh—maybe I've seed him around. There's so da—so dern many of 'em around, a feller can't keep track."

"After you're through with Kopper King, look around for Chimp. He's getting along in years and looks like a monkey. Find out where he's working. And keep your mouth shut. Don't mention my name. I'll see you in the morning."

No need to worry about Stiffy's delivering. He'd find old Chimp if he had to go down all the rat holes.

Later at the clubhouse Mr. Maddox saw Gloria Gerryman and her friends. Sam Harmsworth wasn't there. Gloria looked sulky, angry.

Mr. Maddox was gratified. "Her boy friend stayed with Jeanne and it's burning her. Good for Jeanne."

Meanwhile Joe Maddox had his bookie business—and it was work. He was weary when he entered the hotel suite after nine that evening and found Oscar dialing the radio and enjoying a Scotch.

"Build me a double one," Mr. Maddox said, collapsing in the easiest chair and grunting as he unlaced his shoes.

"Lady friend of yours called three times," Oscar said as he went to the tray holding the mixings.

Mr. Maddox looked up alertly. "Jeanne Cavanaugh?"

"Nope. That Norlene Bell who put half a grand on Jeanne's Hope."

"I'm not in tonight," Mr. Maddox growled.

Oscar squirted bubbling soda into the glass. "She'll call again. Says her boy friend's in town and wants to talk some important Derby money."

"Not tonight," Mr. Maddox repeated. "Not if they've got gold sacked and waiting." Mr. Maddox grabbed the glass, sloshed the ice cubes, drank deeply, and relaxed with a sigh of relief. "I work harder than a ditch-digger, Oscar."

"Sure," said Oscar skeptically, sitting down with his drink.

"I wouldn't go out again tonight for ten grand!"

"I'd sprout wings and fly out for ten grand," said Oscar.

A news broadcast was on. European news, national news, then local items. About the Derby, track gossip, the incoming crowds....

"A record number of automobiles are arriving," the drawling voice stated. "The Chief of Police has requested motorists and pedestrians to be unusually careful. The first traffic death of Derby Week occurred this evening. The body of an unidentified Negro was found shortly after dark beside the Bardstown Road, killed by a hit-and-run driver. There were no witnesses. Police are holding the body and state that a missing left ear is the only clue they have...."

"*Missing ear!*" Mr. Maddox exploded, jumping up.

"Are you nuts?" Oscar asked in amazement as Mr. Maddox slapped the glass on the table and snatched for his shoes.

"I'm suspicious!" Mr. Maddox snapped as he yanked on the shoes and feverishly tied the laces.

"You going out?"

"Yes!"

"Since when did a one-eared corpse look better than a bag of gold?"

"Since it was a corpse!" Mr. Maddox snapped as he caught his hat and made for the door. "Stick around! I may need you tonight!"

CHAPTER THREE

THE CORPSE WITH
THE MISSING EAR

THE MORGUE room smelled of formaldehyde. Shadows cast by the dim light had a cold bleak look. The morgue attendant was matter-of-fact as he pulled out the slab.

"Get it on the radio an' folks start coming in. Lots of them just for a look. Here he is. Know him?"

Mr. Maddox looked and nodded. "His name is Chimp. Works around the stables at the track. When the broadcast said he had one ear, I wondered if it weren't Chimp."

A patrolman who had come in with them whipped out a notebook and pencil. "What's the initials, mister?"

"Just Chimp."

"Funny name. How's it spelled?"

"It's just short for chimpanzee. But as far as I know, that's the only name he ever had."

"Hell of a name. He work for you?"

"No. But I've seen him around the tracks for years."

The patrolman noted the imposing, prosperous figure and a note of respect entered his voice. "Do you own a stable? I'll have to take your name as the identifying party."

Someone chuckled behind Mr. Maddox. "He owns a stable—and there's not another one like it in the country. Eh, Joe? I saw your Kopper King put on another comic this afternoon."

"Cassidy," Mr. Maddox guessed without looking around. He was sarcastic when he faced the grizzled, stocky man behind him. "Bad place for you, Cassidy. Someone might get your number and lay you on a slab. Were you following me?"

"I'll get around to it," Cassidy promised. "Since when did you get interested in morgue stiffs, Joe?"

"Since I knew you," said Mr. Maddox blandly.

"Do you know this nigger, too?" the patrolman demanded of Cassidy.

Cassidy flipped open a small leather pocket case. "Masterton Agency. Track detective."

"Oh, sure—glad you dropped in on this," the officer said readily. "This gentleman says the nigger worked at the track."

"That's right," Cassidy agreed.

"I got to find out who he worked for."

"Someone at the barns can tell you." Cassidy pursed his lips and looked down at the slab. "So somebody smacked old Chimp with a car and left him on the road?"

"Caved in the back of his head and scratched him a little," the morgue man said. "I've seen 'em come in here all busted up. When a train hits 'em—oh, my! This fellow was lucky."

"Every man to his own kind of luck," Mr. Maddox commented. "That's all I know about him. Cassidy here can give you my pedigree. We're old friends."

"Old acquaintances, anyway," said Cassidy. "His name is Maddox. Joe Maddox. Staying at the Hollister House. He'll be easy to get if you want him. Wait a minute, Joe. I'm going your way."

"I was afraid so," Mr. Maddox growled as Cassidy fell into step beside him. "So you've been watching me again?"

"How's the book doing?"

"Who said I was making a book?"

Cassidy smiled grimly. "There's plenty who'll say it."

"And prove it?"

"Maybe I'll have to do the proving."

THEY were on the sidewalk now and Mr. Maddox stopped, put a heavy blunt finger against Cassidy's chest. "Cassidy, I brought horses here to run. Like Vanderbilt. Like Whitney. Don't bother me by trying to make a pinch on any grounds!"

"Vanderbilt, Whitney—and Maddox," Cassidy said and chuckled. "Don't make me die laughing, Joe. If an owner's badge and privileges didn't go with those nags you ship around, you'd peddle them for lion steaks at the first zoo."

"Like hell!" Mr. Maddox denied with the first genuine irritation he had displayed.

"Maybe you wouldn't at that," Cassidy was graceful enough to admit. "Look, Joe—cut the stalling. Any particular reason for coming around to look at old Chimp?"

"The radio mentioned his missing ear. It reminded me of Chimp."

"That all?"

"Any reason why it shouldn't be all?"

"No-o-o," Cassidy admitted slowly. "I just wondered. Running into you at the morgue and all. Listen, Joe, I never thought you were a fool."

"Thanks for nothing."

"You're pretty smart, in fact."

"If it's a touch," said Mr. Maddox with resignation, "don't bother to lay it on so thick. I'm a sucker for a touch."

"You can keep your mouth shut," Cassidy finished. "Listen, Joe. Homicide knows who Chimp is. He smelled of horse liniment and had horse hairs on his clothes. With the track open now, they didn't have to guess. A few questions at the stable gate proved Chimp belonged there. They got in touch with our agency."

"Then why the phony broadcast—and a cop watching the body?"

"Murder," Cassidy said. "He was socked on the back of the head.

He'd done his bleeding and was plenty dead when he was chucked from a car out there on the Bardstown Road."

Mr. Maddox swore softly. He and Cassidy had started walking.

Cassidy went on with a hard grim edge to his voice. "Who'n hell'd want to kill old Chimp? I've seen him around the bangtails since before I went with the Masterton Agency. He was so damned ugly, and having only one ear made him easy to remember."

"Maybe," said Mr. Maddox, "it was trouble over a crap game. Maybe he just got into an argument."

"Maybe," said Cassidy.

"Who was he working for? So far, all they've heard is that Chimp was doing odd jobs for anyone who needed a hand."

"Not much to go on."

"Not much," Cassidy agreed. "I was hoping you might know something about him, Joe."

Never had Mr. Maddox looked more like a bland, regretful Buddha. "Sorry, Cassidy. My horses are at the track—but I don't spend much time with them."

"You're telling me."

"I'll leave you here. It's been a hard day," said Mr. Maddox. "If I run across anything you can use, I'll let you know."

Cassidy was rubbing his chin, staring blankly as they parted on the corner.

MR. MADDOX was scowling, thinking, as he walked in the opposite direction and hailed a taxi. Chimp murdered! What could you think of it after Chimp's agitation early in the morning at the track? Slim Pasternik seemed to have been the cause. And Pasternik was man-of-all work for Honest John O'Toole. All dirty work. And O'Toole was handling money for Gloria Gerryman. And there had been some hidden meaning when Gloria Gerryman spoke to Jeanne Cavanaugh.

"The girls had been talking about O'Toole," Mr. Maddox muttered. "Gerryman cracked about thieves and swindlers and Jeanny cracked back. Did they really mean something—or was it only a couple of the girls sharpening their claws?"

Granted there was meaning in the smiling exchange of words between the two girls, would common sense suggest a connection between black Chimp's death and Gloria Gerryman?

Mr. Maddox entered the Hollister House and was crossing the lobby when a smiling young woman stopped him.

"You are Mr. Maddox, aren't you?"

"That's right, sister," Mr. Maddox admitted after a quick look.

"I'm Norlene Bell."

She was young enough, dressed well enough—if extremely. But life hadn't been too easy with her. The marks were plain to see under the make-up.

Mr. Maddox couldn't recall her—which was unusual. She'd told Oscar that she'd bet with the Maddox book before. But then thousands could say the same thing. Mr. Maddox couldn't remember them all, he supposed, though he didn't miss on many.

She knew him by sight. She'd bet five hundred cash on Jeanne's Hope. Which might mean anything or nothing. She'd suggested to Oscar that there'd be more. Anything connected with Jeanne's Hope was of interest at the moment.

Mr. Maddox smiled warmly. "I hear you've been telephoning for me, Miss Bell. You placed a bet this afternoon, didn't you?"

"I certainly did. And the way somebody on your phone has been stalling me sounds like I'm poison, or trying to borrow my money back instead of betting more."

"Sorry," said Mr. Maddox regretfully. "Commissions are always welcome. I've been out. Now," he finished with a flourish of gallantry that might have thawed even Gloria Gerryman, "I'm entirely at your service."

"It's about time someone trotted out the old oil," Norlene Bell told him briskly. "My gentleman friend's in town with a couple of his friends and a pair of bank-rolls that need a soft spot in the Derby. They want to talk to you."

"We like that kind of business," said Mr. Maddox heartily. "Any time tomorrow that you suggest."

"Tonight," said Norlene Bell firmly. "And if you don't get it quickly, I'll find a bookie who will. There's a big crap game at the Broadway Hotel. My friends are having some drinks out on Third Street and talking about rolling dice before they go to bed. If they get in that game, they won't have horse money left."

"They'll get action, at least, if it's Duke Major's game," Mr. Maddox commented. "It's at the Broadway, I hear, and the word is out that only high-rollers are wanted."

"The boys are waiting for me," she said impatiently. "And I'm taking a bookie back to get their horse money tonight if I have to kidnap one!"

Mr. Maddox had already made his decision. "If you'll allow me a few moments upstairs, Miss Bell, I think we can settle this quickly."

"Now you're talking," she said, pleased and obviously relieved. "Make it snappy, before the boys run out on me. I'll be in that chair."

AS MR. MADDOX entered the room, Oscar turned off the radio. "That dame called again, says she's waiting downstairs, Joe. She's getting hot. Did you collect the dead man?"

"Ixnay on the wisecracks!" Mr. Maddox snapped. "I'm in a hurry! This lady collared me in the lobby. I'm going with her and smoke out a couple of bankrolls. Listen to this.

"Get Stiffy, out at the barn. He may be asleep. You may have to take a hack out there and find him. Or wait for him."

"What's up?" Oscar asked alertly.

"How do I know? I'm trying to find out! Ask Stiffy what he discovered about the colored fellow. See if he found out who Chimp was working for, and any other dope he got about him."

"Chimp? You brought a bet in under that name!"

"He's dead. Stiffy'll probably know about it already."

"I knew it!" Oscar exclaimed. "It's that damn radio report! Listen, Joe, are we going to have more trouble? What business have we got with a one-eared black man who got clipped by a hit-and-run car?"

"It was murder!"

"My God! That makes it worse! Joe, we're here in Louisville! The Derby's day after tomorrow! There'll be enough dough around town to sink a river barge! Ain't that enough to worry about, Joe, without you up to your old tricks? And over a one-eared black corpse!"

"I know what I'm doing!" said Mr. Maddox, not quite accurately. "Here's something else for you. Find a fellow named Jerry Cavanaugh. He works in a local bank. Must be living in town. If he's not in the directory, you might find out though his sister, who owns Jeanne's Hope. Stiffy can find where she's staying. Or you can telephone the Cavanaugh Farm. It's out on the Bardstown Highway near Mt. Washington.

"Bardstown—Bardstown! The Cavanaugh Farm and the Gerryman

Farm are both on that road! I wonder if that has anything to do with Chimp's being pitched out on the Bardstown Road?"

Oscar begged: "Does any of this make sense? I don't like it, Joe!"

"Get through to Jerry Cavanaugh some way, if you have to yank him out of bed," Mr. Maddox ordered energetically. "Tell him I want to see him tonight. If he won't come here, I'll go where he is. But I want to talk to him."

"O.K." Oscar nodded. "But I don't have to like it—and I don't! You going out with that Bell girl now?"

"On Third Street, she says. I won't be gone long. She's cornered a couple of fat bankrolls that are itching to buck the dice tonight."

"I hope you have luck there anyway," said Oscar. He shook his head sourly as Mr. Maddox headed out again. "Ten grand wouldn't have got you outa here a little while ago—and a dead nigger with one ear starts you charging around like a college cheer-leader! If I had my way, I'd get you outa town so fast—"

The closing door cut off Oscar's voice….

AS THE elevator let him out in the lobby, Mr. Maddox's frown changed to his usual broad, beaming good nature.

"We'd better hurry," Norlene Bell said as they left the hotel. "I called the apartment. The boys are sore because I'm not back. They've had a few drinks and want to get going." And as Mr. Maddox stepped to the curb for a taxi, she said: "My car's parked around the corner."

Mr. Maddox kept pace with her hurried steps. He had forgotten that he was tired. Part of his mind was on the dead Chimp, part on Jeanne Cavanaugh, Honest John O'Toole and the Cavanaugh horse.

"So you like Jeanne's Hope?" he remarked.

"*I* do. My friend doesn't."

That suggested her five hundred on Jeanne's Hope had little significance. She was only another customer. But if her friends had good money to cover tonight, this inconvenience would be justified.

She unlocked a sleek new sedan, drove expertly, hurried through traffic to Third Street, and turned south. "What do you think of Jeanne's Hope?" Norlene Bell questioned.

"Maybe a chance."

"Don't kid me. Is that all?"

"No horse in the Derby has much more than a chance."

"That's baloney," she retorted scornfully. "You bookies have a good idea what's going to happen."

"But we don't all agree," Mr. Maddox chuckled. "If I could nail the winner, I'd retire after the race. The dope makes El Conde a stand-out."

She sounded the horn vigorously, shot past a car ahead. "That's what they think," she said flippantly.

"Why shouldn't they think so?" Mr. Maddox asked, on guard quickly from the tone of her voice.

She laughed. "Don't pump me, big boy. I don't know anything."

Mr. Maddox tried again to remember her, and couldn't. But she knew her way around. She was as hard-boiled as they come.

"What did you say your friend's name was?"

"I didn't say," she parried. "It'll surprise you. Here's the place just ahead."

Apartment houses, mostly brick, three and four stories high, set back from the sidewalk, were scattered along this tree-lined stretch of South Third. The building before which they parked was like many others along the street.

The Bell girl brushed the horn button as she took out a cigarette and turned. "Got a match?"

Mr. Maddox gave her a folder and reached for the door handle. The match flare lighted her face for an instant. Mr. Maddox paused, looking sharply at her.

The matchlight revealed her hard, knowing smile. Her look through the flame was triumphant. She blew the match out. Her voice had a faint mocking edge that might not otherwise have been noticeable.

"Thanks for the match. Thanks for coming," she said. "I didn't think you would."

She started to get out. She'd pulled the emergency brake and left the motor running. That brief sound of the horn might have been a signal.

Something was wrong. Mr. Maddox wasn't sure just what. But he was suddenly certain that he had made a fool move in leaving the hotel like this.

He shoved the door open to get out and the answer was there on the curb before him….

The man standing there must have come from a parked car behind them. He hadn't been there when they stopped, hadn't come out of the apartment house. "Stay in there, Maddox," he said. He was reaching under his coat.

It didn't need this much to recognize a heist. And by the time a man could lunge out of the car, the stranger could easily clip him. Mr. Maddox did the next best thing.

He obeyed, stayed in the car. Yanking hard on the door handle, he slammed the door shut, pushed the handle to lock position and threw himself across the seat behind the steering wheel to the other door through which the Bell girl had vanished.

Outside the automobile, in the street, he'd have a chance. The girl probably had a gun too. She might shoot. Mr. Maddox still carried the day's bankroll, and plenty of it.

Ordinarily he wouldn't have taken a long chance against stick-up guns. Too often bandits killed when the victim made a break. Joe Maddox knew he could always get a new bankroll. But Joe Maddox was finished, through, if a startled and angry gunman or gun-moll cut loose with a clip of metal-jacketed bullets.

But when you'd been taken for a sucker ride like this, you blew up....

The girl tried to shut the door. Mr. Maddox struck it with his hand and shoulder. The door flew out again, carrying her stumbling back.

That much Mr. Maddox saw as he started out to where he could straighten up and have room. Only then, from the corner of his eye, did he see the man turning from the handle of the rear door and bringing up an arm.

It couldn't be the man he'd just ducked back from. That one couldn't have gotten around the automobile so fast. Two men had come up beside the car, evidently.

Mr. Maddox ducked and tried to guard his head.

The blow glanced hard off his arm, crushed in his hat in a glancing swipe, knocked his head down.

Off-balance, dazed, Mr. Maddox still tried to fight out of the car. He was rolling forward when the man lunged into him and shoved him back. Mr. Maddox grabbed the coat, tried to drag himself out and up. The man swore at him.

The Bell girl wrenched out with a trace of hysteria: "You'll kill him, Dave! You'll kill him!"

"I'll cave his head in!" Dave said furiously. The second blow he struck clashed hollowly against the metal edge of the car roof, skidded down the side of Mr. Maddox's head, crushed his shoulder into numbness.

It felt like pipe and rang on the car-top like iron or steel instead of lead. In the quick, savage, almost silent melée, one white-hot thought raced through Maddox's mind.

Pipe like this must have caved in Chimp's head! Probably the same pipe, the same man! Joe Maddox was slated to be next!

The thought helped him hang onto consciousness and keep fighting to get out of the car.

Suddenly his neck was grabbed from behind. He was hauled back in against the seat. Strong fingers dug into his windpipe.

Mr. Maddox released the coat, tried to tear the hands away. He couldn't reach the man, who must have jumped into the back of the car from the curb.

The two of them pushed, wrestled him back to his side of the seat. He was gasping, fast weakening from lack of breath.

"Keep still, Maddox, or you'll get it sure as hell! Right here!"

Mr. Maddox stopped struggling. The hands cautiously loosened their grip.

"Someone's coming!" Dave panted. "Hold him! Shove him down in the seat!"

THE GIRL stayed behind. Maybe she had already left, walking to another car or hurrying across the street. Doors slammed. The motor was still idling. Then the car was away from the curb smoothly, swiftly, and if anyone was aware of the trouble, or suspicious, they made no sound that Mr. Maddox could hear—or that the two men noticed.

Gasping, gagging, Mr. Maddox tried to get his breath through a painfully congested throat. Head, arm and shoulder hurt from the dull, heavy blows. More alarming was the thought that these two men must already have murdered once tonight.

Another thought almost brought a grim smile. "Cassidy will have a fit if Joe Maddox is found out on the Bardstown Road and brought back to the morgue!"

The man in the back seat kept a hand on Mr. Maddox's shoulder, dug a gun muzzle into his back. "Going to take it easy, Maddox?"

"Write your own ticket," Mr. Maddox said thickly.

"Hold still! I'm going to frisk you."

The car turned left off Third Street, shortly made another turn as a hand from behind emptied Mr. Maddox's pockets, made sure he had no weapon.

The dashlight was off. Street lights at the corners showed the man called Dave lounging behind the wheel. The flurry of rage had passed, leaving a deceptive calm. His blunt weapon was not on the seat beside him. Mr. Maddox's exploring hand drew back.

"If it's money," said Mr. Maddox, "you've got it."

"And you," Dave retorted without turning his head.

Mr. Maddox spoke again in a monotone. "You've got my dough and you've got me. So what? Nobody would pay fifty dollars to see me again."

Dave turned another corner. They were, as near as Mr. Maddox could tell, driving toward the outskirts of town.

The man in the back laughed shortly. "You carried enough dough yourself. A slob as smooth as you should have better sense than to walk around heeled like that."

"Live and learn," Mr. Maddox muttered.

The man laughed again. "If you live." His gun muzzle slid over the seat top and prodded between Mr. Maddox's broad shoulders.

"Meaning?" Mr. Maddox said, not turning his head.

The gun jabbed for emphasis. "Meaning we don't like you, Maddox. We don't like that big face. We don't like that big belly. We don't like to see you around."

"I gather you don't like me," said Mr. Maddox dryly.

"That's smart. You're spoiling the Derby for us. We don't like it."

Dave spoke impatiently from the side of his mouth. "Give it to the big lug straight. He'll be kidding you next."

"He'll get it quick enough."

They were fast leaving Louisville, somewhere south and east of the Third Street spot where they'd started.

They passed bright gas-station lights. Beyond each oasis of light the road was a little darker. The outlying tentacles of the city dwindled. Fenced fields bordered the road. The cool night became black beyond the boring headlights.

Mr. Maddox considered jumping from the car. The thought might have been read for the gun touched his back again.

"I'd hate to shoot you, Maddox, if you tried to jump. It'd mess up the car."

"I've been trying to place you two," Mr. Maddox said slowly.

"Help yourself."

That might mean he'd never seen them before. Might mean that it didn't matter whether he did know them.

MR. MADDOX had recovered his hat. Perspiration was damp under the sweatband. His shoulder and head ached, but he ignored the feeling as nerves grew tighter and tighter.

Dave turned into a side road, graveled, narrow, without visible life besides themselves. Fields and trees alternated on a rolling landscape. The car slowed sharply, swung into dirt ruts that led back into a patch of woodland.

Dave stopped, backed out on the road again, and headed the car back toward town before he stopped once more with the motor softly idling.

Dave turned behind the wheel, warily poised.

"You've had time to think it over, Maddox," the man in back said, sharper now and cold.

"I've thought."

Will-power kept Mr. Maddox quiet against the gun muzzle. Straining nerves cried to make a fight of it while there was a chance—if a gun in your back gave you any chance at all.

Dave said: "This is a lotta damn foolishness! Let me take him!"

"I'll handle it!" the cold voice said. "Maddox, you get one chance. No more. Beat it out of town!"

Mr. Maddox relaxed. "Any particular reason?"

"We don't like you!"

"Why bring me out here to say it?"

"We brought you out here for this!" A fist looped from behind, grazing Mr. Maddox's cheek and knocking him over against Dave.

Dave was waiting. Dave slugged the other cheek.

Mr. Maddox drove an elbow into Dave, knocking him back behind the wheel. A grab caught the door handle and the door was opening when the gun slugged Mr. Maddox out into the road.

He fell flat, lay dazed. As from far away he heard the cold voice close above him.

"Get smart, Maddox! If you're in town tomorrow, we'll take you! Lam out of the state while you've got a chance!"

Mr. Maddox was trying to get up. A kick knocked him sprawling again. The car started so fast the spinning wheels drove a stinging shower of gravel. When Mr. Maddox lurched groggily to his feet, the twin red tail-lights were dim through dust and vanishing over the first rise in the road.

His fingers found a cut, bleeding cheek. He was coated with dirt, sick and dizzy. The bright stars and clear sky, the peace and quiet of the lonesome night were a mockery to this hurt and helplessness.

Trembling, Mr. Maddox brushed at the dirt. He lurched when he stooped for his hat. Vague night sounds came out of the trees. Far off across the fields a dog barked. Mr. Maddox's feet crunched heavily on the gravel as he started back to the highway....

CHAPTER FOUR

THE WEEPSTAKES

IT WAS close to midnight when Mr. Maddox returned to the hotel. Quiet had not yet fallen over the streets. There would be little quiet now, day or night, until after Derby Day.

People in the lobby stared. The elevator boy stared. Mr. Maddox had brushed himself as well as he could without a whisk, but his suit still looked as if he had rolled on the ground.

The cut cheek had stopped bleeding, but the elevator mirrors showed a dried smear of blood, the raw cut itself and bruises. The broad bland face of Joe Maddox, usually so smiling and confident, was sadly battered.

In the mirror Mr. Maddox sighted a quick glance of understanding between two men behind him. Their faint smiles said they considered him just another drunk.

In the suite Oscar was smoking, walking about. He stopped, staring at Mr. Maddox. "My God, Joe!"

"Fix me another drink," Mr. Maddox ordered huskily as he stripped off his coat.

"You look like you ran into a buzzsaw!"

"Who gives a damn how I look? Stop babbling like a nitwit and give me a double Scotch, straight. What luck did you have with those calls I told you to make?"

Oscar jerked a thumb at an easy chair drawn up facing the window, its back toward Mr. Maddox. "Get up, punk, and spiel it," Oscar said as he turned to the Scotch bottle.

Stiffy slid out of the chair and eyed Mr. Maddox with wary fascination. Stiffy had donned a wrinkled blue coat, slicked down his hair, but still looked like a stable punk cornered where he had no business to be.

Oscar added: "He said guys out at the track could hear him talking at the telephone, so I told him to grab a taxi and come here."

"I'm glad somebody's using a head around here tonight!" Mr. Maddox said sarcastically. "Let's have it Stiffy. What about that black Chimp? Never mind trying to hide the tobacco in your cheek!"

Stiffy's Adam's apple bobbed in his long thin neck as he swallowed and smiled wanly. "I ast that damned—" Stiffy went mute, backing to the shelter of his chair. "Hit ain't my fault, Mist' Joe!" Stiffy pleaded. "Comes when I ain't a-lookin'! I was tryin' to think fast—"

"Never mind this time. What about Chimp?"

"I snooped like you said. Plenty knowed that ole crop-ear dinge. Nigger gal with a razor sliced his ear off when he two-timed her. She yelled if them black cats liked him so well she'd cut him into cat meat for them. Hit scared the bob-tailed hell outen him an' he lit runnin' with his ear in his hand and kept going!"

Stiffy swallowed. "He'd bought her a marriage license, too. He never set eye on that damned ear again. Oncet when he was goin' through town on a freight he mighty near hopped off an'—"

"Never mind Chimp's past history," Mr. Maddox snapped. "What was he doing at the track?"

"Workin' around," said Stiffy. "Mostly around them Green Acres Farm horses."

"The Gerryman Stable?"

"Uh-huh."

"I'll be damned!" said Mr. Maddox. "Doubly and triply damned! Here's ten dollars!" Mr. Maddox scowled in remembrance as he failed to find the usual fat billfold inside his coat. "Oscar, give him a tenner. Give me that drink. Go on, Stiffy!"

"Gosh! Thanks!" Stiffy grabbed the money that Oscar handed him. "I reckon that's all. There's a nigger works for the Green Acre Stables 'at's some kin to this ole Chimp. He's the one told me how-come him to lose that there ear."

Mr. Maddox almost choked on the double whiskey. "Chimp's got a relative working for Gloria Gerryman?"

"Uh-huh. Name of Yaller Sam. He come with the Green Acre Farm when it was sold. Yaller Sam's a high-steppin' little nigger. Says he ain't claiming the dead 'un for kin so's they can't make him pay for the buryin'. Told me that hisself. I mighty near hung one on him for being so derned smart."

"Did you get Miss Cavanaugh's address?"

"I got it," Oscar said.

"That's all, Stiffy," Mr. Maddox decided. "Keep your mouth shut about this."

OSCAR waited until the door closed behind Stiffy. "I couldn't find a Jerry Cavanaugh in the phone book, Joe. So I long-distanced the farm. A sleepy nigger woman answered. She was all tangled up about what I wanted, but she finally got the idea. She hunted around a little and came back with an address and telephone number. It's on that paper by the telephone. South Third Street."

Mr. Maddox winced almost visibly. "Did you call Jerry?"

"Yes. A man answered and said he wasn't Cavanaugh. Said he didn't know when Cavanaugh would be back. He asked me who I was and I stalled."

"Who was he?"

"How should I know? All he said was he wasn't Jerry Cavanaugh. Anyway a dame came to the phone a moment later and started trying to find out who wanted Cavanaugh."

"And you didn't find out who she was either?"

"You didn't say to get the dope on everybody who answered Cavanaugh's telephone," Oscar complained. "She sounded too anxious to get a line on me. I stalled her, too—and when she said she didn't know when Cavanaugh would be back I told her I'd call later."

"Did you mention my name?"

"I wouldn't until I got Cavanaugh. I was getting ready to call again when you came in."

"Which shows how smart it is to be too smart—and maybe you were right after all," Mr. Maddox growled, turning to the Scotch bottle again. "I've got to change clothes and get patched up. Call a doctor."

"Joe! Are you going out again?"

"I am!"

"Next time you'll come back on a shutter," Oscar warned sourly. "And by the looks of you, it almost happened this time! I knew that one-eared nigger in the morgue would get you into trouble!"

"Get my clothes!"

"You didn't have ten bucks to give that boy. Where's your bankroll, Joe?"

Mr. Maddox hurled the empty whiskey glass on the floor. "I wish I knew! I wish I knew a lot of things! I wish you'd cut that damned bleating! If it'll make you feel any better, I got snatched, beat up and robbed! And warned that if I'm in town tomorrow, I get knocked off! Does that make you feel any better?"

Oscar groaned. "I knew it was too good to last! Fine weather, plenty of dough for the book! Everything hotsy-totsy—and this has to happen!, Want me to start packing, Joe?"

"Get my brown suit!" Mr. Maddox snarled. "We came here for the Derby, didn't we?"

THE THIRD STREET address of Jerry Cavanaugh was another red brick apartment house, severe, dignified. When a taxi deposited Mr. Maddox on the curb, it was so late most windows were dark. There was not much traffic on the streets either.

Apartment 3, Oscar's information said. The foyer mail box for Apartment 3 bore a small card lettered: *D.H. Crowder—J. Cavanaugh.*

The telephone, Mr. Maddox guessed, was listed in Crowder's name. Crowder must have answered Oscar's call. The woman could be anyone, wife or friend of either man.

A bell button and speaking tube were above the mail box. Mr. Maddox ignored them and walked heavily up the stairs.

Apartment 3 was at the back.

Mr. Maddox lifted the small brass knocker, let it fall with a bang.

A thumb lock turning quickly inside suggested the person had been waiting for a caller. Then the opening door framed the anxious face of Jeanne Cavanaugh.

She gasped slightly at sight of Mr. Maddox. She was uncertain, astonished, quickly fearful.

"I—I didn't expect to see you!" she said.

"Ditto." Mr. Maddox smiled ruefully. "May I come in?"

"Why—yes. I'm waiting for Jerry. You—you wanted to see Jerry?"

A yellow dinner dress threw gold in Jeanne's hair, now caught most properly on her head. She was a little lady in her own right now, with a slim natural grace that Gloria Gerryman would never have. For it was an inner grace that money and beauty salons could never attain.

"Sam Harmsworth should see," Mr. Maddox thought as he lumbered into the small living-room. "The boy's a fool if he can't tell which is the thoroughbred filly." But aloud, he said: "Jerry? Yes, I hoped I'd find Jerry."

Jeanne was looking at Mr. Maddox's face. "You've been hurt?"

"Slightly." Mr. Maddox chuckled. "So we're both waiting for Jerry. When do you expect him?"

Jeanne sat down opposite him. Her small strong hands moved nervously in her lap. "I don't know," she confessed, watching him. "What—what do you want with Jerry?"

She was worried. Afraid too. And she had no cause to fear Joe Maddox. It had to be fear for her brother.

"Are we alone?"

Jeanne nodded. "Sam Harmsworth brought me here and left a little while ago."

"Fine young fellow."

"Yes," said Jeanne. Color rushed into her face.

"So it's that way," Mr. Maddox thought. But to Jeanne he said: "I wondered what Jerry was doing to help—and what I could do."

"I thought so," said Jeanne. "Please—I told you this afternoon—"

"None of my business, eh?"

Jeanne stood up, as if nerves cried against calm. "There's nothing you can do."

"Except buy your horse," Mr. Maddox supplied calmly.

"You won't—can't. Please forget everything."

"Jerry might have an idea," Mr. Maddox mused.

"I don't want you to say anything to Jerry!"

Mr. Maddox said casually: "Sam Harmsworth has plenty of money. Perhaps—"

"No!" said Jeanne passionately. "Not one word to Sam about this! I—I hardly know him! Today is the first time we've met for years!"

"He seemed to like it." Mr. Maddox smiled. "Didn't I hear something about an engagement he had tonight at Green Acres Farm?"

Jeanne's face was flaming. "Leave Sam out of this!"

Mr. Maddox chuckled again. "If that's the way you feel about him."

"I didn't say I felt any way about him! Please stop insinuating such nonsense!"

"I seem to be saying all the wrong things," Mr. Maddox said, with contriteness somewhat spoiled by the understanding amusement in his eyes. "But while I'm here, can I ask a few questions?"

"About what?"

"Do you know a black stable hand at the track called Chimp? Has one ear."

"No. Why do you ask?"

"It's sort of a game. D'you know a thin-faced fellow called Dave?"

Jeanne thought a moment and nodded. "I know the Reverend David Jones, in Mt. Washington. He's tall and thin."

"Not the man, I'm afraid." Mr. Maddox chuckled again. "How about a woman who calls herself Norlene Bell?"

"I don't know her. I don't see what all this is leading to."

"Neither do I," Mr. Maddox admitted. "Here's one more. Do you know Slim Pasternik?"

"Slim Pasternik?" Jeanne repeated sharply. The fear was dark in her eyes again. "Who is *he?*"

"Gunman and gambler."

JEANNE'S mouth opened. Then she turned to cigarettes lying on the wall table. The match flame trembled in her unsteady hand. She was looking down at the table, toying with the cigarettes, when her strained voice answered.

"I guess I've heard the name. That's all."

The easy chair creaked softly as Mr. Maddox got up and stepped to her. Jeanne looked up at him. She was pale.

"So Slim's got a hand in it?" Mr. Maddox said quietly. "Jeanny, don't lie to me now. I was a friend of your father's. I'm your friend. What about Slim Pasternik? There was a murder tonight."

"A murder? Ah—*who?* Jerry—"

"Not Jerry. A colored stable hand. But it was murder. Where is Jerry?"

Jeanne's laugh had a hysterical note. She was near to tears. "You startled me. Jerry wouldn't know anything about a murder. I—I don't know this man Pasternik. The worst that Jerry can be doing tonight is gambling. I'm not even sure of that. I—I'm only afraid he is."

"Gambling?" repeated Mr. Maddox. "And Jerry works in a bank?"

Jeanne's tears were unshed but glistening. Her chin trembled. "Jerry's not working at the bank just now. He—he—" Jeanne groped for a handkerchief.

Mr. Maddox, towering above her, looked concerned and thoughtful. "Jerry's out of the bank now," he mused. "And you need a lot of cash quick. And Jerry's been gambling? That makes a picture, Jeanny. How long has Jerry been gambling?"

"Several years," Jeanne admitted in a stifled voice. "At first he won a lot of money. Then he lost. He—he wins a little and loses a lot. And keeps thinking that he'll win a lot any time. Jerry's always been reckless. He'd never listen to others, not even his father. He doesn't drink—but this gambling is like a fever. And he loses and loses."

"You sold El Conde to Gloria Gerryman to get money for him?" Mr. Maddox guessed.

Wearily Jeanne said: "Jerry has a half-interest in the farm. El Conde was half his. And I'd do anything if it would help him. Most of our horses are gone. The farm is mortgaged. And—and Jerry keeps thinking he'll help with his gambling and only makes it worse. He's in trouble now."

"At the bank?" Mr. Maddox guessed again. "Jerry took some money?"

Jeanne wiped her eyes. "Just a little at first and then a lot more. They discovered it several days ago."

"And now Jerry pays it back quickly or gets a stretch in stir?"

Jeanne nodded. "Unless it's paid back or—or I give Gloria Gerryman a bill of sale by tomorrow for Jeanne's Hope."

"What the devil," Mr. Maddox exploded, "does Gloria Gerryman have to do with it?"

"Jerry took the money from the Gerryman account and thought he could cover it up for a time," Jeanne said wretchedly. "Gloria discovered the shortage and told the bank she didn't want Jerry arrested until she thought it over. The bank thinks she's doing it because our two farms are close together. Because we're neighbors. The bank thinks it's kind and generous of her. The Gerryman account is so large that the bank is glad to do almost anything Gloria demands."

Mr. Maddox growled under his breath. "If I'm any good as a guesser, that gold-plated little tart never did anything generous unless she got plenty out of it. So she wants your horse, kid?"

JOE MADDOX was a kindly man, and never was more so than at a time like this. A moment later Jeanne was crying softly against his coat.

"She m-means to win this Derby no matter what she has to do. She told me so. And she's heard that Jeanne's Hope has a good chance of winning. She says she'll pay Jerry's shortage at the bank and keep him out of prison if I give her a bill of sale for Jeanne's Hope and let Jeanne's Hope run under the Gerryman colors, too!"

"If I know the lady, your horse wouldn't stand much chance of winning under the Gerryman colors," Mr. Maddox growled. "There's too much Gerryman money bet on El Conde to win. That girl is sharp and hard. That means El Conde had better win."

"Jerry thinks so, too," Jeanne said wearily. "He doesn't think Gloria would let Jeanne's Hope win. And he says Jeanne's Hope has to run and win. He won't hear of anything else. He's sure our horse will win. He says we'll have plenty of money then—much more than the purse—enough to pay the bank back and take care of any trouble. He made me promise not to say anything until he saw me again. Oh, I don't know what to do! I tried to sell Jeanne's Hope for cash to pay the bank—and I couldn't!"

"How much did Jerry take?"

"About nineteen thousand—from the Valley Trust Company."

"And Jerry's out gambling tonight, letting you worry?"

"He told me not to worry when I talked to him on the telephone tonight. He said he'd be too busy to see me, but everything would be all right. He sounded excited and confident when he hung up."

Jeanne's gesture was helpless. "He wouldn't tell me anything. All I could do was come here, have the janitor let us in and wait."

"How about this Crowder, whose name is on the mail box?"

"That's Dick Crowder. They went to college together. Dick's out of town."

Mr. Maddox thought a moment, and then smiled and patted her shoulder. "You've done enough worrying. Turn in here and get some sleep. Maybe Jerry's right. Maybe everything will be all right."

"How can it be?"

"Let Jerry and me worry about it," chuckled Mr. Maddox. "You get your beauty sleep—and tomorrow keep an eye on your horse and Sam Harmsworth."

"I won't be seeing Sam again. I told him so tonight."

"And what did Sam say?"

"He got mad when I wouldn't tell him why."

"Don't blame him," said Mr. Maddox. "If he's got any sense he won't even listen to you. But if he's fallen in love with you he probably is dizzy and not thinking straight."

"Sam's not in love with me! He's practically engaged to Gloria Gerryman!"

"So you're going to dog it in the stretch-run and let her have him," Mr. Maddox snorted. "What kind of racing is that? You're crazy about him!"

"I always have been. And I've cried all over you and I feel better. Sam won't want to see me again after Gloria tells him about Jerry. So let's all forget it."

"If Gerryman's as smart as I think she is, she won't blab to Sam until she gets him," Mr. Maddox said shrewdly. "Forget it and go to sleep. I'm going. Good-night."

MR. MADDOX was smiling as he left the apartment—and scowling as he hurried downstairs. He'd given Jeanne encouragement that even Joe Maddox could hardly justify. He didn't have twenty grand to help. Borrowing such a sum at this time was almost impossible. Word would flash over town that Joe Maddox was borrowing and must be broke. A bookie was only as good as his prosperity. And if the book was tampered with, if reserve cash was used and the book couldn't pay off after the Derby, there's be hell for Joe Maddox to face.

Jeanne had told him things he didn't know or suspect—and it only made more puzzling the things that already had happened.

Swearing softly under his breath Mr. Maddox hurried out of the apartment house to his waiting taxi. He had taken only half a dozen steps from the door when a familiar voice spoke behind him.

"In a hurry, Joe?"

"Where," said Mr. Maddox irritably as he swung around, "in the devil did you come from, Cassidy?"

Cassidy joined him, bulking in the shadows. "Out of the shrubbery, Joe."

"Following me, huh?"

"Just watching you, Joe," Cassidy said with a hint of grimness. "What was the idea of stalling me about going from the morgue to bed?"

"Any law against staying awake—or dropping around to see a friend?"

"When you came back from your first trip out, you looked like a little law might have helped you," Cassidy said sarcastically. "Who put the slug on you, Joe? And why?"

"So you were watching me then too, were you?" Mr. Maddox growled.

"Murder," said Cassidy, "always did make me curious. The way you're acting tonight makes it worse. Who was the girl you went out with after you shook me near the morgue? I got the license number, but you two ducked into the car so fast you got away before I could follow."

"What is that license number?" Mr. Maddox asked quickly.

"Who's the woman?" Cassidy countered.

They eyed one another.

"Maybe we can help each other," Mr. Maddox reluctantly decided.

"Yeah?" said Cassidy suspiciously.

"She said a couple of her men friends wanted to talk horses. We came out here on South Third—and it was a stick-up. They drove me out in the country, warned me to get out of town in the morning, slugged me and left me to walk back."

"You looked like it," Cassidy grudgingly admitted. "Did you report it?"

"Not yet. Maybe that car license will give me a chance to find out who it was."

"Or me," said Cassidy. "Come clean, Joe. You got heisted and slugged. But you don't fall for a trick like that without a reason. What else?"

"Can I trust you, Cassidy?"

"Sure you can, Joe. Why ask?"

"It's a waste of breath," admitted Mr. Maddox. "I know the answer. But my nose is clean, Cassidy, and I need some help. Maybe I can help you, too. I'll deny this if some of your copper friends start asking. But that one-eared nigger laid a bet on a Derby horse with me this morning. Two hundred and forty dollars. Big money for him. And later in the day comes five hundred on the same horse from this dame who drives me to the stick-up. Cash money she laid down. It sounded like a straight story when she said her boy friend had a roll of cash he wanted to lay. So I went with her."

"How much did they get off you?"

"Somewhere between eight and nine grand. Everything but my diamond."

Cassidy laughed with grim amusement. "Not bad. Not bad at all, Joe. Five hundred to take nine grand. That's better odds than you like to pay off."

"They didn't know I'd be carrying a roll. They wanted to slug me and warn me out of town."

"Why?"

"You tell me," suggested Mr. Maddox. "The girl called herself Norlene Bell. One of the men is called Dave."

"Never heard of the woman. There's a million Daves. Know anything more?"

"If I knew, I'd tell you," said Mr. Maddox virtuously. "They half killed me."

"Tough, Joe. Tough. But thanks for coming clean, even if you did have to be slugged to make you talk. My taxi is back up the street. You turning in now?"

"Why not? Now that you're working on it, I'll sleep like a baby."

"I don't like the sound of that," said Cassidy suspiciously as they parted.

Mr. Maddox was smiling grimly as he reentered his taxi. "Broadway Hotel," he said to the driver.

CHAPTER FIVE

MR. MADDOX HOCKS HIS LUCK

IT WAS two o'clock of the new day when Mr. Maddox entered the Broadway lobby. The desk clerk did not flick an eye at Mr. Maddox's question. He knew the answer automatically.

"Mr. Major's suite is Six-sixteen."

On the sixth floor people were still awake. A radio or two was audible and voices in some of the rooms. Six-sixteen was at the back.

Two men came out as Mr. Maddox approached. A third man looked out, closed the door quickly on a chain and looked through the narrow opening.

"Tell Duke it's Joe Maddox."

Several seconds later another man looked out, said, "Hello, Maddox," and unchained the door.

Duke Major looked like a well-bred Englishman, quiet, keen.

The first man and another, both posted inside the door, were harder looking. A practised eye could mark gun bulges under their arms.

In an adjoining room voices murmured. Duke Major opened the door and the voices were plainer, tobacco smoke thick. But there was not much noise.

Fifteen to eighteen men stood around a portable dice table, intent on the game. Some were in shirt sleeves. Tables around the walls held liquor bottles, glasses, ice, plates of sandwiches, carafes of drinking water.

It was not very impressive until one looked over shoulders and saw thousand-dollar bills, five-hundreds, hundreds, fifties scattered on the table, and wads of the same kind of money held carelessly by the players.

Most of the year Duke Major held forth in New York. His game changed location every night or so. But the play was always high cash play, honest dice, and no trouble.

Mr. Maddox knew some of the faces. You'd meet them in New York, in Chicago, Miami, Frisco. Some gambled as a profession, some liked their excitement high and costly, and could afford it. Most of them were here in Louisville because the Derby would be run tomorrow.

MR. MADDOX grunted with satisfaction when he saw Honest John O'Toole, in shirt sleeves, cigar in mouth, rolling the dice.

Slim Pasternik was across the table, dapper, smiling as usual, missing nothing with shrewd cold eyes. Not betting himself, Slim was watching Jerry Cavanaugh toss a fifty on the table.

A look told Mr. Maddox it was the same Jerry Cavanaugh that Cap'n Jim had turned over a knee. A young man now, rather handsome, and reckless, headstrong.

The dice rolled and Slim Pasternik looked up. He saw the big bland impressive figure coming around the table. His eyes narrowed. He shot a look at O'Toole, who was rolling dice again and missed it.

"Hello, Jerry," Mr. Maddox said.

Jerry threw a quick look and blankly replied, "Hello," before he looked back at the table.

Jerry might have had a few drinks by the edge of excitement that gripped him, by the way his fingers nervously clutched a thin sheaf of twenties and fifties.

"Jeanny wants you," Mr. Maddox said.

O'Toole lost. Jerry snatched his money off the table before he looked around. "Anything wrong with Jeanne? Say, your name is Maddox, isn't it?"

"That's right. I want to see you for a few minutes."

"I'm busy now," Jerry said impatiently.

Mr. Maddox stopped smiling. "Son, your sister is worried. I want to talk to you."

Slim Pasternik thrust an elbow between them. "Scram, Maddox! You ain't wanted here!"

"You *will* be tough, Slim..." Mr. Maddox said almost regretfully.

His big fist traveled only a few inches to Slim's cheek, but Slim hit the floor well back from the table. He was up like a snarling cat, reaching under his coat.

Moving with astonishing speed for such a big man, Mr. Maddox caught the hand as it was coming out. A twist made Slim yell with pain. A small automatic clattered on the floor.

Mr. Maddox caught up the gun and stepped back, blandly chiding: "Some day your lousy tricks will get you into trouble."

The players had crowded back from the fracas. Jerry Cavanaugh was angry, bewildered.

"Are you crazy, Maddox? He's with me!"

"Never mind—we're leaving," Mr. Maddox said coldly.

The hard quiet voice of Duke Major demanded: "What's the trouble, gentlemen?"

Duke Major was flanked by the two door-guards holding automatics. They'd been in the room within seconds after trouble broke out.

O'Toole snapped: "That tin-horn bookie started all this! I saw him!"

Mr. Maddox said calmly: "This is Slim Pasternik's gun, Duke. I'll have a word with you."

Duke Major was brittle as they faced one another in the entrance hall. "You know my rules, Maddox. No trouble."

"Has young Cavanaugh been losing or winning?"

"I don't know. Losing a little, I think."

"A local bank where he worked caught him in a shortage the other day. He'd been gambling. Pasternik and O'Toole are playing him along for reasons of their own. His sister is badly worried."

Duke Major did not hesitate. "Pasternik brought him. I assumed he could afford this and knew what he was doing. Just a moment please."

Duke Major was suave as he stepped into the other room. "Gentlemen, I regret this slight misunderstanding. Mr. Cavanaugh, your friend is waiting outside."

Hotly Jerry said: "He's no friend of mine! I don't want—"

"I don't believe you understand me," Duke Major said easily. "Your friend is waiting for you."

"I'll go with him! Gimme that gun!" Slim Pasternik raged.

"In fifteen minutes, Pasternik. You know my rule. No weapons. You'll not be admitted again. Wait your fifteen minutes in the hall. Gentlemen, the game is open again."

The two armed men added the one grim touch. Grim enough for obedience. Jerry Cavanaugh was red with mortification as he left with Mr. Maddox. "Damn you, Maddox, I ought to—"

"You ought to have some sense by now," Mr. Maddox cut in coldly. "What's the idea of bucking dice on borrowed money?"

"I won't talk to you, Maddox!"

"You'll come with me or have more trouble."

"I think you're crazy!" Jerry said bitterly.

AS THEY walked away from the hotel, Mr. Maddox broke the silence. "I was a friend of your father's, Jerry. I'd like to help you. What kind of a proposition is Slim Pasternik offering?"

Jerry walked in tight-lipped silence.

"Son," said Mr. Maddox, "Slim's a crook. So is O'Toole. Why do you want Jeanne to run her horse in the Derby, even though Gloria Gerryman will have you pinched if Jeanne does?"

Jerry's silence continued.

"O'Toole's got a hand in it," Mr. Maddox mused. "And O'Toole has been placing the Gerryman money on El Conde. Is it reasonable that O'Toole wants Jeanne's Hope running against El Conde?"

"Who said he did?" Jerry burst out.

"If not, why are you so damn set on risking arrest just to see Jeanne's Hope run the Derby for your sister? Let Jeanne sign her horse over to Gerryman, settle your trouble, and then start over again right. It'll make Jeanne mighty happy."

"I know what I'm doing!" Jerry said angrily. "El Conde hasn't a—I mean, our horse will take the Derby. We'll win far more than the purse and have our horse too! There'll be money enough then to make the bank listen to reason! I can stand a day or so in jail to get that!"

"Mmmm," said Mr. Maddox. "So El Conde hasn't a chance to win the Derby? Maybe, son. Maybe. But a fist full of cash won't always quash an air-tight case of embezzlement. Sometimes the bank, and prosecuting attorney, have ideas of their own, even if the money is returned."

"I'll gamble on that!"

"You've had a hell of a lot of luck gambling so far, haven't you? Why don't you get wise and cut it out? Suppose your horse doesn't win? Where'll you be then?"

"He will! I've got a hunch! I know what I'm doing! I know what's best for myself and Jeanne! We hardly know you! We're not interested in you! Just keep your hands off our business!"

Mr. Maddox shrugged regretfully. "I know now why Cap'n Jim was whaling hell out of you the last time I saw you. I was going to take you to my hotel for the night. I guess I won't bother. Go on with your sucker gambling."

OSCAR was sitting up in pajamas and dressing-gown when Mr. Maddox returned. "I lose," said Oscar with relief. "You got in without a shutter under you. Cassidy, that Masterton cop, telephoned for you a few minutes ago. I said you weren't here, and Cassidy said that was all he wanted to know and hung up."

Mr. Maddox chuckled as he telephoned Jerry Cavanaugh's apartment, and waited. "I don't believe Cassidy trusts me."

Jeanne Cavanaugh's voice came on the wire.

"Mr. Maddox, Jeanny. I just left Jerry. He'll be all right, even if he doesn't call you or show up. He was gambling a little but it's over for tonight. Better get some sleep."

"Oh, thank you. I will now!" Jeanne said with relief.

"So it's a woman now," said Oscar accusingly as Mr. Maddox took off his coat. "You got to mix a woman in this and ask for more trouble when the Derby's almost on us!"

"Not much time left," Mr. Maddox agreed. "Why wouldn't El Conde have a chance to win?"

Oscar did not hesitate. "I'd give him plenty of chance. You win the Derby on form, not hunches or whispers. What's this Jeanne's Hope show as a two-year-old?"

"He seems to have rounded into form lately."

"So has Father Time," said Oscar. "My money goes on past performance."

"Then why shouldn't El Conde have a chance?"

"He *ought* to have a chance."

"That's what I'd like to make sure of," said Mr. Maddox enigmatically, as he started toward his bedroom.

MR. MADDOX slept late in the morning, and went down to the coffee shop for breakfast. He was not greatly surprised when Cassidy slid on the stool beside him, lifted one of the fat black cigars from Mr. Maddox's breast pocket and asked: "Sleep like a baby last night, Joe?"

"I didn't cry once," said Mr. Maddox modestly.

"After slugging Slim Pasternik!"

"Followed me again, did you?"

"A friend who was there told me. And so this Cavanaugh that Duke ran out with you has a piece of Jeanne's Hope?"

"Has he?"

Cassidy lighted the cigar. "I hear that Cavanaugh was with Pasternik and Honest John. The three of them wouldn't be greasing an ace for the Derby tomorrow, would they? Jeanne's Hope maybe not running like he ought to? With O'Toole placing the Gerryman money on El Conde, he wouldn't be trying to scuttle the next best horse, would he?"

"Ask him," Mr. Maddox grinned. "How about that car license?"

"I wired and just got an answer. Florida tag issued to a phony Miami address. The local police are watching for it. Where do you come in on this Cavanaugh-Pasternik-O'Toole play, Joe?"

"I'm trying to raise enough money to buy Jeanne's Hope," Mr. Maddox answered.

Cassidy got up disgustedly. "Don't hand me baloney, Joe! And if I catch you or these others monkeying with the Derby, God help all of you!"

That raised another angle to consider. At noon Mr. Maddox was no nearer a solution when he paid off a taxi at the track barn where Jeanne's Hope was stabled and turned to see Sam Harmsworth stalking around the end of the barn.

"This," said Mr. Maddox quickly, "is luck. I've been wanting to see you, Mr. Harmsworth."

"Don't talk to me about luck today!" Harmsworth snapped. "This cab vacant?"

The driver was already opening the door. Sam Harmsworth jumped in and left. Mr. Maddox was not surprised to find Jeanne sitting listlessly beside the tackroom door.

"Something wrong with Sam?" Mr. Maddox asked innocently.

"I made him go away."

"Love," decided Mr. Maddox, "would make a sucker out of any handicapper."

Jeanne said stonily: "Gloria Gerryman saw me this morning. She was furious because Sam spent the evening with me. If I see him again, or tell him she said anything, she'll have Jerry arrested. And she wants a bill of sale for Jeanne's Hope by six this evening."

"Going to give it to her?"

"I can't. Jerry is half-owner by law. This morning he refused to sign any bill of sale until after the Derby. I don't know what to do. Six o'clock isn't far away—and she'll have Jerry arrested!"

"Then you'll be free to spend the evening with Sam," Mr. Maddox pointed out. "Gerryman will do you every dirty trick she can. Claw her back. Take Sam away from her."

"I don't want Sam just to hurt her. After Jerry's arrested, Sam won't even want to see me."

"Let Sam say that. Jerry isn't arrested yet. And it's about time," said Mr. Maddox sternly, "that you shook Jerry off your apron strings. He knows what he wants to do. If he guesses wrong, it may teach him the lesson he needs. Wringing your hands and messing up your own life won't help him. What do you think Cap'n Jim would do if Jerry tried this hard-boiled damn foolishness on him?"

"He'd tell Jerry it was his own race and he'd have to run it," said Jeanne after a moment. "And—and he'd be right, I suppose." Jeanne drew a long breath and stood up. "All right. I wash my hands of Jerry in this. I'll run Jeanne's Hope to win no matter what happens."

"Good girl! Now get Sam!"

"Sam's out," Jeanne said firmly. "I'll not let Jerry's guilt smear Sam with disgraceful publicity as a—a friend of Jerry's sister. It would do just that. Sam is too prominent. The Cavanaughs will wash their dirty linen alone. I won't see Sam again—and that's that!"

"Gloria Gerryman will get him."

"I know," said Jeanne. "But maybe I'll win the Derby: That would be something, wouldn't it?"

Mr. Maddox glowered at Jeanne's unsteady smile—and suddenly exploded: "You're a fool, kid! Just the kind of a game little fool young Harmsworth needs! Stick around here this afternoon until you hear from me!"

THE GERRYMAN horses were several barns over. Maddox found the man he wanted currying a chestnut colt. Yellow Sam was a small mulatto, younger than Chimp, dressed like a dandy in striped silk shirt and high-waisted slacks.

"Boy," said Mr. Maddox, "I hear old Chimp was kin to you."

Yellow Sam broke off humming the *St. Louis Blues* and turned uneasy. "Naw, suh."

"Too bad. Chimp laid a bet with me on the Derby. I won't have to pay off then."

Yellow Sam blinked. "Is I kin, do you pay me do he win?"

"If you prove to the police you're kin to Chimp. And if the horse wins, which I doubt. Chimp bet two hundred and forty dollars on Jeanne's Hope to win. I gave him twenty to one."

"An' you pays on dat?"

"If Jeanne's Hope wins."

Yellow Sam threw down the currycomb and cut a buck and wing. "God'lmighty, I got rich! After tomorrow I never hit a lick no mo'!"

"You're damn sure Jeanne's Hope will win," said Mr. Maddox dryly.

Yellow Sam's face lost expression as he picked up the currycomb. "Naw, suh—I jus' hopin'. Where I get de winnin' money do I win?"

"I'll bring it around," Mr. Maddox said as he started on to the barn which housed his own modest racing-string. There he spoke briefly to Stiffy.

"Here's twenty for expenses. From now until the Derby starts, keep an eye on that Yellow Sam, over at the Gerryman Stable. Watch who he talks to, what he does every minute. But don't let him know."

The next thing was a telephone call to Oscar, asking: "How much cash is in the room and down in the hotel safe?"

"Twelve thousand in the safe," Oscar said. "Thirty-eight hundred and seventy up here."

"Put it with the twelve grand. I'll want it all shortly."

Oscar was instantly apprehensive. "You lost over eight grand last night, Joe! Are you going to lose this? It's the pay-off dough!"

"You'll get more in this evening and tomorrow morning."

"And we'll still have to pay off after the race!" Oscar said with growing anguish. "Joe, don't do anything foolish!"

"Only a fool can afford to be foolish," Mr. Maddox chuckled. "Maybe that makes me a fool." He hung up on Oscar, waited a moment and called Duke Major at the Broadway Hotel.

"Will you be there until I can taxi in from the track, Duke?"

"I'm having lunch in the Club House restaurant," Duke Major said. "Can I see you there?"

IT WAS almost an hour later when a waiter summoned Duke Major from a luncheon party at the Club House to the table where Mr. Maddox sat alone.

People were fast filling the seats, boxes and the big inner courts of the grandstand. Most of the Club House tables were already filled or reserved. Tomorrow was Derby Day. By the hour, by thousands upon thousands, the mighty Derby crowd was pouring into Louisville.

Mr. Maddox was smiling faintly as he twisted the glinting diamond ring off his finger. "How big a loan on this, Duke?"

Duke Major whistled softly. "Broke, Maddox?"

"Business is too good," said Mr. Maddox calmly. "I need more cash."

Duke Major examined the diamond. "I've heard this ring is your luck. Taking a chance on letting it go at this time, aren't you?"

"I'm using it for luck this time."

Duke Major nodded understandingly. "Five thousand is the best I can do. I'll have to give you a check on the Valley Trust."

"Perfect."

IT WAS almost two o'clock when Mr. Maddox collected the bankroll from the hotel safe.... Almost two-thirty when the lean president of the Valley Trust Company shook hands, eyed the prosperous smiling visitor and warmly asked: "What can I do for you, Mr. Maddox?"

Smiling, Mr. Maddox laid a neat stack of thousand-dollar bills on the desk and tapped them with a big finger.

"You can accept this money for a release on young Cavanaugh."

Stafford, the president, was startled. "Cavanaugh gave me to understand he couldn't make good. We haven't quite decided what to do about him."

"Miss Gerryman might make good and she might not," Mr. Maddox suggested blandly. "This—er—regrettable affair will make bad publicity for the bank. Young Cavanaugh comes from a fine old Kentucky family. It seems a pity to proceed on the uncertain whims of a headstrong young Yankee girl who might change her mind at the last minute. Wouldn't your stockholders prefer to have the money back without question now...."

It was five minutes to three when Mr. Maddox emerged from the Valley Trust Company with a sealed envelope which he dispatched to Jeanne Cavanaugh at the track, by Postal messenger, together with a telegram.

NOW DO WHAT YOU WANT TO DO STOP NOT A WORD OF THIS TO JERRY STOP GOOD LUCK AND CLAW HARD AND FAST.

Oscar was sitting at the tables which held telephones and betting-sheets when Mr. Maddox strolled in some time later. Oscar was just answering one of the telephones.

"Just a minute. Here he is," Oscar said, and put a hand over the mouthpiece. "This guy's called several times for you, Joe."

The gruff voice on the wire had a familiar ring.

"Never mind having this call traced, Maddox. So you got tough and stayed on in town? What's the idea?"

"No cheap gunmen can run me out of any town," Mr. Maddox said grimly. "I'm making my book and to hell with you! What happens now?"

"We're giving you two more days! See that you stick to your book and nothing else! We're watching you!"

The wire went dead. Mr. Maddox swore softly as he put the handset down. "Now what did he mean by that!"

"What did who mean by what?" Oscar demanded. Oscar was jumpy. He shoved over a stack of five-hundred-dollar bills.

"You'd better hear about this first. Young Cavanaugh bet this on his horse, Jeanne's Hope. Five grand. I took it because we figured El Conde's got the edge. But I've been sweating. Cavanaugh must know something. He seemed damn sure his horse would win and it'd do him plenty of good to win from you. I telephoned Jersey City and Chicago. The play there is on El Conde. Plenty of it. No big money on Jeanne's Hope yet. What do you make of it?"

"Jeanne's Hope will be in there to win. Maybe he'll take the Derby."

"And then what? Have we still got the bankroll?" Oscar stared, and with sudden uneasiness, demanded: "Joe, where's your ring?"

Mr. Maddox looked down at his bare hand. A smile started on his broad face, and turned into a rising chuckle that shook the vast expanse of his well-fleshed figure.

"I traded the bankroll and the ring to Cupid for a sharp set of kitty claws that I hope will scratch like hell."

"Kitty claws? Cupid?" Oscar gulped with growing horror. "My God, Joe, what have you done? We're sunk! I gotta feeling! We're sunk this time!"

Still chuckling, Mr. Maddox agreed. "If Jeanne's Hope wins, we're scuttled. And we might as well make a hell of a splash as we go down. From now until the Derby starts, cover every dollar of Jeanne's Hope money that you can find. And may the Lord have mercy on us!"

CHAPTER SIX

HONEST JOHN O'TOOLE

OUT AT Churchill Downs the afternoon races ended—the last races before Derby Day. And as twilight deepened into night, the track crowd joined the host of newcomers pouring in from all parts of the country.

Hotels had no rooms, no beds. Lines of people waited patiently for restaurant tables to be vacated. Traffic tangled and crept along on the downtown streets. All through the night more cars, more trains, more people would be coming. In the morning, highways leading to Louisville would be filled with speeding cars.

Joe Maddox had seen it all many times before. But always there was the same pulse-tingling excitement, even for a hardened old bookie.

And in thirty years there never had been a pre-Derby evening like this for Joe Maddox. On the streets and in the hotels were an ever-increasing number of familiar faces. An increasing tide of money to be bet. There were greetings and handshakes, talk of past races and the Derby on the morrow. There was everything that Joe Maddox lived for.

And there was hardly an eye keen enough to mark the undercurrent of grimness behind Joe Maddox's broad beaming smile. Grimness such as Joe Maddox had never known before.

For this was the first time—the first time in thirty years—that Joe Maddox had gone so far out on the surface of disaster. For the first time in thirty years Joe Maddox had deliberately put himself in a position where there was a good chance he couldn't pay off.

Old friends, old patrons who trusted Joe Maddox as they trusted their bankers, had cash money to bet, and did. They bet with Joe Maddox on the street, with Oscar at the hotel. They slapped Joe Maddox's back, shook his hand, and went their way certain that if their choices won, they'd get their winning money.

And Joe Maddox had to take that money. To refuse would make disaster certain. Too much money already had been bet with the book, and it was gone.

In the Brown Hotel lobby Mr. Maddox met Jerry Cavanaugh, sarcastically smiling. "Will you cover more money on my horse, Maddox?"

"Take it up to Oscar," Mr. Maddox directed. "Any amount."

"Since you know so much," said Jerry, "notice that I'm still at my affairs. Tomorrow I'll be in the clear."

"El Conde may settle you," Mr. Maddox said grimly.

"Not a chance!"

The jeering voice was Jerry Cavanaugh's. The words and money came from others. Doubt grew on Mr. Maddox like a mist of gloom. There were only a few hours left to discover why El Conde didn't have a chance.

An hour later Mr. Maddox looked in on Oscar and the betting-sheets.

"Cavanaugh brought fifteen grand more on Jeanne's Hope," Oscar said huskily. "And that Harley Smith repeated with four grand. He wanted to go on the cuff for three grand more and I said cash."

"Take all the cash he brings."

Direly Oscar muttered: "Somebody knows something. If we ain't being taken to the cleaners, I've never seen it done before."

"Any word from Stiffy yet?" Mr. Maddox asked.

"I called the barn. He ain't around. That Masterton cop said he'd be down in the lobby for a while and wanted to see you."

"I'll go down," Mr. Maddox decided. "Have me paged if Stiffy calls."

Cassidy was at the cigar counter in the lobby. "Every dip and con man on the circuit is in town," he growled. "I'm tired of collaring them. For two cents, Joe, I'd have you vagged."

Mr. Maddox produced two coppers. Cassidy irritably waved them away.

"I hear a nigger nephew has claimed old Chimp's body. Says Chimp didn't have any enemies. But that isn't why I wanted you. I hear that Cavanaugh and Slim Pasternik are laying heavy money around town on Cavanaugh's horse. What's your idea of that?"

Mr. Maddox chuckled. "How would I know? I only brought a racing-stable to town." And as Cassidy reddened, Mr. Maddox said abruptly: "That boy's paging me. I'll see you in a few minutes."

MR. MADDOX got out of the elevator and was jovially greeted by a plump, smirking man waiting to go down. "Hello, Joe. Glad to see you, Joe. I just came from your room. Business is fine, eh?"

"Rushing," said Mr. Maddox shortly. "Got a horse you like tomorrow?"

"You ask me that, Joe? After the money I've left with you on Jeanne's Hope? A fine horse, Joe. I've been watching him."

"So?" said Mr. Maddox. "Maybe I'd better watch him too."

And just then an elevator took Harley Smith away, and Mr. Maddox hurried to the suite, where Oscar had an open telephone waiting. "Stiffy," Oscar said.

Stiffy's voice over the wire was husky with earnestness. "I was a-watchin' that nigger, Boss, an' I lost him."

"What did he do before you lost him?"

"He worked around the barn all afternoon," said Stiffy. "And then he rode in a street car to town an' seen the police, an' then he come back an' et supper, an' it wasn't till he took him a walk after dark an' talked to a guy drivin' a big white car that I lost him."

Carefully Mr. Maddox asked: "Was it a big cream-colored sedan, Stiffy?"

"Uh-huh. Yaller Sam took him a walk over past Central Avenue, an' clumb in the auto an' talked with a feller inside. It was dark along there an' I snuck up behind to see what they was a-doin'. Before I got me a chance to duck, that damn nigger jumped out an' the car started off an' I lost him."

"I see. He saw you standing there?"

"Hell, no!" denied Stiffy. "I ain't that dumb. I clumb on the rear bumper an' rode that white car clean around the corner an' the nigger never even knowed I'd been there. But my dern foot got caught in the bumper," Stiffy said apologetically. "Wasn't nothin' to do but hang on till the damn thing stopped. Wasn't far or I'd fell off an' been drug along the street. The driver went in a house an' never seen me back there. So I figured I'd better tell you, Boss."

"Stiffy," said Mr. Maddox almost prayerfully, "could you find that house again?"

"I ain't only two blocks away now, at a drug store."

"Give me the address and wait on the corner!"

"More trouble, I suppose," Oscar commented sourly as Mr. Maddox put the telephone down. "And if it'll make you feel any better, Harley Smith bet another three grand on the Cavanaugh horse. Must of cleaned him, too, by the looks of those greasy twenties he had to dig up."

Mr. Maddox glanced carelessly at the dirty, worn, much-folded bills Oscar indicated. Suddenly he snatched them up and examined them. He jerked one out that had a slightly torn corner.

"I remember this one! I got these twenties from old Chimp! They're betting my own money back with me! Where do I find that dirty crook, Harley Smith?"

"He didn't give an address," Oscar said weakly. "Joe, is this dough part of that bankroll you lost last night?"

Mr. Maddox was already leaving, swearing as he went…. There was no sign of Harley Smith in the crowded lobby or outside where Cassidy followed Mr. Maddox.

"Why charge around here talking to yourself, Joe?"

Mr. Maddox snarled: "I just saw some of the money that was heisted off me last night! He left it upstairs!"

Cassidy stared—and then began to grin. "Joe, that sounds like somebody bet your own money back with you.... By God, *it's so!* What a story this'll make! And you can't prove it on him unless you admit running an illegal book here in Louisville!"

Red-faced, glaring, Mr. Maddox realized the trap he was in. A shout of laughter would roll across the American racing circuits when this story on Joe Maddox started circulating.

Cassidy was snorting, shaking as the full humor of it struck him.

Mr. Maddox eyed him wrathfully, and then speculatively. "Suppose, you laughing hyena, I could tip you off about a hocus that's being cooked up in the Derby tomorrow?"

Cassidy stopped laughing. "Don't kid me, Joe!"

"A little help about my bankroll, and a tight lip about it afterward might pay you odds."

Now Cassidy was alert in his role of a track detective. "If you know anything, Joe, write your own ticket. I'll keep my end of it. It's a promise."

"Let's find a taxi and I'll tell you about it while we ride," Mr. Maddox decided.

STIFFY said huskily: "There's the damn car still a-sittin' there." The cream-colored sedan was parked before a bungalow not far from Churchill Downs.

"Wait here," Mr. Maddox ordered.

"O'Toole's car all right," Cassidy muttered as they came abreast.

Cassidy was hard and serious now, after all he had heard in the taxicab. Crooked work in the Kentucky Derby, with the murder of old Chimp in the background, was big, important. A crooked coup in the Derby would deal a smashing blow to racing on all American tracks.

"Stiffy didn't see who was driving," Mr. Maddox husked. "Maybe we can see through a side window."

The bungalow porch was empty. Lights were on in the front of the house. A radio was playing inside. Cassidy cursed softly under his breath, and then jumped as Mr. Maddox's warning hand caught his arm.

Another automobile was driving up in front. They crouched at the side of the house as two people hurried to the front door and entered.

Mr. Maddox risked a look as the door opened. He swore softly as it closed again.

"That's Harley Smith and the girl who decoyed me to that heist last night! So they're close to O'Toole—and feeding my own money back to me! I'm going to try the back door!"

The radio was turned off as they went to the back of the house. There was a small screened back porch. The back rooms were dark.

The porch floor-boards creaked. Cassidy tried the back door and it opened. The dark room inside smelled of cooking. Voices carried in the small bungalow. Mr. Maddox recognized Harley Smith speaking.

"They took it all and no questions. I almost laughed in the big sap's face when I met him at the elevators. O'Toole was smart to let him stay over a day and make his book. I'm like O'Toole. If you have to take a guy or shut him up, get his dough first. Slim, are you sure everything's right now? We've all socked every dollar on that Cavanaugh horse."

Slim Pasternik's thin voice answered. "I gave the stuff to the nigger. He'll slip it in the morning feed. We've used it before. It's sure-fire and won't show in the saliva. El Conde will run, but he won't be a Derby horse."

"Are you sure about that nigger?"

"Sure. He's smart. And he won't get careless, since Dave and Harry here fixed the old nigger I caught listening to us that night at the track. Dave, it looks like that old Chimp told the truth, too, before you conked him. He only bet a few dollars with Maddox. Didn't talk. And after Maddox pays off, Maddox won't have a chance to think it all over and make a squawk. I'll get him myself."

Another voice, a cold familiar voice said: "O.K. about El Conde. But supposing this Cavanaugh horse doesn't win—with all our dough on him?"

"Stop crying about your dough, Harry!" Slim Pasternik snapped. "Look at O'Toole—over a hundred grand on the same horse! Every dime he can raise and borrow, and all the eighty grand he was supposed to have placed out for the Gerryman girl. He was sitting pretty—eighty grand to the good. All he had to do was keep the Gerryman horse from winning."

"Honest John O'Toole!" Mr. Maddox breathed.

Cassidy jabbed him with a warning elbow as Slim Pasternik talked on. "The Gerryman girl tipped O'Toole. Her trainer had been watching the training track on the Cavanaugh farm and putting a stop-watch on this Jeanne's Hope when he worked. He was a flash, and no one else knew it. The Gerryman girl began to worry and blabbed to O'Toole. To check it I came to town a month ago and made a pal out of Cavanaugh himself. It wasn't hard. He's a sap, too. And short of cash. So when I told him I had dough looking for a good Derby shot, and I'd split with anyone who could steer me right, he fell for it and told me about the hot shot they'd been nursing along. El Conde was the only one that figured to beat him."

Slim laughed scornfully. "When I told Cavanaugh I had inside dope from the Gerryman stable that El Conde wouldn't last the Derby distance, he swallowed it. He said it must be so because the Gerrymans wanted to run Jeanne's Hope in the Derby as a Gerryman horse. He decided it was proof they didn't have a Derby winner in El Conde. So he's been playing along with me. I've been handing him O'Toole's dough—and he's been placing it as his own for a cut. It's perfect. There won't even be questions about O'Toole's betting heavily against El Conde. And with El Conde muffing the race, we'll all clean up."

"And Cavanaugh gets a cut?" the Bell girl questioned.

"Are we dumb?" Slim countered. "Cavanaugh's screwy about gambling. We've already got a play ready to take his purse money from him. And maybe his horse too. It's perfect, I tell you. We'll take everything like Grant took Richmond. Let's have a drink on it."

"I need one," Harley Smith said.

WITH no more warning than that, footsteps approached the kitchen door. Mr. Maddox moved hurriedly, but before he could leave the kitchen, the door opened. An overhead light flashed on—and suddenly the Bell girl was screaming.

"Dave! Harry! Men in the kitchen!"

Cassidy reached her, swung her stumbling, screaming across the kitchen to Mr. Maddox.

She kicked wildly. Her sharp fingernails clawed Mr. Maddox's broad face as he caught her. Cassidy had plunged toward the front of the house.

"Keep quiet, you hell-cat!" Mr. Maddox panted as he twisted her around and held her arms from behind.

A gunshot crashed in the front part of the house, then another. Swearing, Mr. Maddox pushed the girl away and charged toward the trouble.

A short hall opened into a front room that ran clear across the house. Two more shots followed—and Mr. Maddox met Cassidy stumbling back into the hall. Cassidy had dropped his gun. He'd been shot in the right arm.

Slim Pasternik's thin voice raged in shrill alarm: "Don't kill him, Dave! This'll wreck everything, you fool! He's a track cop!"

"No cop takes me and sends my prints to Washington! I'll fix him!"

Cassidy lurched down to catch his gun with his left hand.

"I got it!" Mr. Maddox snapped.

A crouching figure with a gun jumped opposite the hallway door as Mr. Maddox scooped Cassidy's gun off the floor. "Maddox!" the man yelled in recognition. It was the voice of Dave. And as his gun blasted, someone flipped a light-switch and plunged the front room into blackness.

Mr. Maddox flattened against the wall. He could see Dave's gun muzzle spurting fire in the dark. He fired once, twice, automatically counting Dave's shots. Dave was as blind as he was. And now Dave's gun went silent. A chair clattered over. Dave's gasping voice cursed.

Out front automobile engines were racing.

"They're lamming!" Cassidy blurted, and shouldered Mr. Maddox aside as he got into the front room first.

Another piece of furniture clattered over. Dave's oaths in the darkness sounded strangled, almost sobbing. And suddenly the lights were on again. Cassidy was wheeling from the switch.

Dave had just staggered away from an overturned floor-lamp and clutched a chair to keep from falling. His empty gun lay on the rug. A hand pressed his side and when he coughed, blood showed on his lips. He looked dazed.

"He'll keep! Gimme that gun! They're getting away!" Cassidy snapped.

House doors had opened all along the street. People had run out in alarm. The two automobiles had reached the next corner and were swinging clumsily around out of sight.

Stiffy's wildly excited voice yelled: "When I heard the shootin',

Boss, I stuck my damn pocketknife in their tires! They ain't goin' anywhere fast with flat tires!"

In the distance a siren wailed. Cassidy excitedly blurted: "Boy, you hung it on them! They won't get out of town now! Joe, watch out here while I telephone for a guard to be put on El Conde."

CHAPTER SEVEN

KENTUCKY KICKBACK

THE MORNING papers had it in black headlines. Only the girl and O'Toole were missing… and the rising, electric excitement of Derby Day pushed it all in the background. From midmorning on the great crowd went surging toward Churchill Downs.

Mr. Maddox was rocky from answering police questions and lack of sleep, but he was there. Cassidy was there, too, arm bandaged and in a sling, a satisfied smile on his face as he edged into the box where Mr. Maddox was sitting.

"Well, Joe, I saved your skin on this. How does it feel to be a hero instead of being pinched for making a book?"

"I'll tell you when I see if the Cavanaugh horse wins or not," Mr. Maddox said grimly.

"Cavanaugh was lucky his contact with Pasternik was based on good faith instead of guilty knowledge," Cassidy observed. "If he and his sister win the Derby, he'll come out of it better than ever. I wouldn't worry about him."

"Who's worrying?" Mr. Maddox said shortly. "I'm thinking about the dough I'll have to pay out if his horse wins."

The first races on the card had been run. The clear notes of a bugle floated through the yellow sunshine. The murmuring movement of the vast crowd heightened.

"Here they come!" Cassidy exclaimed as the red-coated leader rode out of the paddock tunnel, followed by the long file of slowly pacing horses and diminutive jockies gay in bright racing-silks.

Flags were fluttering in the slight breeze. Bursts of handclapping spread as the post parade moved slowly along the track.

The band struck up *My Old Kentucky Home.* And a lump came into Mr. Maddox's throat and the sentiment of the moment wiped out all thought of profit or loss or disaster to Joe Maddox. This was the great moment before the Derby start.

Then, very quickly it seemed, the horses were at the starting-gate... backing, plunging, fighting the assistant starters... and suddenly the roar of the crowd marked the start of the race.

Eager eyes and then binoculars could follow the pack of horses fighting for position on the turn. The amplifiers were calling: "Mad Money is taking the lead... Cantwell second... Jeanne's Hope third... El Conde fourth...."

The lengthening field swept down the back stretch, carrying the hopes of owners and millions of listeners out over the airwaves of the world.

Tiny horses, now, seen across the green infield, carrying tinier jockies.... And it was hard to believe that the fate of Joe Maddox ran there with one horse and its crouched rider....

"Jeanne's Hope first... Mad Money second... El Conde third."

Now there was a madness in the roar of the great crowd. Mr. Maddox caught himself shouting too. *"Come on, Jeanne's Hope!"*

Then he realized what that tiny running horse leading on the stretch-turn meant. Wealth and fame to Jeanny Cavanaugh—money for Jerry Cavanaugh—and ruin for Joe Maddox.

The race swept into the stretch. Jockey whips began to rise and fall. And the inexorable loudspeakers called fate for Joe Maddox.

"It's Jeanne's Hope by half a length... El Conde second... Clydesdale third... Mad Money and Sir Sam...."

The crowd was on its feet, delirious and screaming. Mr. Maddox and Cassidy were up.

"El Conde closing... Jeanne's Hope by a head... Jeanne's Hope by a nose...."

Cassidy was beating Mr. Maddox's arm. "Look at that black horse run! Look at that El Conde! What a horse! *What a horse!*"

El Conde was running under the whip like a smooth black machine, like a great ghost flashing faster each length to the wire....

"El Conde!" Cassidy whooped. "Jeanne's Hope couldn't hold it long enough! What a finish, Joe! What d'you think of it?"

Mr. Maddox was standing quietly, like a man who had faced doom and watched it move away. Mr. Maddox shivered slightly, and then a growing smile spread across his broad bland face, and he was himself again. He stood for a few moments watching El Conde come back to the horse-shoe wreath of flowers for his victorious neck, to Gloria Gerryman and the waiting photographers. To enduring fame and world-wide publicity for horse and owner.

"I'm thinking," said Mr. Maddox almost dreamily, "of the lesson Jerry Cavanaugh has learned, and all the dough I've made today, and of what that eighty grand of Gerryman money would have won if O'Toole had bet it as he was ordered."

A MOMENT later Mr. Maddox jogged Cassidy's elbow. "Look this side of where Gloria Gerryman's getting her picture taken! There's Jeanny Cavanaugh and Sam Harmsworth holding hands!"

"I see them!" said Cassidy. "You know, I feel kind of sorry for her, with the Gerryman girl getting the Derby after all."

Mr. Maddox chuckled.

"Don't feel sorry for Jeanny. Gloria Gerryman won the race—but I'm thinking Jeanny Cavanaugh really won the Derby. Let's go down and congratulate her—and Sam."

THE BOOKIE AND THE BLONDE

BOWIE IN THE SPRING—AND MR.
MADDOX AND OSCAR, HOMING
NORTH WITH THE BIRDS FROM
THE RACES IN MIAMI HAD THE
SEASONAL FEVER IN A BIG WAY.
AT LEAST MADDOX DID. THAT
BLAND BUDDHA OF THE BANGTAIL
CIRCUIT WAS POSITIVELY
WELLING WITH IT—EVEN IF OSCAR
HAD HIS USUAL JAUNDICED
EYE COCKED. THEN THEIR CAR
CRASHED INTO THE LIMOUSINE
OF THE PODDER'S PIXIE PICKLE
TYCOON AND WINTER WITH ITS
CHILL BLAST WAS BACK AGAIN—
ALL AT ONE FELL SWOOP—SCARING
HELL OUT OF THE HOUNDS OF
SPRING WITH MAYHEM, MURDER
AND ASSORTED CRIME.

CHAPTER ONE

MR. MADDOX AND
THE HOUNDS OF SPRING

IT **ALL** started with a dented fender. On this sunny day, with the big blue sedan rolling through the last mile of the long, cross-country trip, Joe Maddox, the bookie, was entirely unsuspecting.

Spring had rolled north ahead of the long sleek automobile. North from Miami and the neat horse barns at Tropical Park. North from New Orleans, from Hot Springs, where March rains had made the Oaklawn track a paradise for mud-runners. North toward Louisville and St. Louis, toward the Delaware, New York and New England horse tracks. And this day spring was bright with promise over the stately Capitol dome in Washington, over the smoky brick factories of Baltimore—and over the straight green pines circling the Bowie track, midway of the two cities.

Spring lilted in the off-key whistling of Mr. Maddox as the big car left Washington before noon. As he swung off the highway on the blacktop road through pine woods to the Bowie stables and track, a difficult treble note flatted sourly and Mr. Maddox stopped whistling and said cheerfully to Oscar: "Well, here we are."

Oscar's pint-size lacked the vast good-humored assurance that Mr. Maddox gave the world. Oscar was cynical as he glanced out the window and retorted: "Yeah? So what?"

Mr. Maddox grinned. "Spring in Washington. The birds and bees, the flowers and trees. Look at those pines."

"I don't like pines—and I had to look at Florida pines all winter," Oscar retorted. "Now it looks like we're heading for a lumber camp."

Crinkles of humor spread over the Florida tan as Mr. Maddox chuckled. "If it's lumbering," he said, "we'll chip off a few splinters for the bankroll. The local talent is hot this year, if those we met in Miami are an example."

"Washington makes me think of G-men," Oscar said. "And G-men make me think of trouble. And when I think of trouble, I want to move on. The feds put the heat on in Miami this year. Maybe bookies are poison around Washington this spring."

"The pickings will be sweeter," Mr. Maddox chuckled. "There's gold by that thar Potomac, friend. And what could be nicer in the spring than gold?"

Oscar snorted. "Spring's got you daffy! When you're like this, anything can happen! And it usually does!"

The next moment Oscar yelled: "Look out!"

A low ridge blocked the view ahead. At that moment a gleaming gray automobile was rushing past from the rear. In the same moment a third car, traveling fast, shot over the top of the rise.

Somebody would crash....

Mr. Maddox stamped on the brakes, saw that wouldn't be enough and wrenched the blue sedan over to the right. The gray car swung

"Holy cow!" Mr. Maddox exploded as he
saw a flicker of fire, then a sheet of flame.

hard over also in a desperate effort to escape a head-on collision and
fenders clashed and crumpled.

It happened in split seconds. Tires sliding, car bucking, left front
fender already smashed, Mr. Maddox drove off the road.

"That dumb-bell!" Oscar yelled, clutching the door handle and bracing against the dash as the bouncing, reeling automobile threw him forward.

They skidded to a stop. The motor *chunk-a-chunked* and died. Mr. Maddox filled the sudden silence with an explosive breath, followed by an even more explosive oath.

"Springtime!" Oscar said hollowly.

"I'll murder that dope!" Mr. Maddox choked. "A bottle baby would have known better than to pass us!"

The ditch was shallow. The sedan probably would back out under its own power, but Mr. Maddox was still furious as he kicked the door open and shouldered out.

The gray car had stopped ahead of them with two wheels down the slope of the shallow ditch.

The third car, ancient and battered, which had almost smashed head-on into the gray car, had stopped far over on the right-hand side of the road, where the ditch was deep enough to have wrecked any machine running into it at high speed.

The wizened face and peaked cap of a stable-hand poked out the window. "Why don't you slugs learn how to drive? You almost wrecked me!"

"No one would have missed you!" Mr. Maddox snarled. "Come out and mix in this if you think it'll do you any good!"

The wizened face took a good look, spat again, said something uncomplimentary and drove on. Mr. Maddox glared at his crushed fender and went to meet the offending driver of the gray car.

"My dear fellow! I'll never forgive myself...."

"Listen!" said Mr. Maddox violently.

"Say anything and it won't be enough! It was stupid of me! Are you hurt? My card, sir. Colonel Roscoe Daggett, sir, wishing to do anything about this that you may desire."

"Er—uh," Mr. Maddox fizzled weakly. His red-laced anger was evaporating before the apologies of this rather amazing Colonel Roscoe Daggett.

The engraved card was impressive. The colonel himself was even more so. Nearly as tall as Mr. Maddox, the man had a square-shoul-dered, military bearing, a distinctive shock of white hair, a close-clipped white mustache, jaunty and crisp. Smartly tailored gray tweeds and a gay feather in the band of his soft hat marked Colonel Roscoe Daggett as quite obviously a wealthy sportsman of the old school.

Such men were dear to the heart of Joe Maddox. They were prodigal in betting on the Sport of Kings. And it was inevitable that a man like Colonel Daggett would have friends of similar habits.

A fat bankroll and well-heeled friends would have mattered little to an angry Joe Maddox. But the profuse apologies were like the spring sun on ice.

"Not at all," Mr. Maddox heard himself saying. "The other car wasn't visible. And—uh—the fellow was driving too fast. My name is Maddox, Colonel, and we'll think no more of it."

Something suspiciously like a snort came from Oscar, eyeing the damaged fender.

A SECOND man came from the gray automobile. He was a gray spare man about the colonel's age, an uneasy man whose eyes seemed to pop a little with surprise behind gold-framed glasses. His gray suit hung without much fit, shirt collar was comfortably loose over a prominent Adam's apple that bobbed and dipped as he spoke with annoyance.

"Damn it, Daggett! This was careless and unnecessary! Almost gave me another heart attack! Might have killed all of us! What are you going to do about this man's car?"

The colonel was already smiling under his crisp white mustache.

"We're settling it amicably, Podder. Mr. Maddox, my very good friend, Mr. Luther Podder."

"Podder?" repeated Mr. Maddox as he shook a cautious hand. "Did you buy First Spry from the Manlove Farm last month?"

Luther Podder blinked behind his glasses and looked slightly embarrassed as he nodded. "Nice horse, they tell me," he mumbled. "Always liked nice horses."

Colonel Daggett chuckled. "I see, Maddox, that you know about the racing string Podder has been putting together."

"Of course," Mr. Maddox smilingly agreed while he rapidly searched his memory for scraps of information he might have picked up. "Er—Podder's Mayonnaise," he quoted tentatively from an obscure cranny of his memory. "Uh—Podder's Canned Soups, eh?"

"And Podder's Gold Star Preserves," Colonel Daggett helped out.

Luther Podder's eyes had brightened with quick gratification. His Adam's apple bobbed up as he added: "Podder's Pixie Pickles also, gentlemen. They've always been my favorite."

Mr. Maddox beamed. "I've enjoyed Pixie Pickles. Er—nothing like them, eh?"

Luther Podder was not the first man to be impressed by the vast and prosperous assurance of Mr. Maddox, not the first stranger to warm and then thaw to that masterful approval. Podder indicated the dented fender.

"Daggett, we'll have to do something about this."

"I'll accept a drink some afternoon at the track," Mr. Maddox informed them. "And that is positively all."

And as sportsman to sportsman—of the old school—the matter was settled on that basis. Hands were shaken, the cars backed out on the road and proceeded.

"Pixie Pickles! What are they?" Oscar demanded.

"Search me," Mr. Maddox chuckled. "But they buy thirty-thousand-dollar stake horses—and that makes them hay."

"It makes you goony," Oscar corrected. "Old Pickles was offering you a new fender and you tossed it away. Where's the percentage in that kind of nuttiness?"

Mr. Maddox turned left into a still narrower road that led to the horse barns, already visible through the pine trees. On their right they could see the track fence and the high bright structure of the Bowie grandstand rising impressively in the setting of green pines.

"Percentage is what you make it," Mr. Maddox said. "Maybe we can make something of this. I'm trying to place Colonel Daggett. I've a hunch I've seen him before."

"He looks like a big-shot."

"He might be. But he gives me a feeling...."

Mr. Maddox let the idea fade out as he skirted the stable lines, parked the car and searched out the barn whose end stalls housed Kopper King and the other three horses of the somewhat less than distinguished Maddox Stable.

OLD POP HARVEY, the Maddox trainer, got up from a bale of straw and greeted them. "I been lookin' for you two. There's a nice little spot for Kopper King next week. Mile an' a sixteenth an' ten pounds allowed for a non-winner this year."

"Give that goat Kopper King ten pounds for every year he hasn't won a race and he'd start without a jock," Oscar commented sarcastically.

Mr. Maddox ignored all that. He was looking toward the other end of the long, low barn. A thin little man had emerged from a stall, barked an order at a colored swipe and turned toward them on the bowed legs of an ex-jockey.

"Are we stabling next to Mynie Sampson and his platers?" Mr. Maddox asked sharply.

"Nope," said Pop, squinting down the line of stalls. "We drawed Mynie—but the hosses is good hosses. Mynie's training for Baden Manor Farm, that's owned by a feller name of Podder."

"What?"

"Podder," repeated Pop. "Baltimore man with scads of dough an' some purty good hosses. He's had 'em at this Baden Manor Farm all winter an' they're comin' to taw now for the summer tracks."

"Does Podder know about Mynie?"

"He hired him," said Pop dryly, as if that were proof of Podder's ignorance, and continued: "I see Jack Podder, the son, hangin' around Mynie's girl Annabelle some. The Podders might have some reason for makin' a big-shot outa Mynie."

"I smell vanilla," Oscar murmured. "Or is it pickles?"

"Huh?" Pop said.

Mr. Maddox called: "Hullo, Mynie. Is *this* a surprise!"

"What's surprising about it, Maddox?"

Mynie Sampson's thin face was sallow, his necktie a violent purple, his manner nervous and breezy. And men versed in the ways of racing, like Mr. Maddox, could tell you that Mynie Sampson had missed being barred from a dozen tracks by the fringe of his scanty blond eyebrows.

A long memory could recall when Mynie Sampson had booted them home with the best. And then a horse had gone down in a race and the doctors had set Mynie down for life.

Mynie had turned halterman—and not even the shrewd memory of Joe Maddox could say when Mynie Sampson had turned shady. A bad year, unpaid feed bills, no getaway money in sight near the end of some race meet probably had started it.

Once done, the second bit of crooked work had come easier—and Mynie Sampson had become a shady little halterman with a string of plugs that barely earned a scant living with every crooked trick that a lifetime on the turf had absorbed.

That was Mynie Sampson—and here was a belligerent Mynie training the new stable of a wealthy pickle-potentate.

Mr. Maddox suppressed a caustic retort, shrugged and answered placatingly: "I was only talking, Mynie. Glad to see you. We just met your boss down the road."

Mynie's sharp face reddened. His fists clenched. Mynie Sampson was suddenly a dangerous little man, raging at them.

"I had a hunch old man Harvey'd write you to stir up trouble for me!" Mynie roared furiously.

"I never wrote no such thing!" Pop Harvey shrilled.

"Pop's right, Mynie."

"Don't lie to me, you big sack of clabber!" Mynie raged. "I'm telling you! Make trouble for me here an' I'll take you down to size if I get the chair for it!"

From the corner of his mouth Oscar warned: "He's got a gun on his belly, Joe!"

Mr. Maddox nodded and shrugged at the furious little horse trainer. "Mynie, I didn't even know you were working for Podder until I saw you come out of the stall there. Take a cooler before you talk yourself into real trouble."

"I'm telling all three of you!" Mynie choked. "Don't make no trouble or it'll be the last dirty trick you—"

Mynie stopped with a mighty gulp. It was almost a gasp. Mynie looked stricken. The cause was at his side an instant later.

"Dad!"

They'd appeared at this end of the barn in time to hear Mynie's last words—Podder and a young man, an older woman, a younger woman, and this girl, who had hurried to Mynie's side with her low exclamation.

MR. MADDOX placed the girl as he removed his hat. She must be Mynie's Annabelle—that kid that Mynie had bragged about when he'd been booting them home for fame and money.

Now the "kid" was twenty or twenty-one at least, an inch taller than Mynie, with looks to match any woman in the club-house boxes. Mr. Maddox could remember Mynie boasting in the past of the fine schools his girl would attend. She'd evidently done just that.

Then Luther Podder was beside them, saying a trifle sharply: "Sampson, you're not having trouble with Mr. Maddox, I hope!"

Mynie swallowed. He seemed tongue-tied. The glance he flicked at his daughter was miserable with an unspoken message.

Mr. Maddox filled the awkward moment with a quick chuckle. "No trouble at all, Mr. Podder. Merely a friendly argument. I've known Sampson for years. Quite a coincidence to find my horses in this barn also, eh?"

"Quite," said Luther Podder. He was not uncertain now, in dealing with a man on his payroll. He was short and curt about Mynie. "Sampson has had words with several people lately. I've asked him to watch his temper."

Mynie swallowed again. He was twisting his hat brim and trying to smile. The strain showed white at his mouth corners. When he spoke, there was a grating attempt at humor in his voice.

"This ain't the first argument with Mr. Maddox. He—he's always sure he knows everything about horses. We get to arguing pretty hot."

Mr. Maddox caught Annabelle's quick breath of relief. She'd been afraid. More afraid than Mynie. When she'd turned the barn corner and heard Mynie, she'd hurried forward with the sharp fear of trouble. Now she looked almost weak with relief. Pale, too, from the strain. And then grateful as the young man came to her side, smiling easily at Mr. Maddox.

"I'm Jack Podder, if no one will introduce me. I don't know too much about this business—but I'm a good listener whenever you can spare the time."

No glasses on this young man. Not much resemblance to the pickle-and-preserve manufacturer. Jack Podder might have been All-American in college. All muscle and bone, features a bit on the ugly side, now radiating warmth with a smile and hearty handshake.

Then the young man's smile grew slightly puzzled as the younger of the two women behind them gaily warned: "The gentleman will teach you about horses, Jack. His lessons come high—but they're not easily forgotten."

Mr. Maddox's broad bland smile concealed quick wariness. This girl was older than Annabelle. A blonde. A stunning blonde—sleek, chic, self-assured. And on the metallic side, Mr. Maddox decided as his shrewd eyes tried to place her.

Luther Podder had lifted his eyebrows. Jack Podder's smile continued puzzled.

"How is that, Diane? Mr.—er—Maddox seems to be just the sort of teacher I need."

"I doubt it," said Diane dryly. She was smiling maliciously at Mr. Maddox. "We haven't met. I'm Diane Wall."

An instant of hesitation, and then Mr. Maddox placed the name. "You were on Broadway several years ago, Miss Wall?"

"Five years ago." Diane Wall shrugged. "Just long enough to find out I was a long way from being an actress after all."

Luther Podder cleared his throat almost irritably. "Diane, what is this about teaching Jack? I don't like mysteries."

Diane Wall laughed. "Mr. Maddox isn't a mystery. Sometimes he's a calamity. Or am I wrong about bookmakers, Mr. Maddox?"

"It depends, Miss Wall."

Mr. Maddox was still bland and cheerful as he explained to Luther Podder and his son. "Miss Wall is saying that I cover race bets at times for certain friends who wish the convenience. Those who lose are sometimes wiser afterwards."

Audibly in the background the older woman said: "A bookmaker!"

The one word placed Mr. Maddox and all like him in the category of stable-hands and shady race-track followers.

She might not have meant it to sound so, but she felt that way. Her next words were hurried and positive. "If you don't mind, Luther, I'd like to see that horse before we have lunch."

She was well into the forties, but hardly looked it. A little too young to be Jack Podder's mother. Obviously wealthy. Probably well-known in society. Bookies, you guessed instinctively, came to her back door—if they came at all.

Luther Podder looked uncomfortable as he turned away with a nod at Mr. Maddox. He might as well have put it into words. He'd thought the vast and impressive Mr. Maddox more than a bookie. The discovery made a change.

Diane Wall still had the malicious smile as she said: "Coming, Jack? Good-bye, Mr. Maddox. Don't take me too seriously."

"Not at all," Mr. Maddox said blandly.

He was watching Jack Podder say something under his breath to Annabelle. Watching Annabelle, pale and smiling, bite her lip as she nodded. Then the Podders, father and son, walked on with the two women.

Mynie Sampson waited a moment, and then spoke huskily. "Baby, I'm—"

"It doesn't matter," Annabelle said. "I—I'll see you at lunch."

Annabelle whirled and hurried around the end of the barn. She was near to tears or Mr. Maddox had lost all his perception.

Mynie turned slowly and looked after the Podders. When he faced back, he was a pinched, white-faced, venomous little man.

"Before God, Maddox, watch your step! Keep away from me! Keep your damn mouth shut about me and my affairs! I'm warning you!"

Mynie swung on his heel and walked after the Podders, a bow-legged little man in a worn leather jacket, with thin shoulders weighted by something more than his years.

Pop uncomfortably cleared his throat. Oscar snorted under his breath.

For some moments Mr. Maddox stood motionless, looking after Mynie and the Podders. A red flush crept like a dangerous wave over his broad face. Some inner thought made the jaw muscles stand out in ridges as Mr. Maddox turned in the same dangerous silence and walked to the tackroom.

CHAPTER TWO

D.C. G-HEAT

OSCAR WAS the first to speak when they entered the warm dim little room that reeked of liniment, leather and horses. He literally exploded: "Can you tie it? High-hatting us! Bookies ain't good enough for them! And that little gyp Mynie threatening to knock someone off!"

Pop Harvey added shrill indignation. "Crazy, that's what he is! Drunk as a coot or jist plumb crazy! They oughta run that little crook off the tracks years ago!"

Mr. Maddox bit hard through the end of a thick cigar. He was still red with anger and his eyes were hard and calculating. "Mynie was always cool enough. Now he's carrying a gun and blowing his top. What do you make of it?"

"I told you! Drunk or crazy!" Pop snorted.

"Crazy like a fox," Mr. Maddox differed curtly. "His daughter seems friendly with young Podder."

Pop snapped: "Give you odds she's trying to hook him!"

"Pickles," Oscar sneered. "A million dollars' worth of pickles—and Mynie Sampson playing that girl of his for a come-on!"

"Mynie used to boast what a great kid she was. He was crazy about her," Mr. Maddox said. And as if questioning himself, "Is Mynie skunk enough now to use her for sucker-bait?"

"Mynie'd do anything!" Pop snapped. "I ain't had no use for him since he turned crooked. When I seen we had the same barn, I tried for new stalls. Told Mynie I was trying. He knows how I feel."

"Have you seen this Colonel Daggett around here?" Mr. Maddox asked. "Big fellow. Looks like a million."

"Twice," Pop nodded. "A blow-mouth. Sounds like he knows all about hosses."

"He'd sound that way," Mr. Maddox said grimly. "Pop, sit on the lid here. Keep away from Mynie. Do you know who that older woman is?"

"She was here with Podder t' other day," Pop said. "I asked Mynie's girl if that was Missus Podder. She ain't. He's a widower. She's one of them Washington blue-bloods. Widow of a big senator that died two-three year ago. Feller from out West named Trumpet er close to it."

"Trumbull," Mr. Maddox guessed after a moment. "Senator Ogden Trumbull. So! A gee-gee stable and Washington society. The pickle man is stepping out. Come on, Oscar. Let's drive over to the clubhouse and eat."

Mr. Maddox was dangerously calm as they returned to the automobile. "Oscar, there was something about that fellow Daggett."

"Cream," Oscar said. "Smooth as cream."

"I placed him while they were talking," Mr. Maddox said. "Years ago Daggett was out on the Coast. He was thinner then. They called him Duke Snyder. He passed for a Britisher and could outbluff a British clubman to his face. His pal was called Frisco Dick."

"So he's only a mug!" Oscar said with satisfaction.

"Just a mug," Mr. Maddox agreed. "The Duke and Frisco Dick were con men around Hollywood and Frisco, with blackmail on the side. Smooth and big-time in everything they tackled. The Duke finally slipped up and drew a stretch. I heard later he got out and left the country. Now he's back carrying lard and a belly and passing for a horsey colonel. Nice, eh?"

"And Podder's the sucker," Oscar guessed the obvious. "Serves him right. I hope the colonel takes him like a dip going through a lush. Can you imagine that pickle punk and his lady friends giving us the eyebrows while they've got the colonel in their hair?"

"I can imagine a lot," Mr. Maddox said grimly. "And before I'm through, I'll know a lot. Including why Mynie Sampson is carrying a gun and ready to use it on me."

Mr. Maddox parked on the broad lot at the side of the grandstand as Oscar protested: "Maybe it ain't worth bothering with, Joe. Maybe you'd better forget it."

"Let's eat," Mr. Maddox said grimly.

BOWIE racing days brought out Washington and Baltimore society, senators, congressmen, diplomats, the wealthy and fatuous of the Virginia and Maryland bluegrass. And the season brought out the mob too, milling before the grandstand, crowding seats, pushing in lines before the mutuel windows under the big grandstand. Long race trains had brought them from Washington and Baltimore. Buses, automobiles and even trucks had brought them. The sun was bright, spring was a glorious tang in the air. Sleek fast thoroughbreds prancing to the starting stalls made hearts beat faster and money move recklessly. Race by race through the afternoon the mutuel handle climbed higher.

Mr. Maddox even bet a couple of tenners himself. The busy summer was just ahead. Familiar faces greeted Joe Maddox, the veteran bookie. There was lush promise of business in the days to come. But Mr. Maddox remained grim and unsmiling.

The Podders had a box. Annabelle Sampson was not with them. Diane Wall happened to be looking when Mr. Maddox passed the box. Her smile of recognition again might have been malicious. At least with Jack Podder at her side, she looked pleased with herself.

The fourth race was coming up. Oscar, at the bar beside Mr. Maddox, was lifting a beer glass, when Mr. Maddox grunted with satisfaction.

"There's Frisco Dick! That's what I wanted to know!"

"Where?"

"By the door."

Oscar's glance flicked to the spot. The distinguished-looking Colonel Daggett had paused beside a thinner man, well-dressed, well-tailored, with a pearl-gray hat tilted correctly on iron-gray hair.

Both men might have stopped there by accident, paying no attention to each other. Only sharp eyes would have caught the slight movement of Frisco Dick's lips behind the hands cupping a match to his cigarette.

"Class," Oscar admitted with reluctant admiration.

"Mugs!" Mr. Maddox growled. "And I'll make bigger mugs out of them!"

Oscar's quick objection was almost violent. "Lay off, Joe! We're on our way up to the Big Stem! We don't want trouble! Look, Joe—it's spring now, Joe! You said so yourself."

Mr. Maddox pushed his half-empty beer glass away and held up a hand—the left hand, on which a great blue-white diamond glinted coldly in a massive ring of yellow gold.

"Look at it."

"I've seen it," Oscar shrugged.

"Blue-white and honest," Mr. Maddox said in the calm dangerous manner which had cloaked him since lunch. "Horses gave it to me. I do business around the horse tracks the same way. When stuffed shirts like Podder, and mugs like Mynie Sampson, Duke Snyder and Frisco get in my way, I run over them."

"Tell it to the stewards, Joe."

"Tell them what?" Mr. Maddox growled. "First I've got to find out what's being cooked up. I'll be seeing you a little later."

THE AFTERNOON'S racing was over as far as Mr. Maddox was concerned. He felt the old surge of excitement and anticipation as he joined Pop Harvey back at the stables.

"Where's Stiffy?"

"Hangin' on the track rail, I reckon."

"I want him—and I want a talk with you."

Pop grew alert. Faded blue eyes looked for a moment before Pop nodded, stepped over to one of the stalls and sent a diminutive colored swipe for Stiffy.

Mr. Maddox was chewing on a cigar when Pop rejoined him.

"I want Podder's horses watched, Pop. All the dope on them. Especially any horse that's entered in a race."

"Kinda sudden interest in Podder's horses, ain't it?" Pop asked shrewdly.

Mr. Maddox ignored Pop and continued. "I want Mynie Sampson watched. Everything he does. Everyone he sees. Any gossip about him. When he leaves the track, I want to know where he goes. I want the tag numbers of any car that brings someone to see him."

Pop slapped at a droning horsefly and nodded. "It'll be good riddance t' the little crook if you ask me!"

"I'm not asking you," Mr. Maddox said curtly. "And if you stick your neck out and let Mynie suspect anything I'll make you sweat."

Pop searched the broad grim face behind that level warning and smiled wryly. "I reckon you will," Pop agreed. "And I don't aim to sweat. Not over Mynie. Here's that young hellion."

Stiffy was a raw-boned youngster with tobacco bulging one cheek, a big Adam's apple in a scrawny neck, ragged clothes, a hard-boiled swagger. The previous fall he had come over from Pimlico in a horse-van with an endless stream of talk, hard-boiled acquaintance with stable life and a fierce devotion to the racing game.

His past was a blank. Stiffy slept in a vacant stall on straw, asked for no pay, worked hard and made himself a part of the Maddox Stable for better or worse.

Now Mr. Maddox wasted no words. "Stiffy, you talk too much."

Stiffy looked furtively at Mr. Maddox's broad face and nailed a busy beetle with brown tobacco juice.

"Nope," Stiffy denied. "I ain't even got a tongue, s' help me."

"You'd better not have," Mr. Maddox said. "Pop will tell you what I want. Rent yourself an old car somewhere that you can use any hour of the day or night. I remember last fall you had a Maryland driver's license. Pop will give you the money."

"An' I'll make sure what he does with it," Pop snapped. "You, Stiffy, hear me?"

Stiffy had hastily discarded his chewing. Now he blinked at Pop, licked his lips and nodded. "Yessir."

Very little would escape the eyes of Pop and Stiffy. There remained Frisco Dick and Duke Snyder, posing as Colonel Roscoe Daggett. Mr. Maddox returned to the grandstand.

TWICE in the next quarter of an hour Mr. Maddox almost stopped men whom he knew, then let them pass on. The cashiers were paying off for the fifth race before he found what he wanted.

The man was reedy, wasp-waisted, somewhere past thirty. His long woman-like hands were disconsolately riffling an assortment of mutuel tickets when Mr. Maddox strolled past without stopping.

"Tail me, Larry," Mr. Maddox said from the corner of his mouth, and passed on without looking around.

Down at the end of the two-dollar windows Mr. Maddox brought the man to his side with a jerk of his head.

"How's tricks, Larry?"

"Tough, if I gotta say so, Mr. Maddox. Got anything good up your sleeve?"

"I might have a little job."

Black eyes glinted with interest. Larry Kent shot his cuffs, canted his hat to a more rakish angle and said briskly: "Why not make it a steady job? There ain't a better bookie-runner out than me, if I do say so. If I had a bankroll—"

"You'd blow every dime on roulette and dice," Mr. Maddox finished. "I don't need a runner. But do this job right and I'll treat you right."

"I'll see you on it."

"There's a couple of men I want tailed. I don't know where they're staying or what they're up to. Chances are they won't leave the track together. But I want all the dope on them. Use all the help you need. I'll pay."

Narrow-eyed, Larry Kent said: "Trouble?"

"Not if you watch your step."

"And if I don't?"

"You're smooth," said Mr. Maddox. "That's why I'm offering this to you. And no matter what happens, I don't know anything about it."

"I gotcha. Sweeten me with a C-note and I'm ready."

Mr. Maddox had the hundred-dollar bill in his hand a moment later. And a warning with it. "No dice, no ivory balls."

"O.K.," Larry Kent agreed as he reached for the money. His smile was crooked. "It's a toughie, I guess. I'll do what I can. Show me the men and tell me where you're staying. I'll call you when I get something."

"Matahowan," said Mr. Maddox, naming one of the bigger hotels, near the Treasury in Washington. "Tail me now and I'll give you the nod on the men. The fat one calls himself Colonel Roscoe Daggett. You'll have to find out what handle the thin one's using."

Not many minutes later Larry Kent had had his sight of the Colonel and Frisco Dick. He would stay with at least one of them. The sixth race was over and Mr. Maddox once more was smiling blandly when he rejoined Oscar and asked: "Ready to go?"

"I know that look," Oscar said suspiciously. "You've laid an egg on this Podder business!"

"Forget it."

Oscar snorted. "I'll have nightmares now. I don't know why I'm sucker enough to wait around for the blow-up!"

THE MATAHOWAN manager would have disapproved violently had he known why the large gentleman in suite 4-B was making so many telephone calls after dinner.

Bookies and the Matahowan had little in common. But then any casual glance would have said the same about the prosperous and genial Mr. Maddox.

Business, however, was business, and the little black notebook which Mr. Maddox held while he was telephoning, contained the names and addresses of some of the most distinguished and wealthy people in the District of Columbia.

They'd placed bets with Mr. Maddox in past years. They'd be eager to bet again. Some were old contacts, friends from other cities over the country.

Joe Maddox, the veteran bookie, with his big flashing diamond ring, infectious humor, his willingness to lay against any money, any time, was always welcome to the friends of the turf world. An evening of telephoning would bring all the money Joe Maddox cared to handle while in Washington.

Oscar, whose work with the betting-sheets and telephones would start in the morning, came stamping in with the first editions of the morning papers a little after nine.

"Look!" said Oscar, slamming a folded paper beside the telephone. "Take a look at that!"

"Quiet, you numb-wit!" Mr. Maddox snapped. He took his big hand off the receiver and chuckled: "Of course, Congressman. Any time. Write your own ticket—the same as in Chicago. And it's been a pleasure to speak with you again."

Oscar was speaking again as the receiver went down. "That dame writes as poison as she speaks! If she keeps this up, we'll have the feds in our laps before we can jump."

The column Oscar indicated was headed—*Diane Wall's Diary*. Mr. Maddox read with interest. Mostly it was social gossip. Diane Wall had a canny, biting style. Two comments on politics, from the woman's angle, read as if authentic and from an informed source. Oscar's ire centered on a bit near the bottom of the column.

> An exciting day at Bowie. Beautiful horses—among them First Spry, the latest addition to the fast-growing stable of Luther Podder and his son, Jack, Baltimore's favorite young sportsman. The bookmakers are also with us again. Some with racing stables of their own. Now is the time, ladies, to restrain your husbands. Or should the bookies be restrained?

Oscar blurted: "She might as well have said Joe Maddox was in town an' the cops ought to do something about it! I coulda told you at the track she was poison!"

Mr. Maddox reached for a cigarette. He was smiling.

"Squawking won't help. If our noses stay clean, we'll be all right. This isn't the only book in town."

"It's the only book that's carrying a racing-stable! Next time maybe she prints names, Joe! And then what? This town is where the G-boys grow. And they traveled clear to Miami this winter to put on the heat. That dame might be building a fire under you in Hoover's office right now."

Mr. Maddox nodded, frowning at the thought. "She might. She could, if she wanted to be nasty."

"And then what happens? Remember where they go from the District of Columbia when the judge hands it out?"

"I ought to," Mr. Maddox chuckled. "They've already put some Washington bookies on ice in Atlanta, what with everything being a federal offense in this town."

The thought almost made Oscar shudder. His plea was from the heart. "I've got a hunch that trouble at the track today was just a starter. Let's pack an' head for Broadway. Spring ain't the time to be rolling dice against the G-men in Atlanta!"

Mr. Maddox stood up, bulking above Oscar as he chuckled. "Spring in Atlanta might not be so bad. They have flowers in Atlanta too. Take a shot of Scotch for your nerves. We'll be all right. I might even leave if it looks like the lovely Diane is gunning for us with her newspaper column and her contacts."

"Does she have to put a gun in your face before you get wise, Joe? Let's lam while we can pass a cop without ducking. Ship the horses to New York or New England. That'll leave us sitting—"

The telephone bell interrupted. Mr. Maddox was still smiling as he answered. Oscar could not hear the low urgent voice in the receiver, but the smile vanished from Mr. Maddox's face. The stiffening of the big well-fleshed figure warned Oscar that something important was happening.

"I'm calling Joe," the voice said. "Is this Joe?"

"Who is it?" Mr. Maddox countered.

"I'm talking for Larry. You know Larry?"

"Maybe. Where's Larry?"

"He's busy. He's gotta have you and a couple more C-notes if you want some action. You know what I mean?"

"Where are you?"

"I'm calling from the airport. There's a night-club over here. Larry's busy inside. Bring them C-notes, Larry says, and your car. And don't lose any time. This is hot. I'll be standing at the end of the bridge."

"I'll see you," Mr. Maddox said and hung up.

"What is it?" Oscar demanded suspiciously.

"Business."

"I know the signs. Look, Joe, are you gonna lay off that Podder business?"

"Those mugs," Mr. Maddox said as he started for the door, "are going to get the surprise of their lives."

"Maybe I'd better go along, Joe."

"It's bad enough hearing you squawk in here," was Mr. Maddox's parting shot.

CHAPTER THREE

TWO-WAY RIDE

PENNSYLVANIA AVENUE was an imposing sweep of bright lights to the base of Capitol Hill as Mr. Maddox wheeled the big blue car to the right on Fourteenth Street. He was smiling with grim satisfaction as the light-bathed shaft of the Washington Monument appeared off to the right a few moments later.

Washington might be the front yard of the F.B.I.—but the Bureau didn't know everything. It didn't know why a little race-track crook like Mynie Sampson had started to carry a gun. It didn't know that two smooth workers like the pseudo-Colonel Daggett and Frisco Dick were working under their very noses.

The G-men didn't know a lot of things that Joe Maddox would know before long. Larry Kent was a fast worker. If it took two C-notes, and more, to get to the bottom of this, the price would be cheap.

They were printing money behind the lighted windows of the Bureau of Printing and Engraving as Mr. Maddox drove by. The pavement made a sweeping curve that ended on the brightly lighted Potomac River bridge, with the Virginia shore on the other side.

A man stood at the Virginia end of the bridge. He looked to be in his middle twenties, with a hat pulled low over a thin sharp face. He stepped forward as Mr. Maddox stopped.

"Joe?"

"Yes."

He jumped in and closed the door. "Turn right," he said bruskly.

"That's not the way to the night-club!"

A quick movement—and a gun was in Mr. Maddox's side. "That's the way for you! Turn or I'll blast you!"

Tires protested as Mr. Maddox swung sharp and hard to make the turn. A descending grade brought them out on the Mt. Vernon Memorial Highway, paralleling the Virginia shore of the Potomac along there, from Arlington Cemetery and the Robert E. Lee mansion to Mt. Vernon, below Alexandria.

"So it's a stick-up?"

"Stop for that guy—and get in the back seat!"

A second man, young also, and taller, with a topcoat over his arm was loitering beside the highway. For a hair-raising moment Mr. Maddox debated making a fight for it. Scattered traffic was passing, moving fast. No other help was in sight to keep Joe Maddox from getting shot or slugged.

"Take the dough," Mr. Maddox offered. "Drop the car across the river. If I lose, I lose."

"Shut up and get in the back seat! Watch him, Monty!"

Mr. Maddox got into the back seat with the sheepish realization that Oscar had been right after all. Joe Maddox had made a fool move—and here was the payoff.

Monty followed him into the back seat, gun in hand. The other one took the wheel, started on, and chuckled over his shoulder.

"That's ten you owe me, Monty. I told you he'd be sucker enough to fall for it."

"I guess the bigger they are the harder they tumble," Monty retorted. "Eh, Maddox?"

"What do we do now?" Mr. Maddox asked.

"You get down on the floor there an' stay quiet. And no lip about it. Go on."

Lights glinted on the smooth surface of the Potomac. Over there across the river the white-lighted shaft of the Washington Monument thrust toward the dark night sky. Over there was the White House too, and the business district, and the big stone building a little way down Pennsylvania Avenue that held F.B.I. headquarters.

And none of it was any good to Joe Maddox, here on the Virginia side of the river. A big airliner coming in low overhead to a landing at the airport was no help. Or the purring automobiles that rushed past as Mr. Maddox wedged his bulk down into the cramped space on the floor.

Monty threw the topcoat over him and callously pushed him down with a foot. "Now stay there or I'll slug you!"

Under the coat Mr. Maddox huddled raging and helpless. Larry Kent had handed back a double-cross. In no other way could these men know about Larry, the hundred-dollar bill, and Joe Maddox.

Mr. Maddox could tell when they turned off the Memorial Highway, across the bridge that carried traffic past the stately Lincoln Memorial, back into the District of Columbia, into the city.

Minute by minute this looked less like a stick-up. An ominous, growing feel of danger began to prickle nerve-ends.

The car made many turns, entered fairly heavy traffic. There were stops, presumably for traffic-lights, more turns. Mr. Maddox lost all sense of direction.

THEY were still on city pavement some fifteen minutes later when the car swung up a slight incline and slowly entered a building. The driver jumped out and closed garage doors.

"I'll be back in a minute," he said and vanished through a side door.

Mr. Maddox tried to sit up. The foot shoved him down again. "I'll tell you when," Monty said curtly.

The driver returned. "Tie this around his face an' bring him in."

A coarse Turkish towel was secured around Mr. Maddox's face. One leg was almost asleep. He limped as he was guided out of the garage.

Steps followed…. Then the warm quiet of a house closed about them. Monty led him to a second-floor room and nudged him with the gun-muzzle to a sitting position on a bed.

"Take it off now if you want to."

A light-switch snapped. The room was dark when Mr. Maddox freed his face of the heavy towel-folds. A dazzling flashlight beam struck his eyes, blinding him, hiding the man behind the flashlight. But it was Monty's voice behind the light.

"We know Larry's side of it. What's the idea of paying that punk to stick his nose in other people's business?"

"And I thought that rat was a square-shooter," Mr. Maddox growled.

The light kept him blinded. He had the feeling someone else was in the room. He saw a cigarette tip glow briefly behind Monty.

Sitting there on the soft bed with slitted eyes, Mr. Maddox smelled the tobacco smoke. And also a faint pervading perfume that suggested a woman's presence. Perhaps not at the moment—but a woman had been in this room.

The bedspread was silky—such as a woman would use. So this was a woman's bedroom somewhere in Washington.

The chill prickle of danger continued. Balancing it was the savage satisfaction that there was some crooked reason for Mynie Sampson's carrying a gun. Crooked work was centering at the Podder stable. Crooked enough to justify this.

"How much did you pay Larry?" Mr. Maddox asked.

Monty snapped: "What's the idea of hiring the guy?"

Mr. Maddox was still angry at himself for going wrong on Larry Kent, for walking into a trap like this. Joe Maddox who knew all the tricks and dodges, who'd matched wits with some of the smoothest crooks in the country, falling for a sucker telephone call.

He had been weighing the odds. Now he came to a decision and stared full at the light. "Listen," Mr. Maddox said in a flat heavy voice.

"Keep that light in my face all night if you like. Get tough with me if you've got time to waste. If I go out of here in a morgue wagon. I've said it all. Now, to hell with you!"

Threats should have followed—and violence. Mr. Maddox had no illusions. But Monty seemed nonplussed.

The silence drew out. Behind Monty a low voice said: "Watch him." The man who had been standing there walked out of the room and closed the door.

Monty swore softly. Mr. Maddox denied himself the luxury of a grim smile. The bluff had worked for the moment.

Monty stepped back and lighted a cigarette. His face was visible for an instant, pinched at the nose, hard at the mouth, black hair, dark blue suit, wiry build. Monty drew on the cigarette and growled: "You oughta be pitched in the river, Maddox."

Mr. Maddox said nothing.

"I've handled guys like you before," Monty sneered. "They all talk."

MR. MADDOX sat solidly and impassively. Monty cursed him again, as if nerves were getting jumpy. The flashlight beam moved here and there. This was a woman's bedroom, with silk-covered period chairs, etchings on the wall, flowers on the dressing-table where triple mirrors threw back the light.

The smooth silver frame around a man's photograph glinted on the dressing-table. The passing light-beam showed enough of the picture to startle Mr. Maddox.

He wanted to order the light back on the dressing-table. Tensely Mr. Maddox waited. The light roved jerkily, coming back to him, moving away. Monty flicked ashes off the cigarette and moved restlessly.

Then suddenly the light was on the table again—and Mr. Maddox chortled savagely.

The Adam's apple was there, the gold-frame glasses over slightly popping eyes. Luther Podder beyond any doubt, in a large silver-mounted frame on this feminine dressing-table.

Never mind where the house was located. Never mind who Monty or the other man were. The tie-up with Podder was enough.

"Funny, is it?" Monty sneered.

Mr. Maddox wiped the quick hard smile away. Plenty of mystery here—but if Joe Maddox lived, he'd get to the bottom of it now. He looked up alertly as a man came in.

"Bring him out."

This might be the payoff. Mr. Maddox obeyed watchfully while one man held the flashlight and the other knotted the towel back into place.

They guided him from the room, down the same stairs, outside to the automobile. Once more he was ordered down on the floor in the back. The topcoat was thrown over him. Monty sat there with his gun ready while the other man drove.

Once more the automobile zig-zagged through the city. Joe Maddox knew too much. He was dangerous. Frisco Dick and Colonel Daggett weren't fools. Strange that so little had happened in that house. They'd trapped him, taken him to the house, uttered a few threats, and apparently decided to accept his refusal to talk.

It didn't make sense. Not with these men—unless they'd decided to rub Joe Maddox out. This might be a trip into the country where that little matter could be accomplished at leisure.

Then abruptly the car pulled to the curb and the driver got out. Monty said: "Don't move, Maddox!"

He took the topcoat with him. Mr. Maddox lay for a moment considering, and cautiously raised up.

An automobile just ahead pulled away with a rush. Mr. Maddox lunged up to his knees, grunting at cramped muscles. Through the windshield he saw receding tail-lights.

The car whirled around the corner and was gone. Swearing, Mr. Maddox clawed for the door handle, stumbled outside. And it was too late to do much of anything.

Other automobiles were parked for the night along the quiet tree-shaded street. Red-brick houses were in a solid row from corner to corner. No pedestrians were in sight. Not a witness to what had happened.

The ignition key had been left. He'd been given freedom and his automobile back. They hadn't even asked for his billfold.

Mr. Maddox slapped dust off his trousers. He was in one of the older sections of Washington. He drove to the corner and the street sign said that he was on Fifteenth Street in Northeast Washington.

Deep thought as he drove back to the hotel only heightened the mystery and made him wary with growing apprehension. There was more to this than Joe Maddox could see at the moment. But what?

CHAPTER FOUR

THE BOOKIE AND THE BLONDE

MR. MADDOX left the automobile with the hotel doorman and went up to the suite, scowling thoughtfully. Oscar was waiting. Mr. Maddox walked in, exclaiming: "Build me a drink! I need it!"

"Yeah?" said Oscar. "Shall I make one for the lady too?"

"Lady?" Mr. Maddox snapped.

"A lady at all times, I hope," a woman's voice said lightly.

The blonde Diane Wall stood up from the easy chair where she had been sitting almost out of sight. Her smile had a brittle edge.

Danger here—but the smile Maddox covered it with was as broad and welcoming as any lady could desire. "This is a pleasure, Miss Wall."

"I'll not feel so guilty then. Your Mr. Oscar hasn't seemed too happy about my visit."

"The lady," Oscar said sourly, "said she'd wait until you showed up."

"And said she had all night to wait," Diane Wall added lightly. "I'm rude and I'm stubborn and Mr. Oscar is angry about the bit in my column about bookmakers. I *am* sorry."

Oscar looked skeptical. Mr. Maddox was blandly forgiving as he chuckled.

"Undoubtedly we should be grateful for the publicity, Miss Wall."

"Thank you. You *are* nice. Did I hear a drink mentioned?"

A glance sent Oscar into the next room on that errand. Still smiling, Mr. Maddox indicated the chair again and suggested: "Of course I'm curious, Miss Wall."

She shrugged as she sat down. "I was on my way out to a house party at the Podder farm and thought I'd satisfy a little of my own curiosity."

"No trouble locating us?"

"I called a friend. A track detective named Cassidy."

"Ah—Cassidy!"

"Nice, isn't he?" Diane Wall said. Her smile might have meant anything. It was Mr. Maddox's guess that it meant trouble.

Cassidy hadn't been in evidence at the track. But the fact that he was in town and knew where Joe Maddox was stopping showed that Cassidy was on the job. And Cassidy, and other detectives of the Masterton Agency, who covered all the race-tracks of the country, were a more potent threat than any police headquarters.

Diane Wall was probably aware of that by the way she was smiling. She had the looks, the assurance, the hardness, maliciousness and brains to be dangerous.

"What can I do for you?" Mr. Maddox asked bluntly.

"What was the trouble at the stable today?"

"Trouble?"

"There *was* trouble—and I must know."

"So you can print it?"

"No."

Mr. Maddox lifted his eyebrows.

She was not offended. "Please believe me."

"In any case, I don't see—"

"—that it's any of my business," Diane Wall finished coolly.

Neither was smiling. Both seemed to realize an undercurrent of seriousness. Mr. Maddox's nod agreed that it was none of her business.

"Would it make you feel any different if I assured you this meant a lot to me?" Diane Wall asked gravely.

"In what way, ma'am?"

She bit her lip.

Oscar came in with Scotch and soda, two glasses, and went back into the other room.

MR. MADDOX drank slowly, pondering the girl before him. She seemed to need the drink. Color had left her face. Over the glass she said: "I'll have to tell you. It's Jack Podder. I've waited a long time for someone like him—and now I'm going to fight for him."

"So!"

His tone caused her eyes to widen. "You don't like him?" she said, as if finding it surprising, hard to believe.

"I didn't say so." Mr. Maddox shrugged. "How can my talk with Mynie Sampson have anything to do with you and young Podder?"

The Scotch was bringing a faint flush back to her cheeks. Loosening her tongue a little. "That girl is young, but she's clever. She wants Jack, too. And she's not good enough for him. Her father is no good. I know all about him, although I haven't said anything to Jack."

"Decent of you."

Diane Wall laughed shortly. "Not at all. You know better. It's clever of me. I don't know enough about the situation to be convincing. I'd only make Jack feel sorry for her. He's the kind who *would* feel sorry."

Mr. Maddox regarded her with a reluctant admiration. Clever, dangerous, yet he was beginning to like her in spite of himself.

"Is it young Podder or his money?" he abruptly questioned.

Diane Wall did not hesitate. "Both."

"You're frank, at least."

Diane drank from her glass again. Color was deeper in her cheeks. "My family had money and lost it. I've done without. I've had my share of disappointment. The stage, for instance. I wasn't good enough. I work hard now for what I earn. I wouldn't marry a poor man."

"Not even if it were Jack Podder?"

"I doubt it. But Jack's not poor. And I happen to be in love with him. I'm going to marry him."

"And you want something on Annabelle and her father to scuttle the competition."

"Yes."

Mr. Maddox smiled wryly. "You're still being frank, at least. I like it."

"Thanks, I believe you."

"But I'll not help you do Mynie Sampson's girl a dirty trick," said Mr. Maddox, rising and putting his glass on the table. "As far as I've seen, there's nothing wrong with her. Why don't you check up on the Podders?"

Diane Wall looked startled. Her eyes had a greenish light that seemed to brighten at a hint of danger. "What do you mean, Mr. Maddox?"

"Does it matter? You say there's a house party at the Podder farm. I'm driving out there too, on a little business of my own."

"Then," said Diane Wall, standing up, "I'll leave my car in town and go with you. Jack can bring me back in the morning."

"Good technique," Mr. Maddox chuckled. He telephoned for his car to be brought to the front. And when Oscar looked in the room said: "I'm driving to the Podder farm."

"I've been listening," Oscar said. "Do you have to be clubbed over the head to get any sense? Lay off this, Joe!"

Diane Wall was watching them both alertly.

"Forget it," Mr. Maddox told Oscar. "And don't wait up for me."

DIANE WALL was subdued as they drove away from the hotel. "I might have known it wouldn't work. But I suppose when you get desperate, anything seems reasonable. You'll not say anything about this to Jack?"

"Sister," said Mr. Maddox, "I'm not a heel." And then added: "But when I meet a heel, I treat him like one. Remember that."

"Why? Are you referring to Jack?"

"I don't know, sister."

"Then there is trouble!"

"Forget it," Mr. Maddox said blandly. "Tell me about the farm."

Baden Manor, the Podder farm, Diane Wall said, was something over fifteen hundred acres fronting Chesapeake Bay, near Annapolis. Mostly woodland and pasture, Baden Manor house overlooked the Bay. New stables had been built when Luther Podder started buying thoroughbred horses.

"He's a strange man," Diane Wall confessed. "Sometimes I think he's a little bewildered by all the money he's made."

Mr. Maddox said nothing. He was thinking about the picture of Luther Podder on the woman's dresser, about Cassidy, who must be watching him, and about Colonel Daggett, Frisco Dick and Mynie Sampson. He was wondering what the mystery was hiding. And wondering if Diane Wall knew more than she pretended. She was clever enough.

They followed Pennsylvania Avenue out and took the Upper Marlboro road. Beyond that sleeping little country town a rear tire blew with the speedometer above fifty. Mr. Maddox wrestled the car to a stop on the road-edge.

"The first tire trouble since last fall," Mr. Maddox said philosophically. "And it'd have to happen tonight."

"I'll help," Diane offered. "I can change a tire as well as a man."

"I'm gray-haired and fat," Mr. Maddox chuckled. "But I can manage. You hold the flashlight."

Some women would have been annoyed, helpless. Diane Wall was humming under her breath as she held the light and Mr. Maddox unlocked the luggage compartment. "In a few minutes," he said, "we can laugh about it."

Diane Wall screamed instead.

It was a thin, stifled scream of fright and horror. Not loud. No louder than the oath which ripped from Mr. Maddox at the same moment.

They both had seen the same sight as the lid came up. The body in the compartment was bent and doubled up in a gruesome huddle. A hand slid limply down over the floor-edge. The fingers looked unnaturally white in the light—and long and slender like a woman's.

"Gimme the light!" Mr. Maddox said thickly and swore again in a strangled voice. His heart hammered in great thumps. Sweat broke on his face as the full implications dawned on him.

Larry Kent hadn't double-crossed. Larry hadn't sold out. Whatever had made Larry talk had ended in this.

The mystery house no longer was a mystery. This explained the snatching of Joe Maddox. Larry Kent must have been dead before the telephone call. They hadn't wanted to question Joe Maddox. They didn't care what he knew. They only wanted his car for a short time.

They'd led Joe Maddox into the house, asked a few questions to divert suspicion, and while he'd been in that upstairs room, they'd loaded Larry Kent's body into this trunk compartment. And they'd put Joe Maddox back in his car, carried him across town and given him his freedom, his automobile—and Larry Kent's corpse.

MR. MADDOX breathed heavily. His was the explaining now. He had the body. More than one person at Bowie track must have seen him talking to Larry Kent.

Behind him, in a stifled voice, Diane Wall gulped: "Who did it?"

Mr. Maddox swung around. His heart still hammered. His throat was dry, tight, as he faced this new danger. This girl, this newspaper woman, could start Joe Maddox to the electric chair the moment she reached a telephone. Mr. Maddox remembered with something close to despair that he'd refused his help when she'd opened her heart to him. What could he expect from her now?

"Looks like I killed him, doesn't it?"

If there was room for surprise left, it came now. Diane Wall was pale. The horror still showed on her face. But she stammered: "I d-don't think so. You wouldn't have shown him to me this way."

"Thanks," Mr. Maddox jerked out. "No—I didn't."

"I—I don't understand. Who is he?"

Mr. Maddox turned the light back on the body. Never had his brain seemed so numb.

"It's your car, isn't it?" she persisted.

"Yes."

"Don't you know anything about it?"

She sounded on the borderline of hysteria. Cool, she might be, clever and assured—but she had a woman's nerves and they were fraying.

"Take it easy," Mr. Maddox said gruffly. "Yes, I know who he is. Maybe I've got an idea who did it. But I can't prove much of anything."

"If you can't prove anything—they'll say you did it!"

"I suppose so."

"Oh, it's terrible, isn't it?"

Mr. Maddox growled assent.

"You're a newspaper woman. It's your duty to report this—to print it."

"I—I know."

"I can't ask you to keep quiet. The cops would hold you, too, if they found out."

"I know," Diane said again, huskily.

"It'd finish you with Jack Podder."

She had no answer to that. But she was thinking of it. The strain showed on her pale face.

"On the other hand," Mr. Maddox muttered, "it might help you hook young Podder. Might be just the thing you need."

The quick turn of her eyes considered that. And the idea was a thread so slender that Mr. Maddox had no thought of trusting his life to it.

"It doesn't matter in any case," he commented. "The Podders are somewhere behind this. Jack Podder may be tarred with a dirtier stick than you."

"I don't believe it! Not Jack! Not his father! They wouldn't! They couldn't!"

"That," said Mr. Maddox heavily, "is something I'm going to know. If young Podder is innocent, the truth will clear him."

"He can't possibly know anything about this!"

"What do we do?" asked Mr. Maddox evenly. "Go to the police now or let me have a chance to get at the truth?"

"I don't want Jack hurt! The public never forgets. They always think the worst!"

"Can you keep your mouth shut and leave everything to me?"

"I can try," Diane said.

"Hold the light while I change the tire," Mr. Maddox said grimly.

TWICE the trunk lid had to be lowered while cars passed. Each time fear that the strangers would stop mounted to a tense climax and gave way to relief.

Mr. Maddox was panting when he finally put the punctured tire and the tools back in the trunk. "Let's get away from here," he said thickly as he climbed in the car. "Keep your chin up. You look half dead yourself. Where do you live?"

"On California Street."

"Apartment or a house?"

"In an apartment. Does it matter?"

Mr. Maddox ignored her question. "I understand Luther Podder isn't married. Is he interested in any woman?"

"I don't think so. Not seriously."

"Who was the woman with him today?"

"Marcia Trumbull. Her husband was Senator Ogden Trumbull."

"Wealthy?"

"I think so. Ogden Trumbull made a fortune in Western mines. Marcia has plenty of money."

"Does she have an apartment also?"

Diane looked over her shoulder, shuddered visibly at the hidden passenger behind them, and said: "Marcia has a house in Georgetown."

"Does it have a detached garage?"

"Why—I think so. Why do you ask?"

"I'm just talking."

"You know something! I've got to know what it is!" Diane sounded close to hysteria again.

"Stop it!" Mr. Maddox ordered sharply. "Either you help me or you blow up as soon as we reach the Podder place! Which?"

Diane drew an unsteady breath. "Silly, isn't it? I thought I was hard-boiled and able to face anything. I'll be all right if I know exactly what to do."

"Wipe it out of your mind. When you get to the Podders' be yourself. Easy and natural. You won't know where I'm going or what I'm doing."

"I'll try if you think it will help."

"It will. Do you know how Mynie Sampson happened to get a job training for Podder?"

Diane was silent for a moment, thinking. "Last winter Jack said something about a friend of his father's recommending the man."

"Know the friend's name?"

"I'm not sure. I think it was a Colonel Daggett."

"So?" Mr. Maddox said.

Diane was thinking about something else. "This Sampson girl pretends she's helping her father. That's how she met Jack, staying near the horses so that she could see Jack constantly."

"Horses," said Mr. Maddox, "have always been a part of Anabelle's life. She'd naturally be found around the stables while she's living with her father."

"I'm not a fool! She's clever and scheming!"

Inwardly Mr. Maddox damned young love and its complications. This was bad enough without Diane Wall's judgment being warped by Annabelle Sampson. Maybe she was right. What did it matter while a gruesome corpse rode damningly in Joe Maddox's automobile?

A faint salty tang entered the night air. They'd left the Annapolis highway some time back. Now, following Diane's directions, they came to white-washed board fences and turned through stone gateposts to the long tree-shaded driveway of Baden Manor.

IT WAS called a farm—but Baden Manor house, blazing with lights could have belonged only to a man of Luther Podder's wealth. White-painted brick blended new and old construction. Architecture was Georgian. The house wings were spacious. Beyond the driveway trees was a boxwood hedge, flowers, lawns green and smooth. And just before the automobile swung around in front of the house, the headlights drove on back to a great white horse-barn and smaller outbuildings.

Mr. Maddox stepped out.

Diane Wall joined him, speaking under her breath. "It's a lovely place. There's been a house here for two hundred years."

Mr. Maddox shrugged. Other cars were parked before the house. A man-servant had opened the door and stepped out. After him came hurrying the muscular figure of young Jack Podder.

"Hello! Is this Mr. Maddox?" Jack Podder called as he came off the porch.

"Good guess," Mr. Maddox retorted. "You must be a mind-reader."

"Diane! I'd no idea you were coming with Maddox! Washington is calling on the telephone, Mr. Maddox. This is the third try, just as you came up. So you see how we knew you were coming."

"Who is it?" Mr. Maddox asked as they went to the house.

"The man didn't say. Telephone's there in the corner. Diane, you're using the same room."

Mr. Maddox saw half a dozen guests through a doorway on the left, heard others. Diane Wall was lightly mounting a graceful old staircase as Mr. Maddox lifted the telephone receiver with a sense of foreboding.

Oscar's sharp, anxious voice, verified the feeling. "Joe?"

"Yes!"

"Looked like you'd never get there. Joe, just after you left Cassidy came here!"

"Why?"

"Anyone listening there?"

"No."

"Cassidy walked in smooth as a greased eel with the old malarky that he wanted to welcome us to town. He asked for you. I told him you were out."

"That all?"

"I wish it was," said Oscar dismally. "The big flatfoot made a couple of cracks about you being out rustling business—and I cracked back that you was out to see that rich guy, Luther Podder."

"Always trying to help, eh?" Mr. Maddox said sarcastically.

"I know," said Oscar with unexpected meekness. "I knew right away it was a dumb break. But it was too late then."

"And what happened?"

"Cassidy eased out like he had his hand in your pocket already. I been telephoning since then to let you know."

"Anything more?"

"Ain't that enough?"

"If I get back," Mr. Maddox promised with bland vitriol, "I'll tell you what I think about it. Wait there until you hear from me!"

LUTHER PODDER had joined his son in the front hall. A dinner jacket fitted Podder no better than the gray suit he'd worn before lunch. Podder's eyes still seemed to be slightly popping with surprise behind the gold-framed glasses. His manner held no enthusiasm.

"We weren't expecting you, Maddox."

Mr. Maddox hunched his wide shoulders and stared at the smaller man from hard, estimating eyes. He was thinking of Podder's picture on the woman's dressing-table. And of Cassidy, the Masterton Agency's crack detective. And of Larry Kent's corpse out there in the automobile.

Cassidy must know something. If he did he was coming fast at this moment. That was the way Cassidy worked. Nerves knotted under Mr. Maddox's belt as he thought of Cassidy appearing suddenly and searching the big blue sedan outside.

"Not too glad to see me, are you?" Mr. Maddox said slowly.

Luther Podder's mouth hardened. "I didn't say that."

"You didn't have to."

The prominent Adam's apple inside the turned-down collar bobbed as Luther Podder snapped: "Usually our guests are invited. Certainly they don't come in this unfriendly manner."

Tight raw nerves drove Mr. Maddox out of his usual calm. "I came to ask you some questions, Podder. They'll have to wait—but I'll be back shortly."

"Questions about what?"

"We'll go into it when I get back," Mr. Maddox growled, ignoring Jack Podder's perplexity and the father's distinct irritation. Diane Wall came down the stairs as Mr. Maddox started for the door. "You're not going?"

"I'll be back."

"I'll thank you for the ride then. Be with you in a minute, Jack."

Diane was smiling as she caught Mr. Maddox's arm. She was speaking rapidly under her breath as they went down the front steps together. "Colonel Daggett is here!"

"I might have known!"

"I opened the wrong door upstairs. He was inside using the telephone. It's an extension. I think he was listening to your conversation. I don't know why he should do such a thing but—but I thought you should know."

"Smart thinking, sister. Keep an eye on him, will you?"

"Yes. But—why?"

"He's a phony," Mr. Maddox growled. "A crook. I'm coming back. Just don't miss anything!"

CHAPTER FIVE

IN THE SPRING
A FAT MAN'S FANCY—

A S HE started the car and Diane returned to the house, the tight knot of danger was still heavy in Mr. Maddox's middle. Diane Wall wasn't the type to juggle murder, guilt and danger too long. Worry was eating at her courage, her poise.

A moment later Mr. Maddox had something else to worry him....

Automobile headlights had appeared on the road where he was heading. The first stabbing flashes of light were visible through the driveway trees. They were still some distance from the driveway entrance—but coming fast. Coming like the driver might be trying to catch up with someone. Cassidy, for instance, trying to catch Joe Maddox!

If that was Cassidy, he'd know Joe Maddox's big blue sedan. When they passed, Cassidy would probably turn and follow. A wild race might lose Cassidy. Probably not. And Joe Maddox couldn't explain Larry Kent's body to Cassidy.

Mr. Maddox yanked on the wheel, dimmed the headlights, swung toward the big white horse-barn.

The barn was dark. No one seemed to be up at this hour of the night. Which was not surprising. Stable help arose at daybreak, turned in shortly after dark.

A big horse-van stood near the barn. Several yards behind the van was a small sedan. Mr. Maddox cut the lights and motor, coasted near and leaped out.

The speeding automobile had whirled into the driveway and was rushing toward the house. It proved to be a coupe that swung out of sight before the portico.

The man, whoever he was, would be in the house for at least a few minutes. Mr. Maddox clawed open the luggage compartment. Larry Kent was no stripling—but Mr. Maddox in this moment had strength he'd never suspected.

He grunted with the strain and the rear door of the small sedan creaked slightly as he opened it with a handkerchief over his hand. Seat cushions and springs gave out faint sounds as the weight of Larry Kent's body went on them.

Mr. Maddox closed the door quietly and a moment later had the flashlight beam back in his own luggage compartment.

There was no visible sign that Larry Kent had ever been in there. Mr. Maddox locked the compartment.

He was breathing hard from the exertion and strain, and was grimly conscious that the danger was greater than ever when a hoarse whisper made him jump and whirl. "Boss!" the whisper said.

Mr. Maddox used the flashlight recklessly. Nerves had almost let go with a yell. The light struck Stiffy, scrawny, ragged, grinning uncertainly.

"What the hell!" Mr. Maddox exploded under his breath, and then thought to turn the light off.

"You coulda knocked me over with a horsehair when I seen it was you!" Stiffy confided in an excited whisper. "How didja know I was back here, Boss?"

Mr. Maddox groaned. "Where did you come from?"

"Wasn't no trick," Stiffy boasted. "When that guy Sampson drove off in a van, I follered him in a durned old jalopy I rented from a stable dinge. Buck-a-day an' the gas I use."

"What van are you talking about?"

"That'n right there," said Stiffy. "When he turned in here, I parked the jalopy in the weeds an' snuck over acrost the field."

"So Mynie vanned over himself?"

"Come for a boss named Sandy O that's running tomorrow," Stiffy husked. "I heard a couple swipes in the stable say Sandy O was a dog an' it was wastin' time to haul him to the track."

"Where are the men now?"

"They said it'd be an hour before Sandy O was loaded an' they was gonna hit the straw again." Stiffy chuckled under his breath. "Wasn't till you come back here to the car an' throwed the light in the back that I figgered it was you."

Stiffy was a threat also now. Mr. Maddox wondered how much more of this a man could stand. "Stiffy, how much do you know?"

"Nothin'," said Stiffy cheerfully. "And I ain't a rat neither."

"Beat it back to the track then," Mr. Maddox said. "Forget you were here tonight. You didn't see me. You haven't any idea where I was tonight."

"I ain't got any idea about anything," said Stiffy. "So long, Boss."

Stiffy vanished in the night as soundlessly as he had appeared. Mr. Maddox was weak as he got back into the car.

"Hiding behind a kid now!" Mr. Maddox thought savagely. "And if the cops ever grab him for questioning about this, I'll have to take the rap to help him!"

A moment later the big car, lights still off, purred softly away from the barn. The small coupe that had arrived so hurriedly was parked directly in front of the house.

MR. MADDOX was halfway to the road before he switched on the lights. He was almost at the road when the rear-view mirror showed dimmed headlights swinging away from the house and coming after him.

"Cassidy, or I'm a liar!" Mr. Maddox jerked out.

Tires skidded, the car reeled into the wider road and the snoring motor built up speed. Lights leaped on full behind him. The coupe made an equally fast turn out of the driveway and came racing after.

Mr. Maddox had the heavier, faster car. But only savage emotion could have made him put the speedometer above seventy as he did now. And the headlights stayed doggedly behind him.

Six—eight miles registered on the speedometer. Signs warned of a cross-road. Mr. Maddox stamped on the brakes, slid tires, jerked the heavy car to the right, and found himself on a dirt country road.

He was bouncing and slamming along that dirt road when the furiously driven car behind drew close, horn blaring peremptorily. Mr. Maddox grinned suddenly and slowed.

The coupe bounced up abreast. A shout came through the open window.

"Damn you, Maddox! Stop that car!"

Mr. Maddox stopped. The coupe did the same, exactly abreast of him.

"I thought you wanted to pass," Mr. Maddox called blandly. "Do I know you?"

"Do you know me?" repeated the loud angry voice. "You're damn right you know me! Get out of there, Joe! I've got a gun if you try anything funny!"

Mr. Maddox opened the door, chuckling. "If I could trust my ears, I'd say that ugly voice sounded like Cassidy."

"Well, you can trust your ears!"

Cassidy lunged out between the two cars, with a flashlight. He was a grizzled, stocky man, hat askew, voice crackling with anger.

"Try to lam away from me, will you? You're under arrest, Joe!"

"Why?"

"Never mind why! That was a slick trick you pulled back there! Laying low until I got in the house and then trying to sneak out! They told me a Washington telephone call was waiting! It was that little weasel, Oscar, tipping you off, I guess."

"Was it?" said Mr. Maddox blandly. "Why the high blood pressure, Cassidy?"

"Almost wrecked myself twice trying to catch you!" Cassidy exploded. "Served you right if you'd piled against a telephone pole! What's in that car, Joe?"

"A half-pint in the dash pocket," Mr. Maddox grinned. "If I'd known you were following me, I'd have stopped and had the cork out."

"Never mind the cracks, Joe! You wouldn't have been driving like a maniac if you hadn't slipped up this time! I'm warning you I've got a gun! Don't try to get away!"

Sadly Mr. Maddox said: "I tried to get out here in the night where I could think. And you have to turn up in my hair, Cassidy. Go ahead and I'll think anyway. I'm trying to decide whether to claim a horse tomorrow."

"Yeah?" Cassidy sneered. "Do I look like a sap? You won't need horses where you're going! Stand there while I look around!"

Mr. Maddox lit a cigar while Cassidy directed his light into the sedan. "Unlock the trunk, Joe."

"Anything to please," Mr. Maddox murmured.

A heavy silence fell as the trunk lid in back came up and Cassidy threw light into the empty compartment. Cassidy's voice came with a baffled choked sound.

"By God, if I've been kidded tonight! Is this one of your damn jokes, Joe?"

"Is what?" Mr. Maddox asked kindly.

"You know what I mean! That telephone call that—that—" Cassidy swore. "It must be! You trick me down to Chesapeake Bay—and then run hell out of me over the countryside! It's your lousy idea of humor!"

"You're talking Greek to me," said Mr. Maddox cheerfully. "What telephone call? About what?"

Cassidy was breathing heavily. "Never mind. I don't want to talk about it! Joe, so help me, some day I'll make you sweat for this!"

Mr. Maddox locked the trunk again. He had never been more bland and cheerful. "Cassidy, it's a hell of a note when an honest horse-owner can't drive out in the night to think about a horse he wants to claim."

"What horse?"

"Podder owns him. Sandy O. He's running tomorrow. I drove down tonight to pick up any dope Podder might let loose about the horse."

"Podder's horses are at the track!"

"Sandy O's at the farm. They're moving him to the track tonight. Drive back with me and have a look."

"Damn the horse!" Cassidy said blackly. "I've had enough tripe tonight!"

In that vile humor Cassidy got back in his car, turned it and departed with an angry clash of gears and no farewell.

MR. MADDOX watched the receding tail-lights and chewed hard on the cigar. The bland cheerfulness lingered, like faint hope that he was reluctant to put aside.

No need to wonder who had made an anonymous telephone call to Cassidy. Or why. They'd tried to make certain the noose would tighten fast on Joe Maddox's neck. Mr. Maddox growled aloud. "Mynie Sampson would know Cassidy would jump at a hint he could corner me. I'll break that little rat Mynie's neck before I'm through with this!"

Cassidy had vanished when the sedan got back to the blacktop road. It took will power to turn again toward Baden Manor Farm—and Larry Kent's body in the small automobile by the big white horse-barn. Maybe they'd already found the body.

Cassidy must have returned to Washington. His coupe was not in front of the manor house or back at the barn. Neither was the horse-van. Neither was the small sedan! The headlights showed no life stirring at the barn, no excitement.

Mr. Maddox went to the house. His nerves were crawling again as the dignified manservant admitted him and stated: "Mr. Jack Podder said that if you returned, sir, he wishes to see you in the library. Will you step this way, sir?"

Jack Podder entered almost soundlessly by another door, saying: "I didn't know whether you'd return or not, Mr. Maddox."

The boy seemed grave, worried behind his estimating look. And when Mr. Maddox did not speak directly, Jack Podder added: "A detective named Cassidy was here looking for you. There seemed to be some trouble."

Mr. Maddox chuckled. "I've known Cassidy twenty years. He has brain-storms. What's on your mind, son?"

Jack's match paused in lighting a cigarette. "I'm wondering why you came here in the first place. Diane's suspiciously vague about it. She says she just happened to run into you and asked for a lift."

"Correct, son. I drove down to ask your father some questions."

"About Sampson?" Jack asked with a quick challenge.

"Perhaps."

Keener eyes than Jack Podder's would have been baffled by the bland cheerfulness of Mr. Maddox.

Jack Podder was big and muscular, with his share of intelligence—but he faced a man who had sharpened wits against canny race-fans for thirty years. Worry, visibly gnawing at the boy did not help him now.

"There's some kind of trouble," he nervously insisted. "I think you know what it is. I shouldn't be surprised if Diane knows too. She's acting strangely."

Mr. Maddox lifted his eyebrows. "Trouble?"

Jack Podder gestured impatiently. "I'm not a fool. That wasn't a friendly argument we interrupted today. I think this visit tonight has something to do with it. It means a lot to me, sir." A forced, apologetic smile warmed the unhandsome face again.

"Are you worried about Annabelle?" Mr. Maddox asked shrewdly.

Jack Podder looked sheepishly surprised. "How did you guess?"

THIS TIME Mr. Maddox did not have to force his chuckle. "I'm not a fool either, son. She's a nice girl."

"Nice?" said Jack. "Why—why—" His gesture replaced the mild word with superlatives mere speech could not encompass. "I want to marry her, sir."

"So?" said Mr. Maddox. "That bad, eh? *Hmmm…* I was wondering if it wasn't Miss Wall."

"Diane's a good scout. We've had fun together. But I'm not in love with her."

"Well, you're the one who's in love, son. So you think Annabelle's in trouble?"

"I know it!" Jack said positively. "And I can't find out what's wrong. It's doing things to her. She won't tell me about it. She insists nothing is wrong."

"She might be right, son."

"I told you I wasn't a fool, Mr. Maddox. A little while ago I asked Annabelle to marry me—and she started to cry. She said the answer was no, for there wasn't a chance for us to be happy."

"Young folks," said Mr. Maddox, "get the damnedest ideas. When did you ask her?"

"When you left I went back to Sampson's house to tell Annabelle you'd come here, and ask her what she knew about it. I begged her to marry me then."

"Houseparty here and Annabelle back in the hired help's house, eh?"

Jack flushed. "She wouldn't come tonight. Don't you think I want all our friends to see and admire her?"

Mr. Maddox nodded. "Son, it strikes me I'd better let your father wait, and have a talk with Annabelle first. Might be she and I could settle a lot of things. Maybe she'd feel different afterwards. Suppose you take me to her."

"She's gone. Her father brought a truck over from the track to get a horse that's running tomorrow. He drove off while we were talking—

and then Annabelle asked me to let her alone so she could think, I came back to the house. I'd just got to the front door when Annabelle drove away in her car."

Mr. Maddox felt his face freeze. "Uh—what kind of car was she driving?" he asked huskily.

Jack looked at him curiously. "A gray Chevrolet sedan. It was parked back at the barn."

Mr. Maddox started to reach for a cigar. The hand felt unsteady. He thrust it into his coat pocket. The boy was looking at him. Something had to be said. "Is Sandy O the horse that Mynie's hauling?"

"As a matter of fact he is. You're well posted."

"Sandy O is entered tomorrow, son. Why is he here at the farm until the last minute?" Bookie shrewdness helped Mr. Maddox suggest: "Been keeping him under wraps so you can spring something?"

Jack smiled wryly. "No such luck. We had to take Sandy O to get another horse. Got him for a song. He's a four-year-old and didn't run better than second as a three-year-old. Sampson has been working with him and thinks he might show something in a thousand-dollar claiming race. It's Sampson's idea. I'm not even enthusiastic about starting him."

MR. MADDOX nodded with a show of interest. Inside he was thinking of that small shabby automobile that Annabelle had driven away into the night. She was alone. At any moment she might look in the back seat and discover the grisly passenger. Or someone else might make the discovery and place the guilt of murder squarely on her shoulders.

For a moment Mr. Maddox was tempted to tell Jack Podder. The boy had a right to know.

Common sense stopped the impulse. You couldn't tell what a young fellow in love would do. He might blow his top, might rush to the telephone and call on the state police to help prove the girl's innocence. Certainly he'd not waste much thought on what happened to Joe Maddox. And there might yet be time to catch her.

"Son," said Mr. Maddox hurriedly, "I'll stop by the track and see Annabelle. I've got a hunch she'll be there with her father. Maybe talking it over with him."

"I'll go along."

"You'd do more harm than good. Let me see what I can do."

Behind Mr. Maddox a dry, irritated voice demanded: "What will you do for my son, sir?"

Luther Podder had stepped into the library and overheard the last words. Mrs. Ogden Trumbull was with him. It was Mr. Maddox's quick guess the woman had egged the elder Podder into this interruption. She had that air of disdainful satisfaction.

Mr. Maddox took his first good look at her. For her age she was attractive, if you could forget the thin lips, the little, almost invisible face lines of will and determination that could be dangerous in a clever woman. For her benefit as much as Jack's father, Mr. Maddox spoke truthfully—to a point.

"We were talking about Sandy O's race tomorrow. I'm interested in his chances."

"He has none," said Luther Podder promptly. "He shouldn't have been entered, and I told Sampson so."

Mrs. Trumbull spoke with scathing conviction. "You see, Luther, Colonel Daggett was right. He's forced his shady business into your own house. I thought something like this might happen."

Only caution held back Mr. Maddox's temper. He was seeing that dressing-table with the silver-framed picture of Luther Podder. And the men who'd had him snatched and who had killed Larry Kent. The colonel, for instance, who had used the extension telephone to listen in on Oscar's warning.

Mr. Maddox managed to resurrect another of the bland smiles. "I'll not thank Colonel Daggett for his interest. And you, madam, might feel differently if you knew everything."

"I don't understand you."

Mr. Maddox bowed gallantly. "Just as I thought. Mr. Podder, I came here for information, not money. Your son's bankroll is safe."

"Dad, he's right. Money hasn't been mentioned."

Luther Podder irritably waved that aside. "Maddox, I suppose you've heard that a detective came here looking for you. I don't like it. We're interested in a racing-stable—not bookmakers, betting, and detectives snooping in the middle of the night."

Mr. Maddox said curtly: "I'll try to find out exactly what you are interested in."

He had a quick conviction he'd startled the Washington society woman. And he took that thought out of the library. Jack Podder followed him with some embarrassment.

"I'm sorry. Perhaps I should have explained everything. Er—I didn't want Annabelle coming into the argument."

"Forget it, son," Mr. Maddox advised.

JACK showed him to the door—and in a moment it closed on the gay Podder houseparty that seemed a mockery of all that was happening tonight.

And a moment later, on the other side of his automobile, Mr. Maddox found Diane Wall nervously pacing. She burst out: "I had to see you! A detective came here for you!"

"I saw him. He's an old friend," Mr. Maddox said with another slight distortion of the truth.

"What—what happened to that…?"

"Young lady," Mr. Maddox admonished, "I thought I told you not to worry."

"I can't help it," Diane confessed miserably. "I keep seeing that body and wondering what's going to happen. Jack has noticed that something is wrong. And that detective! What are you going to do?"

"You'll have to leave it to me, sister. If you go to pieces, everything blows up."

"Jack too?"

"Yes."

She drew a long breath. "I—I'll try to keep it out of my mind. I'll do anything to help Jack."

Mr. Maddox started to open the car door. And then stopped. He had a conscience. It was bothering him now. There was something likable about this Diane Wall and the way she felt about Jack Podder. No pretense. All her cards on the table. She was hard-boiled and practical—but she was in love. And it was hopeless. She was going to have a rocky time of it when the truth exploded in her face.

"You've been around, sister. Can you take it?"

"What do you mean?"

"I'm wondering how you'll feel if you miss out on young Podder."

She tried to see his face. She was still for a moment. Then with a slight catch in her voice she said: "You're trying to tell me something. You've just seen Jack.…"

"He thinks a lot of you, sister. But—"

"But—" said Diane Wall. She guessed instantly, bitterly: "So I've made a fool out of myself!"

"No," said Mr. Maddox. "Not a fool. Not with a fine young fellow like Jack Podder thinking the world of you. But you can't handicap love. It just—"

"That girl—"

"Either you can take it or you can blame her," Mr. Maddox reminded. "Jack Podder's no fool. You couldn't lead him around by the nose. Why think another girl could? Jack spoke to her about it tonight and she turned him down. Does that look like she's on the make? Maybe you still think enough of Jack to give him a boost now when he needs it."

"So now I'm to *help* them!"

"Hurting Jack Podder won't make it taste any better." Diane stood silently.

Mr. Maddox moistened his lips. He'd taken a long chance. Maybe he'd wiped out everything that would keep her silent. Maybe she'd head for the first telephone and call the police, hoping there was still a chance to remove Mynie's girl as a rival.

Diane laughed shortly. "All right. I know when I'm licked. Maybe I was a fool to fall for Jack in the first place. I should have chosen his father. Maybe I can like him as well, if I try. What am I supposed to do now?"

"Nothing," said Mr. Maddox. "Forget everything. Will you do it?"

"Why not?" said Diane. "I'll have to forget a lot of things, won't I? I might as well start on this."

She walked toward the house, a little blindly, Mr. Maddox thought. But her head was up, and her eyes were probably dry. Mr. Maddox swore under his breath as he started the car.

"Love plays hell with all the odds!" he growled aloud. "And I have to sit in the middle with my neck in a sling! If I ever get out of this, I'm cured!"

CHAPTER SIX

A HORSE CALLED SANDY O

THE PINES near Bowie track looked dark and gloomy as Mr. Maddox drove up. When he parked and got out, silence hung over the darkened stables. Crap games had long ended. Swipes, exercise boys and stable attendants were sleeping against the dawn rising-hour. A lantern moving in one of the stalls probably marked a sick horse someone was doctoring.

The barn that held the Podder and Maddox horses was dark and quiet. Stiffy was not in sight. Mr. Maddox directed his flashlight into the stall where Stiffy slept. The cot was vacant.

Kopper King nickered softly in the next stall as Mr. Maddox walked to the tackroom. Pop Harvey was sleeping alone there.

A shake brought Pop up yawning and startled when the flashlight showed Mr. Maddox. "Pop, where's Stiffy?"

"Ain't he here?" Pop mumbled. "Whassa matter? Wha' time is it?"

"It's late. Did you hear Mynie Sampson come in a little while ago?"

"He took a van out afore I went t' sleep," Pop said, standing up in long cotton drawers. "Stiffy went off after him. Ain't they back yet?"

"They ought to be. Both of them," Mr. Maddox muttered.

"I been watchin'," Pop stated as his wits began to function. "Only visitors Mynie had was that there Colonel Daggett right after the bosses come back from the last race. They talked a couple minutes was all. Wasn't no chance to hear what was said. Mynie looked like he'd seen a ghost when the feller went away. I eased over to pass a word an' he cussed me an' walked away. Poison, that's what that little crook is these days."

"Crooked! That's right. Damn crooked, or I'm a liar. I wonder what happened to Mynie."

The flashlight was off. They were standing in darkness. The floorboards creaked as Pop shifted uneasily on his bare feet. "He's runnin' a hoss tomorrow," Pop said.

"I know."

"This all looks dern funny t' me," Pop grumbled.

Mr. Maddox lifted his head and stepped to the door. The heavy drone of a truck motor was drifting through the night. The truck turned toward the stables. Drew nearer. Swung toward the barn.

"Mynie!" Mr. Maddox muttered, and closed the tackroom door.

The truck lights swept past. The truck halted some yards farther on.

"Stay in here," Mr. Maddox husked to Pop, and stepped out into the darkness.

The side door of the van was being opened. The footboard thudded down. A flashlight winked on and the short bow-legged figure of Mynie Sampson entered the van.

"Easy, boy, easy now," Mynie's low voice addressed the horse. "You're all set now. Take it easy."

Annabelle had not come with her father. Mynie certainly had no knowledge of the gruesome passenger his daughter had carried out on the highways. Mr. Maddox stepped into the doorway of the van and spoke easily.

"Keeping kind of late hours, aren't you, Mynie?"

Mynie whirled from the horse's head and swung the light-beam at the doorway.

"Maddox!"

"The old neighbor himself," Mr. Maddox agreed blandly. "Good-looking horse. Where'd you get him at this ungodly time of night?"

Mr. Maddox hadn't expected a welcome. But there was an unexpected deadliness and threat in Mynie's silent advance to the door, with the light held steady on Mr. Maddox's broad face.

"Still snooping, huh, Maddox? Still looking for trouble!" Mynie's voice shook with a sudden rush of rage. The sleek brown Sandy O moved uneasily, as if he sensed the little trainer's emotion.

Mr. Maddox bulked there in the doorway and chuckled softly. "What's worth snooping about a horse arriving at a barn? Matter of fact, I was looking for Annabelle."

"She's home where she belongs! What the hell do you want with her?"

"She *was* home," Mr. Maddox corrected. "She drove off after you, Mynie. That's why I kind of thought she'd turn up here."

MYNIE cursed under his breath. The light bobbed as he made a quick move—and a nickel-plated revolver muzzle slid into the light like a venomous fang. Mynie's thin voice sounded venomous too. "So you were at the farm snooping! I warned you what'd happen, Maddox, if you didn't lay off me? Did you think I didn't have the nerve to blast your guts open?"

One thing a bookie learned was men and their moods. Mynie meant what he was saying. Fear and rage had pushed Mynie to the desperate verge of a killing.

But this was danger a man could face with his wits and strength, danger that a man could get his hands on at close quarters. Mr. Maddox had never bulked with so much smiling assurance as he did now in the glare of Mynie's flashlight.

"I didn't doubt it, Mynie. Only I didn't think you'd blast me for trying to help your girl. She's a fine kid, Mynie. Too good to let you mess up her life with your crooked tricks."

"*You* help her?" Mynie choked.

"Yes," said Mr. Maddox. "And I mean help her. She's in trouble. Things are all messed up for her. I'm damn sure some of your crooked tricks have done it. It's none of my business—but I'd like to straighten her out so she'll marry young Jack Podder. He asked her tonight and she started crying and refused. Did you know that, Mynie? Or does that crooked little heart of yours give a damn?"

Behind the light Mynie gulped. It was audible. The gun wavered and the glinting muzzle swung down out of the light to Mynie's side. "You're lying, Maddox! Damn you, you're lying! What do you know about Annabelle and young Podder?"

Mr. Maddox shrugged. "Stop calling names. I told you I just came from Baden Manor. Jack Podder told me. He's pretty upset. You know how it is—crazy to get married and his girl crying about it and refusing to tell him why she won't marry him. And him unable to find out what's wrong."

"But—but she's in love with the guy!"

"So I assume," Mr. Maddox dryly agreed.

"She—that's all she was hoping! That he'd ask her!"

"Well, he did."

"Maddox, are you telling the truth?"

Inwardly Mr. Maddox relaxed a little at the note of pleading that had entered Mynie's voice. A man wouldn't shoot you while he was arguing. "The truth, Mynie."

They were speaking in low voices. Mynie's next words were little more than a husky whisper, roughed with despair. "Why'd she do it?"

"Maybe you know, Mynie."

"Everything I've been tryin' to do was for her. So there wouldn't be any hitch between them."

"What have you been trying to do? Tonight you left Baden Manor before I did. But I got to the track before you, Mynie. And you weren't anywhere in sight along the road. Don't kid an old-timer like me. I know the tricks. Where'd you go? What happened while you were off the road?"

"Keep outa this, Maddox!"

"Annabelle followed you away," Mr. Maddox reminded coolly. "Maybe she knows. Maybe that's why she's not here now. Maybe that's one of the reasons she's not saddling herself and a little crook like you on Jack Podder. How about it, Mynie?"

"I told you, Maddox! Keep outa this!"

"I'm in it," said Mr. Maddox. "Want to know why, you little rat? Want to know about Duke Snyder—or Colonel Daggett—whichever you call him? And Frisco Dick?"

Mynie gasped. Mr. Maddox let him have the rest of it. "Don't stand there and tell me you were ganging up with those mugs to help your daughter with a piece of murder?"

"Murder?"

"Murder!" Mr. Maddox snapped. "A hell of a mess to hang around your daughter's neck! No wonder she wouldn't marry the boy! No wonder she went all to pieces!"

"Oh my God!" Mynie groaned. "I don't know what you're talkin' about, Maddox! I don't know about any murder! But I gotta believe you! I gotta! You know them dirty crooks!"

Mynie's voice shook. "If they killed someone an' Annabelle followed me from the farm, maybe something's happened to her!"

"Maybe," agreed Mr. Maddox. "But is this the horse you hauled away from Baden Manor?"

"Look at him!"

"He'd better be," said Mr. Maddox. "Because after he runs tomorrow, he'll get a fancy going-over to make sure he's really Sandy O. I'll keep the wires hot to every big booking-spot in the country, and watch the track money. If he carries a load of cash tomorrow and wins, Mynie, he'd better be Sandy O. Because if you went off the road between here and Baden Manor, and switched Sandy O for a ringer to run in his place and win, you're sunk before you start. I'm telling you, Mynie! I hate a crooked race—and it wouldn't be the first smooth trick you've pulled on the talent!"

MYNIE'S light went out. Mr. Maddox swiftly crowded against the side of the door. He had a hunch he'd hit a bull's-eye—and now Mynie might use the gun.

But Mynie's shaking voice admitted: "You're too smooth, Maddox. You always was. God help me, this horse ain't Sandy O. They've been building up to it all winter. Ever since they got me the job training for Podder. I tried to back out an' they wouldn't let me. I told them my girl was falling for Jack Podder an' I couldn't pull no crooked work now. And they used it against me. Swore they'd let Podder know about my record an' get me and Annabelle both kicked out.

"They said there wouldn't be any trouble if I played ball like we agreed in the first place. And if I didn't play ball and tried to double-cross them, somebody'd take me for a little ride some night. That's when I started carrying a gun. I been having nightmares about it—thinkin' of what it'd do to the kid if I didn't make all the moves right."

"Who got you the job? Daggett?"

"Yes," said Mynie huskily. "An' how'd I know Annabelle and Jack Podder would fall for each other? I was about busted and wore out trying to make a living with them cheap horses I had. Hard luck all the time, no matter what I tried. So when Duke Snyder looked me up last fall an' said he had a sweet spot all framed up for me in this new stable, and we'd all make plenty of dough working the Podder horses right, I fell for it. How'd I know I'd hurt my baby instead of getting plenty of dough for her? The Sandy O switch was the first play they had figured out. All winter this ringer's been on a place they rented between Podder's farm an' here. It didn't take but a little work to make him match Sandy O to a hair—and he's good enough to take them platers tomorrow in Sandy O's place.

"I near went crazy trying to figure a way out of it. Annabelle knowed something was wrong from the nightmares I had and the way I acted. She figured right that it was crooked. And I couldn't tell her. She knowed too much about me already. And was shamed by it. I sent her to good schools. The girls there didn't have fathers like me. But she stuck to me just the same. And now when she fell for a swell young fellow like Jack Podder, I couldn't tell her I'd took the job crooked in the first place and was hooked. Wasn't nothing I could do but play ball with them crooks until she got married—an' then when they couldn't hurt her, tell 'em we'd all take a rap for this Sandy O trick if they didn't lay off. I figured I could hook them like they had me hooked."

"You would figure out a way like this," said Mr. Maddox. "Pull a crooked trick to nail the other crooks. Mynie, I almost feel sorry for you. But not quite. You buttered your bread and now you're stuck in it. But your kid deserves better. Close up this damn van. I think Pop Harvey has got an old gun around somewhere. We'll drive back for Sandy O and see what we find. And this is one time I'd be glad to see that big flatfoot Cassidy. He'd help. He's got plenty on the ball, even if I'd hate to tell him so."

And then Mr. Maddox froze as a voice spoke dryly outside the van doorway.

"I'll say the same thing for you sometime, Joe. This has been interesting. I've got a gun. Let's get started—and we can do our talking on the way."

MR. MADDOX snapped on his flashlight. So did Mynie—and Cassidy's grizzled, stocky form loomed up threateningly on the down-slanting footboard just outside the door.

Cassidy was smiling with hard satisfaction. He could have men barred from all American tracks. Could jail them. Could send them through the courts to the ultimate penalty. Prison… hanging… the chair.

That was what Cassidy's presence meant—and he had them cold. A hard note of enjoyment was in Cassidy's voice.

"I thought if I slipped over here to the track I might turn up something. So it was really murder after all, Joe? Where's the body?"

Mynie stood there in stricken silence. Mr. Maddox shrugged to the inevitable. "I might have known you'd pull an ace out of your sleeve, you lug. I don't know how much you heard—but maybe you can help now."

"I heard plenty," Cassidy assured them. "Everything. Get this van closed up, Sampson. We'll start this ringer back where you got him. And see what's there."

Mynie's groan sounded as if Mynie were near a state of collapse. "I mighta known it'd end like this! I don't know anything about a murder! Maddox'll have to tell you that! All I want now is to help my girl!"

"It sounds like she's in it deep," Cassidy said gruffly. "Come on, let's get going."

CHAPTER SEVEN

BLAST-OUT

THE THREE of them crowded on the truck seat, and as they passed through the dark pine trees once more, Cassidy lifted his voice. "I'll get at the bottom of all this one way or another. Sampson, you might as well come clean. Who got you this job and framed all this?"

Mynie was too crushed to evade. He answered mechanically as he hunched over the steering wheel.

"This guy that calls himself Colonel Daggett got me the job with Podder."

"Daggett," said Mr. Maddox, "used to be Duke Snyder, out on the Coast. Maybe you remember him. His sidekick was Frisco Dick."

"No," said Cassidy.

"They've both got records. They were smooth workers. They're better now, evidently, from the way Podder fell for them."

"I've got Podder's number," said Mynie wearily. "He woke up one morning an' realized he was rich an' wasn't making much of a splash for his money. He was a sucker for a big front. Colonel Daggett, Mrs. Trumbull, and folks like that had the shine he needed. So he got thick with them."

Cassidy countered: "Who's Mrs. Trumbull?"

"Ogden Trumbull's widow," Mr. Maddox said. "The crusty senator who made so much trouble about silver. He died several years ago."

"That guy? Sure. So his widow's a pal of this man Podder?"

"She's got a house in Georgetown," Mr. Maddox said. "And a silver-framed portrait of Podder on her dressing-table."

Even Mynie turned his head in surprise at that. Cassidy snorted. "So you get into bedrooms too? When did you get so thick with the lady, Joe? I thought you just came up from Miami."

"I get around."

Mynie moved his hands uneasily on the steering wheel and cleared his throat. "I never could figure that dame. Jack Podder told Annabelle that Mrs. Trumbull made a play like she meant to marry old man

Podder. He wasn't interested, but she's hung around as a friend. Jack didn't go for her as a new mama. He told Annabelle that the Trumbull woman introduced Colonel Daggett to them. I never was told that, but there it is, like Jack Podder said."

"Nice going, Mynie," Mr. Maddox murmured. "Remember that, Cassidy. And now, you big flatfoot, I'm coming clean on what happened today. It's got to be proved—and I think we can do it."

The truck headlights pushed along the deserted highway while Mr. Maddox talked. Cassidy hunched on the right side of the seat and listened without comment.

Mynie Sampson was the one who cried out with rage and protest. "You put that stiff in the car my baby was going to drive!"

"I'm sorry, Mynie. I didn't know she'd ever see the car. That's one reason I came looking for her so fast."

"She's out all alone with a dead man!" Mynie almost sobbed. "Damn you, Maddox! I could put a bullet in you!"

Cassidy erupted profanely. "Cut out that talk! It's what you get for going into a crooked deal! Take his gun, Joe! He'll pull something screwy yet!"

Mynie started to resist, and then let Mr. Maddox have his revolver. "Everything that happens makes it worse!" Mynie blurted helplessly.

"You asked for it," Mr. Maddox said with scant sympathy. "Who's at this farm?"

"I only been there two-three times," Mynie mumbled. "Mostly it was a guy named Kicks Liggett who used to ride the half-milers. He turned tough. It was him and this Frisco that said I'd find myself on a spot if I didn't play ball with them. They was both there tonight."

"How much farther is it?"

"Five-six miles."

"Stop a couple miles this side," Cassidy directed. "Maddox and I'll get back with the horse. When you drive in, act like you came back alone. Tell 'em you decided it was too risky to go through with. Tell 'em you've got your daughter to think about. Keep them talking outside the truck, so I can hear what they say. And God help you if you ball it up and give us away!"

"That ain't doing anything about Annabelle!"

"She'll turn up! A dead man'll scare the hell out of her, but he won't hurt her!" Cassidy snapped. "We'll get the body later. First we want the men who killed him."

CASSIDY must have sensed Mr. Maddox's thoughts. He added: "Don't get me wrong, Joe. You had the body. It's your baby until you can lay it on someone else. I've heard a lot, but I ain't seen anything to back it up."

"The older you get the harder your head gets!" Mr. Maddox snapped. "Have it your way—and I almost hate to have to wish you good luck!"

"I can guess," Cassidy agreed.

Mynie was the next one who spoke. "It ain't far. You can shove over that panel in back of you an' crawl through. Or use the door."

"The door," Cassidy said. "But open that panel first and leave it open. And don't get any ideas. There's murder mixed up in this and I ain't taking chances with you."

"I've got my kid to think about," Mynie reminded bitterly.

Mr. Maddox chuckled in the pitch-black interior of the van as the truck lurched on. "Cassidy, I'd have to have a light to tell you from the horse!"

"Never mind the cracks!"

The detective had posted himself inside the open panel where he could watch Mynie and the road ahead. A gun could reach Mynie easily. An agile man could get through into the front seat. It would not be so easy for Mr. Maddox.

The cavernous interior rumbled hollowly, creaked, groaned, lurched and swayed. The floor shook under their feet. The horse snorted, moved uneasily.

Motion and sound grew worse when Mynie turned off into a side road. It was another dirt road, rough and rutty.

They passed more pine woods and then the truck wheeled off the dirt road into a side lane, with woods on one side, brush on the other and a turn in the road hiding what lay ahead.

Cassidy husked through the open panel: "Sit in that seat and argue! And if you hear me give the word, get down and open that side door. Make an excuse so it looks natural. I don't give a damn what."

Mynie nodded without looking around.

Mr. Maddox was at Cassidy's shoulder. He saw the headlights thrusting around a curve in the rutty lane. Cleared ground was ahead.

Not much of it. Brush, weeds, long uncut grass had grown up around an unpainted, weathered, rotting, little frame house—an old barn.

The house windows were dark. The place might have been deserted. But no place where three automobiles were parked could be deserted. Two of them were shiny, expensive cars. The third was a small sedan.

Mynie saw the sedan and wrenched out: "Annabelle's here! That's our car!"

"Shut up!" Cassidy snarled through the open panel. "Swing the damn truck this side of them so they can't back out!" And in an aside to Mr. Maddox, Cassidy said gruffly: "Ain't this sweet? We draw a full deck!"

"And plenty of trouble!" Mr. Maddox guessed. "They're killers, you dope! And here we are cooped up like baboons in a cage! Suppose Mynie tips your hand? What chance have we?"

Cassidy was holding to the panel-edge as the truck lurched around in a sharp turn that brought it behind the parked automobiles, close to the house. Without turning his head, Cassidy spoke through his teeth. "He'd better not rat!"

But that was only Cassidy talking. Getting Mynie wouldn't help much if they were caught in here. And Cassidy suddenly ducked back from the open panel as a man leaped onto the running board without warning and directed a bright flashlight beam full into Mynie's pale face.

"What the hell are you doing back here?" an angry voice demanded.

THE TRUCK stopped with a jerk. The motor died. Mr. Maddox had crowded back into the front corner opposite Cassidy. Each was holding a revolver. Cassidy's stiff-legged tenseness showed that Cassidy realized this was more than detective work now. This had all the elements of a trap.

Mynie's voice sounded little better than a croak. "You scared hell outa me, Liggett! I wasn't looking for no other cars here!"

"T'hell with them! What's the idea of coming back here?"

"I—I thought I'd better come back an' talk it over. I told you I didn't want to go through with this, Liggett! I brought the horse back."

"Dick! Duke! Come here! This guy has turned yellow on us!"

They must have been waiting just inside the house door. They were beside the truck a moment later, invisible from the inside, but audible.

"What do you mean, yellow?"

"He brought the horse back! Says he's running out on us!"

"Damn him! Sampson, what's the idea?"

"I'm thinking about my girl!" Mynie said miserably.

"We've been all over that! Let her marry the guy! This won't hurt him!"

"If he ever found it out...."

"He won't. I could slug you for blowing up at the last moment this way!"

"Wait a minute, Dick." That was the smooth unflurried voice of Colonel Roscoe Daggett, as rich and convincing as ever. "I wonder if something hasn't changed Mynie's mind for him. How about it, Mynie?"

Mynie's voice shook. "I told you before how I felt about it."

"I know, and in a way I sympathized with you," the rich voice said. "But everything's lined out for a killing, Mynie. You saw it that way. You switched the horses tonight. Got clear to the track with this horse, didn't you?"

"Uh—well, yes."

"You didn't see anything there? You didn't talk to anyone? This man Maddox, who's in the same stable with you? He headed that way a little while ago."

"I ain't seen him," Mynie denied.

Mr. Maddox inwardly damned the lack of conviction in Mynie's voice. But Mynie still had a certain courage, and it burst out now.

"I saw my car as I drove up! What's Annabelle doing here? Where is she?"

Daggett's voice clipped back. "How do you know she drove that car? It was still at Baden Manor when you left in this truck!"

"No one else ever uses it! Where is she?"

Frisco Dick's sharp-edged voice said: "I'll handle him! He might as well get the works now!"

Colonel Daggett differed. "I want to know what made him change his mind at the last minute this way."

"That Maddox has got you jittery! Sampson has been working up to this for weeks!"

"Maddox," complained the colonel, "is all over the place. You had your chance to stop him—and look what happened. He turned the tables on you. He's wise to plenty now. He's dangerous!"

"Sure he is," Frisco Dick agreed with a rasp. "If I'd known how dangerous, I'd have had the boys fix him while they had him. But Sampson and this girl of his are making the hell now. Look, Sampson— we were coming after you anyway. Your daughter's here!"

"I got to talk to her! Where is she?"

"I'll talk first," Frisco said coldly. "Did you know she followed you here? Parked her car in the bushes and was watching when you switched horses. She heard the talk. She was plenty wise when you drove off. And if Daggett hadn't driven in from Baden Manor and got a flash off the metal on her car with his headlights, she'd have lammed away and pitched a monkey wrench in everything. She told us so!"

"Sure she would!" Mynie threw back with a quick flash of spirit. "She ain't a crook! She wouldn't stand for your dirty tricks!"

"By God, you sound like the little tramp yourself! Here's where you get smart or else! She was hauling a dead man in her car! Get it! A dead man! She fainted when we showed him to her! Are you both going to get smart and play ball—or do we turn that tramp over to the cops on a murder charge? Come on, take your choice!"

MYNIE should have wilted. He was little and crooked and he'd been given the works where it would hurt most. His girl's future. Mr. Maddox, perhaps, could have warned them. Joe Maddox had had some chance to look into the small shriveled soul of Mynie Sampson, where Mynie's girl was concerned. But Maddox was in the dark cavernous van and Mynie was alone on the front seat—and there were three men, and perhaps more, outside the truck. And Mynie should have kept his head for a little while longer.

But that might have been the bright and shining side of Mynie's soul, that fierce devotion to the girl he'd raised. The howl of sheer rage that came now from Mynie was blood-curdling.

"Call *my* girl a tramp and frame her for murder! *You* killed that guy! I know! Where is she? I'll get her home safe if I walk to the hot seat with you! Where is she?" Mynie sobbed the last as he hurled the door open.

Colonel Daggett shouted: "He must have seen Maddox! He knows!"

Another voice bawled: "Look out for that wrench he's got!"

The truck cab was dark now. The flashlight snapped off and on outside. Feet scuffled. Oaths spat. Mynie's incoherent rage keened on the night.

Cassidy was swearing under his breath as he beat Mr. Maddox to the panel opening and started to fight through into the cab. The two gunshots that hammered fast outside the truck made the racehorse snort and plunge in fright. Colonel Daggett's voice rose stridently.

"You fool, Dick! You killed him!"

"Yeah—I meant to—the little rat! He's no good to us anyway now. Nobody heard the shot!"

"What will we do now?"

"Fix the girl and clear out! There's time to move the truck and get rid of them before daylight!"

Cassidy got through the opening. Mr. Maddox dived after him.

"What's that in the truck?"

The flashlight found Cassidy looming in the cab doorway that Mynie had left open. "You're pinched!" Cassidy bawled.

A gunshot answered Cassidy. The light disappeared. Colonel Daggett yelled: "There's another one coming out! The truck's full of men! Get out—"

Gunfire cut off the rest....

Mr. Maddox never did know how he got his bulk through the small opening. Guns were blasting as he slid over the seat, barked shins and shoulder in his dive out the door. He half stumbled to his knees as he hit the ground.

Mynie's revolver was in his hand. He came up shouting: "Where are you, Cassidy?"

"Stop that car!" Cassidy yelled.

The gunfire had stopped. An automobile starter was grinding. The motor raced alive as Cassidy spoke. Headlights glared against the house. The car leaped back toward Mr. Maddox.

Reflected light showed Cassidy snapping a twister on the kneeling figure of Frisco Dick. Near them a second man writhed weakly on the ground.

Rear wheels spun hard, throwing dirt and debris over Mr. Maddox. The car lurched ahead in a sharp hard getaway turn. Not a chance to catch it on foot. Maddox fired three shots at the gas tank—and as the car lurched and skidded on around, the muzzle-flash of a gun spat back at him. Then the automobile circled the other side of the truck and headed into the rutted lane.

Mr. Maddox swung toward Cassidy, panting: "Who was it? Daggett?"

"Yes! And another one, I think! Hold this fellow! He put a bullet through my leg! I oughta—"

Cassidy broke off as the horn of the fleeing automobile blew wildly. A tremendous crash followed. Then silence.

"Holy cow!" Mr. Maddox exploded and plunged toward the spot.

He saw a flicker of fire, then a sheet of flame. Where the lane swung around into the trees a spreading pool of erupting gasoline showed the big automobile tangled with a small dilapidated coupe.

Gasoline evidently pouring from the bullet-punctured tank had ignited and was burning fiercely.

COLONEL ROSCOE DAGGETT staggered dazedly out of the blazing car as Mr. Maddox approached. He saw Mr. Maddox in the fire glare and tried to run down the lane. But he limped badly.

Mr. Maddox saw a second figure huddled on the car seat as he ran past. He caught up with the colonel fifty feet beyond the wreck, got a handful of coat collar and jerked the hobbling figure back against the revolver muzzle.

"Do I give it to you?" Mr. Maddox panted.

"My knee's broken, I think! That fool boy ran right into us!"

"Boy?" Mr. Maddox got breath into his laboring lungs and called: "Stiffy!"

Out in the bushes a thin uncertain voice answered: "That you, Boss?"

"Come here, Stiffy!"

Brush crackled. Stiffy came into sight cautiously, and started talking fast when he saw that the prisoner was safe.

"I followed that truck when it come from the Podder place, an' I was hangin' around for a chance to get that Sampson girl away when the truck come back. I heard what was said, an' when the shootin' started I figured maybe they'd take her away, so I legged it like hell back to my car an' tried to block the road!"

"Tried?" said Mr. Maddox prayerfully. "You almost demolished it!"

"I didn't mean to burn no car up!" Stiffy quavered. "Now I'll hafta pay the dinge for it! An' I'll bet that other guy in the car is gonna burn up!"

"Stiffy, you fool!" Mr. Maddox husked fondly. "Help get that other man out before he burns up! We'll settle all this later!"

It was some minutes later before Mr. Maddox got back to the horse van with Colonel Daggett and the young man named Monty, who had been trying to get out of the blazing car when they reached it.

Stiffy had run on ahead with an automatic that Mr. Maddox had taken off the second prisoner.

The truck lights were on. Stiffy and the automatic were valiantly guarding the handcuffed Frisco Dick. The man who had been writhing on the ground lay the slack inert fashion of the dead.

Mynie Sampson was there too beside his horse van. The wrench lay on the ground where Mynie had dropped it. And Mynie Sampson, little bow-legged and crooked, would never again drive the horse truck, never hold the wrench.

Mynie's girl, kneeling beside the quiet form, was weeping bitterly while Cassidy sat on the truck running board and tied a handkerchief around his leg through a slit he'd cut in the trousers cloth.

Cassidy stood up, favoring his wounded leg. "They had her locked up," he said heavily. "She got out. There's no phone here. Better drive to the Podder place, Joe, and call the state police. Take the girl, too. And hold that Trumbull woman."

Cassidy nodded toward Frisco Dick.

"I took a chance and told him the Trumbull dame had ratted on them. So he ratted back a little. She was a come-on for the old con mob before she hooked the senator into a marriage years ago. When the senator died, he was almost broke. The lady gets a pension from the government, but it wasn't enough. She made a play for Podder and got nowhere on marriage, so what did she do but call her old con pals in to take him?

"It was her Georgetown house all right that they used tonight. They caught the fellow that you hired tailing them, grabbed him and made him talk. And when he tried to bust out, some guy called Monty slugged him too hard on the back of the neck and ruined him. So they fixed to frame you with it. Better call a doctor too, Joe. This leg of mine's going to get bad. And take Sampson's daughter. She won't be any help here."

Mynie's girl got slowly to her feet, fighting for control.

"No!" she refused huskily. "Not there. I never want to go back there. I don't want to hear what they'll say about my father. I don't ever want to see them again. He wasn't all he should have been—but I l-loved him."

Cassidy spat. He was gruff. "That don't make sense to me, young lady. Mynie shot square with his boss and got this helping us catch these crooks. You ought to be proud to hear what people will say."

Mynie's girl stood slim and shaking for a moment. "I don't know what you're s-saying," she stammered. "He was *h-helping* you?"

"What do you think?" said Cassidy gruffly. "Would I lie to you? He came here with us, didn't he? He's been stringing these crooks along to catch 'em cold. And tonight we sprung it. Ask Maddox. Would I lie about it, Joe?"

From somewhere a lump had stolen into Joe Maddox's hard-boiled throat. He blinked once or twice as he looked at Mynie Sampson and Mynie's girl, and at Cassidy glaring at him.

"So help me, Cassidy," Mr. Maddox perjured himself huskily, "in twenty years of knowing you, I've never heard of you lying. You're ace-high. Annabelle, we're all proud of Mynie. Come with me. They're worried about you at Baden Manor."

Maybe Mynie knew what Cassidy had done. The light was bad, but Mr. Maddox found it easy to believe that Mynie Sampson's last expression was a faint smile of contentment as Mynie's girl turned toward the car that would take her back to Baden Manor for good.

BLOOD ON THE BLUE-GRASS

THE BLAND BUDDHA OF
THE BANGTAIL CIRCUIT
KNEW THERE WAS
SOMETHING ROTTEN IN
THE MINT-JULEP BELT
WHEN A HORSE THAT
COULDN'T HELP BUT WIN
WAS DOPED TO CROSS THE
LINE EVEN FASTER THAN
HE WOULD NORMALLY. THE
HANKY-PANKY MAY HAVE
HAD ITS WIND-UP IN OLD
KENTUCK' BUT IT DAMN
WELL WASN'T BRED THERE
AS MADDOX SOON FOUND
WHEN HE FLEW FROM
TIMES SQUARE TO LATONIA
TO BE IN AT THE FINISH.

CHAPTER ONE

CRAZY LIKE A WEASEL

TIMES SQUARE was a long way from the old and famous Latonia racetrack, down there in the mint-julep belt where the broad blue Ohio looped between Cincinnati and Covington. Better than five hundred miles away, to be exact. And yet this hot summer evening Mr. Maddox received a telegram which brought Latonia squarely into his New York hotel.

There was nothing unusual about the wire. Such messages were always coming to the hotel. No matter where Joe Maddox happened to be in the United States, you could always reach him through the Vardon, just off Times Square.

No matter where the horses were running, or where Mr. Maddox and Oscar were making a book, letters and wires to the Vardon were promptly forwarded to him.

But this hot night Mr. Maddox was at the Vardon in person, looking more than ever like an eye-filling symbol of prosperity and bland, cheerful assurance. Tonight Mr. Maddox's linen suit showed the touch of an expensive tailor and the huge diamond ring on his big hand had never glinted more richly as he scooped the yellow envelope off the hotel desk.

Oscar was there too. Oscar, that wizened, sardonic little man who did most of the paper work, who stayed in the hotels and answered the telephones, quoted odds, put down the bets, and did most of the worrying. Tonight Oscar was hot and grumbling as they headed out of the lobby.

"Don't read it," Oscar said, wiping perspiration from his face. "It's too damn hot to think before we get outside a couple of cold ones at Jimmy's."

Mr. Maddox chuckled as they plunged into the noisy hustle and

heat of 44th Street and turned west toward Times Square, grinned as he scanned the telegram…. "Here's where we should be. This is from Covington."

Oscar's thin face registered quick distaste. "Latonia, huh? Throw

it away before you get a yen to jump there and fry in heat worse than this."

Mr. Maddox frowned slightly as he finished the wire and shoved it into his coat pocket. "It's from Pete Cheney."

"Who?"

"Pete Cheney, the jockey."

"That fresh young hot-head who got set down four months last winter for slugging on the stretch turn at Santa Anita?"

"That was Pete." Mr. Maddox nodded. "And it was a good thing for him. Pete had to learn to keep his temper no matter how much dirt the other boys tried in a race. Pete's a natural jockey. I started watching him long before he lost his bug. Pete Cheney will be one of the great riders before he hangs up his tack."

"Maybe," said Oscar sourly, wiping his face again while they waited for a traffic cop's shrilling whistle. They started across the light-blazing madness that was Times Square at the theater hour and Oscar said: "Jockies don't worry me tonight. Gin and lime and frost all over the glass is all I want."

They turned up Broadway. Mr. Maddox walked to the next corner in frowning thought before he said: "Pete wired a thousand-dollar bet on Wink Thrice, in the Hilltop Stakes, tomorrow. On the nose. He says to keep mum."

Oscar leaped nimbly back from a rushing taxi, swore at the vanishing driver, and turned his spleen on Pete Cheney's telegram.

"Jockey dough, huh? Sounds like somebody's cooked up a deal. So that's what a four months' set-down did to your phony Sande?"

"Pete's riding Wink Thrice and likes the horse well enough to put a grand on him." And from the depths of his vast knowledge of racetrack lore, Mr. Maddox said: "Wink Thrice is the two-year-old that's promising to be the Derby horse next year."

"You ought to know. He cost you money at Bowie," Oscar reminded. "And if there ain't a deal, I still don't like the horse. His owner's a politician. I been reading about him. When there's votes behind a horse, anything happens."

"Not to this horse," Mr. Maddox denied flatly. "I've never met Judge Brandon, the owner. He races under the name of Coolgrene Farm. Seems to me he's running for governor this year. Senator Conway in Washington knows him and spoke highly of him when Wink Thrice won at Bowie this spring."

"So what?" said Oscar, mopping his face again as they neared Jimmy's place. "Your jockey's all right and your horse is all right an' his owner may be president next year. But you ain't making a book this week so the money don't do you any good. Wire the guy it's no soap."

"I'll lay off the money for Pete," Mr. Maddox said calmly. "He wants better than track odds, if possible. The track price tomorrow figures to be short. Someone around Jimmy's might like to take a chance on laying a good price."

"Probably," Oscar agreed sourly. "Some of those bandits would take a chance on their grandmother's throat being cut." And as they turned into Jimmy's Oscar settled the matter to his own satisfaction. "You lay the grand and I'll take the gin."

JIMMY'S place, unless you were a regular, lacked the high-pressure color for which tourists searched Broadway. There was no floorshow, no dancing, no uniformed doorman. You found comfortable booths at Jimmy's, sizable tables, walls paneled halfway up in dark wood. More men were in evidence than women.

If you knew Jimmy's like Joe Maddox, you spotted men whose names were known at the racetracks, the gymnasiums and sporting centers across the wide country. Sports writers, promoters, gamblers, boxers, wrestlers, theatrical people. Like met like there—and if a sprinkling of the underworld was often present, it was because no one cared to draw hard and fast lines at Jimmy's.

Tonight the booths were mostly full, although the rush would come later. Mr. Maddox greeted half a dozen friends, let Oscar go on back to a table and the cold drink, and took up the matter of placing Pete Cheney's thousand dollars.

It would have been easy at track odds. Three well known handbook men were in Jimmy's at the moment. More would be in later. And a dozen men, including Mr. Maddox could have reached numerous other bookies with a telephone call.

Pete Cheney's thousand would have been snapped up quickly at track odds. But all three bookies in Jimmy's at the moment were cagey about fixing a price so long before the race. Benny Roos, lean, sharp and shrewd, who had made a book for fifteen years around New York, put it in a nutshell.

"Eight-to-five, Joe, and that's giving you my dough at that. Even the two-dollar trade is wise that Wink Thrice'll take that race tomorrow. They'll murder the price in the mutuels."

"When I can't think of larceny, I call it Benny Roos," Mr. Maddox told Benny and the three other occupants of the booth. "I wouldn't take eight-to-five for a friend's money if I had the certified pay-off check in my other hand."

"O.K." Benny shrugged. "I ain't in business for your health. Have a drink—and pick up the check."

"I'd find your check under it," Mr. Maddox retorted cordially as he turned away to the telephone.

Half a dozen calls over the city gave no better luck. Mr. Maddox was disgusted when he joined Oscar at a back table. "Pete might do better with track odds. They're all afraid of Wink Thrice."

"Benny Roos ducked out after you talked to him, like he had a headache," Oscar commented. "Here's your drink coming. I told him to hold it. Forget that jockey. Ain't this heat enough worry?"

Mr. Maddox sipped the frosty drink, sighed with relief, relaxed in the chair. Five minutes later he was still relaxed and the glass was almost empty when Benny Roos came to the table, smiling and affable.

"Who buys me a drink?" Benny chuckled, wrinkling his sharp nose with humor as he pulled out a chair and sat down.

"You guess," Mr. Maddox invited. "Watch him, Oscar. He's larceny on wheels. Benny, the sight of you is a pain."

Benny Roos grinned. "You'll like it when I'm through. I've been thinking about that grand, Joe. I'll take a chance. What'll you let it go for?"

"Four-to-one."

"My God! On Wink Thrice?"

"He wanted six-to-one," Oscar helped accusingly.

Good humor left Benny's face, went out of Benny's life. Benny groaned. "Joe, you talk about larceny! If I covered money like that, how long would I last?"

"Too long for us," Oscar stated.

Benny put his hands on the tablecloth. "I'm talking business now. I'm sitting there and I get a hunch that tonight's my night to go wacky. So I step back here to take a chance, Joe. And right away you skunk me."

Mr. Maddox yawned. "Four-to-one, Benny. That's what I'm after—and that's what I'll get."

"Would you lay three-to-one?" Oscar questioned narrowly.

Mr. Maddox drained his glass and set it down with a thump. "Not a dime less than four-to-one. Beat it, Benny. You're wasting our time."

"Maybe I am," said Benny, getting up. "I thought you'd be reasonable, Joe, an' I like a hunch now and then. But four-to-one on Wink Thrice? It kills me to listen."

"We'll leave the body in the gutter," Mr. Maddox promised as Benny started to leave.

And then Mr. Maddox's eyes narrowed ever so slightly as Benny Roos hesitated and turned back, looking anguished but suddenly determined. "All right, Joe. When I get a hunch, I get a hunch. I'm a fool and I know it. When I wake up in the morning I'll hate to think about it. But right now I'll lay you four-to-one on Wink Thrice, in the Hilltop Stakes."

"Sold." Mr. Maddox yawned. "You're smarter than I figured, Benny."

"I hate myself already," Benny groaned as he left them. "This'll be my lesson about hunches."

OSCAR waited until the sharp, shrewd little bookie was out of earshot before he chortled. "Can you beat it? If anyone told me Benny Roos'd make a sap play like that, I'd laugh. Some hunch! A couple more like it and he'll be peddling pencils! Four-to-one! Phew!"

From narrowed eyes Mr. Maddox watched Benny Roos return to the booth and waiting friends. And even the length of Jimmy's restaurant was not enough to hide the fact that Benny Roos had lost his anguish. Benny looked very well satisfied with himself.

Mr. Maddox galvanized into alertness. "Hunch hell! Benny never had a hunch in his life unless he had the cash in his hand! Finish your drink. We've got things to do."

"Nix! It's too hot. Ain't we doing all right now? I don't want to move."

Mr. Maddox beckoned for the check and stood up. "Come on. I'm in a hurry."

Oscar drained his glass and regarded it sadly as he stood up. "I never seen it to fail. You settle everything like you want—and then it ain't like you want it. Don't tell me that dough you laid with Benny Roos ain't behind this."

Mr. Maddox made no reply until they were outside, and then a grim under-current of suspicion hardened his words. "Benny is smooth. He thinks he is anyway. He left Jimmy's to find out something. I was giving him the hook when I asked four-to-one—and I didn't have any idea he'd take it."

"I told you he was crazy."

"Crazy like a weasel. Benny knows something. He's so sure of it he couldn't wait to get his hands on the thousand. The nerve of him putting on that act."

"It looked good to me," said Oscar stubbornly. "I'd moan too if I was laying four-to-one on Wink Thrice. What could Benny know? You think something's sour about the horse?"

"I don't know," Mr. Maddox admitted. "But when Benny Roos is so sure a horse like Wink Thrice can be covered at four-to-one—something's sour. The horse was all right less than an hour ago, when Pete sent that wire."

"Maybe there's a sneezer going in the same race that the Coolgrene Stable don't know about," Oscar suggested. "You know how these owners an' trainers get all steamed up over their own nags."

"Four-to-one," repeated Mr. Maddox grimly. "And after Benny slipped out to make a call. Benny would have given six-to-one if I'd held out. That little weasel knows something."

"So what?" said Oscar in exasperation. "He's got the money. It's out of our hands. And here you go down Broadway like you was Wink Thrice making the race. Walk slower. I'm burning up."

Mr. Maddox did not shorten his lumbering stride. "There's only one answer. Benny got a tip that Wink Thrice won't win tomorrow. And when it's that positive about a horse like Wink Thrice, there's something crooked behind it."

"So what?" said Oscar again. "The Coolgrene Stable don't think so. It ain't our money."

"I like Pete Cheney. He's got a great career ahead if he watches his step. And I don't like crooked races. We're going to Latonia and look into this."

"Now you're crazy!" Oscar blurted. "There ain't time to drive it or make it on the train."

"We'll take a plane tonight."

"Not me!"

"You too," Mr. Maddox said flatly. "I might need you."

CHAPTER TWO

BROADWAY TO BLUE-GRASS

DAWN WAS still gray in the east when they emerged from the plane at Dayton, Ohio. Oscar was red-eyed from lack of sleep. He shivered in the dawn chill. "Now we got to catch a train. My God, it's cold. Joe, I wouldn't do this for my own mother!"

Mr. Maddox chuckled. "Save the shakes for this afternoon. You'll need 'em if it gets as hot as the paper promises. We're making it with plenty of time to spare."

"I got all the time in the world to spare. It's your idea, Joe. You worry with it. I want a gallon of black coffee, hot an' strong. God, it's cold!"

But when they were finally registered at a Cincinnati hotel, before eight o'clock, Oscar had recovered enough to eat breakfast. Mr. Maddox ate heartily and with relish.

"You circulate around and grab the dope on Wink Thrice," Mr. Maddox decided as they got up. "I'll call the track and find out if Judge Brandon is in town."

"Going to tell him?" Oscar asked, staring.

"I'd like to talk to him. It's his horse."

Judge Brandon was in town, at a hotel not two blocks away. The judge was in the hotel when Mr. Maddox telephoned. When he heard Senator Conway's name mentioned, he would be very glad to see Mr. Maddox.

That part of it was easy. The judge was smiling when he admitted Mr. Maddox to the suite.

Here, Mr. Maddox decided instantly, you had a politician. A good man, by his looks, rather short and heavy-set. Not bad looking with white scattered through his black hair. But a politician, hearty, deep-voiced, with an enthusiastic handclasp and a welcome to friend and stranger.

"Any friend of Dan Conway's is a friend of mine, Mr. Maddox. Make yourself comfortable. What can I do for you?"

And without doubt, too, the judge had his own favorable impression of this prosperous-looking visitor who might himself have been a senator or a governor. You could see the judge wondering just who this Mr. Maddox might be—and not quite certain that he shouldn't know.

Smiling broadly, Mr. Maddox sat down. "I flew from New York last night to see your horse win today."

"That's quite a trip to see one horse win," said the judge, smiling. "But you'll not be disappointed. If Wink Thrice doesn't win the Derby next year, we'll all be disappointed."

"So I understand," said Mr. Maddox blandly. "And when I heard a rumor in New York last night that Wink Thrice wasn't going to win today, I wondered."

"What's that?"

"A rumor—from sources that are usually right."

Judge Brandon had stopped smiling. A flush of irritation reddened his face. "I don't understand you, Mr. Maddox. There is no reason for such talk. Are you suggesting that the race won't be run honestly?"

"It had that sound," Mr. Maddox admitted. "I wondered if you'd heard anything."

"Certainly not! As a matter of fact, it's no secret that I'm backing the horse heavily! Who is spreading such rumors? How did you happen to hear them? It's nonsense, of course!"

"I doubt it," Mr. Maddox differed. "I know the racing game as an owner and from making a book for a number of years."

Judge Brandon jumped as if he'd been struck. "A bookmaker?"

Mr. Maddox nodded, smiling slightly. "Senator Conway will vouch for me."

"Good heavens! I had no idea! I'm sorry I can't discuss this any further with you!" The judge was already on his feet, bruskly terminating the interview.

Mr. Maddox's broad face hardened.

"You don't like bookmakers, eh?"

"I don't care to discuss it. In my position...."

"I don't give a damn about your position," said Mr. Maddox with equal bruskness. "I'm only interested in your horse."

"My integrity in such matters has never been questioned!" Judge Brandon said excitedly.

"I didn't question your integrity."

"We'll not talk about it any further, sir. Good-day!"

Judge Brandon was already at the door, opening it. And now Mr. Maddox was also red-faced and angry. A hot reply sprang to his lips, but he bit it back and nodded coldly to the judge as he went out.

WHEN the door slammed behind him Mr. Maddox swore under his breath all the way to the elevator—and jabbed the push button so hard the end of his finger hurt.

"The nerve of him!" Mr. Maddox said wrathfully to the speeding cables in the elevator shaft. "Too damned hard-headed to talk with a bookmaker! If it wasn't for Pete, I'd—"

The opening elevator door cut that off. The elevator boy looked with surprised interest at the red-faced scowling man who had ridden up blandly smiling only a few minutes before. Then he reopened the door as a hurried voice in the corridor called: "Down! Down!"

The girl was breathless from haste, still struggling into a summer jacket as she rushed into the elevator. The scowl left Mr. Maddox's face. He relaxed with smiling interest. She was so hurried and distressed that she was buttoning her jacket wrong. She discovered it with an impatient exclamation and a fierce little frown as the elevator dropped down.

She was a leggy little thing with a tip-tilt nose, freckles and no make-up or hat. Evidently she'd run a comb hurriedly through her blonde hair, snatched the jacket and dashed for the elevator. And even a cynical and hardened old veteran of the racing and gambling world like Joe Maddox could wonder what lay behind such youthful haste, such frowning anxiety. Late for her appointment at the beauty shop, perhaps.

The elevator let them both out in the busy lobby and the girl turned to Mr. Maddox and said abruptly: "I'm Gayle Brandon. I—I overheard your talk with my father and I ran to catch you before you got away."

"God bless my soul!" said Mr. Maddox, sweeping off his hat. She had surprised him almost to speechlessness.

Then as he looked down at her, Mr. Maddox recovered his aplomb, and his impressive bulk shook with quick humor. "Young ladies don't usually dash after me. Will your father like this?"

Gayle Brandon smiled a little too. "He wouldn't. I got out of the suite before he knew what was happening. Let's leave the hotel before he has a brain wave and comes snooping."

Somewhat to his surprise, Mr. Maddox found himself taken in

charge and hurried out of the lobby while Gayle Brandon talked a mile a minute. "Pete's told me all about you. I know about the thousand dollars that he wired you last night."

"*Mmmmm,*" said Mr. Maddox shrewdly. "So you know Pete's business, eh?"

"All of it," Gayle Brandon nodded briskly. "Pete's mine and I know everything he does. Anyway, I think I do. I—I hope I do."

"I'll bet you do," Mr. Maddox chuckled as they reached the sidewalk. "Pete's a fine boy. Nothing tricky about him. And if Pete is yours, young lady, that's fine. Pete knows what he's about."

"Pete doesn't know what you told Father. He's sure Wink Thrice will win. We're planning everything on it. Wink Thrice has *got* to win."

"As bad as that?"

Gayle Brandon nodded. "Pete's almost broke," she said candidly. "He'd never saved much money before I met him. The four months he wasn't working used up the little cash he had. It was even necessary to go in debt some. That thousand Pete wired you last night was all he'd managed to save after he started riding again. He had to borrow two hundred of it. Don't you see, he's *got* to win."

"It can't be that bad," Mr. Maddox said kindly. "Pete can go broke again and save up another stake."

Gayle's gesture had all the tragic impatience of youth. "You don't understand. Father's suspicious. He's practically forbidden me to go around with Pete. And—and Pete won't marry me until he can take care of me decently. And I haven't got any money to help him. Father's got it all."

SHE was so tragic about it that Mr. Maddox had to suppress another chuckle. "Pete has the right idea. I'll bet he wouldn't take your money if you had it. You wouldn't want a man who didn't want to take care of you properly."

"I'd want Pete any way." Then her tip-tilt nose turned up to Mr. Maddox above a rueful little smile. "No, I wouldn't. I'm glad Pete's like he is. And that is all the more reason why I want him quickly. What you said to my father scared me. Pete and I have to know more about it."

"I can see you do," Mr. Maddox agreed. "But I'm afraid, young lady, that I said about all I know. I hoped your father might be able to add something. But you heard him."

"He's not really so stuffy," Gayle said quickly. "It's this political campaign. Father's worried. The opposition is attacking him because he owns several race horses and likes racing. They're saying that he races his horses secretly under the name of Coolgrene Farm and his sympathies are with the millionaires who own big racing stables. They've even hinted that he has secret deals with gamblers and I don't know what. Lies, innuendoes," Gayle said scornfully, "that people who know Father well wouldn't listen to for a minute!"

"But plenty of voters will," Mr. Maddox guessed. "I know. Speak of horseracing to some people and they see sin and damnation."

Gayle nodded. "That's it. You see why Father's worried. And why he wouldn't talk any more when he heard you were a bookmaker? He didn't say so—but I know he thought it might be a trick. You might have been sent by the opposition to trap him into some statement or something that could be used against him."

"Hmmmm," said Mr. Maddox.

"And besides," Gayle went on hurriedly, "Father's so sure Wink Thrice will win today that he'd consider anything else preposterous."

"Your father is forgiven," Mr. Maddox said blandly.

Gayle looked at him with indecision. "But—but suppose you *are* right? What can we *do?*"

"We'll have to tell Pete Cheney and see what he thinks," was the best Mr. Maddox could offer.

"Of course we must. Pete was going to stay at the track this morning and do roadwork. *You* come out and tell him," Gayle begged. "I'll pay the taxi fare."

"We'll go in my taxi," Mr. Maddox corrected. "And if Pete can pick horses like he can a girl, Wink Thrice will win that race this afternoon."

"You *are* nice," Gayle said, smiling back.

TO REACH the Latonia track you crossed a soaring bridge over the placid Ohio into Kentucky. And the smaller city of Covington beyond the bridge merged into Latonia, on the southern edge of which was the track.

It was not a great new plant with massive concrete grandstands and lavish landscaping. Railroad sidings lay behind the grandstand and tree-fringed bluffs were beyond. Houses faced two sides of the grounds. The grandstand and the horse barns were comfortably weathered and modest. Latonia was old and placid and satisfied. You had the feeling that tradition, breeding, and the sportsmanship of the Kentucky blue-grass belt was comfortable and at home here.

Mr. Maddox and Gayle Brandon were lucky in catching Pete Cheney just in from his roadwork, still swathed in rubber suit, heavy trousers, woolen sweater. Pete was panting. Great drops of perspiration beaded the ludicrous surprise on his thin face as he met them.

"I wired you in New York last night, Mr. Maddox! I didn't know you were here."

"I wasn't, Pete. I caught a plane last night. Your money is down at four-to-one."

"That's fine…. *Four-to-one?*" Pete whistled, then grinned with delight. "You must be a wizard." His sweatered arm caught Gayle's waist and swung her in a laughing jig for a moment. "We're in the clear, honey! They can't stop us now!"

"Pete, those swipes are looking! Listen to Mr. Maddox. He's been to see Father—and Father wouldn't listen to him. I'm worried."

"Worried?" said Pete, smiling uncertainly. "I don't get it. What's wrong, Mr. Maddox?"

"Maybe nothing," said Mr. Maddox. "Eight-to-five was the best price I could get, Pete. And then one smoothie made a telephone call after swearing eight-to-five was the best he'd give me—and before I could get away, he was back giving me four-to-one. Anything to get his hands on the money. How does that smell?"

Pete Cheney was young, as young as Judge Brandon's daughter, which at the most wasn't over twenty-one. But you grew up fast, you learned fast on the horse tracks. By the time you'd lost your bug and were a full-fledged jockey, you were tough and shrewd, with few illusions. At least about horse tracks and touts and gamblers and the shady fringes of the underworld.

Now Pete's thin perspiring face set in lines of quick worry. "I don't get it. Wink Thrice is all right. I looked at him not two hours ago. He'll be in there to go today and he's never been better."

"I got four-to-one in New York." Mr. Maddox shrugged. "That's all I know, Pete. It smelled bad to me, so I caught a plane to see what was up. But you're riding. It was your money that was covered. You ought to know."

"Yeah, I ought to. I thought I did." Pete moistened his lips. "I don't know what to say. There's nothing else starting in the race that makes it safe for smart money to give us four-to-one. I didn't expect it. It's got me worried. I don't know what to do."

"I don't either now," Mr. Maddox confessed. "You'd better make sure the horse hasn't been sponged—and watch for tricks every minute after the saddling bell rings."

"Yeah," said Pete again. The worry was still on his face as he stared at Mr. Maddox.

Gayle spoke with possessive authority. "Pete, don't stand around in those wet clothes. You'll catch something. We'll go look at Wink Thrice while you're changing. And we'd better not talk about this."

You could see by the way he nodded that Pete trusted his girl's judgment. She was level-headed, alert, intelligent. They'd make a great team after they were married. Pete would go on to be the fine rider that he promised. And if Judge Brandon had half an eye he'd be boosting the two kids instead of trying to keep them apart.

WINK THRICE was a chestnut, with lively intelligent eyes and fine clean power in every line of his big frame. He had developed nicely as a two-year-old. There was every promise of growing into a great horse next year if he didn't break down under the grueling strain of two-year sprints.

Mr. Maddox ran a hand lightly over the chestnut muzzle thrust out inquiringly over the stall door. He spoke under his breath and realized what he was doing and smiled sheepishly at the girl by his side.

"I still go soft around a good horse."

"I know," said Gayle. "A horse like Wink Thrice makes me want to—to choke up inside. It doesn't seem possible that any living thing could be so beautiful and fast and game. Wink Thrice would run his heart out if Pete asked him to."

"And so would you," said Mr. Maddox. "You're a woman and maybe you can't see it. But some women are the same. Lovely and bred fine, with too much heart for the races they're called on to run. You'd never let Pete down, would you?"

Gayle shook her head. Tears were in her eyes. She snatched a handkerchief and wiped them away. "Look at me. I'm just a softy after all. I never thought I'd like being compared to a horse."

"While we're waiting for Pete," mused Mr. Maddox, "I'll walk around and see if I know anyone. I might hear something."

Gayle nodded understandingly and Mr. Maddox left her there. When you had followed the horse circuits for thirty years, you knew most of the old-timers and many of the younger ones.

In half an hour's strolling among the horse barns, Mr. Maddox greeted numerous familiar faces and paused for brief words with many of them. Without exception he found nothing suspicious when he mentioned Wink Thrice. Around the barns it was conceded that Wink Thrice would take the Hilltop Stakes this afternoon.

All very puzzling. When he returned to the Coolgrene stalls, Mr. Maddox was wondering if he wasn't wrong after all. Benny Roos might have just had a hunch, as Benny had claimed. All this might be unnecessary worry for two fine kids like Gayle Brandon and Pete Cheney.

Pete had changed clothes and was a good-looking, slender young man now. And still worried. "Any luck?" he asked when Mr. Maddox found them.

"Nope. I don't know any more than I did. I might as well go back across the river and snatch forty winks. It's up to you now, Pete. Maybe I was mistaken. I hope I am. Anyway, you're warned now."

"I'll be watching," Pete said grimly. "Staying, Gayle?"

"Of course, now that I'm here. Thanks for the taxi ride, Mr. Maddox. Thanks for—everything."

"Good luck," Mr. Maddox said to them both, and he'd never meant it more.

Oscar was in the hotel. "No luck," he reported when Mr. Maddox entered their suite. "This is a screwy chase, Joe. That horse is due to win and you can't talk anybody out of it."

"We've done our best," Mr. Maddox said wearily. "We'll know when the sixth race is over. I'm grabbing some sleep until two o'clock."

CHAPTER THREE

DOPED TO WIN

THE WEATHER reports had been correct. The afternoon was boiling hot by the time Mr. Maddox and Oscar arrived at the track for the finish of the fourth race.

It was the same old scene—always fresh, always new enough to start pulses ticking faster. The crowded grandstand and clubhouse, flags flying, officials at their posts. The smooth track a graceful oval around the lush green infield. The crowd roaring, surging to see better as the horses swept around the stretch-turn and headed for the wire.

Mr. Maddox did not bother to look for Gayle Brandon. She'd be here somewhere, with her heart and her prayers on that smooth-curried track when Pete Cheney rode out in his polished boots and gay racing silks for the slow, stirring post parade.

Wink Thrice was not scratched. There were no jockey changes when the bugle blew for the sixth race and the horses filed from the paddock to the track.

Wink Thrice was Number 3. And Pete Cheney on a breath of a saddle, knees high, leather bat expertly in his hand, looked so cool and confident you'd never think he had a worry in the world. Unless you looked closely at the tight line of Pete's young jaw and the white-ness of his knuckles as he gathered the reins to quiet Wink Thrice, who was showing all the fire and spirit you'd expect from a winner. A fine jockey. A fine horse, that chestnut pride of Judge Brandon's Coolgrene Farm Stable. A little too finely trained perhaps, with the moisture coming out darkly on his coat and the way he tossed his head, worried the bit, rolled his eyes.

Mr. Maddox was standing at the fence near the judge's stand where he could plainly see the stretch and finish of the five-and-a-half furlong dash.

AS THE horses came back past the grandstand on their way around the turn to the starting gate, Pete Cheney lifted his bat in a slight greeting to someone in the grandstand.

No need to wonder whom Pete had greeted. Turning, Mr. Maddox found her in one of the boxes, where she'd evidently come after the saddling. She was in white, with her face small, lovely, glowing with pride under a big leghorn hat. Pete Cheney's girl, waiting for Pete to bring home his winner. Judge Brandon's heavy-set figure and others of the party formed an animated, expectant group. The judge was beaming.

Quickly Pete had been forced to give attention to the lunging, prancing horse. And after that one quick look around, Mr. Maddox, too, gave alert attention to Wink Thrice and the six other horses.

A puzzled frown came to his broad face as the bright racing silks moved around the turn. "I don't believe it," he muttered.

"Huh?" said Oscar at his elbow.

"Nothing."

"Got you talking to yourself, has it?"

"Oscar," said Mr. Maddox, "if I had a million dollars in my pocket and tried to borrow a thousand, what would you think?"

"I'd think you were dizzy," said Oscar. "Joe, this thing's got you wacky," he added tartly. "Your talk don't even make sense."

Mr. Maddox shrugged and leaned on the rail while the minutes dragged and the starters tried to line the horses in the stalls around there on the back of the track. There was delay.

"Wink Thrice broke through," the loudspeakers announced. And a few minutes later: "Wink Thrice is continuing to hold up the start."

Mr. Maddox shook his head and muttered again under his breath.

Oscar grumbled: "He'll leave his race at the gate!" Then Oscar gripped the fence hard as the starting bell rang, and the grandstand erupted in a wave of sound.

They could see the bunched horses breaking along the backstretch like leaves whirling before the first blast of a gale. Keen eyes glued to binoculars high up in top of the grandstand caught the details and relayed through the loudspeakers.

"Ken's Pride takes the lead. Lost Lady and Wink Thrice tied for second by half a length. Trumball four. O.K. fifth…. And now it's Ken's Pride by a nose—Wink Thrice coming fast—Lost Lady third— O.K. fourth…. And going into the turn it's Wink Thrice by a length, moving away fast…. Ken's Pride second…."

But now you didn't need the loudspeakers. The horses were in full view on the turn, stringing out behind the chestnut flash that was fast widening his lead.

Wink Thrice streaking like a brown leaf that had caught the full gale on his heels! Wink Thrice, backed lower than eight-to-five in the mutuels, running the race which all the dope had figured him to run. No—better than that. Running a faster race….

THE CROWD was on its feet, rooting in a frenzy of delight as Wink Thrice blazed into the stretch, two lengths in the lead and going away. Running like a horse possessed. Running head out with flaring nostrils and the dry track dirt plashing in little spurts from pistoning hoofs.

Mr. Maddox leaned over the fence and watched. Pete Cheney wasn't using the bat. There was no need for whipping. Pete Cheney wasn't urging the horse. Pete wasn't even using his weight far forward to help Wink Thrice run his smoothest and fastest. Wise eyes like those of Joe Maddox could spot Pete riding leadenly, stiffly, as a smart jockey could ride to take the heart and speed out of a horse.

It did not slow Wink Thrice. Like a staring chestnut fury, like a horse possessed of a blinding urge to run, Wink Thrice was still going away from the field as he flashed under the wire.

The grandstand was a bedlam of delighted excitement. Even Oscar was infected.

"That'll teach Benny Roos about hunches!" Oscar whooped. "I'd like to see that shyster's face when he hears about this! Who said it wouldn't be a win? What a running fool that baby turned out to be! He's got the Derby in his oat bucket!"

Mr. Maddox ignored Oscar and the noise behind them. Still leaning over the fence, Mr. Maddox was watching Pete Cheney well down around the turn, fighting to stop Wink Thrice and turn him back toward the judge's stand.

Wink Thrice still seemed to be possessed of that demon of speed as he tried to run on and on and on....

Mr. Maddox swore and smashed his clenched fist on the fence. "Why didn't I think of it? What a complete cluck I was!"

"Whassa matter?" Oscar demanded. "Are you wacky again? He won, didn't he?"

"He got under the wire first," Mr. Maddox conceded and turned to stare at the judges, who to a man were training binoculars on the turn where Wink Thrice was all over the track as he fought the bit and yanking reins.

"He wants to run it again, Joe! An' I'll bet he could!"

Mr. Maddox nodded and waited. The other horses cantered back. Wink Thrice came bolting up to meet the cheers of the crowd.

Pete hurled his bat away, yanked the rearing horse over to waiting hands that caught the bit. Pete looked pale, drawn, frightened as he dismounted and stripped off his tack.

"We'll see you up here, Cheney!" one of the judges called. "You there, hold that horse where you have him!"

And a moment later the loudspeakers requested: "Will Judge Brandon please come to the judge's stand?"

It had not been a photo finish—but the winning numbers were not promptly posted. The crowd quieted as it sensed something wrong. A tall man carrying a black bag hurried to the judge's stand from the direction of the paddock. After a word with the judges he went down on the track, handed the bag to one of the attendants and began a quick examination of Wink Thrice.

"Ain't that the track vet?" Oscar questioned uncertainly.

"It is."

"What's the idea, Joe? What's wrong?"

"Wait and see."

Judge Brandon had reached the judge's stand. His face was red and angry. You couldn't hear what they were saying, but you could catch glimpses of them all talking. The judges stern, Judge Brandon getting angrier. And Pete Cheney, slim and thin and small beside the larger men, standing there with the drawn pallor plain on his face. Pete nodded once or twice, spoke to them, shrugged helplessly.

The veterinary had taken forceps and cotton gauze and swabbed deeply into Wink Thrice's mouth. He put the soaked gauze into a glass bottle. He was sober, grim as he took a last look at Wink Thrice and carried his bag back into the judge's stand.

By now ominous murmurs were rising behind Oscar and Mr. Maddox, were coming in a discordant wave out of the grandstand as the crowd began to suspect the reasons behind the delay.

Oscar clutched Mr. Maddox's arm. "Joe, they're actin' like that horse was doped!"

"Look at him," Mr. Maddox growled. "Look at his eyes. Look at the way he's acting. Look at the way he held up the start and the way he ran. It exploded in just right at the gate, and he's still loaded to the ears. He must have been given a double dose."

Angry shouts and boos thundered from the grandstand as the results were posted. Number 5, Ken's Pride, was first. Number 1, O.K., was second. Number 7, Lost Lady, was third. Number 4, Johnny Come Quick, was fourth.

Wink Thrice had been disqualified.

"I thought of everything but that!" Mr. Maddox said savagely. "There was a horse good enough to win—and he was loaded with so much dope that there's evidence for a blind man to see. Benny Roos didn't have a hunch. Benny got a tip that there would be a disqualification no matter how Wink Thrice finished in the race. Benny knew he had a sure thing when he came after Pete's thousand!"

Oscar's wizened face was a study against the angry shouts of the crowd.

"So that's what you meant when you asked about having a million an' borrowing more dough. Wink Thrice had plenty to win an' he was doped anyway."

"Don't get smart on me now," Mr. Maddox said irritably. "We should have caught the rats who doped that horse. This may finish Pete Cheney as a rider. What a lousy thing to happen to those two kids."

Oscar caught Mr. Maddox's elbow. "Get that, Joe!"

The loudspeakers were calling. "Will Mr. Maddox come to the secretary's office? Mr. Joseph Maddox is wanted at the secretary's office immediately if he hears this!"

"They ain't spotted you, Joe! They ain't sure you're here at the track! Let's get back across the river! This ain't our business now. We don't want any of it!"

Mr. Maddox hesitated. He was in full sight here by the judge's stand but evidently hadn't been noticed. The case of Wink Thrice was now serious. It would have stern repercussions.

Oscar warned: "The Masterton Agency dicks will be asking questions. You'll be plastered in the newspapers, Joe. No telling how bad it'll be—and it ain't even our turkey. Let's get back to New York an' forget it!"

Pete Cheney was leaving the judge's stand for the jockey room. Pete looked bad. A crushing weight seemed to bow his shoulders inside the green-and-orange racing silks of the Coolgrene Farm. Pete must have been suspended again.

If they decided Pete had any knowledge, any part of the doping, Pete might be barred from all tracks for life. Those hard young years of learning his trade would be smashed. Pete would be just another young bum who hadn't been smart enough to keep out of trouble.

Judge Brandon, even more haggard now than Pete, came out next and met a barrage of boos and furious shouts. The judge held his head high with angry pride but his movements had a woodenness that suggested he was still stunned.

It was that grandstand box to which Mr. Maddox looked while he hesitated. That box where Gayle Brandon's young face had been glowing under the leghorn hat. Her hat was still there, bent over now so that her face was hidden—but even that could not hide the abject misery that had engulfed her. Mr. Maddox made his decision. "Come on, Oscar."

"Where?"

"You know damn well," said Mr. Maddox. "Wait by the ten-dollar windows while I'm in the secretary's office."

FIVE stern track officials were waiting when a Masterton detective at the door admitted Mr. Maddox. Judge Brandon was there also, and as Mr. Maddox came in, the judge rasped: "There's the gambler who knew about this damnable outrage!"

"Not a gambler," Mr. Maddox corrected. "A bookmaker. Gentlemen, I heard my name called." Mr. Maddox smiled wryly at a small, elderly man with snow-white hair and a white rosebud jauntily in his coat lapel. "Ah, Major James. A raw piece of business, wasn't it?"

This was Major Tom James, one of the track owners, a noted breeder and sportsman in the blue-grass country.

Stony-faced, the major nodded. "Maddox, I can't believe you had knowledge of this, as Judge Brandon charges."

"So he charges, does he?" Mr. Maddox bit the end off a fat black cigar and reached for a match. "He's got a nerve, after I warned him."

"That is what interests us," said George Lanier, the track secretary, who had lost his usual brisk pleasantness and was frowning behind his glasses. "Mr. Maddox, you evidently knew something about this."

In past years it had been "Joe" to George Lanier. "Joe and George" when the Maddox horses had stabled here at Latonia. Now it was "Mister" Maddox.

Mr. Maddox smiled rather grimly. "Don't let it get you down, George. All I had was an idea. Call it a hunch if you like, that something might happen today. But if I thought anything, I thought an attempt might be made to keep Wink Thrice from winning. I went to Judge Brandon. He refused to discuss it. What more do you want?"

"You know more than that!" Judge Brandon exploded heatedly.

"Do I?" said Mr. Maddox blandly. "You had your crack at me this morning. Now it's your racing stable, your horse and your trouble. Don't try to shove it in my pocket."

"You—you had guilty knowledge!" the judge spluttered. "I demand to know what friends of yours were behind this! I'll take it into the courts! I'll—"

"Will you now?" said Mr. Maddox, and his bland blue eyes were suddenly frosty and his broad face harder.

Major James broke in. "I've known Maddox a long time. His word is good enough for me. If he knows nothing about this, I believe him."

"He warned me, Major! It's clear presumption of guilty knowledge!"

"Not at all," said Mr. Maddox coldly. "Only a hunch. I did all I could when I took the trouble to warn you. What precautions did you take against your horse being doped? Did you check your trainer and stable hands and the spot where you bet money on the horse? You bet a lot of money, didn't you?"

"That has nothing to do with it!"

"Maybe not," said Mr. Maddox. "And maybe it had. How do I know? You're the one who should know the answers. I haven't covered a bet in weeks. But if I held all the money on your horse, would I want him doped to win?"

Dryly Major James remarked: "He lost."

"It worked out that way," Mr. Maddox conceded. "Only a fool would hop up a horse like Wink Thrice and expect to get by with it. And that's all I can do for you, gentlemen."

"Er—just a moment," Major James said as Mr. Maddox turned to the door. "We wanted your side of the matter, since Judge Brandon said you'd spoken to him. If you can help us get to the bottom of this, I'll be obliged, as an old friend."

The hardness left Mr. Maddox's face as he turned back to the white-haired gentleman. "Thanks, Major. You understand that my business calls for a lot of guessing. I made a guess this time. I've no proof of anything. I've nothing that will do you any good. I've been in New York. What goes on here I don't know. That's all I can do for you."

"If you say so, Maddox," the major accepted almost sadly.

Judge Brandon snorted, but no one else broke the uncomfortable silence as Mr. Maddox walked out of the room.

BEFORE the door closed, they all heard the sharp voices of newspaper men who had gathered outside.

"Here's Joe Maddox, boys! What goes on in there, Joe?"

"Give us a statement, Maddox, will you?"

"Was Brandon hooked up with the gamblers?"

"Joe, were you covering any dough on this race?"

"Over here, Maddox! How about that million-dollar smile?"

Camera bulbs flashed brightly as the door closed.

Judge Brandon winced, spoke bitterly. "They'll crucify me politically. And without reason, without cause!"

And George Lanier, the track secretary, snapped with equal bitterness: "Oh, yes, they'll play it up big. This will give racing a black eye all over the country. And God knows what it will do to us here at Latonia!"

Major Tom James drew a troubled breath and shook his head. "I expected more from Maddox. He's shrewd and honest, with an uncanny way of knowing things. When I heard he'd gone to Judge Brandon with a warning, I thought we'd get to the bottom of this without much trouble."

"Don't tell me he's honest!" Judge Brandon said angrily. "A bookmaker! A—a gambler! And he might as well have stood there and laughed at us!"

The Major sighed. "I don't pretend to understand his position in this. If it were anyone but Joe Maddox...."

"Talk!" Judge Brandon said thickly. "The man's gone now and so far there has only been talk. What will be done to clear my name?"

Mr. Maddox heard none of that, although he could have guessed most of it. And he was not surprised by the newspapermen gathered outside the door. It had been a sure bet they would not neglect this story. They'd be in full cry after names, information, suspicions that would throw light on the drugging of Wink Thrice.

They'd make the most of Joe Maddox, the widely known bookie who had been thrown into the forefront of the scandal by the blaring loudspeakers which called him out of the crowd. But Joe Maddox had never looked more like a big bland Buddha as he faced them, and shook his head.

"Nothing to say, boys. I don't know a thing."

It wasn't enough. It didn't satisfy them. They hurled more questions. Two cameramen ducked around in front of Mr. Maddox and the blinding light of their flashbulbs struck his broad face as camera shutters snapped.

Joe Maddox—name, background and photograph—would be in the newspapers. Bad publicity which Maddox had always dodged like the plague. And now nothing could be done about it except smile and walk on until the press boys turned back for better game in the secretary's office.

"So you finally slipped up, Joe!"

"Cassidy!" Mr. Maddox exclaimed violently, even before he turned— and he was right.

The stocky grizzled man who had touched his elbow was Cassidy of the Masterton Agency. Cassidy, who had sworn for years he'd get Joe Maddox—and now was smiling with satisfaction.

"It was raw, Joe. You're going to deserve all you get."

"Murder wouldn't deserve you!" Mr. Maddox snapped.

"This was almost murder," Cassidy said. "This morning I heard you'd been at the barns talking to the jockey. I figured something was rotten but I didn't think it'd be this raw."

"A flatfoot like you never had a thought," Mr. Maddox sneered. "Have you got a warrant? Are you going to make a pinch and let me prove you're a fathead?"

Cassidy choked. "Fathead, is it? Listen, you cheap horse layer! I'll pin this on you before morning! This time I've got you! Think it over while you're trying to cover up!"

"Nuts!" Mr. Maddox sneered, and shouldered past.

CHAPTER FOUR

BLIND DATE

AT THE ten-dollar windows Oscar's thin face showed relief at the shortness of the interview in the secretary's office. "Everything all right, Joe?"

"No!" said Mr. Maddox, and his inner emotions made the denial almost savage. "What's right about a dope case? What's right about getting my name and picture on the press wires and in the headlines across the country? How many folks will be wondering now if Joe Maddox is on the level?"

"Yeah, I suppose," Oscar agreed and then caught himself hastily. "It ain't that bad, Joe. People who know you won't pay any attention to it." But Oscar seemed to realize that he lacked conviction and hurriedly changed the subject. "What did they say? What'd they want?"

"They wanted to know whom to pinch. Brandon had put the finger on me. They had an idea I could squeal everything."

"Wouldn't they believe you?"

"I wouldn't have believed myself!" Mr. Maddox snapped. "That's what a bookie can expect when anything crooked turns up. So I walked out and bumped into that Masterton cop, Cassidy. Even he couldn't hold me. But he's trying to pin it on me. He'd break his neck to get a court to throw the book at me." Mr. Maddox was plowing through the crowd toward the exits as he talked.

Oscar, pushing and shoving to keep at his elbow, said morbidly: "I had a hunch we shoulda stayed in New York."

"Never mind hunches now!" Mr. Maddox growled.

A taxi carried them away from the track and in less than a mile Mr. Maddox spoke sharply to the driver.

"Turn over three streets and then go on to the bridge. I think we're being followed."

The driver turned right at the next corner, and in the second block exclaimed: "Another hack made that turn! Want me to lose him?"

"Never mind."

"Cassidy," Oscar guessed.

"Probably," Mr. Maddox agreed.

You could be sure Cassidy would be trying. He'd sift Joe Maddox's actions, fine-comb his contacts, dog his movements....

A few minutes after they reached the hotel, Oscar rejoined Mr. Maddox in the air-conditioned cocktail bar. "Joe, there's a 7:17 plane for Washington and the main stem."

Mr. Maddox looked darkly over a Scotch and soda and shrugged. "We might as well take it. I'll come up to the room in a little while. Get the first papers that carry the story."

The late afternoon rush was filling the cocktail bar. Sitting behind a small table, back to the wall, Mr. Maddox overheard references to Wink Thrice. Oh, they were talking about it. Sport fans from coast to coast would be talking about it.

"Keeping busy these days, Maddox?"

A look placed the breezy speaker who pulled out the other chair and sat down. Hewett was his name. Acey-Deuce Hewett to intimates in Detroit, Chicago, St. Louis. Acey-Deuce, because those slim nervous fingers were never far from a deck of cards and a sucker to clean.

Surprisingly Mr. Maddox smiled. "What'll you have, Acey?"

"Lemonade. Doctor's orders."

"Still using that gag?" Mr. Maddox chuckled. "Relax, Acey. Relax."

Acey grinned. "Make it a short Tom Collins."

TRIMLY built, well-barbered, well-dressed, Acey looked like a well-to-do young businessman who might be a leader of the country-club set. And in fact Acey was no stranger to country clubs. Or to night clubs and those furtive hot spots outside the cities, where sporty citizens brushed elbows with the underworld.

Acey's rackets were streamlined, chromium-plated, to suit the modern age. Smooth rackets like blackmail, con games, bribery, crooked politics. And a respectable stranger meeting Acey wouldn't have believed any of it. Acey's weakness was a swaggering conviction that he could pick winning horses.

"Working in town?" Mr. Maddox questioned.

"A little," Acey nodded. "I heard your name called at the track this afternoon. Did the stewards spot your book under their noses?"

Mr. Maddox beckoned for another drink and winked. "Stewards don't bother Joe Maddox's book. They were hot about that sixth race."

Acey looked slightly startled. "Were they trying to pin that stinker on you?"

Mr. Maddox winked again. "Maybe, son. Maybe they just wanted some answers."

"And you had answers to give?"

"Maybe," Mr. Maddox chuckled.

"You must be a pal of Judge Brandon."

"Wrong guess," Mr. Maddox chortled. "I don't know the gent." Mr. Maddox scratched a match with painful care, puffed a thick cigar alight, and smiled contentedly through the smoke. The broad happy face was hot and flushed from too much Scotch, the tongue a trifle thick, eyes the merest bit glassy, to a shrewd eye like Acey Hewett's.

"When Joe Maddox gets ready to talk, he talks. But not until he's ready." Mr. Maddox was expansive as he picked up the fresh Scotch. "That's what I told 'em, Acey. Joe Maddox don't talk until he's ready."

Acey leaned forward. "What'd they say, Joe?"

"Wha' they say?" Mr. Maddox gulped a third of the drink and smacked his lips. "Swell! I go for good Scotch. Nope, they can't push

Joe Maddox around. I told 'em and they had to take it. So I walked
out and bought a drink."

"You were always smart, Joe."

"Too bad I ain't making a book," Mr. Maddox regretted. "You're a
sucker for an odds-on favorite, Acey. But I don't need your dough
now. I've got plenty dough." Mr. Maddox lifted his big hand and
admired the great flashing diamond that was cradled in a massive
gold ring. "Look at it, Acey. Cost me plenty. It's my luck—and am I
lucky?" Mr. Maddox grinned past the ring. "Wait'll I get through
collecting. There'll be folding money to stuff a mattress. You don't
believe me? It's smart money and Joe Maddox has got it, son."

Acey's supple fingers were turning the cold glass from which he
had barely sipped. His bright eyes were glowing. "Sure, Joe. But all
that don't tell me anything. Where you getting all this smart money?
I don't tumble."

Mr. Maddox chuckled hugely. "Sure, you don't. Nobody tumbles.
I told 'em over at the track an' that's the way it is. Finish your drink
and have another."

Acey looked at his wrist watch. "I've got to see a fellow. Going to
be around tonight?"

Mr. Maddox gestured expansively. "I'll be everywhere. 'S night for
Oscar an' Joe Maddox to howl. We're smart, Acey, an' now we're cel-
celebratin'."

Acey blinked as if he couldn't believe this was Maddox. A thought
struck him. He wet his lips and grinned. "Sounds good, Joe. How
about cutting me in? I know some girls who'd like to step out."

Mr. Maddox shook his head. "No tramps."

"Nothing like that, Joe. These girls are regular and like a good time.
You'll have a lousy evening mooching around by yourself."

Mr. Maddox wavered and then yielded. "Bring 'em along. Tell 'em
Joe Maddox is spending the dough and if they aren't tramps they can
write the tickets."

"Eight o'clock?"

"That'll do."

MR. MADDOX lit a cigar and looked unblinkingly through the
smoke while Acey Hewett's trim figure walked out of the crowded
room. And when Acey was gone, Mr. Maddox paid the check and
also left, moving lightly, with a spring of energy that had not been

present through the long hot day. He was whistling between his teeth as he entered the fourth-floor suite where Oscar was glumly scanning a newspaper.

Oscar gestured toward a second paper on a chair. "You won't feel so damn cheerful when you get a load of that. They shot the works."

The headlines of the sports edition were black and bold.

BRANDON HORSE DRUGGED
Widely Known Bookmaker Questioned
Crowd in Uproar at Latonia

Thousands of turf fans angrily watched their money vanish in the sixth race at Latonia this afternoon when track judges disqualified Judge John Brandon's Wink Thrice, the apparent winner.

A track official who asked that his name be withheld, stated that the judges had no choice other than disqualification when confronted with a clear case of doping, apparently resorted to in an effort to make certain that Judge Brandon's Wink Thrice would lead the field home in the Hilltop Stakes.

Track experts were unanimous in stating that the Brandon horse could probably have won without resort to drugs. "Drugging would only have seemed necessary," one expert stated, "when a large sum of money was involved and a win had to be certain."

Judge Brandon, prominent in turf circles and politics, vehemently denied participation in the criminal drugging of his horse. At the same time Brandon partially and reluctantly confirmed rumors that large sums had been bet on Wink Thrice by himself and close associates.

Track stewards, in what was termed a preliminary statement, revealed that Judge Brandon and his trainer, Dennis MacGilvery, have been barred from racing at Latonia pending further action by the stewards and the Kentucky Racing Commission. Jockey Pete Cheney, who rode Wink Thrice, has also been suspended. Track experts recalled that Jockey Cheney had only recently ended a long suspension by the stewards of Santa Anita Track. Jockey Cheney refused a statement. Federal narcotic officials expressed interest in the case, which apparently involved illegal possession and use of narcotic drugs.

Joseph Maddox, widely known bookmaker for many years, was questioned by track officials as to his knowledge of the crime. Maddox refused to say how much, if any, of the money bet on Wink Thrice passed through his hands. Kentucky and Ohio racing circles were immediately in an uproar. Swift punishment under all state and federal laws was promised by track officials for the person or persons guilty.

Mr. Maddox looked up wryly from the paper. "The guy who wrote this had poison in his needle. He doesn't say flatly that Brandon is a crook—but he dares you to think anything else after he's through. I'd say this newspaper doesn't like Judge Brandon."

"It doesn't like you any better," Oscar stated sourly. "Take a look at the picture page on the back."

Across the top of the page were news shots of Judge Brandon, Major Tom James, Joe Maddox. The cameras had shot low and up at Mr. Maddox, making him look huge, brutish, arrogant as he walked out of the racing secretary's office. The picture was captioned: *Notorious Bookmaker Questioned in Brandon Scandal.*

Still smiling wryly, Mr. Maddox tossed the paper on the chair. "That's nearer assassination than poison."

"Sibera won't be far enough to lose federal narcotic men," Oscar said bitterly. "It gets worse, Joe. We shoulda stayed in New York. Look what happens when we butt into something that ain't any of our business."

Mr. Maddox chuckled. "If we can't make Sibera, we might as well stick around."

"Wha's at?" Oscar's head came up with startled alarm.

"We'll stick around and see what happens."

"Not me! Not on your life!"

Mr. Maddox hummed a few notes as he removed his coat. "We'll celebrate tonight."

"Celebrate *what?*"

"Everything," said Mr. Maddox. "Benny Roos had a hunch. Now I've got a hunch."

"Joe! You ain't going any deeper in this?"

"Acey Hewett is bringing a girl for you tonight."

"A girl? Acey Hewett? That St. Louie hoodlum?"

"Tut-tut," Mr. Maddox reproved. "She's something extra. A lallapalooza. Probably wrapped in cellophane and ribbon. All yours—and all evening to enjoy her."

"A blind date an' a St. Louie hoodlum!" Oscar all but moaned. "And the blind dates I draw would gag an ostrich! Joe, I don't want no blind date! Ain't we had enough? Have we got any dough risked? We're through! Let's lam before it gets worse!"

MR. MADDOX came out of his shirt and his broad face had

hardened. His voice had an edge few people ever heard. "You miss the point. We've more than money risked here. Joe Maddox and thirty years of making a clean book have got the mark now. What about decent racing and fine horses like Wink Thrice that can be dirtied by crooks and rats? What's money got to do with it?"

"Sure, Joe, but—"

"Some things you don't know and maybe can't help," Mr. Maddox growled. "You never tumbled to kids in love."

"Kids?" Oscar repeated weakly. "Kids in love?"

"What does a forty-minute egg like you know about two kids dreaming of marriage?" Mr. Maddox threw across the room. "When did you ever look at a boy and know he belonged to you and you couldn't see anything ahead but heaven and rosy dreams?"

"Not no boy," Oscar denied uncomfortably. "Listen, Joe—"

"So I waste time with you!" Mr. Maddox snapped. "I'm speaking of Pete Cheney and his girl. The Brandon girl. You didn't meet her. I did. I saw her with Pete Cheney."

"But her old man—"

"Damn Brandon. She can't help it if he's her father. He pushed his stubborn chin out and got nailed. And now those two kids are washed up and sunk through no fault of theirs. And if I know anything about crooked work, there's little that Brandon and the track stewards and the whole blasted Narcotic Bureau can do about it. This thing was smooth. This was planned and there'll be no loose ends lying around to unravel. So what are we going to do about it?"

"O.K., Joe," Oscar said wearily. "I'll be a cluck. What do we do?"

"We get the dirty crooks out in the open and nail them."

"O.K., Joe. But do I have to nail them with a blind date?"

"You're dated, sucker. Climb in your rags and meet her and like her."

Oscar gave back one final spark of defiance. "I don't have to like her."

"Act like it anyway. That's all you have to worry about."

Maybe so—but Oscar had an uneasy premonition when he saw Mr. Maddox take from the bottom of his suitcase a little object he seldom carried—a small cylinder of heavy lead, some three inches long and half an inch through.

"What kind of an evening's this going to be?"

Mr. Maddox dropped the heavy little cylinder into his coat pocket, where the weight made a slight sag. He was cheerful again. "How do I know? When rats come out of their holes, anything can happen."

Acey Hewett finally telephoned. "All set, Joe? The girls are here in the lobby and hopped to go."

"Coming down," Mr. Maddox hung up and jerked a thumb at the door. "The little lady's waiting."

"For my own mother I wouldn't do this," was Oscar's last blurt of protest.

CHAPTER FIVE

STORM AT THE CABIN CLUB

HER NAME was Dottie and she was an inch shorter than Oscar, blonde and pretty like a coaxing little doll. Empty-headed like a doll, perhaps, but an eyeful nevertheless. Acey Hewett had, surprisingly, delivered the goods.

Oscar took one look and was a different man. "Kid," Oscar told her, "you're what the doc ordered. Don't be bashful tonight."

Dottie giggled. "Listen to him, Lois. I'm going to like this."

"I can see that, honey," Lois said.

Lois was older, black-haired, smartly sophisticated. You could find her type on the green clubhouse lawns of any big track. Some were wealthy. You'd see their names in the social columns next day. Some—and they were often hard to spot—would never be on any society page.

This Lois was no stranger to folding money, however she got it. Mr. Maddox judged her with one sharp look and was satisfied. Not even Acey's vivacious blonde, Marie, was a match for Lois. And Lois had come to meet Joe Maddox.

Jovially Mr. Maddox asked, "Where do we eat?"

Dottie giggled again. "They have swell champagne on the Tournet Roof. Oscar, do you like champagne?"

"Kid," Oscar said gallantly, "I never get enough. You can have gallons tonight."

"Gee, Lois! Hear him! Gallons of fuzzy water! Hurry, hurry!"

That set the evening. Plenty to drink. Something doing every minute. The girls were expecting it. Acey, Oscar and Mr. Maddox were willing.

Acey Hewett had his own car, a flashy blue sport model with the top down. On the Tournet Roof they found music, gaiety, food, wine and dancing.

Oscar was enchanted with his blonde. Few people had ever seen Joe Maddox so pink-faced, so jovial, so quick to reach for wine, so talkative, expansive, hugely enjoying himself, even to the point of drinking too much.

Acey Hewett drank little. A shrewd observer might have sensed lurking strain behind Acey's talk. Not that Mr. Maddox noticed or cared, so obviously was he enjoying himself.

Lois suggested the drive out on the north side through Avon Field Park. And after the park it was Lois who wanted to drive on along the Lebanon Pike through the open country.

Acey, hatless at the wheel, whistling with the swing music on the radio, called over his shoulder: "How about it, Joe? If it rains we can put the top up in a couple of minutes."

"Anything, Acey."

Lois laughed by Mr. Maddox's side. "Nothing slow about you, Joe."

"Not when I'm celebrating, sister."

"What are you celebrating?"

"Money," Mr. Maddox chuckled. "Folding dough that would choke a horse—the easiest I ever got my hands on."

"I'll bet it's the race this afternoon," Lois guessed shrewdly.

"Acey's been talking, has he?"

"I read the newspapers."

"I'm a clam," Mr. Maddox chuckled.

"But I'm curious."

Mr. Maddox shook with the joy of his secret. "The stewards were curious. Ev'body's curious. An' ol' Joe's a clam."

"Don't be that way," Lois coaxed. "I won't tell anyone."

"Not even Acey?"

"Him? Why should I?"

"Search me. Take a tip from old Joe Maddox, kid. Never loosen up until it's worth something to you."

"Acey was right when he said you were smart."

"It looks like rain," was all Mr. Maddox said.

THEY were beyond the city limits now, speeding into the open country, the sultry night air whipping about them. Cool enough while the wind lasted, but you could feel storm in the air, like the pressure of a threatening hand. From the front seat Dottie shrilled: "Who's buying me a drink? Li'l Dottie wants a drink!"

"Got to get the kid a drink!" Oscar shouted. "Wha's matter, no drinks for Dottie?"

"Hold it!" Acey called. "Friend of mine's got a place a few miles ahead."

Green neon writing topping a rustic arch said: *Cabin Club.* The building was well back from the road, with trees intervening, so that only dim lights were visible from the highway. Faint music if you stopped to listen. Ahead of them another automobile had made the same turn and a noisy quartet emerged as Acey parked among many other cars at the side of the building.

The inside was rustic—rafters, beams, sidewalls, bar, booth, tables and a rustic railing around the small crowded dance floor. Strings of little colored lights made a dim false gaiety. The music was loud, talk and laughter louder. The waiters were busy.

"Just a joint," Acey told Mr. Maddox carelessly as a waiter seated them. "But there's money in a place like this when the pay-off isn't too high."

"I've heard."

"You haven't heard anything," Acey boasted as they sat down. "You wouldn't believe the names that drop in at joints like this. They like to drive out and let their hair down."

"Gambling?"

Acey grinned. "When the fix is right. Joe, a string of joints like this makes a horse track look like small change. The track gets them for a few weeks and then closes. These joints run all the time. Get a string of them with the fix in—and you wouldn't believe the take over a year."

"The tracks do pretty well."

"Maybe. This is a better racket. You could do yourself good in it, Joe."

"How?"

Oscar and his blonde were noisily ordering drinks. Acey's girl, Marie, was helping them. Lois showed no interest as Acey shifted his chair over and spoke confidentially to Mr. Maddox. "Look, Joe, this is on the cuff. These boys operate in four states. They're smart. And not pikers. They make it and they spend it. They'll pay if you want it. You wouldn't believe the connections they've got."

"Guys after my own heart," Mr. Maddox beamed—and even as he said that he almost lost his poise at the sight of Gayle Brandon sitting alone at one of the small wall tables.

Gayle was toying with a drink she had hardly tasted. The chair opposite her had not been occupied. And she was pale, tense, even under the false gaiety of the dim colored bulbs. She was staring furtively at the cigarette girl who was hawking her tray several tables away. The cigarette girl moved on. Gayle's glance followed....

Acey was saying: "Come back and meet one of the boys. Al Costigan, from St. Louis. He's got a big piece of this racket. He'd like to talk to you."

Mr. Maddox nodded, and as he and Acey got up, Oscar complained: "We ain't leavin' already?"

"Not yet," Mr. Maddox said brusquely. "But keep out from under the table, you mug. No telling what we'll be doing next."

"I'm ready for anything," Oscar boasted.

Acey paused beside the cigarette girl and helped himself to cigarettes from her tray. His greeting was audible. "Hello, Babe. How's tricks?"

"Swell, Acey.... Everything all right?"

Acey said something in a lower voice. She replied in a whisper. Mr. Maddox missed their expressions for Gayle Brandon was startled, uncertain as she saw him. Mr. Maddox frowned, shook his head slightly, and then followed Acey Hewett, with questions prodding his thoughts.

Gayle Brandon hadn't come to this roadside hot spot for amusement. Not alone. Not on this night when her world had crashed about her. Not with that pale, strained tenseness, that interest in the cigarette girl whom Acey had familiarly addressed as Babe.

Pete Cheney might be coming. Mr. Maddox doubted it. Gayle didn't look as if were waiting for anyone. She looked alone and purposeful. Almost desperately purposeful.

Acey skirted the small dance floor. Mr. Maddox brushed by a girl and her escort. The girl glanced at his face and visibly gasped with recognition. The music stopped and some of her words floated back.

"...*man... paper....*"

Even the women in places like this knew Joe Maddox now. From

Frisco to Miami they'd know Joe Maddox by name and newspaper pictures, by the clever printed words that suggested Joe Maddox was a notorious racetrack hanger-on and crook. Thirty years of playing the horse game straight—and now they'd done this to Joe Maddox!

ACEY passed through a doorway. At the end of a short hall a second door let them into a small office where a man rose quickly behind a desk and dismissed a second man with a wave of his hand and a curt: "See you later, Phil."

Phil greeted Acey as he went out and flicked a sharp, guarded glance at Mr. Maddox. He was another well-dressed, smooth young man with an honest face that cried denial of crookedness. Every year the successful crooks got smoother, harder to spot. But Joe Maddox seldom made a mistake.

Mr. Maddox's face was beaming as he shook hands with Costigan. Al Costigan, from St. Louis—and other cities and states where his rackets operated. Still another smooth one, this Costigan. Older than Acey, older than Phil, as old as Mr. Maddox, but slender, well-tailored, with handsome touches of gray at his temples, and teeth that were white and even when he smiled. And you could guess that Costigan's bright restless eyes missed little.

"Glad to meet you, Maddox. I've heard about you."

"From Acey, probably, after he bet on the wrong horse," Mr. Maddox chuckled. Inwardly he tried to place Costigan and could not. But then you couldn't meet everyone around the country.

"I heard your name called at the track," Costigan smiled. "No trouble, I hope."

"Not yet," Mr. Maddox boasted as he sat down.

Costigan sat down too. His smile narrowed. "There'll be trouble about that race. Looks like you're close to the heat, Maddox."

"They're trying to put on the heat," Mr. Maddox admitted.

Costigan was studying him. "Look," Costigan said abruptly, "why don't you get wise? You're going to need-connections. You need to hook up with the right people. Cut yourself into the real money and stay safe."

Behind Mr. Maddox, Acey spoke quickly. "That's an idea, Joe. I didn't think of it. Al's got the right slant."

"Not bad," Mr. Maddox agreed blandly. "Where do I find the right people?"

"I can fix that," Costigan admitted. His manicured fingers were tapping the desk blotter. His eyes were nervously intent.

Thunder rolled in the distance. A whirring fan in the corner failed to keep the air from feeling moist and oppressive. Perspiration beaded Mr. Maddox's forehead but he had never looked blander, less worried as he shrugged. "It's an idea. I'll think it over—but I'm doing all right."

The thunder rolled again, nearer. Costigan continued to tap the green blotter. Harder now, as if inner emotion were escaping through his finger ends. And doubt drew two fine lines down Costigan's forehead as he watched Maddox's smiling face.

"I'm going to St. Louis in the morning," he said abruptly. "There's a set-up ready that won't mean nickels and dimes. It's the spot for a smart bookie. Take it and you won't be sorry."

"I'll bet not," Mr. Maddox beamed. "But I'll have to know more. What are the angles?"

Costigan looked annoyed. "You'll have to cut in on it before there's any talk."

"I was afraid so. Forget it. I'm doing all right."

Costigan stood up and opened a desk drawer with a quick, decisive motion. "It was a damn fool idea to start with, Acey! Now we'll do it my way! Take him!"

Mr. Maddox came out of the chair fast, dodging to one side. But he was not quick enough. Acey Hewett was standing behind him— and not even Mr. Maddox had supposed they'd be so raw and hurried about it.

Only a gun in Acey's hand could have jammed so hard in Mr. Maddox's back. Acey's voice was suddenly all brittle threat. "Take it easy, Joe! Get 'em up!"

MUSIC was throbbing again in the front part of the big rustic building. And lightning glared brilliantly outside. A hard flurry of cooler air blew through the open window as Mr. Maddox lifted his empty hands and spoke calmly. "What's the idea? Art you two trying to kid me?"

Costigan turned with a gun in his hand and lowered the window and drew the curtains. When he swung back his rapid questions were cool and searching. "What happened at the track this afternoon? What did they want with you? What did you tell them? What did you know to tell them? Where did you muscle in on that race?"

"Did I?" Mr. Maddox countered.

Acey's gun prodded him. "Don't stall, Joe. You shot off your mouth plenty to me."

"I thought you were a pal," Mr. Maddox said over his shoulder.

"Sure," Acey agreed. "I'm a pal. Go on and talk."

Mr. Maddox shrugged. "There's nothing to tell. I had a few drinks and talked some. None of it meant much."

Costigan came around the desk. He was still quiet. Nothing rough about him—and yet Mr. Maddox forgot the gun in his back as he watched the man. "In New York you laid money on that race," Costigan said. "A few hours later you're here at the track being questioned by the stewards. And you take a few drinks and start broadcasting how smooth everything worked. Don't kid me. You got a line into that business some way. Now spill it while you've got a chance."

"Better loosen up, Joe," Acey advised in the same brittle, threatening voice.

"So Benny Roos has a hole down into the same rat's nest," Mr. Maddox said thoughtfully. "You've been in touch with Benny since the race. You're jumpy about me. You don't know what's happened. You don't know what's going to happen. The only thing you can figure is to grab Joe Maddox and make him talk."

"And we mean *quick!*" Acey warned.

Mr. Maddox's lip curled "Rats aren't smart, Costigan. They get caught in traps and eat poison. They duck when the light comes on. The hardest job is to get 'em out in the open to get at them. You rats came out easier than I hoped. Too easy. Acey was so clumsy about it that I wasn't sure at first."

Behind him, Acey bit out: "Why you—"

Costigan's gesture silenced Acey. Costigan had reddened. His narrowed eyes were bright, hard, and now going uncertain if you looked close and knew men. "What do you mean, Maddox?"

"Do I have to draw a picture?" Mr. Maddox said scornfully. "Acey took the bait. Did you crooks think I didn't know what I was doing? Hell, I didn't even bring a gun. That's what I think of rats."

"He means it!" Acey said huskily. "Al, we'd better get him out of here! Get 'em both out of here! Maybe we were tailed. Maybe—"

"Shut up!" Costigan snapped. His wire-tight voice still lacked Acey's edge of panic. Which was to be expected, or Acey probably would have been giving the orders.

"This was your fool idea!" Costigan added roughly to Acey. "Look how it turned out. I'll handle it now. Go get—" Costigan broke off as the door opened.

A girl's hurried voice said: "Excuse me. I— Acey, I've got to see you!"

"What is it?" Costigan demanded.

Mr. Maddox looked around. It was the cigarette girl, without her tray, flustered now, excited, uncertain as she replied to Costigan. "I got a phone call. I—I don't know what to do."

The guns were out of sight in coat pockets. She didn't notice that anything was wrong. The telephone call was filling her mind—and the call was bad enough if her manner was any indication.

"Talk to her outside," Costigan directed.

Mr. Maddox put a hand carelessly in his own coat pocket as Acey followed her out and closed the door. "More trouble?" he asked with amusement.

"Keep out of this!" Costigan told him viciously.

BEHIND the desk, hand on the gun in his pocket, Costigan eyed the door and waited.

In a moment Acey was back, speaking hurriedly. "That punk telephoned her. He's in town and wants to see her. Don't want to wait until she's off. Says he'll hire an auto and come out here. She stalled him. He's on the phone. Want him out here?"

"No!" Costigan denied sharply. "She can see him in town. Better take him to Solly's place. Tell Babe to ask him to wait on some corner and she'll drive by." Costigan sucked in a short hard breath. "You and Phil drive her in and see that everything's settled."

"Solly's place?" said Acey.

"Yes!"

Acey licked his lips, jerked his head at Mr. Maddox impersonally. "What about this one and that drunken lug who came with him?"

"I'll handle them. Find Duke. Tell him I want him. Then get in town quick with Babe. I want that settled fast."

"It's settled," Acey said as he turned to the door.

As the door closed behind Acey, a thunder-crash outside shook the building. With a rush and roar the storm broke so furiously that the orchestra music faded to a distant whisper beyond the small office.

Mr. Maddox mused: "If you kill me, Costigan, you'll burn."

Costigan's teeth again showed white and even. "I haven't burned yet."

So others had died. And after Joe Maddox there would be more. Why not? A string of hot spots like this kept a fix in with sheriffs and other law officers, retained good lawyers. The baffling web of the underworld obscured, entangled, stopped outsiders. And you could be sure this present business was big enough to rate murder.

Mr. Maddox sighed. "Never mind the gun, Costigan. I'm not armed. Maybe we can make a deal."

"We'll make a deal," Costigan agreed.

"Fine," Mr. Maddox said. "Let's talk it over."

Mr. Maddox pulled his chair around to sit down—and his big hand suddenly brought the chair up off the floor. Pivoting, Mr. Maddox hurled the chair in an underhanded swing.

Costigan tried to dodge. He was snatching out the automatic at the same time. And the chair struck him legs first and drove him back against the desk. And as the automatic blasted a wild shot the thunder crashed again outside.

Mr. Maddox followed the chair with astonishing quickness for a man of his bulk. The wild shot missed him. The chair-back fell down to the floor, with the legs and frame still pinning Costigan against the desk. Blood was starting from Costigan's gashed cheek.

Mr. Maddox's hand had come out of his coat pocket. His big fist slammed over the chair and Costigan was too rattled to duck. The blow flattened Costigan's nose and teeth broke behind Costigan's lips. Costigan's head snapped back. He sprawled back over the desk as Mr. Maddox snatched the gun from him.

Mr. Maddox took time for a grateful look at the heavy little cylinder of lead that had been clenched inside his fist. "Nice gadget!" he panted and kicked the chair aside and dragged the feebly struggling figure off the desk. Costigan's nose and mouth were bleeding as Mr. Maddox steadied him upright.

"For once," Mr. Maddox said harshly, "I'm going to like this!"

Costigan's eyes rolled wildly as a big fist whipped to the jaw with studied accuracy. And that was all Costigan saw. Mr. Maddox yanked him behind the desk and he collapsed limply.

WIND and rain were beating on the window when Mr. Maddox cautiously opened the office door. The short hall was empty. The orchestra was still playing and when he emerged from the hall the dance floor was crowded. It was hard to believe Costigan lay back there behind his desk. Hard to believe the automatic dragging in Mr. Maddox's coat pocket had been fired to kill a few moments back. Only the storm and the music had kept all these people from hearing the shot.

Mr. Maddox wiped at a smear of blood on his bruised knuckles as he skirted the dance floor. Acey Hewett wasn't in sight. But Acey might have been delayed. He might still be around. Even now he might have spotted Mr. Maddox and be going for help. And the man named Duke who was to come to Costigan's office would be there any minute. He'd find Costigan. He'd have help and gunmen in no time....

Mr. Maddox stopped, swearing under his breath, as Cassidy's stocky figure came opt of a chair just ahead. Cassidy had been sitting alone— and Cassidy's smile was sardonic with satisfaction. "Nice going, Joe. When did you and your stooge start picking dames and stepping out in joints like this?"

"You guess!" Mr. Maddox invited. "How long before you get smart, Cassidy? You're wasting time tailing me."

"Sure," said Cassidy cordially. "Have a drink, Joe. Tell me about that mug you and Oscar are with tonight. He acts like he's got a piece of the joint—and I'll bet everyone on the payroll has got a record."

"Where is he?"

"I should know," said Cassidy. "Who is he?"

"I wouldn't know."

Cassidy's smile was thin-lipped. "You look jumpy, Joe."

"You're having another dream, Cassidy!"

With a quick motion Cassidy lifted Mr. Maddox's hand. "Where'd you get the smear of blood, Joe?"

Mr. Maddox snatched the hand away. "You're balmy!"

Cassidy looked at the doorway at the rear of the big room. "You slipped up there, Joe. Those knuckles haven't bled—but they've been used. What's going on back there?"

Eyes all about them could note every move of the two men standing in full view. Oscar and the girls were still at the table. Gayle Brandon had just settled her check and was hurriedly leaving her table, leaving the building with some purpose in her mind. Mr. Maddox thought he knew. And if he was right, his sudden surge of apprehension was justified.

"I'll go back and have a look," Cassidy decided. "Maybe there's a pal back there who don't like getting punched. How about it, Joe?" Cassidy's narrowed eyes were waiting for a sign. And when you knew Cassidy of the Masterton Agency, you knew he was dangerous in moments like this, when the kinks of a case were just ready to break from some unexpected move.

"Nothing back there," Mr. Maddox denied. "Why don't you get smart, Cassidy, before you make another dumb mistake?"

That was enough. Cassidy's hard smile broke as he started back. "I said I'd get you by morning, Joe. Better lam while you've got time. This looks like the payoff!"

And when Cassidy looked back, his smile went grim with satisfaction. Joe Maddox was hurrying to the front exit with reckless haste. A man so well known could always be found and pinched. Cassidy went on back to find the cause of Joe Maddox's flight—and Mr. Maddox barely caught Gayle Brandon as she was starting out the front door.

"Miss Brandon!"

She paused, showing no surprise that he should have followed her. "I wanted to see you, Mr. Maddox—but I can't wait now."

"Where are you going?"

"That—that girl is leaving. She just went out."

"Got your automobile?"

"Yes."

"Get it! I'll be out front in a jiffy!"

It took seconds only to get back to Oscar, still hilarious with the blonde. "Snap out of it!" Mr. Maddox ordered, slapping Oscar's shoulder.

"Si' down, Joe."

"You ain't had a drink!" the blonde accused. "Lois, make 'im sit down! Wha's matter? We wanna party!"

Mr. Maddox threw a twenty on the table. "Here's your money for the check! Come on, you lush!"

The dark-haired Lois was sober, watchful as Mr. Maddox plucked Oscar out of the chair. "What are you doing?" she called across the table.

"Ask Hewett," Mr. Maddox threw at her as he propelled Oscar toward the door.

"Leggo, Joe! Where's Dottie? I wan' Dottie!"

"You pickled Romeo! I'll give you Dottie under the chin if you don't hurry!"

CHAPTER SIX

STABLE PUNK'S BABE

A LAST look back as they left the big rustic room showed Lois also hurrying toward that door at the back, toward the office and Cassidy and Costigan.... She and Acey had been the plant. The other two girls didn't matter. Now Lois would have men after them quickly.

Oscar protested again as he was shoved out into the beating, blowing rain. "This'll drown us, Joe!"

"I'll give you worse than drowning!" Mr. Maddox retorted savagely. "Walk in it! I bring you along for help—and you get lushy over a cheap little tart who wouldn't wipe her feet on you if someone else had five bucks in his pocket. I should have let you stay and get shot."

"Wh-whazzat?... Shot?"

"You heard me! I just took a gun away from one man!"

Oscar staggered. Mr. Maddox held him up while headlights swung out from the parked cars. The light sedan slid to a stop beside them. "This ain't Acey's car!" Oscar protested.

Mr. Maddox already had the door open. He shouldered in, dragged Oscar after him, explaining: "This mug is with me! Step on it!"

Gayle Brandon started on before the door was closed. Oscar almost fell back out. Mr. Maddox grabbed him, leaned over and slammed the door.

"They've gone!" Gayle said excitedly. "But I saw the car! It's blue with a canvas top! It can't be very far ahead!" Driving recklessly toward the highway, Gayle exclaimed: "It's out of sight already! And I don't know which way it turned!"

"I know the car," Mr. Maddox told her coolly. "They're heading toward the city."

Gayle threw a quick look. "You know a lot."

"Never mind that now. Why'd you come out here? What's so interesting about the cigarette girl?"

The sedan reeled, skidded in a fast turn onto the highway. Gayle was driving recklessly. When she answered Mr. Maddox, her voice was jerky, husky with strain. "I couldn't sit helplessly and see everything smash. Father's political future. Pete's future. Everything Pete and I had planned."

"It's not that bad." But Mr. Maddox knew she didn't believe him. He could understand, he could sympathize—but he couldn't do much for the black hopelessness of hurt youth.

"Everything's messed up," Gayle said wretchedly. "Pete says he hasn't anything to offer a wife now. He'll probably never have. The judges said if he wasn't guilty too, why didn't he tell the starter when he noticed something wrong with Wink Thrice. They'll bar him from the Kentucky tracks! The racing commissioners in other states will do the same. They support one another. Pete won't have a chance!"

"Did Pete know something was wrong with the horse before the race started?" Mr. Maddox asked sharply.

"He was honest enough to tell the judges and the stewards," Gayle said defensively. "The horses were on the track before Pete suspected something might be wrong with Wink Thrice. Even then he wasn't sure. They were at the starting gate before Pete had any idea of the truth."

"Pete should have told the starter."

"Pete couldn't believe it. Why should anyone have doped Wink Thrice? He was good enough already. Pete had been watching for something that might lose the race. And even at the gate he wasn't sure. Father and his friends had bet heavily. Pete had all our money down. The crowd was backing Wink Thrice. You know the rules. The horses were at the gate. All bets were valid, no matter what happened. All that money would have been lost if Wink Thrice hadn't run. How could Pete disqualify his horse for something he wasn't sure about? Even at the gate Wink Thrice wasn't so bad. Pete says the drug didn't take hold fully until they were running. And then it was too late. Pete couldn't have held Wink Thrice back if he had tried. The judges would have seen him and taken action. All Pete could do was ride the race and hope everything turned out all right."

Gayle tore her eyes off the road long enough to demand fiercely: "What would *you* have done?"

"Watch the road!" Mr. Maddox warned hastily, and then admitted: "I'd probably have done the same thing. Pete didn't have much choice. But what about you? What brought you out here tonight?"

JAGGED lightning brought Gayle's face into sharp relief. The thunder-crash that followed blocked her reply, and when it died away she spoke while her eyes peered into the sheeting rain ahead. "Pete was sure that cigarette girl had something to do with it. I was useless. I wasn't helping any, so I slipped away and came out here to look at her and—and perhaps think of something."

"What does Pete know about that girl?"

"It was a hunch more than anything."

"Hunches!" Oscar said loudly. "We had a hunch! Look at us!"

"Go on," Mr. Maddox told Gayle.

"Pete doesn't know much about her. Saturday, a week ago, Pete and I saw Danny Locklin out with her. The next morning Pete kidded Danny about her. And Danny boasted that she was crazy about him and said she worked at a night spot out north of Cincinnati."

"Who is Danny Locklin?"

"Our exercise boy."

Mr. Maddox was alert. "A kid? A punk around the barns?"

"Danny's eighteen," Gayle said. "He wants to be a jockey. Father hired him about a year ago."

"Go on. What's the girl got to do with it?"

"It was only an idea," Gayle confessed. "Pete said she obviously knew her way around. She was pretty. She must make good money where she worked and have all the dates she wanted. Why should she bother with a stable hand like Danny Locklin?"

"I'm wondering the same thing."

"Pete didn't think anything about it until after the race today. Then he wondered. It seemed queer she would be out on a Saturday night with Danny. She would have some other night off. Not Saturday, the busiest night of the week."

"Smart thinking. Has this punk done anything suspicious?"

"Not that we know. Danny was questioned this afternoon like everyone else around the barn. Pete said they didn't pay much attention to him. Danny looks younger than he is, and goodnatured and harmless. We all like him. He was hungry when Father gave him a job—and he's worked hard."

"Was he around Wink Thrice before the race?"

"Naturally. But that wasn't any reason to suspect him. Pete just had a hunch that something was queer about Danny's having dates with this girl."

"Pete was right. Where's this Danny Locklin tonight?"

"At the track, I suppose," Gayle said. "I had an idea he might see the girl again tonight. But mainly I wanted to investigate her. I went to three other places before I found her." Gayle struck the steering wheel with her palm. "And now she's left her job in the middle of the evening and gone out with two men! I caught only a glimpse of them. But I saw enough of her in there. She's clever and selfish and hard behind all that make-up—and I'm going to see what she's doing tonight!"

"Where's Pete?"

"He said he'd be busy tonight. I—I think he didn't want to be with me. He made it plain."

"The young idiot!" Mr. Maddox said bluntly. "The one night he should have been with you! Pete'll have his lesson when he hears how close you got to real trouble."

"I'm not in any trouble!"

"You should have had better sense than to circulate alone in joints like the Cabin Club! Mixing in things a girl like you doesn't know anything about! Starting out like this after a brace of rats who'd put you out of the way quick if they suspected what you were doing!"

"You don't have to talk to me like that!" Gayle protested. "I know what I'm doing!"

The storm, the wetting, the fresh air and the excitement were sobering Oscar fast. "Lady, we don't know what we're doing," Oscar said.... "Hey, Joe—watch that gun! It makes me jumpy!"

Mr. Maddox was holding Costigan's automatic in the light from the dash. "Here's what we're up against," he said gruffly. "Pete Cheney and all of us. A bullet from this just missed me back there at the Cabin Club. The man tried to murder me."

GAYLE looked at the gun, gasped—and let the speeding sedan swerve to the road-edge. The outer wheels struck water, mud...., Gayle was suddenly fighting the wheel as the car skidded.... Reeling and sliding, they whipped back on the road—and almost crashed into another car that shot out of the storm with a sudden wild blare of a horn…. In seconds the strange automobile vanished in the night behind them, traveling fast the other way.

"If I ever get safe home to Times Square," Oscar promised wildly, "dynamite won't blast me out!"

Gayle let the sedan slow down as she looked again at the gun. "It startled me," she said shakily. "Did someone really shoot at you? Is—is that your gun?"

"It's mine now, sister. And if I know trouble, there are guns in that car we're following. And ready to be used. This isn't tea and cakes. This is the McCoy. They mean business. You wouldn't have had a chance if they'd caught you following them."

"I don't think I understand," Gayle said weakly.

"Don't try. Catch that car if you can. They're meeting someone who telephoned that cigarette girl. Some punk, they said. And when they meet him, he'll get more than love or kisses."

It took a moment for Gayle to grasp that. Even then she hardly understood. "You—you sound as if they might be meeting Danny Locklin."

"Now that I'm wise to the kid, I think so," Mr. Maddox agreed. "Who else would it be? Locklin's got his date with the girl friend. And five to one it's his last date."

"She won't see him again?"

"She won't—and no one else will either. If we're right about him, he knows too much."

"You mean they're going to hurt him?"

"Maybe it won't hurt," Oscar said gloomily.

"We don't know how much the boy knows. How guilty he is," Mr. Maddox admitted. "But if I know the men with that girl, they'll not let a stable punk worry them like they seem to be worried now."

"I—I didn't realize," Gayle admitted uncertainly. "Hadn't we better tell the police?"

"What good would it do? We don't know where Locklin is. We're not sure they're meeting him. We don't know where they're going. Did you ever hear of Solly's place?"

"No," Gayle denied.

"Then we don't know anything," Mr. Maddox said. "The cops couldn't help if we called them. And we'd lose that car ahead. All we can do is tail it and see what happens. The rain's letting up a little. Step on it."

The thunder and lightning were receding in the distance. The headlights were reaching out farther through the slackening rain as Gayle drove faster. And she made only one more comment, miserably. "It's all so confused. None of this seems to make sense—any more than doping Wink Thrice made sense."

Mr. Maddox was dryly practical in his reply. "It doesn't have to make sense. It's happened. It's happening. That's all we have to worry about."

"Ain't them tail-lights ahead?" Oscar asked.

THE RED tail-lights were barely visible… then clearer as Gayle's sedan drew closer. That car ahead was rolling fast, but not recklessly, through the rain.

"Better pass it," Maddox directed. "Oscar, get down out of sight. If it's the one we want, they may be looking."

"And if they see your mug, they'll cut loose," Oscar guessed. "And I'm sitting on their side. I'll get it first."

Mr. Maddox chuckled. "It'll be your chance to help. Too bad you aren't twice as big, so you'd cover me better."

Oscar's reply was a mumble, probably unprintable, as he jack-knifed down out of sight. Mr. Maddox hunched low in the seat as Gayle blew the horn and went past the other car with a rush. It was a blue sport model with a canvas top and the windows up. Its headlights glared in the sedan's back window as they pulled ahead.

"What do we do now?" Gayle questioned.

"Slow down a little," Mr. Maddox directed. "If we catch up with another car, let it hold us back until that sedan passes us again. Then keep it in sight. We're coming into the city. There'll be more traffic. I doubt if they'll be watching for a car to be trailing them. There wasn't any reason to think they'd be followed."

"I'm wet. My leg's going to sleep!" Oscar groaned. "Joe, do you have to do this?"

"Keep quiet," Mr. Maddox said unfeelingly.

The rain slackened steadily as they entered the city and heavier traffic. Mr. Maddox had been right. Acey's car soon passed them. Gayle had no great difficulty in keeping it in sight.

They skirted Avon Fields Park, continued on into the city, observing speed laws, stopping for traffic-lights. And the blue sedan was not far ahead on Main Street, when it swung to the curb at the corner of Government Square and let following cars continue by. The big post-office building loomed just ahead as Gayle turned quickly to the curb and cut off the lights.

"Is this right?" she asked.

"What are they doing? I can't see," Mr. Maddox said.

Gayle looked out the window on her side. "Someone's getting in. A man. He must have been waiting there on the corner.... Now they're going on."

Two automobiles passed in the misty drizzle. "Pull out behind them with your lights off!" Mr. Maddox snapped. "Then dim your lights and don't lose—"

Gayle's gasp broke in. "That's Pete's car pulling out ahead of us!" The small coupe to which Gayle referred had been parked beside the post office. Mr. Maddox had seen it pull out into the traffic with a purposeful rush.

"Are you sure? How d'you know Pete's car?"

"Do you see that rear reflector shaped like a horseshoe? That's Pete's. He had it made from one of the racing plates Racasas wore when he won the Withers Mile last year. It was the first big winning race that Pete had ridden. He said it was when his real luck started. He wanted a souvenir to bring more luck." Gayle's voice caught. *"Luck!* I hate that word now!"

"Then Pete was watching that fellow on the corner. He's following him!" Mr. Maddox said. "So it must be your Danny Locklin. And Pete—" Mr. Maddox broke off, scowling at that twinkling horseshoe-shaped reflector moving ahead of them. He'd been about to say that Pete Cheney didn't know murder was in the air tonight. But if Gayle didn't think of it, so much the better. No telling what she'd try to do if she coupled Pete and murder. "Tag Pete. He'll keep them in sight," Mr. Maddox told her. "They'll not notice his car if he's careful."

Oscar made gloomy comment. "You can't kid guns, Joe. I don't like this."

"Keep quiet!" Mr. Maddox snapped.

But the damage was done. "Pete doesn't know they have guns!" Gayle realized in a frightened voice—and had to stop just then for a red traffic-light.

AN OFFICER on the corner was looking at them. The twinkling red horseshoe on Pete's car receded swiftly beyond the intersection. "I'm going to run the light!" Gayle decided desperately.

But that was denied her even before Mr. Maddox could agree. Cross traffic made the intersection impassable. They had to wait with a dismal sense of failure closing about them. When the green light finally came, Mr. Maddox rasped: "Try to catch them!"

But it was an order that lacked conviction. Pete's lucky horseshoe had vanished in the night ahead. The river was only short blocks away. All traffic had to turn to right or left to cross one of the river bridges. A right turn for the bridge to Covington and the race track.

"We might find them in Covington," Mr. Maddox hazarded.

"You won't," Oscar differed abruptly. "That red horseshoe turned left at this corner."

Gayle made a reckless turn into the cross-street she had been about to pass, but Mr. Maddox was not convinced. "This is no time for gin guessing! D'you know what you're talking about, Oscar?"

"I've got eyes," Oscar said irritably. "You two were watching the cop and that red light. I know a horseshoe, don't I? I know right from left, don't I?"

"You didn't when you left that blonde," Mr. Maddox retorted.

"Here's the Interurban Terminal," Gayle said, slowing. "Could they have come here?"

"Why should they?" Mr. Maddox asked. But he was baffled enough to add: "Stop a minute. I'll make sure."

The terminal had been built for the electric cars running to points out of the city. And here now were taxis, automobiles, people. It was a long chance—but anything was worth trying. Gayle stayed with the car. Oscar got out with Mr. Maddox.

The last misty spits of rain were ending. The damp night had an invigorating freshness. Oscar drew a long breath. "I can walk straight anyway, Joe. Don't never throw any more blondes at me. I can't take 'em."

"They can take you, sucker."

"You don't have to rub it in."

Acey Hewett's flashy automobile was not in sight. They entered the terminal, and inside it was Oscar who exclaimed: "Ain't that the cigarette dame you want?"

Mr. Maddox looked and drew a breath of relief. "We're all right now. I'll do the talking."

She was looking impatiently at a wrist watch when Mr. Maddox loomed beside her and said: "Hello, Babe."

The startled hardness on her young face showed instant recognition. Mr. Maddox's hand on her arm stopped her quick step away. And her reaction was like an angry cat as she tried to twist free. "What do you think you're doing? Keep your dirty hands off me!"

"Where did they go, sister?"

"I don't know what you mean!"

"Acey and Phil. You know what I mean."

She knew. The guilt of it was in the quick pallor behind her make-up, the dart of her eyes around for some way of escape. But Mr. Maddox loomed over her, grimly careless of who might see him holding her arm.

"Do you come clean—or do you take the rap for it?"

"I'll call a cop!" she warned furiously. "I'll bring this whole damn station around!"

She could do it too. A policeman was loitering at the other end of the waiting-room. Two women nearby had noticed the little by-play and were watching curiously. Oscar looked jittery and apprehensive. More people would be eying them in a moment. If the girl screamed....

Mr. Maddox inwardly winced at the thought of what would follow if she screamed. She might even get by with it. How much chance was there to prove that a gun had been pulled on him at the Cabin Club? He had the gun—but it wouldn't help to be caught with it. You could lay hard money that Costigan, from St. Louis, had never bought the gun. And if Joe Maddox was in the headlines for molesting a girl and carrying a gun, it would look bad.

There was still time enough to back out. Still time to play safe. Oscar was almost audibly and prayerfully wishing to retreat. Mr. Maddox thought of all that—and rolled the dice for what they were worth.

"If it's murder, sister, you'll take the rap with the others. Go on and yell. Call that cop. You might as well be pinched now as later."

She looked like a cat at bay—a bold-faced, rouged little cat, frantic to use her claws. And afraid to. For she didn't scream. She didn't call the officer—and Mr. Maddox knew now how to handle her.

"Where were you going?" he demanded.

"None of your business!"

"Come on. Let's find Acey. And if you squawk, I'll call the cop myself."

For one dangerous moment she seemed about to scream after all. Then sullenly she went with him, his hand on her arm and Oscar walking gingerly on her other side. "I don't know anything!" she denied angrily. "You're wasting time bothering with me!"

"We're going after Acey, sister."

"I won't do you any good!"

"You didn't do Danny Locklin any good either, did you?"

That made her stiffen, look fearfully at him. Mr. Maddox growled at Oscar: "She's guilty as hell—and she'll come clean or else!"

"Call a cop and get rid of her," Oscar said bitterly. "She'll be screwy enough to start yelling and get pinched anyway."

"I think not. Sister, where's Solly's place?"

"I don't know!"

Sullenly, unwillingly she was crossing the wet street between them. And her denial had a ring of truth when you knew Acey Hewett's kind. Girls like this were told as little as possible and kept out of the way when not needed.

This girl had been needed until her boy friend was in Acey's car. That finished her part. She'd be better out of the way, out of town. She didn't have the polish, the smoothness of a girl like Lois. She was all right for a stable punk like Danny Locklin—and little more.

"Sure you don't know where Solly's place is?" Mr. Maddox demanded as they reached Gayle's car.

"I told you I didn't!"

"Is Acey coming back for you?"

"Nobody's coming anywhere for me!"

"Get in the back seat." Mr. Maddox stepped in the back after her and spoke to Gayle.

"She won't talk. We'll have to turn her over to the police. Drive out toward the airport while I give her one more chance. Pete was heading this way. Maybe he kept on toward the airport."

Gayle was fearful as she started the motor. "How do we know what's happening to Pete? We've got to do something quickly!"

"We'll go to headquarters if she won't talk," Mr. Maddox promised.

Gayle waited while another automobile passed them and parked at the curb ahead. They were pulling out and abreast of the other car when the girl beside Mr. Maddox suddenly screamed....

The girl had put the window down on her side—and that had seemed all right. But now without warning she was fighting to open the door and screaming through the window opening at the car they were passing.

"Duke! Duke! Get me!"

Mr. Maddox grabbed her. Through the open window he glimpsed a well-groomed young man emerging from the other car. And peering from the back seat was Costigan, of St. Louis. And another man, possibly two, were in the car with Costigan.

Babe, the cigarette girl, was all the wildcat that she had threatened to be, kicking, clawing as she fought to get out.

"Drive around the block and find a cop!" Mr. Maddox threw at Gayle. "Fast! We can't handle that bunch!"

CHAPTER SEVEN

MUDDY WATERS

GAYLE PICKED up speed in gear with a rush. Mr. Maddox caught Babe's arms, and pushed her down hard on the seat. "You aren't going anywhere, sister! It's a pinch for you now!"

She was swearing and kicking. The hard fast turn at the corner threw her against Mr. Maddox. She bit his arm. One hand jerked free and she clawed his face.

"Sock her!" Oscar yelled from the front seat. "Throw her out, Joe! They're taking us!"

Behind them tortured rubber shrieked in a racing turn. Mr. Maddox had been afraid of just what was happening. Costigan's car was fast. The driver was hot. Too hot for Gayle Brandon in a mad race like this through the city streets.

"Faster!" Mr. Maddox urged.

Headlights coming behind glared through the back window. Costigan's car was rocketing in second gear and closing fast. Gayle had to brake hard before making the turn at the next corner. Even at that she went around fast and recklessly. But not fast enough. Once more—tortured rubber behind them shrieked a mockery of her driving.

Costigan's car was over toward the far curb and almost up with them after it made the turn.

Mr. Maddox saw the car reeling and straightening out. And then the powerful motor of Costigan's car took hold and the car shot ahead, swerving back across the street. It passed them and cut in ahead, forcing Gayle to the curb. Her tires slid as she stamped hard on the brake pedal and wrenched over to the right to avoid a smash.

The front wheel hit the curb and snapped on around. The light sedan careened up on the sidewalk and crashed fender and wheel against an iron light-pole. Costigan's car slid to a stop ahead of them.

"Jump out and run like hell!" Mr. Maddox rasped at Gayle. "I'll hold them!"

He and the girl had been thrown off the seat. Mr. Maddox let her go, snatched at the door handle on his side and lunged out, drawing the gun.

Dismayed and helpless Gayle might be—but she obeyed without question. She was coming out from behind the wheel as Mr. Maddox lunged from the back seat. A sweep of his big arm sent her back of him. A gunshot crashed toward them. Mr. Maddox shoved the front door wide open and stood behind it.

Three men had boiled out of Costigan's car. Their purpose was plain. Mr. Maddox fired through the window opening… and then hell erupted on the night as three guns opened up at him. Costigan and his men were dodging forward, shooting as they came.

The metal door clanged and shook as bullets tore through it. The windshield smashed in little radiating lines around bullet holes. Lead struck other parts of the car. And lead drove through the flimsy protection of the door and hit Mr. Maddox's leg above the knee.

Mr. Maddox was measuring his shots. His third bullet dropped a man. He thought it was Costigan. Oscar had vanished. Gayle was gone. Mr. Maddox saw the cigarette girl darting behind the gun-men and entering the other car. The wounded man was trying to crawl back to the car.

Mr. Maddox squeezed the trigger again—and nothing happened. The clip hadn't been full, apparently. He swore helplessly and crouched behind the door. They'd pot him like a rabbit if he ran. They'd close in and riddle him if he waited helplessly here behind the door.

And a policeman's whistle shrilled loudly back at the corner. The two men still on their feet stopped shooting, grabbed the wounded man by the arms, shoved him into the automobile and bolted in after him. They retreated in a rush of gears and snoring exhaust.

The policeman fired one futile shot after the tail-lights, saw he could not stop the car and came on at a run. And the tail-lights of Costigan's car whirled around the next corner and vanished.

"Joe, are you all right?" Oscar called from the other side of the car.

"I guess so. Did they hit you?"

"They scared hell outa me. My God, Joe, we're in it now! Every cop in town will be on us!"

"Here comes the first one!"

MADDOX tossed the gun on the pavement and limped to the rear of the car. His wounded leg gave out flashes of pain but there was no time to bother with it now.

Gayle Brandon was returning. She seemed to be all right and it was a vast relief. Mr. Maddox had felt agonized guilt at bringing her into danger like this. He should have put her out at the post office and driven the car himself.

The cop dashed up, panting, waving his gun. He was raw-boned and young, and belligerently excited. "Get 'em up! What the hell's going on here? You, on the other side there! Come out here!"

"Never mind that rod," Oscar complained bitterly. "I've been shot at enough tonight!"

With his hands up, Mr. Maddox spoke no less harshly, urgently. "Get an alarm in for those men quick, officer! They attacked us! Three of them!"

"There'll be an alarm! Where's your gun?"

"On the pavement there."

"Got a permit?"

"Not for this state. The gun isn't mine. I was on my way to turn it in to the police!"

"Yeah? Stand back against the car! Both of you!"

"You're wasting time!" Mr. Maddox said harshly. "Look at the car here! You can see how they ran us into the curb! If you don't act fast, you'll be helping murder! It may be too late now!"

A flashlight glared over Mr. Maddox. The light shifted to Gayle as she reached them, breathing hard from her flight and hurried return. She was pale, but panic evidently had not unsettled her. Pete Cheney was on her mind as she appealed to Mr. Maddox. "They've gone after Pete, haven't they? They'll—they'll kill him!"

"Hear that, officer? She's talking about Pete Cheney, the jockey who rode Wink Thrice today, if you read the papers! He'll be next if those men aren't stopped!"

"That guy? That jockey? Sure I know who he is! He cost me ten dollars today!"

"Not Pete Cheney," Mr. Maddox denied. "He's a square-shooter on any horse. He was framed today. We were following the crooks who had Wink Thrice doped. Judge John Brandon, the owner, is this young lady's father. You can check all that. But do something now about those gunmen before it's too late!"

The light was full on Mr. Maddox's face as he spoke. "Isn't your name Maddox?" the officer demanded.

"Yes."

"I thought so, now you bring up that horse race! Your picture was in the paper this evening! Maybe you're talking straight after all!"

"D'you think I'd be standing here with a bullet in my leg kidding you?" Mr. Maddox demanded. "What do I get out of having those men stopped? We're safe here now. Do you know where Solly's place is?"

"Never heard of it.... What about this jockey, Cheney? Keep back, you people!"

TWO PASSING cars had stopped. People on foot were running to the spot. A siren was wailing just around the corner. From the next corner a second policeman was coming at a run. And Mr. Maddox talked fast, sketching with brief curt words the background that had led up to the shooting.

The officer turned to the first man out of the patrol car. "Do you know where Solly's place is?"

"Who's Solly? What happened here?... Say, Ed, you know where Solly's place is?" Ed was the driver who had jumped out on the other side and hurried around the front.

"Solly?" Ed repeated. "Never heard of it.... Wait a minute—you don't mean Solly's Fish Dock?"

"That might be the place," Mr. Maddox said quickly. "Where is it?"

"Out Eastern Avenue. Up the river, this side of Le Blond Park.

Fellow named Solly has got a float there on the bank. Kind of a houseboat at one end. He rents out boats and takes out fishing parties and buys and sells fish. I've been there. He used to bring moonshine down the river and peddle it off the float. He was picked up a couple of times and beat the charges in court. I remember when they put him through the line-up."

Now all that Mr. Maddox had said bore fruit. Even the newspaper publicity helped. The young officer did more than Mr. Maddox had hoped. "Maybe you two had better take Mr. Maddox, here, to this Solly's place. It won't take long. If Maddox is right, you haven't got any time to waste."

Gayle wanted to come. They wouldn't let her. Blood was still wet and warm on Mr. Maddox's leg as he sat on the front seat of the speeding patrol car.

Once more Mr. Maddox talked fast to cops who were hardboiled and not very impressed at first. It might have been the bullet-furrowed leg or Mr. Maddox himself, big, grim and urgent, that turned them grimly purposeful too.

The wailing siren cleared a way for their rush out of the business district and past freight yards on the river-front. The short-wave radio was growling words. Automobiles swerved aside to let them by. Pedestrians stopped and stared.

Now they were in a drab street lined with old brick houses and small stores. In past years Mr. Maddox had come this way to and from River Downs racetrack, a few miles up the river.

The driver's question was curt. "There's three in one car and two in the other?"

"If they didn't pick anyone up or drop anyone. I put a bullet in one man. I don't know how badly he's hurt."

"Nice going—if your story is true."

Mr. Maddox leaned forward. The growling monotone of the police announcer was describing Acey's car. Followed a rough description of Costigan's car, with orders for all members of the force to stop both automobiles on sight.

The information must have come from Oscar and Gayle Brandon, back there at the scene of the shooting.

The patrol car slowed abruptly, turned right into a narrow, unpaved street leading toward the river. And at the first cross-street an automobile stood before the corner house. The red glint of a horseshoe reflector showed above the license plate.

"That's Pete Cheney's car!" Mr. Maddox exclaimed. "He might be in it!"

The driver stopped short, backed up enough to turn over beside Pete's car. It was empty.

"We're right anyway," Mr. Maddox said. "Pete must be over by the river—if he's alive."

They lost less than a minute inspecting Pete's car, and half a block beyond, on the right, a crude board sign said: *SOLLY'S FISHING DOCK—Boats for hire. Fishing Parties.*

A painted arrow pointed toward the river. A last cross-street had a final row of drab brick houses, with yards, sheds, old fences straggling to the slope of the river bank. A last overhead light seemed dim and useless in the black sweep of night that reached out over the broad river. The down-sloping riverbank was scarred by past high waters and dotted with useless, flood-borne debris.

The fishing dock was an old float moored to the bank. A plank shanty bulked at one end. Small boats were tied against the float like sleeping ducklings. And the cop at the wheel exclaimed: "There's your two automobiles!"

The police spotlight lanced down the river bank to Acey Hewett's sporty touring car and Costigan's automobile, parked near the float with lights off. The spotlight shifted to the float like light spraying on an unreal stage where distant figures milled in quick confusion.

A gunshot came hard and sharp off the float. From the confusion two figures plunged off the outer edge of the float. The splash burst up like molten silver in the police beam. A burst of gunfire tattooed briefly on the night at the figures which had vanished into the river.

Then men were running off the float toward the parked automobiles and the police car was lurching, bouncing down the uneven river bank.

Acey's car was the first to start moving.

"Take the other car, Ed!" That was the cop at the wheel—and Ed went out the rear door in a reckless leap as the police car skidded and reeled over to the left to cut off the forward rush of Acey's car.

MR. MADDOX wrenched open the door and jumped before the crash. The wounded leg threw him into a sprawling fall that skinned hands and ground his cheek into the damp, smelly bank.

The patrol car stopped Acey's car with a mighty crash a few yards away as Mr. Maddox rolled over, spitting dirt. And what Mr. Maddox expected to happen did happen. Acey Hewett bolted from behind the steering wheel with his gun out and blasting. And the cop was getting out on the other side of the patrol car, the far side, where he couldn't stop Acey.

Mr. Maddox came up out of the dirt in a limping rush, reaching into his coat pocket. Acey saw him, thought he was drawing a gun, and fired wildly at the new threat. And missed....

Mr. Maddox was already swinging a big fist clenched on the little cylinder of lead. Acey stumbled. The fist hit his neck with Mr. Maddox's weight and rush behind it. The second shot from Acey's gun raked Mr. Maddox's side as Acey went spinning groggily back against his car.

Other guns were racketing on the night. The girl in Costigan's car was crying out shrilly as Mr. Maddox grabbed Acey's hand and gun, jerked Acey upright and hit the pale blob that was Acey's face. And hit it again and again until Acey collapsed, moaning.

The other guns had gone silent when Mr. Maddox yanked Acey around by the coat collar and gouged a gun muzzle into Acey's shrinking back. "Don't shoot, Joe! Don't, Joe!"

"I wish I could!" Mr. Maddox panted. "Where's Pete Cheney? Where's that stable boy?"

"I dunno!"

"You rats shot them and pushed them into the river when you saw us, didn't you?"

"They jumped," Acey mumbled.

"We saw it, damn you! It was murder!"

The police driver appeared behind Acey's car, yanking the young man called Phil by a handcuffed wrist, and holding a cringing little man in soiled white trousers and shirt. "Here's the guy who owns this fish dock! Who else we got?"

Costigan's car had not been started. One man, shot down before he reached it, was groaning on the ground. A second man stood near him with hands in the air. Babe, the cigarette girl, was sobbing as she got out. Death before her eyes had done what Mr. Maddox had not been able to do. Unnerved her, put her close to hysteria.

Mr. Maddox called: "They murdered Pete Cheney and the boy Pete was following! The bodies are in the river! Shut that girl's mouth! Where's that rat Costigan? Isn't that him kicking inside the car?"

MR. MADDOX shoved Acey over with the other prisoners, opened the back door of Costigan's automobile. Feet which had been kicking the door inside lashed out again as the door opened and lights came on inside.

For an instant it looked as if the floor space in back was filled with one huge misshapen body. Then it resolved into two figures crowded down out of sight in the cramped space. Al Costigan was one. His pale face was just inside the door. He was breathing heavily. Eyes were closed. A froth of blood stained his lips.

The other man had been kicking the door. His gagged face was red from exertion as he tried to shoulder Costigan's weight off his chest and sit up. Arms had been bound behind him. His wrists were tied to the foot rail, so that he could raise only a little in a twisted, strained position.

Mr. Maddox took one look—and chuckled in spite of the grim business about them. "Cassidy!" Mr. Maddox said. "I could tell by the feet!"

Cassidy's rage was choked to inarticulate sounds by the gag as Mr. Maddox called Cassidy's identity to the police and hurried around the car to the other door where he could get at Cassidy's wrists.

"Don't tell me," Mr. Maddox soothed as he worked on the cords. "It's a new way to slip up and pinch me. And a smart idea to gag yourself. You always did talk too much."

Cassidy was swearing thickly as his hands came free and he tore off the gag.

"You knew I'd walk back into something like this at the Cabin Club, Joe! You knew I'd get clipped as soon as they saw me!"

Cassidy's legs were cramped, stiff. Mr. Maddox steadied him as Cassidy stumbled out. And Mr. Maddox was sober in his denial. "Not this, Cassidy. I didn't think they'd put the mark on a Masterton cop like this. I'm not that kind of a louse. But you were crowding me and too bull-headed to listen."

"You're a louse," Cassidy said sourly. "But maybe not that bad, Joe. I was on the floor there when they were shooting at you downtown. Where's the guy who shoved a gun in my face when I looked in that office? He drove this car."

Ed, the policeman, called out violently on the other side of the car before Mr. Maddox could answer. "Who's that down there by the water?"

"Don't shoot!" a voice called weakly. "It's Pete Cheney and Danny Locklin!"

THEY staggered out of the river, a hundred yards downstream, as Mr. Maddox ran toward them and Cassidy, and Ed, the burly cop, followed. Pete was helping his companion. Both boys had been shot. Pete in the left arm. Danny Locklin in the shoulder. And Pete Cheney could still talk and even grin a little now as he faced them.

"Maybe I'm dumb. I sneaked up to see what Danny was doing— and when I heard him trying to beg off from getting in a boat, I jumped in to help him. They knocked me cold before I could punch twice. Danny figured they were going to kill him—and he was right. Only it was both of us after they got me."

"So it *was* murder?" Mr. Maddox said.

"Plenty of it," Pete said. "They were heading us into a boat when the other car came up. The men jumped out and said to get the hell out of here because somebody named Costigan was in the car dying and they had a Masterton detective in there too and the cops were coming.

"Two of them wanted to take us out in the river. The fellows that drove up last wanted to fix us there on the float and throw us in. Then your car showed up. They all looked at it. I hit the fellow beside me, pushed Danny in the river and jumped after him. They shot us when we hit the water. Danny couldn't swim. We almost didn't make it back to shore."

They reached the automobiles as Pete finished. "Do you know now who doped your horse?" Mr. Maddox asked.

Pete nodded, staring at the girl who was sitting miserably on the running board of Costigan's car. "I had a good idea when I started out tonight. Danny spilled everything while he was begging them not to take him out on the river. That tart introduced Danny to this guy," Pete said, nodding at Acey Hewett. "Danny had a brother who was doing life under another name. This guy knew the brother and knew Danny from him. They had a deal worked out with a man who was sure to be elected governor if Judge Brandon didn't beat him. Danny's brother would be pardoned if the man was elected. But if

Judge Brandon was governor, there wouldn't be any pardon. So they were framing the judge so he couldn't be elected."

"And Locklin was the boy?"

Pete nodded. "Around the barns we all thought Danny was all right. Maybe he was if his brother had been left out of it. I guess when you know your brother's doing life and you can help him, you'll take a chance. Anyway, Danny fell for it. Wink Thrice lost. Judge Brandon was in a hell of a mess. And then Danny lost his nerve and telephoned his girl that he wanted to see her before he skipped town. I didn't know that, but I was following Danny to see what he was up to. And when they drove here by the river I knew it wasn't kosher. I heard them say that the guy who owns the boats here is a big shot among the local dope peddlers. He got the dope they used on Wink Thrice."

"Is this a break!" Cassidy exclaimed. "The agency wants that fellow! Joe, maybe you'll get flowers out of this after all!"

"I'll look for a rock when I get them, Cassidy," Mr. Maddox said. "Better give the flowers to Pete Cheney and his girl. It turned out I was only following them while they did the hard work."

"Gayle's at home," Pete retorted. "She doesn't know anything about this."

"Gayle," said Mr. Maddox calmly, "almost got shot in the gunfight we had downtown. I met her at the Cabin Club out north of town where she'd gone to have a look at Danny Locklin's girl friend. Gayle's too swell a kid to be trying such things, Pete. Don't let her do it again."

"Where is she? Is she all right?"

"She's pinched," Mr. Maddox said. "Judge Brandon will probably be there, too, by now—and what he'll say doesn't matter. Hang onto that girl, son."

And even Oscar couldn't have been too cynical if he had heard Pete Cheney's husky promise. "Just watch me!"

TROT OUT YOUR MURDER!

WHEN THAT BLAND BUDDHA
OF THE BANGTAIL CIRCUIT
UNDERTOOK TO TURN A SPOILED
DARLING OF CAFÉ SOCIETY
INTO A FEMALE JORROCKS HE
NEVER DREAMED BLACKMAIL
AND MURDER WOULD REAR
THEIR UGLY HEADS TO PUT
HIM BEHIND THE 8-BALL. BUT
MURDER CAN GO AT A TROT
AS WELL AS A GALLOP—AND
YOU'RE JUST AS DEAD WHEN IT
CATCHES UP WITH YOU BETWEEN
THE SHAFTS OF A SATAN-
DRIVEN SULKY OR MOUNTED ON
A POSTAGE-STAMP SADDLE—
AS MADDOX SOON LEARNED
THE RACE-DAY HE DROVE
GOSHEN GA-GA TO KEEP THE
HAMBLETONIAN CLEAN.

CHAPTER ONE

A HORSE MEETS SOCIETY

THIS WEEK-DAY, about noon, Mr. Maddox drove swiftly up the Hudson River Parkway in speeding triple lines of traffic. To the right, Riverside Drive reared fabulous man-made cliffs to face the high stone cliffs across the great smooth river. And to the rear, the mid-Manhattan skyline formed dizzy peaks above the maelstroms at their feet.

And it was easy to believe that few other places on the wide earth could spawn so exotic a product as the girl who lounged beside Mr. Maddox in bored indifference.

Broadway, Fifth Avenue, Park Avenue and the night-club belt had spawned her. The Waldorf and the Ritz had given her background. An exclusive coiffeur had worked perfection with the tawny sheen of gold that was her hair. World-famous fashion experts had designed her hat and dress. And her smooth, oval, lovely face, her deep, brooding, long-lashed eyes could make even a hardened old bookie like Joe Maddox catch his breath every time he looked at her.

She was the ultimate in all that a great city could do for a woman— and she sat in smoldering, bored indifference as the big car carried her out of the city.

"The river's mighty pretty today," Mr. Maddox commented genially. "Look at those white yachts and gray battleships anchored out there. Like a painting, aren't they?"

She glanced indifferently at the wide sweep of river. Her yawn was a masterpiece of delicacy.

"Yachts," she declared, "bore me dreadfully."

Mr. Maddox loomed big and solid and richly impressive behind the gray plastic steering wheel. His chuckle was one of those vast

Tim's body rocketed off the sulky in a helpless plunge that carried hard against the inside fence.

deep spreading waves of humor that welled up into smiling crinkles on his broad bland face.

"Yachts bore you, do they?" Mr. Maddox said. "*Mmmmmm*—think of that."

The girl did not look as if she were thinking. With all her exotic

loveliness, her face was a bored blank as the big sedan rolled swiftly across the George Washington Bridge.

Highway 2 was a broad white concrete slab that carried them northward through the green Jersey countryside. When they crossed over into New York State again at Suffern the traffic was still heavy and the hand of the city was still hard upon them.

But the country grew more open, and in a little while—not much over an hour from the bridge—there was a broad flat field over to the right, below the level of the highway.

Tall trees were graceful and green at the far edge of the field, and a town was beyond. Under the first trees were long low green-painted horse barns and a small grandstand. And the white boundary fences of the racetrack formed a graceful oval under the early afternoon sunlight.

"There we are," Mr. Maddox said. "If we're lucky, Tim Lonergan's somewhere about the barns."

"Does it make any difference?" the girl said indifferently. "I came to get the horse—not this Lonergan person."

Mr. Maddox chuckled again.

"Tim Lonergan makes a lot of difference, anywhere. And Tim's not going to like this. Take it from Joe Maddox, Tim's not going to like this."

She shrugged, and few women could have so dismissed, obliterated, wiped out an unseen man with a mere shrug.

When you turned right off the highway at the filling station, you were driving into Goshen, New York—and the hard hand of the city had suddenly lost its grip upon you, if you were one of the elect, partial to harness racing.

As he straightened the blue sedan into the shaded roadway leading into Goshen, Mr. Maddox took his foot off the gas, his big hands off the wheel, and exhaled pleasurably as he reached for a cigarette.

"It's going to be a great Hambletonian this year. Nothing like the Hambletonian. I haven't missed one for over twenty years."

The girl yawned and opened a hand-chased platinum vanity case and inspected her flawless features. A crimson fingernail that was a work of art in itself made little delicate touches at eyebrows and eyelashes.

Mr. Maddox smiled ruefully. "You just don't like horses, eh?"

"I suppose they're all right," she said absently. "Heaven knows they must be all right, by the way the photographers and columnists flock to Belmont."

"Mmmmm—horses have gone social in the last few years all right," Mr. Maddox agreed.

THEY were in the little tree-shaded town of Goshen now. Automobiles were behind them and ahead of them as Mr. Maddox turned right into an old narrow street and followed other cars toward the small racetrack.

And it was a small track, neat and old and rather shabby when you were used to the great multi-million-dollar flat-racing tracks near the metropolitan centers.

To all outward appearances the city had come here to the little Goshen track in surprising numbers. Rows of sleek cars were already parked on the green grass behind the small grandstand.

Well-dressed men and women were thronging about the grandstand, strolling around the barns and standing at the low track fence to watch the piston-drive of trotters and pacers between the shafts of dainty, bright-colored sulkies.

But there was a difference if you knew horse racing and horse tracks. It was in the air and all about. Not even Saratoga, home and heart of the thoroughbred world, had this friendly, leisurely, country-fair atmosphere.

At Hialeah and Santa Anita, at Washington Park and Bowie and Churchill Downs, the horse barns were away from the crowd, unnoticed, unthought of for the most part. Sleek, dainty thoroughbreds appeared in the saddling sheds of those tracks. Diminutive jockeys in gay racing silks were hoisted on the postage-stamp saddles, paraded before the grandstands, raced briefly, and vanished from the sight and interest of the crowd.

But here at Goshen the stables were close beside the grandstand. Horses, drivers, stable help and spectators were one friendly unit drawn together by the common bond of harness racing.

And in all the gathering crowd this afternoon there was no man more distinguished than the big, well-fleshed figure of Joe Maddox. No face more friendly and beaming than that broad bland face known from coast to coast among the racing fans and betting fraternity.

And in all the crowd this afternoon there was no woman so gorgeous, so exotic and breathlessly lovely as the girl who walked rather distastefully to the horse barns beside Mr. Maddox.

Many eyes turned to follow them. And Joe Maddox, for all his shrewd wisdom and experience, might have lost some of his friendly smile if he could have dissected the thoughts behind two pairs of those eyes, or could have heard the monosyllabic remarks passed between two men.

But Tim Lonergan was on Mr. Maddox's mind—and Tim Lonergan they found in the third barn back from the track. Or rather they found Tim Lonergan's loud emphatic voice issuing from a horse stall.

"Toe weights hell! I know what weights she needs! Put those two-ounce ones back on her and she'll step like a lady!"

The smell of straw and manure, of leather and liniment and horses was sweetly rank before the serried stalls as Mr. Maddox called through the doorway.

"Here's a lady, Tim, who don't need toe weights. Brush off your talk and put on your manners. It's a day for the house of Lonergan—and your worries are over."

The loud voice came back disgustedly past the horse blocking the doorway.

"My worries'll never be over while I have to fight with a stubborn, bull-headed banshee's son who stopped thinking when he was hock-high!"

Tim Lonergan came up out of the straw, ducking under the horse's sleek neck. All six feet of Tim Lonergan, in shirt sleeves and soiled khaki trousers, black hair rumpled and bits of straw clinging to the knees where Tom had been kneeling.

"Any lady needs toe weights to keep her pretty feet—"

Tim Lonergan stopped in the doorway in midstride and midspeech. His eyes fixed in startled fascination on Mr. Maddox's companion. A flush struck Tim Lonergan's hard, tanned face. His mouth opened soundlessly—and after a moment his greeting was weak.

"Hello, Maddox. I didn't know it was you."

"Miss Allison—Tim Lonergan," Mr. Maddox said blandly.

Tim Lonergan ducked his head. The flush was still on his face. The slightly dazed look was still in his eyes.

"Miss Allison?" Tim mumbled. "Er—it's Miss Anne Allison, isn't it? Uh—how do you do?"

"How do you do?" she said coolly.

AND YET somehow in the space of a disapproving moment something had happened to her. She was not so bored now. Tim Lonergan had struck sparks against her indifference.

Her long-lashed eyes looked Tim over from soiled trousers to rumpled hair. Her nostrils quivered at the stable reek. And it was plain to see that she resented Tim Lonergan's handsome bulk along with horses and stables and all this business with which she had become involved.

And Tim Lonergan saw it and was puzzled.

Mr. Maddox broke the awkward moment with a chuckle.

"Tim, I see you keep up with the newspapers even if you aren't in New York much. Since you know who Miss Allison is, we can get to the point. Miss Allison wants a horse. And you've got horses to sell, eh? I know you had the other day, anyway."

Tim Lonergan nodded. His dazed look gave way to a friendly grin.

"That's right, Joe. I've still got 'em." And Tim drew a deep breath of satisfaction and spoke eagerly.

"Miss Allison, I didn't suspect you liked horses. And especially harness horses. Say, this is great. I—do you own any already?"

"All I want," said Anne Allison coldly, "is a horse that will win the Hambletonian this year."

Mr. Maddox could appreciate Tim's wondering look.

"That's some order," Tim said with dawning amusement. "A lot of us spend a lifetime looking for a horse that will win the Hambletonian." And Tim grinned indulgently. "You see, Miss Allison, when you have to enter a horse before he's born in a race that's run at three years old, you've got a long gamble that you'll ever get anything that's worth while."

Her shrug dismissed all that.

"I've decided to win the Hambletonian this year. Those in a position to know tell me you have a horse that probably will win this year. I don't remember his name."

"Larkspur," Tim said and his smile was still indulgent. "He's good. But we have our fingers crossed."

"Is he better than Blanche Carter's horse?"

"Well, we think so," Tim said cautiously. "That Peter Kline is some horse. Miss Carter was lucky to get him from Colonel Goodspeed last year. And Lon Wescott is a good trainer. He's brought Peter Kline along mighty well. The public seems to think well of him."

"Too well," Anne Allison said coldly. "You'd think no other horse ever existed and no other woman was ever so clever as this Carter girl in owning that horse. The publicity she's been getting has turned her head. I'm satisfied with the chances your horse has of beating her horse. I'll take him—and show her a thing or two."

"Just a minute," Tim said, and he had stopped smiling. "You want a race horse that will beat Peter Kline, just because the Carter girl is getting a run of publicity?"

Tim's voice gathered volume. "You want to buy Larkspur and win the Hambletonian so you can cut in on her publicity? All the Hambletonian means to you is a chance to get your name and your pictures in the papers more than you appear already as one of the leaders of cafe society?"

"Don't shout at me," Anne Allison said coldly. "It really isn't any of your affair why I want the horse. I said I'd take him. And I'm willing to pay you liberally to finish training him for the race. I'll even give you part of the purse if you win."

Tim Lonergan's flush returned in a beet-red flood that went clear up into his black hair.

"Larkspur," Tim said in a stifled voice, "is not for sale! And even if he were,"—Tim's voice was rising again—"even if I were down to my last dime and my feed bill cut off and begging for a buyer to take him off my hands, he wouldn't be sold for that purpose, Miss Allison! Why—why—" Tim choked on the surging violence of his feeling.

"Cafe society!" Tim exploded. "Girls like you, Miss Allison, with a fortune on your backs, and faces to stop the heart of any poor fool of a man! And only envy and froth in your empty heads! Deciding to buy my Larkspur like he was a—a blasted new hat, so you can win the Hambletonian and get your picture in the papers! I'm not pleased to have met you, Miss Allison, and a good day to you, ma'am! The lady in the stall here is more to my liking!"

Tim ducked his head furiously in the trace of a bow and was swearing under his breath as he swung around to enter the stall.

And Mr. Maddox stood there mute, flabbergasted, helpless for once in his life. Even knowing Tim Lonergan, he had not expected this outraged explosion at such an early point.

And the worst, Mr. Maddox thought with an inward groan, was yet to come, if he knew Anne Allison and Tim Lonergan. And by now he felt that he did.

CHAPTER TWO

SPOILS TO THE SPOILED

IT WAS doubtful if any man had ever talked so to Anne Allison in all her pampered life. And yet, knowing her father, Mr. Maddox was not greatly surprised to see a furious and suddenly human girl whose fists clenched and who looked as if she would be pleased to claw Tim Lonergan into helpless confusion.

And it was at that precise moment that Mr. Maddox became aware of two men who had strolled around the end of the barn and had been idly looking at horses in nearby stalls.

They were near enough to have heard everything that the raised voices had said. Nevertheless, they were apparently absorbed in their scrutiny of the horse in that particular stall. And the slender elegant build and pale close-shaven profile of one of them was enough to make Mr. Maddox warn under his breath.

"Hold it, Miss Allison! You're saying too much out loud!"

She heard him—his voice, at any rate—for her blazing look went to him for an instant. Only an instant. Then she followed Tim Lonergan to the stall doorway and her voice was sharp and cutting and triumphant.

"I hope, Mr. Lonergan, that horse whose company you prefer to mine is not Larkspur! For if it is, you're not going to have the pleasure very long!"

"Go away!" Tim Lonergan shouted from inside the stall. "Take her away, Maddox! You've got a nerve bringing her here!"

Still the two strangers were not looking. Still they seemed to be absorbed only in the horse that occupied that second stall. And Mr. Maddox swore savagely under his breath.

When a big Broadway gambler and ex-racketeer like Roscoe Knerr stalled with an act like this, something was in the wind. And it would be crooked! For Roscoe Knerr was crooked. And it would not be nice because the word had never been applied to Roscoe Knerr.

Even Knerr's first name was not nice if you knew about it. The underworld had tagged him "Roscoe" because too often gunplay had been connected with his crooked business.

"Miss Allison!" Mr. Maddox begged.

But he was wasting breath. Anne Allison spoke bitingly through the stall doorway.

"You may be interested to know I'm going to take your Larkspur horse!"

"Will you go away?" Tim Lonergan shouted again. "Your old man may own a steamship line and be crawling with millions—but you haven't got enough money to buy a headstall out of my tack! Now go away!"

"I had enough money," Anne Allison said furiously, "to buy up the notes you gave Cary Willard! They're demand notes and my lawyers tell me they're collectible at any time. I suppose this afternoon you have forty-five thousand dollars and accumulated interest! If you have, I'll take it while I'm here!"

That brought even Roscoe Knerr's pallid face around. And by now Mr. Maddox didn't care much. For he knew he was listening to a lovely and furious girl smashing the heart and the hopes of a fine young man.

The silence that fell inside the stall was more eloquent than words. Then Tim Lonergan appeared in the doorway. Tim seemed to have gone pale and haggard all in a moment. He was quiet now, as if all the fire had been quenched.

Tim looked over Anne Allison's head.

"Is that right, Maddox?"

"I guess it is, Tim," Mr. Maddox said uncomfortably.

"You knew it when you brought her here?"

"Yes, Tim," Mr. Maddox said. "I guess I thought something could be worked out. Anyway, it was none of my doing. I've covered money for Miss Allison's father for years, and some for Miss Allison—and the least I could do was to drive Miss Allison out here and hope that something could be worked out."

Tim rubbed his forehead like there was a hurt inside.

"Cary Willard said he needed the money—but I didn't think he'd do anything like this. I told him I'd try to raise the money."

"He had to have cash," Mr. Maddox said. "Miss Allison gave him cash. Cary didn't know what would follow."

"Larkspur is worth more than forty-five thousand," Tim said with an effort.

"Oh, I'm prepared to give you the difference," Anne Allison said coldly. "All I want is the horse. You won't lose anything in spite of this scene you're making. Are you going to be reasonable about it?"

Tim Lonergan looked at her. His eyes were burning. "You win," Tim said in a calm and rather terrible voice.

Tim lifted his strong hands that could hold the reins on the wildest horse and master dangerous melees of racing sulkies on tight turns.

"If you were a man," Tim added thickly, "I'd break your neck! As it is, I'll give you publicity—and not the kind you want. The newspapers will get this story and get it straight! And when I'm through, you'll be a laugh in the headlines! Get out those notes of mine you bought! I'll turn Larkspur over now—and I hope this is the last I'm forced to see of you!"

Item: WALLY WINZER'S PEEP-HOLE

What's this about glamour—lovely Anne Allison overboard from family steamships and the Nities for harness racing at Goshen this month, with good chance of winning the famous Hambletonian?

Item: BARNEY CALLIGAN'S SPORT-TALK

Some buzzing and gab along the main stem and up at Goshen about the sensational transfer of Tim Lonergan's Larkspur to Anne Allison, the Park Avenue Orchid and heiress of the Allison Steamship dough.

Tim Lonergan broadcasts, his horse was snitched from him on a slick squeeze and says he's laughing about having his real Hambletonian winner in the other hip pocket. Candy Kid will pull the Lonergan sulky in the Hambletonian. The wise birds are scratching and wondering.

Item: MANHATTANITES, by Cecelia Havermeyer

Delightfully daring is Anne Allison's assault on harness racing at Goshen this month. Gasps of unbelief greeted photographs of lovely Anne in personal charge of her new racing stable. And *entre nous,* how eyebrows have lifted over whispers of a regrettable feud developing between two of society's now enthusiastic horsewomen. We didn't catch the names—but guesses are in order.

Item: WALLY WINZER'S PEEP-HOLE

It's a toss-up between Blanche Carter and Anne Allison at Goshen. Fast work, say the know-it-alls, for Anne to take that suite at a Goshen hotel and go all-out in her spectacular attempt to win the Hambletonian. Buzz McAllister, whose "rubber" checks never bounce, reported cheering on both the gals.

Item: SHOOTING IT STRAIGHT, by Hank Ristine

The dope's all scrambled on the leather carrying gee-gees coming up for the Hambletonian. What with the Allison heiress shoveling wads of dough to offset her inexperience and get the breaks for her Larkspur. Anyway, there's interest aplenty at Goshen this month and the city slickers are going in a big way for the country-fair type of racing.

We're watching the Lonergan entry. Tim Lonergan has learned many a trick in his wide experience on the "punkin" tracks. When they go under the barrier in the Hambletonian, the Irish Apollo will be driving his horse. A million bucks can't pull a fancy rein in a tight spot.

Item: CLOCKER SCOTT'S SLANT

Get aboard the Lonergan entry in the Hambletonian. There's something going on there. The boxcar dough on Larkspur is owner-dough and the flash workout figures and the odds don't mean anything. Nuf sed.

It was Monday evening and Joe Maddox was riding up in the elevator to his suite at the Vardon Hotel, just off Times Square, when he read that last item of many that had appeared during the past several days. Mr. Maddox folded the paper and swore under his breath.

Pinky, the elevator boy, grinned wisely. "They hit you today, Mr. Maddox?"

"If that was all I had to worry about," Mr. Maddox growled, "I wouldn't be getting indigestion!"

The growl was still in Mr. Maddox's voice and a scowl was on his broad face as he shouldered into the suite, found Oscar in the bathroom shaving, and demanded: "Get any more of that dough on Peter Kline this afternoon?"

Oscar, wizened and sardonic, was the one who answered the telephones, put down the bets, and did most of the paper work for Joe Maddox's book.

And now Oscar turned from the mirror and spoke through a mask of lather.

"Another grand came in. What's the dope on that race, Joe? Are we taking sucker money on that Peter Kline horse—or are we getting the hook?"

"If I knew, I wouldn't be driving up to Goshen and back every day like a damned commuter!" Mr. Maddox snapped. "I hear one thing and I hear another. I read one thing and I read something else. The clockers are flipping nickels to decide what to say. Tim Lonergan is sore at me and won't talk. And the Hambletonian is day after tomorrow."

Oscar tilted his head, went to work with the safety razor and spoke cynically from a mouth screwed out of shape.

"A horse is a horse. Ain't you seen enough of them to dope this Peter Kline out yourself?"

"That's why I'm jumpy. That's why I don't know whether I'm a sucker or a wise guy!" Mr. Maddox snapped. "Larkspur is a better horse than Peter Kline. They're training Peter Kline too fine, from all I can gather. That Carter girl is getting jumpy, I hear, and bearing down on her trainer. She and Anne Allison have got Goshen ga-ga with their feud. The dough they and their friends are putting up don't leave any sense in the odds."

Oscar cut himself, said, "Damn!" and muttered: "Somebody will clean up."

"My private opinion," Mr. Maddox said sourly in the doorway, "is that Tim Lonergan could take a plow-horse and a hay wagon and run circles around these society entries."

"But the smart money," Oscar reminded, "keeps showing up on Blanche Carter's Peter Kline. That grand this afternoon was from Louie Menzie, who runs the Swiss Tavern. He brought it up himself and said maybe he'd have some more. He's no dope."

Mr. Maddox probed for a moment in an uncanny memory, and spoke ominously.

"Menzie's brother-in-law used to be pay-off man for Roscoe Knerr. I remember when he was shot. Don't tell me Knerr hasn't got a crooked finger in this somewhere. I smelled it coming that day Anne Allison took Tim Lonergan's horse away."

"I'm not telling you anything," Oscar mumbled as he scraped under his chin. "I'm asking you, Joe. What are you gonna do about it?"

"If I knew," Mr. Maddox growled, "I wouldn't want a drink so bad before I eat. Where's that Scotch?"

But Mr. Maddox never got to the bottle of Scotch. One of the two telephones rang. And the voice, when Mr. Maddox answered, was low, furtive, hurried.

"Maddox back yet?"

"Who is it?"

"That you, Maddox? It sounds like you."

"This is Joe Maddox."

"I been after you all afternoon. Look, Joe, this is Dandy Hoke. You remember me—Dandy Hoke?"

Mr. Maddox had to think a moment before he placed the name— and then his reply had no warmth.

"I remember you—and none of it's much good. What do you want? I'm too busy to be wasting time with chiselers."

Dandy Hoke took no offense. His furtive voice pitched a shade higher, toward a placating whine.

"O.K., Joe—I know you got no time to waste. Would I be buzzing you like this for nothing? I got a deal for you. It's worth fifty on the line tonight, Joe. Bring half a C over an' talk to me, Joe. I'm in the Carlew. Room 306."

"Listen you!" Mr. Maddox said with cold emphasis. "If it was cigar bands, and you were outside my window, I wouldn't lean out and listen. The nerve of you asking me to bring over half a C. And don't come up here or I'll have you tossed out on your ear."

"Look, Joe—don't take it that way! I'd come over there if I could. So help me."

"Hang up and don't bother me!"

Mr. Maddox was putting the telephone down when he caught Dandy Hoke's feverish words tumbling out of the receiver.

"It's about Goshen—"

MR. MADDOX snatched the handset back. His broad bland face was suddenly hard with attention.

"What was that you said, Hoke?"

"Goshen, Joe."

"What about Goshen?"

"Slip fifty in your pocket an' come over here," Dandy Hoke begged.

"It's worth more, Joe. You'll say so—an' make it right with me. But I gotta have fifty tonight, Joe. You won't be sorry."

"I'd better not be."

"Knock four times on 306, Joe. One heavy an' three light. I'm not using my right name here."

"That," said Mr. Maddox, "wouldn't be anything new. I'll stop by if I get the time."

That was an understatement. Mr. Maddox hung up and was reaching for his hat as he called to Oscar.

"Anybody by the name of Dandy Hoke been trying to get me this afternoon?"

"Nobody gave that name," Oscar said, looking out of the bathroom. "But I forgot, Joe. Some lug telephoned two or three times, asking for you. He wouldn't give no name."

"How do you know it was a lug?"

"I've heard enough lugs over enough telephones since I been taking horse bets," Oscar answered cynically. "This guy was a lug and he had something on his mind."

"I'll meet you at Jimmy's place," Mr. Maddox said as he started for the door.

"Where you going?"

"To see what's in that lug's mind," Mr. Maddox said, and was gone.

The Hotel Carlew was on the other side of Times Square, toward Eighth Avenue. When new the Carlew had not been so very respectable. Now it was not new and glad to welcome most of the dredgings off the shady fringes of Broadway.

A tourist might not have suspected, but a man like Joe Maddox could sort and classify the lobby crowd with a glance or two. And tonight Mr. Maddox was barely inside the door before he made a nimble turn toward an empty lobby chair which held a discarded newspaper.

In another moment he was at ease in the chair, eyeing the desk past the edge of the open paper. That stocky grizzled man talking to the desk clerk was Cassidy, of the Masterton Agency, which guarded horse tracks from coast to coast. Cassidy, who had for years been trying to catch Joe Maddox, the bookie, in some matter outside the law.

Now Cassidy nodded to the clerk and headed for the elevators.

Mr. Maddox thoughtfully muttered, "Damn!" and watched Cassidy enter an elevator and start up.

It was a good bet that Cassidy had been questioning the desk clerk about Dandy Hoke. Now with Cassidy in the elevator, Mr. Maddox glumly resigned himself to Cassidy's seeing Hoke first. Cassidy was that kind of a detective.

No other passengers went up. Mr. Maddox watched for the floor indicator to stop at the third floor. But the hand went on around as the elevator continued upward. And Dandy Hoke didn't belong up there on the eighth floor where the elevator finally stopped.

There was a chance that Cassidy didn't even know that Dandy Hoke was in the hotel. Mr. Maddox smiled grimly crossed the lobby and his big bulk took the stairs with surprising nimbleness. There was at least a chance now to see what Hoke had on his mind. And the stairs held no sharp-eyed elevator operators to remember who had gone up to the third floor.

Room 306 was to the right of the elevators, around a turn in the corridor. Mr. Maddox heard the elevator that Cassidy had taken come back down without stopping. And he made the turn in the corridor just as a girl emerged from 306 and closed the door....

She turned, saw the bulk of him coming toward her. She did not gasp—but she looked as if inwardly she were gasping. And as if she were gripped by the cold hand of horrified helplessness. She seemed to be trying to decide what to do and was not thinking fast enough in a sudden emergency.

Mr. Maddox helped her. The bland good humor of his broad face showed only cursory interest as he walked leisurely past the girl and the room from which she had just emerged. But keen eyes that could note a split-hair change in the odds, the suspicious flicker of a jockey's eye, the shade of staleness in a favorite going to the post, missed nothing about the girl.

She was vastly relieved at being ignored. And behind all that was a dazed, white-faced emotion she was fighting to suppress.

They passed. The girl hurried to the turn of the corridor and was gone. And Mr. Maddox thought hard about her as he walked to the window at the end of the corridor and turned back.

A girl coming out of Dandy Hoke's room would be nothing unusual. Even a girl like this, who was far from the Broadway type. Hoke and his kind chiseled among her kind. They hunted where the bankrolls were fattest.

Hoke would be at his smooth ease with that athletic-looking girl with the wide mouth and high cheekbones. She had the air, the look of money and background. And all unconsciously so, as girls did who had always taken such things for granted.

Oh, yes—the Dandy would be at his ease with her. But he wouldn't be meeting her in one of the shadiest hotels around Times Square. You simply didn't find girls like her slipping in and out of hotels like this.

Mr. Maddox knocked on 306. And knocked again. And for a moment wondered if he had the right room.

The Carlew was an old hotel, without spring locks on the doors. Mr. Maddox tried the knob. The door swung in on a darkened room. Which might have meant anything.

Mr. Maddox stepped in and fumbled for the light switch to see what it did mean. He blinked as the light went on. And then for a long moment stood staring at the disordered room—and finally reached for the doorknob and closed the door and moved into the room, staring about with narrowed, hardening eyes.

CHAPTER THREE

HOMICIDE OF A HEEL

THE ROOM had been ransacked. Thoroughly. Dresser drawers were pulled out. A coat and trousers lay in the clothes closet doorway. They had been pulled off the hangers, searched and dropped. On the bed was a man's Panama hat. The contents of a tan traveling bag had been lifted out and tossed on the floor.

And Mr. Maddox was in the center of the room, taking in everything, when his breath sucked harshly and his eyes riveted through the open doorway of the bathroom.

A man was in there. Mr. Maddox had no slightest doubt that the foot and the leg hanging over the edge of the bathtub belonged to Dandy Hoke.

This was the horror that had been behind the girl's pale fright when she slipped out of the room. No wonder she had gasped inwardly, had stood in frozen indecision when she unexpectedly faced a stranger as she left.

Wire-tight nerves warned Mr. Maddox to follow her fast. Get out of the room, out of the hotel quickly and inconspicuously. This was no place for Joe Maddox. No place for a nationally known bookie whose normal business forced more contacts with the underworld than he relished.

But instead Mr. Maddox stepped into the bathroom and switched the pitiless glare of overhead light on white tile and porcelain.

Dandy Hoke was in the bathtub and the Dandy would never bathe again. He had not been bathing this time. He was fully dressed in a light tan worsted summer suit, pale tan silk shirt and expensive white-and-tan summer shoes. Carefully, tastefully dressed, as Dandy Hoke and his kind were usually certain to be. And Hoke looked as if he had fallen back into the tub hard, clumsily, helplessly, before he died.

The white-tiled floor showed no blood. But there was blood on Dandy Hoke's coat front and silk shirt. And powder marks on the coat and a small round hole over the heart.

Mr. Maddox swore softly.

The Dandy had moved about in the tub before he died. Blood was crimson on his right hand where it had fumbled at the death wound. Finger smears were gruesomely vivid on the back side of the tub, where the Dandy's fingers had aimlessly pressed before he died.

Mr. Maddox's foot was touching a damp bath towel, scorched and stained in spots. He picked up the towel and held it full length.

The stains were powder stains around small holes down the center of the towel. Bullet holes, of course, scorched at the edges by the fiery muzzle blast of a gun.

The powder smell still hung in the air. The wet towel spoke for itself. Mr. Maddox muttered aloud for the comfort of the sound in that bright-tiled little room of death.

"Wadded a towel around the gun to stop some of the noise—and maybe keep Hoke from seeing what was coming! The cloth started to smolder and was dunked under a faucet! And while Hoke was dying here in the tub, his room was frisked!"

A purse had been tucked under the girl's arm as she went out. With the first surprise over, Mr. Maddox could think with grim detachment. He had called the Dandy a chiseler. He could have called him worse.

More than one woman—and man too—probably had reason to

wish Dandy Hoke dead. Blackmail was not the least source of Dandy Hoke's shady livelihood. There could be plenty of reason for the girl coming here to see Hoke and killing him and frantically searching the room for evidence which had given Hoke a hold on her.

Mr. Maddox bent over the tub and felt the dead man's wrist. The flesh was still warm. Blood had barely started to congeal. The Dandy had been dead only a little while.

And then, still leaning over the tub, Mr. Maddox uttered a startled grunt and twisted the better to see something he had not noticed before.

Hoke's bloody right hand had made crimson marks on the front side of the tub. But not aimless marks. Mr. Maddox was looking down at crude, wavering letters which the Dandy had traced while he died. Letters placed so that one had to be leaning over the tub before they were clearly visible.

Ann Alisn

THE LAST *n* was crude and wavering off into illegibility as if the Dandy's life and strength were going fast. But there it was, smeared vividly against the white porcelain.

Anne Allison—accused by the last move of a dying man. Anne Allison—who was in all the headlines for her latest publicity stunt at Goshen. And Dandy Hoke had telephoned Joe Maddox in high agitation about some business that concerned Goshen....

Mr. Maddox straightened, reached for his handkerchief and mopped his broad face. He felt as if perspiration were breaking out.

It was not hard to believe that the Dandy had been afraid this might happen. He had been hiding here in the Carlew under another name, without money. Oh, it was easy to believe this black-haired, narrow-shouldered young crook had been hiding.

But not easy to believe he had been hiding from Anne Allison. Anne was not the girl who had hurriedly left the room. Anne was staying at Goshen these days. Anne Allison couldn't possibly have done this!

Mr. Maddox bent again to study the damning blood letters....

There they were. There the Homicide men would find them. There police cameras and newspaper cameras would record them for evidence and the headlines. There in crimson blood on porcelain and steel was the final payoff of publicity that would engulf and destroy lovely Allison.

Mr. Maddox cursed. He didn't want to believe it—and there it was. There crumpled in the bathtub was Dandy Hoke and the blood-stained finger that had damned Anne Allison.

Up there in Goshen was Anne Allison and her petty feud with the Carter woman over gossipy publicity. And over on Park Avenue, in a costly apartment, was old Buck Allison, bulwarked behind his ships and his millions.

Money and success had not changed Buck Allison a great deal from the broad-shouldered, heavy-fisted young fellow who had started out with a couple of old lumber schooners on the Pacific Coast.

Buck Allison had never been a good picker of horses. But he had laughed when he lost and laughed when he won. And the girl who had not been born those long years ago on the Coast would bring no laughter to Buck Allison if this hit the headlines.

It would probably be a waste of time to search Hoke's room again. And each minute Joe Maddox wasted here made his own risk more acute. But Mr. Maddox had never been more grimly, deliberately calm as he took a hand towel off the rack, wet it, rubbed on soap, and bent over the tub.

When he was through the towel was stained and Anne Allison's name had been wiped out of the headlines. For a short time at least.

With the same towel Mr. Maddox rubbed the light switch he had touched and put out the bathroom light. He wiped the light switch in the bedroom and the inside doorknob.

He listened for sound outside in the hall, heard nothing, and used the towel to open the door. He rubbed the outer knob hard, tossed the towel back in the room, and with his handkerchief closed the door as he went out.

He descended the stairs without encountering anyone.

The girl was not in the lobby. Mr. Maddox had not expected her to be. Cassidy was not in sight either. There could be nothing suspicious about the big bland man who came unnoticed off the stairs and strolled leisurely to the street.

Only when he reached the sidewalk and turned toward Times Square did Mr. Maddox draw a slow breath of relief. And then he almost swore aloud as Cassidy's familiar, stocky figure came up from behind and fell into step.

Cassidy was smiling—and the thin smile might have meant anything.

"I didn't know you were staying at that dump, Joe," Cassidy said.

CHAPTER FOUR

CASSIDY ASKS THE TIME

MR. MADDOX smiled too, and it was an effort. "Who said I was staying there? Where did you drop from?"

Cassidy's smile continued.

"I was just passing. You're not staying at the Carlew?"

"Stop stalling," Mr. Maddox said. "You know I stay at the Vardon. Why so much interest?"

"Habit, I guess. Who do you know in the Carlew, Joe?"

"No one."

"No one?"

"That's right."

"Just wandered in there, I suppose?"

"Something like that," Mr. Maddox nodded. "I wanted the time. Any more questions?"

"Well, who's going to win the Hambletonian day after tomorrow?"

Mr. Maddox chuckled with some sincerity. "If I could answer that, I'd make some money, Cassidy. What's your sudden interest in the Carlew?"

"I was looking for a fellow."

"I don't know him."

"I'll bet not," Cassidy nodded. "Seeing much of the racing at Goshen, Joe?"

"Some."

"How is the money being bet on the Hambletonian?"

"How should I know?" Mr. Maddox replied from force of habit. For years—too many years—Cassidy's sharp wits had been trying to catch Joe Maddox taking illegal bets around the big horse tracks. And now Cassidy was plainly driving at something.

"If you don't know, nobody knows," Cassidy said idly. "I hear you drove that Allison girl to Goshen the day she took Larkspur away from Tim Lonergan."

"Did you?" Mr. Maddox said noncommittally.

"That's a funny situation," Cassidy mused.

"Is it?"

"Tim Lonergan swears she can throw money ankle deep around the track and still won't win the Hambletonian with his Larkspur. Lonergan's got a fine hate on her. And *vice versa*."

"Interesting," Mr. Maddox said blandly. "You're keeping up with things, aren't you, Cassidy?"

"I hear things," Cassidy shrugged. "That Miss Carter's Peter Kline has got a lot on the ball. It ought to be a race, Joe."

"It usually is."

"Three big owners. Three good horses. Big money being bet. Plenty of room for crooked work, Joe."

"Show me a horse race and I'll show you room for crooked work," Mr. Maddox murmured—and inwardly he was thinking of the body in that third-floor bathtub.

Already a maid might have entered the room. Already the police might be coming, to search, probe, ask pointed questions. If not now, then any minute, any hour. And Cassidy's oblique, carelessly misleading questions were driving at some point that was hot and hard in Cassidy's mind.

"You know how the Masterton Agency feels about horse races and crooked work, Joe."

"You've caused me enough trouble in the past with your hunches and ideas," Mr. Maddox said bluntly.

"I just thought I'd mention it," Cassidy said amiably.

They had reached the bright lights, the crowded streets and walks of Times Square. Cassidy stopped. "What time have you got, Joe?"

Mr. Maddox glanced instinctively at his wrist watch. "Eight twenty-five."

"Thanks," Cassidy nodded, and his smile was thin, his voice gentle. "Did you say you went into the Carlew to get the time, Joe?"

That was Cassidy, casual—and deadly. You never quite realized when the big Masterton detective was at his deadliest. And yet Mr. Maddox had never looked more like a bland and smiling Buddha as he parried the thrust.

"Did I say that? I went in to set my watch. It had stopped."

"I see," Cassidy nodded, still smiling. "Well, so long, Joe. I'll be seeing you."

"I don't doubt it," Mr. Maddox agreed.

HE WAS smiling as he left Cassidy. The smile lasted until he was out of sight. Then Mr. Maddox wiped his face. He felt as if he might be close to a chill.

But when Mr. Maddox walked into Jimmy's place, farther up Broadway, he was smiling again.

Jimmy's place was not Broadway, unless you knew Broadway. Nothing gaudy and garish appealed to the passing public. And inside there was no entertainment. Only paneled walls, comfortable tables, booths, and good food.

But at any hour of the day or night in Jimmy's place you could find the sporting world, theatrical world, newspaper world—and often the underworld.

Nothing exciting about them, nothing to interest strangers. They would merely be eating, talking, trading gossip, information. Strangers would never guess that headlines were often planned inside the smoothly paneled walls of Jimmy's place.

Mr. Maddox was big, broadly smiling and hearty as he greeted acquaintances on his way back to a booth where Oscar was already eating.

Oscar looked up from a forkful of steak.

"Find the lug?" Oscar asked without much interest.

"Yes," Mr. Maddox said, and when a deft waiter appeared, Mr. Maddox remained standing and gave his order briefly. "Double Scotch."

Oscar's eyes widened. When the waiter was gone, Oscar asked uneasily: "Trouble, Joe?"

"Lugs," Mr. Maddox said, "are always trouble. I've got to make a telephone call."

Jimmy's telephone booths, in a back corner, were for a clientele that did much secretive telephoning. There were two booths, roomy, comfortable, absolutely soundproof. Padded stools let one sit at ease during long conversations.

Mr. Maddox telephoned the Park Avenue apartment of J.P. Allison. A maid answered, said that Miss Allison was not at home, and to another question readily said that Miss Allison was at Goshen, New York.

Mr. Maddox hung up with relief. He had been afraid Anne Allison was in town for the evening. Goshen would be an alibi that would go far toward shielding her from hasty accusation.

Not that any alibi would have countered that grisly accusation of a dying man. All Buck Allison's money could not have prevented the police taking Anne into quick custody, could not have stopped screaming headlines.

But now, for better or worse, there was time to dig into the grim mystery.

The double Scotch was waiting when Mr. Maddox joined Oscar again. And Oscar was alert now.

"What's the trouble, Joe?"

"Plenty," Mr. Maddox said as he slid into the booth. "He was dead."

Oscar gulped on his steak. "Holy cow! Sudden, wasn't it?"

"Evidently," Mr. Maddox said. "He was murdered."

Oscar choked, grabbed for the water glass and cleared his throat. "Were the cops there yet? Did anybody guess you came to see him?"

"I walked into the room and found him." Mr. Maddox eyed the big glinting diamond on his finger. "Cassidy saw me leaving the hotel."

Oscar groaned. "I had a feeling that lug meant trouble when he kept telephoning for you. Tell me—what's the payoff, Joe?"

"I don't know," Mr. Maddox confessed. He swallowed the double Scotch and let the smoky bite stay in his throat. "He had some dope about Goshen. And before he could talk, he was murdered. It must be about the Hambletonian. I'm driving back to Goshen tonight."

Oscar protested instantly. "Don't be a sap! If one guy gets himself killed, two can get killed!"

"Easily," Mr. Maddox admitted.

"You're getting set to be the next one!" Oscar warned, and leaned forward. "Joe, get some sense for once in your life! If that guy got knocked off in his hotel room, think what may happen if you stick your neck out asking for the same!"

"That," Mr. Maddox said lightly, "is what interests me. If I don't stick my neck out, maybe I'll never know."

"You're crazy, Joe!"

"Probably," Mr. Maddox agreed. "And I'm in a hurry."

Oscar looked regretfully at his steak and put his napkin on the table. "O.K., Joe. Let's go."

"You," said Mr. Maddox, "are staying here with the book. And you don't know where I am. You don't know anything about me. You don't know what I was doing this evening. Especially if Cassidy comes around asking you a lot of questions."

"Will he be around?" Oscar asked uneasily. "That big mug always means trouble."

"No telling what Cassidy will do after that body is found," Mr. Maddox said. "I want you to watch the money that shows up on the Hambletonian. And pick up any dope you can get on Roscoe Knerr."

"Joe, do you think Knerr—"

"I've stopped thinking," Mr. Maddox said. "If I'm not back tomorrow, I'll telephone you."

CHAPTER FIVE

MADDOX MAKES A BOW

GOSHEN, NEW YORK, by night, was a far cry from Broadway and Times Square. Only a few dim lights were visible at the racetrack. Most of the town was asleep. But bright lights still burned in the Old State Tavern, not far from the railroad tracks.

The Tavern was a small, old-fashioned hotel and coffee shop where Anne Allison had taken rooms. For years the Tavern had been where the harness racing fraternity congregated of evenings.

Now, a little before midnight, a phonograph was playing loudly in the coffee shop when Mr. Maddox entered. The babble of voices was noisy through drifting tobacco smoke. The unaccustomed odors of expensive powder and perfume clashed with the good honest smell of straw, liniment and horse stables usually noticeable when the harness world converged on Goshen each year.

Mr. Maddox smiled faintly as he looked about the room. The Tavern, tonight, was probably the only spot in America where cafe society could be found rubbing elbows with horse stable regulars.

Anne Allison, at a table in the back, was the reason. Friends of Anne had stayed over from the afternoon's racing or driven up from New York for the evening. Everyone else in the long, low-ceilinged room seemed to have been included in the party. And a party it was.

Tables and chairs had been pushed back to make a tiny dance floor. Talk was loud. Laughter was louder.

Some of the faces Mr. Maddox knew. An ironical smile touched his mouth as he noted the familiar grizzled mustache of Uncle Steve Bendor at the small bar with a girl who probably was no stranger to the rotogravure and gossip columns.

The girl laughed, patted Uncle Steve's arm and moved away. Uncle Steve buried his mustache in a stein of beer and was staring owlishly after her when Mr. Maddox chuckled at his shoulder.

"It's all a dream, old-timer. You'll wake up and be sleeping in the straw again."

"Huh?" Uncle Steve swiped at the foam on his mustache, and then looked foolish as he saw who had spoken. "Howdy, Maddox. Where'd you turn up from?"

"I floated in on a cloud," Mr. Maddox said gravely. "A pink and rosy cloud following a snowstorm of hundred-dollar bills, with pretty girls patting my arm and telling me what a kick they were getting out of harness racing."

"Eavesdropping ain't fair," Uncle Steve complained sheepishly. "If they want to make a circus, I ain't the one to hang back. Look at 'em, Maddox. The boys out at the county fairs wouldn't believe it. Money don't mean nothin' to them. Last night that tall blond young feller back there give Eddy ten bucks for mixin' him a drink he liked. Ten bucks!"

"That young man," said Mr. Maddox, "is Buzz McAllister, whose father controls a large piece of the rubber tire industry. Is he one of your pals now, you old stable goat?"

"Ain't no call to rub it in," Uncle Steve complained. "I'm workin' for Jonas Clearwater. And Jonas is training that horse for Miss Allison. When I'm told to hang around here nights an' answer questions, there ain't anything else to do."

"A night club entertainer, eh? I never would have thought it."

"Neither would I," Uncle Steve admitted. "But it beats washin' a horse. I never seen such goin's on or so much money spent so fast, Maddox. Big cars a-comin' and a-goin' and cameramen takin' pictures of Miss Allison an' her horse and Jonas Clearwater. And a press agent named Crown underfoot with ideas to get printed in the papers. Swells from New York comin' up to look around an' strangers everywhere askin' questions. Jonas Clearwater's got a fire in his britches. He's left the other horses on his training list to the stable help while he fusses around with that Larkspur."

Uncle Steve drained his stein and shook his head.

"You wouldn't believe it, Maddox. No siree—you wouldn't believe it!"

"A press agent and everything," Mr. Maddox murmured. "How about Tim Lonergan? Is Tim around here tonight?"

"Lonergan stays close to the barns." Uncle Steve leaned closer. "He sure don't like Miss Allison. Nor her him. It sticks out all over them when they pass at the track."

"You can't blame Tim," Mr. Maddox said absently. He was looking back at Anne Allison and thinking again how breathlessly lovely she was.

Tonight Anne wore a white linen suit. Just plain white, with the styled simplicity of genius. Every woman in the room must have envied the picture Anne made.

Her table was the center of a small group, some standing. All were hilarious. Most of them had drinks. Anne too. Half the length of the room, Mr. Maddox could see the sparkle and gaiety that made her different from the bored, beautiful girl who had come for Tim Lonergan's horse the other day. This was Anne Allison, the darling of cafe society.

IT SEEMED fantastic now to believe that Anne could be accused of anything by the dying Dandy Hoke.

But she had. And it was murder, calculated, deliberate. The bath towel through which the shot had been fired was proof.

Anne was looking toward them. She beckoned.

"She's a-wavin' at me," Uncle Steve said complacently. "More fool questions outa them friends of hers, I reckon. See you later."

But Uncle Steve had barely reached the table when a pink-faced, briskly smiling young man reached Mr. Maddox's side.

"Miss Allison tried to catch your eye, Mr. Maddox. She'd like you to meet her friends. I'm Terry Crown."

"The press agent," Mr. Maddox smiled as they started back.

Terry Crown laughed.

"We don't admit it. Press agents are supposed to be read—not thought of."

Anne was gay with her greeting, her introductions to the others around the table. A Miss Kane, a Mrs. Blythe, Loretta Rolande, who was a Broadway star and a good one.

Buzz McAllister, Mr. Maddox knew. Blythe and a Tom Fortune were strangers. Hilliard Stone, tall, dark and lean, he had heard of. Polo and yachting kept Stone in the headlines. The Stone banking interests were internationally known. And there was Eddy Hickman, thin, alert, with a slightly sardonic, chestnut-tanned face. Eddy Hickman's by-lines were beginning to be noticed in the sport pages of the *Globe*.

"You'll all have to bet with Mr. Maddox," Anne told them gaily. "He's almost a family institution. He used to be Dad's bookmaker in California before I was born."

"Friend of Lonergan's too, aren't you, Maddox?" Eddy Hickman asked slyly.

"I'm everyone's friend," Mr. Maddox told him blandly.

"How do you dope the Hambletonian?"

"There's always a chance for the best horse to win."

They thought that was funny. The Kane girl's laughter was shrill and too loud. She'd been drinking too much. Her eyes were getting glassy. But Eddy Hickman was sober. A faint smile stayed on his dark face.

"Only a chance?" Hickman asked.

"Anne has the winner," Terry Crown put in briskly. "It'll be a walk-away. The trainer's certain. How about it, Maddox?"

"I'm not Jonas Clearwater," Mr. Maddox evaded genially. "If I can believe all I read, Larkspur will win in straight heats on publicity alone."

They also thought that was witty. The Kane girl screamed with laughter.

"Anne, darling, he's precious! He's got to be my bookmaker, too! Joe, what odds will you give on Anne and Blanche Carter?"

"And this Lonergan person and the squirrelly-looking horse he's going to race?" Buzz McAllister called across the table.

"Tim Lonergan's a fine driver," Mr. Maddox told them. "You never can tell what Tim will do."

Anne had lost her smile. And abruptly she pushed back her chair and stood up.

"'Night, everybody. I'm going to bed."

The Kane girl cried protest.

"It's early, Anne! We drove clear up here to see you and waited—

and you come in for one drink and run off again. It's hardly twelve. You haven't been to bed this early since you left Miss Cattlett's school!"

"Pour them in their cars, Terry," Anne said, and waved at them, including Mr. Maddox, and ignored the further protests as she left.

"Anne was up at five this morning to see about her horse," Terry Crown explained cheerfully.

"To see about her publicity, you mean," the Kane girl corrected loudly. "This is the last time I'll drive up to see her! Come on, Tom, let's start back."

Mr. Maddox rubbed his chin and spoke to Terry Crown. "I thought Miss Allison had been here all evening."

The brisk young press agent gave him a quick look. "Anne had an errand to do and a flat tire delayed her." Terry Crown moved on around the table to speak with Eddy Hickman. He might almost have been dodging further questions.

Mr. Maddox was impassive as he walked away and entered the Tavern lobby. Anne had gone upstairs. The sad-eyed desk clerk said that Miss Allison had the three front rooms on the second floor. Her sitting-room was the middle door.

A maid opened the door when Mr. Maddox knocked. She was middle-aged, capable and brief. "Miss Allison is retiring and will see no one."

"Tell her it's Mr. Maddox and it's important."

She closed the door again. Anne herself opened it a few moments later. She had started to take her hair down and had caught it up again hastily. The flush had left her cheeks. The gaiety was gone.

"Is it so very important?" Anne asked. "I'm awfully tired."

"I hear you got up at five this morning," Mr. Maddox sympathized.

"Funny, isn't it?" Anne said. "I've often gone to bed at daybreak. Getting up so early seems strange."

"You won't find many cameramen or reporters around so early," Mr. Maddox chuckled.

Anne shrugged. She was not even trying to smile. But she was not bored now. She had changed in the last few days.

"I went to the barn," she said. "It's all strange to me—but I want to be there while Larkspur is being trained. He's so beautiful when he runs."

"That," said Mr. Maddox, "sounds serious."

Anne flushed. Her eyes hardened—if deep long-lashed eyes like hers could be said to harden.

"I said I would win. Usually I do what I promise."

"Mmmm," Mr. Maddox said thoughtfully. "Tim Lonergan was the one you promised, wasn't he?"

Anne's flush deepened. "I'll spend any amount of money to win after the way he talked to me and to the newspapermen! He's going to feel awfully foolish after the Hambletonian!"

"Money," Mr. Maddox suggested, "can't do everything."

"Money can do anything," Anne said with a finality that left no room for argument. Her hand went to the doorknob in a gesture of dismissal. "Was there anything more? I'm really very tired and I'm to be called at five again."

Mr. Maddox looked at her keenly and dropped his voice for her ears alone.

"I wonder if you're too tired to talk about Dandy Hoke?"

CHAPTER SIX

A STRANGE BEDFELLOW

ANNE CLOSED her eyes. Her hand was hard upon the doorknob, as if she needed the support. A tiny pulse in her white throat began to throb madly. And the color drained out of her cheeks as she opened the door in silent permission for him to enter.

But only the faintest tremor was in her voice as she called out to her maid in the next room.

"Mary, will you go downstairs for a little? I'll telephone down when I want you."

"Yes, miss."

They heard the door of the adjoining room open and close as the maid went out.

"Won't you sit down?" Anne asked.

She had taken a cigarette from a package on the old writing table against the wall. Her hand was steady. But she was rigidly, almost fiercely on guard, and doing so well at it that Mr. Maddox wondered if he had ever really known her.

He shook his head and remained standing.

"So you do know Dandy Hoke?" he said thoughtfully.

"I didn't say I did," Anne denied. "Who is the man? Why do you ask me about him?"

"You were in New York tonight."

"Was I?" Anne said. "And what business is it of yours?"

Mr. Maddox sighed. She was so young and lovely. Spoiled and pampered undoubtedly. But admirable too in this moment. Buck Allison himself couldn't have controlled his emotions better.

"Look, young lady," Mr. Maddox said bluntly, "I've known your father a long time. I'm not one of these scatter-brained bar-flies you run around with. This man Hoke is dead. He was shot. Murdered. And he used his finger and some of his own blood to write your name on the side of the bathtub in which he died. It's murder, do you understand? Murder! And he accused you. Now let's hear what it's all about!"

He thought then she was going to faint. No girl could have that ghastly drawn look of frozen horror and stay normal. Her whisper came forced and husky.

"*My* name was put where the police will accuse me of m-murder?"

"Yes," said Mr. Maddox grimly.

"And—and the police are looking for me now?"

"Sit down, kid. Take it easy," Mr. Maddox relented. "I don't think they are. I walked in and found the body and saw your name and washed it off before I left. You're in the clear for the time being."

It was like pouring life back into her. And Mr. Maddox could understand. Hardened old bookie that he was, he had been shaken into a cold sweat at the thought of being tied in with murder. How much worse it must be for this girl.

And then Mr. Maddox could have kicked himself for taking away the full bludgeon of fear that he needed to make her talk freely. For Anne's breasts rose with the shaky breath she caught deeply—and once more she was on guard.

"I haven't killed anyone," she denied huskily. "You can't believe I did!"

"No," Mr. Maddox admitted. "I don't think you killed him. But why did he leave your name?"

"I don't know," Anne said.

"You must know."

"But I don't!"

"You knew him, didn't you?"

Anne went to the table and pressed the cigarette out in an ash tray. She still looked ghastly, but she was calm enough when she turned back.

"I haven't admitted that I knew this man. I won't admit that I even know what you're talking about. But—but I'll tell you about a girl who has been paying blackmail over the usual indiscreet letters."

Anne swallowed and shook her head.

"They were letters to a married man. They should never have been written. I don't think they meant exactly what they seem to say. But a good lawyer could twist them into court evidence. The man's wife would see that they were used. He and his children would be dragged into an unsavory mess. He shouldn't have kept them, but he did, and they were stolen from him."

"This girl paid blackmail to help him?" Mr. Maddox asked curiously. "And he let her?"

"He had no money to pay," Anne said steadily. "It—it seemed better to do the paying and—and keep everything quiet."

Mr. Maddox shrugged. "That still doesn't say why Hoke was killed."

"I can't tell you why," Anne said again. She clenched her hands. "This man Hoke telephoned and said he had to have money quickly. He promised to give up the letters this time. He said he didn't want them any more. But he had to have five thousand dollars within an hour or so. The girl couldn't get the money that quickly. She—she telephoned her best girl friend to get it and go in her place. And the friend went to his hotel room and found him dead and had presence of mind to walk out again and—and say nothing."

"I saw her come out of Hoke's room," Mr. Maddox muttered. "So that checks. And Hoke left your name there before he died. His room was ransacked. He must have believed that you—well, the girl, if you want it that way—had him killed on account of the letters."

"But how could he?" Anne asked in dry tight despair.

"Rats like Hoke can believe anything because they'd do anything," Mr. Maddox said. "Anyway, Hoke believed it. And if those letters were in his room, they're gone now. The room was frisked by an expert."

"Do you think someone else has the letters?" Anne asked tautly.

"Evidently." Mr. Maddox scowled thoughtfully—and spoke his mind bluntly. "This girl had better tell her father. He's needed now. Murder is too serious for any girl to be up against alone."

"He mustn't hear about it!"

"If I know this girl's father, he's all right," Mr. Maddox urged. "He'll understand and help."

"No!" Anne insisted. She was twisting her hands nervously together. Tears were very close to her eyes. "He—he mustn't ever know!"

"Kid," said Mr. Maddox kindly, "I'm old enough to know what's right and what's best in a matter like this. Let me talk to him. I can make him understand."

"You'll go to him! I'll have to tell you now to stop you!" Anne gulped. "You don't understand. This—this girl has the same name as her mother. Most people would think the girl wrote those letters. Her—her mother is dead. And her mother wrote them in the year before she died. She didn't mean all she said. But it's there in black and white!"

Anne's chin was trembling as she let all pretense go.

"Father mustn't wake up some morning and find *her* name in the papers, in—in a cheap divorce court. Can't you see I'm trying to keep his memories as they are? To keep something for him that's terribly precious and dear since she died? They think I wrote the letters. But he'd know. I'll pay—I'll do anything to keep him from knowing about them!"

MR. MADDOX stood there with his throat tight also. He swore helplessly to himself. Joe Maddox had never been up against anything like this before.

You could figure out crooks. You could match move with move. You could take a chance on violence and publicity. You could always fall back on money and lawyers. But what could you do about a girl who was protecting the mistakes of her mother and the memories of a father whose grief must have been great?

Once this hit the headlines there was no hope. Anne couldn't do anything. Buck Allison would have his bitter disillusionment.

"I don't know what to do!" Anne wailed.

And now she wasn't Anne Allison, lovely sophisticate of cafe society. Anne Allison, beautiful, bored and petty about the little spites that ruffled her money-smoothed days and nights.

She was just big Buck Allison's kid, stunningly pretty. But young, very young, under her veneer of sophistication. Young, frightened, helpless in this morass of blackmail and crime that had engulfed her. And yet fiercely protecting Buck Allison and her mother.

"Who else knows about this?" Mr. Maddox asked gently. "Your girl friend, of course. Who is she?"

"Betty Garfield."

"How much does she know?"

"I told her he had letters. Betty believes I wrote them."

"Will she talk now?"

"I—I don't think so. When Betty found him dead in that room, she didn't say anything. She's level-headed. Betty met me in the Pierre lobby, where I was to go as soon as I could drive in from here. She told me what she had found. She was awfully upset. But she agreed it would be best not to say anything. I'm sure she won't, for my sake."

"I hope you know her," Mr. Maddox said under his breath. "Anyone else know?"

"My press agent, Terry Crown, knows a little. He has to know quite a lot about me anyway, to do his work right. He's very clever. I told him I was being blackmailed. He agreed it was better to pay than have bad publicity."

"Does he know Dandy Hoke was doing the blackmailing?"

"Oh, no. But I wanted Terry to understand in case anything did happen."

"Like him that much, do you?"

"Terry's job is to get me the best publicity possible. I thought he should know. And—and I wanted some advice. I had to talk to someone. Terry seemed the most logical person. My interests are his interests."

ANNE wiped her eyes and twisted the handkerchief between her hands. "What shall I do?" she asked hopelessly. "The police may have found something that will make them think I killed him. The letters might be there in the room after all. Or—or if someone else has them, what will they do?"

She was thinking clearly enough. She was right, and it made her helpless fear greater.

Mr. Maddox sighed inwardly. This was bad. Worse probably than Anne thought. But none of that showed on his face.

Mr. Maddox took her hand and patted it with a kindly gallantry that would have astonished many people who thought they knew Joe Maddox, the hard-boiled bookie.

"Kid," said Mr. Maddox, "right now you go to bed and sleep. I'll be here tonight. It probably isn't as bad as you think."

Mr. Maddox tipped her chin up. His broad face was smiling. He had never looked so big, so vastly confident, so humorous and reassuring.

"Smile," Mr. Maddox ordered. "Tomorrow it won't seem nearly so bad. I've got a hunch everything will be all right. Now let me do the worrying and go to bed."

Anne's smile was wan and pathetic—but it was a smile. Gratitude was a bright glow under her long lashes.

"It helps just to hear that and to know you'll be near," Anne confessed. "I'll go to sleep and I'll keep smiling and—and thank you, Joe Maddox."

She still had that wan smile as she closed the door.

And the sad-eyed clerk downstairs was not smiling as he shook his head.

"We haven't any rooms. Won't have until after the Hambletonian."

"Not even a bed anywhere?" Mr. Maddox questioned. "I want to stay here for several days."

"Nope," the clerk said positively. "There's even an extra bed been put in my room and rented to a newspaperman."

"Mmmm—got a room have you?" Mr. Maddox mused. "What are your rates?"

"Four dollars a day, single, until after the Hambletonian. But there won't be anything, mister. I'm sorry."

"So am I," Mr. Maddox said with genial regret. "I'd be willing to pay a fifty dollar bill for a bed for the next three or four days."

The clerk gave him a startled look, and then dipped a steel pen in ink and handed it across the counter.

"I can sleep out in the woodshed for that, mister. But you'll have to be in with that newspaperman."

"Who is he—Eddy Hickman?"

"Grasner's his name. He won't bother you. Got a bag?"

"Out in the car. I'll get it."

The little, low-ceilinged room was in the third floor attic, under the slope of the roof. A light was on inside. A man was bending from the edge of a narrow bed, taking off his shoes, when the clerk led the way in.

"This gentleman'll use my bed for a few days."

"Yeah? Packing them in, aren't—"The man broke off, staring from heavy-lidded eyes as Mr. Maddox walked in. "Make yourself at home," he said, and pulled off the shoe and dropped it on the floor.

The clerk departed. Mr. Maddox tossed his hat on the bed and took off his coat. He had never been more bland and genial.

"Maddox is the name. The clerk tells me you're a newspaperman. What paper?"

"Chicago paper," Grasner grunted. He sat there on the edge of the bed, pudgy, middle-aged, with lax, rounded shoulders. And yet somehow the man gave the impression that he had suddenly gone tense, watchful, wary.

Mr. Maddox was not surprised. Grasner and Roscoe Knerr had been well enough aware of Joe Maddox the other afternoon when they stood within ear-shot of Anne Allison and Tim Lonergan.

And now Grasner looked as if he thought Joe Maddox had taken the other bed in this attic room for some ulterior purpose.

CHAPTER SEVEN

TRICKERY AT THE TRACK

MR. MADDOX beamed in friendly cheerfulness. "I've got friends on the Chicago papers. Which one are you with?"

"*Star,*" Grasner said. He removed the other shoe. His manner was more cordial when he straightened. "I hear you're a bookie. Taking any money on these Goshen races?"

"On the Hambletonian."

"Any limit?"

"I lay off what I can't handle."

"What horse do you like?"

"Larkspur is getting a big play," Mr. Maddox said cheerfully as he busied himself getting ready for bed. "I wouldn't be surprised if he doesn't go to the barrier the favorite."

"I don't like favorites," Grasner said. "They cost me money."

The man seemed to be making an effort to be pleasant. Mr. Maddox met it with a greater pleasantness, bland and smiling. Cordiality was thick in the little attic room until the light was out.

Mr. Maddox lay staring up into the darkness, turning Grasner over in his mind. Roscoe Knerr had a wide acquaintance. Grasner might be a newspaperman from Chicago. And the Hambletonian, as the premier harness race of the year, drew interest from coast to coast.

But Mr. Maddox doubted Grasner as much as the man had apparently doubted him at first sight. He smiled grimly in the darkness at the thought that Grasner was probably lying awake wondering about him.

But there were many other things to think about. Many twisted, threatening threads that made a pattern of trouble and grief. Mr. Maddox fell asleep grappling with them.

The room clerk pounded on the door not long after dawn. Mr. Maddox swung out of bed with the feeling that he had been sleeping at the edge of disaster. And as he drove to the track through the golden wash of sunlight the feeling persisted.

Already dainty rubber-tired sulkies and the slightly heavier training carts were on the track. The fast drum-slap of trotters and the softer rhythm of leather-hobbled pacers came out of the soft gray dust in heart-warming cadence.

Fine horses. Gentlemen drivers. Crookedness had seldom touched this grandest of equine sports. All the long summer around the county fairs and the state fairs of the Grand Circuit the trotting races had thrilled thousands who seldom saw any other kind of horse race.

Here at Goshen tomorrow the season would come to a climax in the Hambletonian, for three-year trotters, with its estimated purse of forty thousand dollars. And another great name would join past immortals of trotting history like Dan Patch, Goldsmith Maid, Directum I, Uhlan and others.

Mr. Maddox stood near the grandstand and watched a drum-rush come down the stretch. The horse was brown and small, with legs that seemed too short and back that seemed too long. He seemed to run off-balance, bobbing his head awkwardly. Yet mane and tail whipped back with the speed of his running and the piston-like drive of his legs was a straight, true blur that seemed satisfactory to Tim Lonergan, sitting easily on the sulky seat.

Unlike the dainty thoroughbreds, these trotters took a lot of running to warm up, to train right. Tim made two more circuits of the track with his Candy Kid before he pulled off the track.

Tim had taken off his white dust coat, silk cap and goggles and was watching Candy Kid being taken out of sulky and harness when Mr. Maddox came up and stopped before him.

"He's good, Tim," Mr. Maddox said.

"Is he?" Tim said coolly.

Mr. Maddox sighed.

"Look, Tim, I didn't take your Larkspur. I didn't have anything to do with it. Come down off your high-horse. With a trotter like that, you've still got a chance to win your Hambletonian."

TIM'S frostiness thawed a little. He watched Candy Kid being led away. His slow smile was contented.

"The ugly little runt," Tim said. "I think he knows what it's all about. He's trotting like a champion since I lost Larkspur."

"That's all you need. That and the breaks, Tim."

"Did you see Jonas Clearwater and the Allison girl at the rail with stop watches?" Tim asked. "Jonas is running a three-ringed circus, with more money than he ever thought existed. Larkspur is a better horse than Jonas ever had in training. And Candy Kid has him worried to death." Tim's smile hardened. "Tomorrow we'll see whether she's as clever as she thought she was."

"Anne's not as bad as you think she is," Mr. Maddox said abruptly.

Tim spat. His tanned young face was expressive.

"She couldn't be," Tim said. "When I walked out of the stall the other day and saw her, I thought nobody like her could help being an angel. I could have stood losing Larkspur, for I owed the money. But the cheap publicity circus she's put on around here finished me. Look at her, coming around early now, as if she's really interested in her horse and the race. There's no place in trotting for phonies like her!"

Mr. Maddox shook his head. "She's not a phoney, Tim. She's young. She's never understood all this. She went into it like she would a social campaign. But she's not a phoney."

"Are you trying to sell her to me, Maddox?"

"What would you do with her?" Mr. Maddox chuckled. "You've got your horses and racing. You couldn't use a girl like Anne, even if she was the angel you thought she was."

"A girl like that, who understood horses—"Tim broke off, frowning, as if what he was about to say didn't belong in his mind. "Look, Maddox, since you think so well of her, tell her to keep that damn press agent of hers away. He hangs around trying to make himself agreeable. He said something about having my picture taken with her, and I almost threw him out. Tell her we're running a training stable, not a headline mill."

"I'll tell her, Tim," Mr. Maddox said. "And I wanted to ask you if you'd noticed anything suspicious around your stalls."

"No. Why?" Tim asked, staring.

"No reason," Mr. Maddox shrugged. "But there's a lot of money coming out on this Hambletonian. You can't be too careful."

Tim's smile was indulgent.

"You've been around flat racing too much, Maddox. We don't have that sort of thing in trotting." And Tim turned away to watch his horse being washed off and rubbed down before being taken out on the track again.

Mr. Maddox thought of Tim's last remark not more than an hour later when Tim brought Candy Kid down the stretch once more and into the first turn in another drumming rush.

Anne was standing there, too, in jodhpurs and dainty leather boots, the golden sun on the tawny gold of her hair and faint shadows of strain and sleeplessness under her eyes.

The New York papers had arrived without mention of a dead body. Anne had said with white-lipped strain: "They must know something. They must be doing something."

"No news is good news," Mr. Maddox had reminded.

And then Candy Kid streaked toward them and Anne forgot her troubles.

"Doesn't it make a picture?" she asked.

"That's Tim Lonergan," Mr. Maddox reminded slyly.

Anne's quick cry of horror was the only reply she had a chance to make—

A wheel of Tim Lonergan's dainty red-and-blue sulky had come off in the turn. The axle dropped down and ploughed a geyser of dirt. Candy Kid broke out of the trot and swerved fast and hard to the jerk of the reins as Tim's body rocketed off the sulky in a helpless plunge that carried him hard against the inside fence.

CHAPTER EIGHT

OUT OF THE RUNNING

IT WAS all over while Anne's cry was still on her lips. Candy Kid swerved across the track kicking at the wrecked sulky. And as Mr. Maddox went over the low fence with a smothered oath, the dust drifted away from Tim Lonergan's limp body.

Other sulkies were pulling up on the track. Men beyond the fence and at the barns were shouting, running. But Mr. Maddox, moving fast despite his bulk, reached Tim first. Anne was only a step behind.

Tim's scalp was laid open in a long gash. Mr. Maddox's keen eyes noted Tim's right leg twisted at a queer angle below the knee. A hand on the leg was enough.

"Is he dead?" Anne asked tightly.

"I doubt it," Mr. Maddox said, and he called to the first men who came running up. "His leg's broken! Better get a stretcher."

Anne had dropped to her knees and was using her handkerchief on Tim's bloody, dirty face. There was enough help present and more coming. Mr. Maddox headed at a jog trot around the turn where a driver had cut over, jumped from his sulky and stopped Candy Kid.

Men from the stables reached the wrecked sulky and trembling horse before Mr. Maddox. The gray-haired, tight-lipped driver called: "Is Lonergan hurt much?"

"Broken leg and a head cut," Mr. Maddox panted. "I think he'll be all right. How's the horse?"

Before anyone could answer an astonishingly ugly, bow-legged little man came up at a plunging run and alternately cursed to himself and crooned soothingly as he hurriedly examined Candy Kid.

This was Monk Magee, Tim's stable boss, with arms too long, shoulders too broad, bowed legs too short for the thick, powerful torso. There was something incongruous in the crooning sounds coming from that beetle-browed, flat-nosed simian face, in the almost feminine, gentle touch of great strong hands on Candy Kid's legs.

Monk cursed when the left hind leg flinched under his touch.

"Bruised himself!" Monk said, and swung around with a plunging motion that brought him to the dirt-crusted wheel spindle of the sulky that Mr. Maddox was silently examining.

Monk jerked up the side of the sulky as if it were no weight at all. His other big hand wiped dirt and grease off the spindle with one hard rotary motion of a calloused palm.

For a moment Monk stared down at the threads on the end of the spindle. Scowling blackly he looked at Mr. Maddox and started to say something. Then he thought better of it and swung back to the horse, rumbling: "Let's get him outa the shafts!"

Mr. Maddox bit off the end of a big black cigar, lighted it and turned thoughtfully away. Monk's look was enough. That lost wheel was something more than an accident.

Tim Lonergan hadn't been killed. Candy Kid hadn't been crippled. But either or both might have happened. And as it was Candy Kid's bruised leg might turn bad. And worse—Tim Lonergan would be laid up with a broken leg tomorrow when the Hambletonian field scored down for the first heat.

Alone there on the track in the bright sunlight, Mr. Maddox swore as blackly as Monk Magee.

"Tim's out of the race, damn them! Damn every crook who ever put a dirty hand on horse racing!"

The next hour was a busy one. Tim Lonergan, still unconscious, had been put into Anne Allison's big automobile and rushed to the hospital at Middleton. Mr. Maddox got the private word he wanted with Monk Magee.

"Funny that wheel didn't come off when Tim went around the track first this morning," Mr. Maddox said.

Monk's big fists clenched. His eyes were red, sultry, dangerous.

"Tim used a cart the first time. He didn't take that little fire wagon until the second breeze. I went over it myself yesterday afternoon. Everything was tight. It'll be a black day if I find who did it." Monk spat. "See about him, will ya? Tell him Candy Kid'll be all right an' I'm waitin' for orders."

Middleton was not many miles down the highway. Anne had already left the hospital. A nurse at the reception desk said that Lonergan was conscious and the doctors were setting his leg. His skull had not been fractured. He would do fine resting in bed while the leg knit.

And Tim would be in a black bitter mood at being crippled out of the race tomorrow. Mr. Maddox left a note to be delivered as soon as Tim could receive it and started back to Goshen. And the day clerk at the Tavern had news that somehow was not surprising. Grasner had checked out.

THERE was one narrow telephone booth at the back of the lobby. Mr. Maddox edged his bulk in, closed the door, and put a call through to the Chicago *Star.* He was not greatly surprised either to hear that Grasner was not known at the *Star.*

It all seemed to be part of a pattern that was shaping up fast now. Mr. Maddox chewed the end of an unlighted cigar as he called the Vardon, in New York, and asked for his suite.

Oscar answered and blurted: "Are you all right, Joe? Have they pinched you yet?"

Mr. Maddox snatched the cigar from his mouth. "What do you mean? What's happened?"

Oscar was anguished.

"Detectives were here about half an hour ago, Joe. They wanted you."

"Did they have a warrant?"

"I don't know. They didn't tell me, Joe. But they asked plenty questions! They wanted to know about phone calls we got from the Carlew Hotel yesterday. The guy who made them has been murdered. They wanted to know what business we had with him!"

Mr. Maddox swore at his stupidity. He had forgotten that the Carlew must have kept a record of Hoke's telephone calls. "What did you tell them?"

"What could I tell 'em, Joe? Calls come in all day long. He must have been asking for horse odds or something, wasn't he? They say he was registered under the name of Murray, but his right name was Hoke. I don't remember those names—and I guess you don't either, eh, Joe?"

Oscar's anguished voice was trying to say that detectives might be listening to their conversation. Mr. Maddox picked it up calmly.

"If his name was Hoke, I talked to him. He was interested in the big race tomorrow. If the detectives come back, tell 'em I'll be glad to answer any questions. Which horse in the Hambletonian has been getting the most play?"

"Peter Kline."

"I'll be seeing you," Mr. Maddox said. "Tell Shorty I'll see him soon as I get in town."

"Uh—oh, Shorty! Sure, I'll tell him, Joe."

Mr. Maddox stepped out of the cramped hot booth and reached for a handkerchief to wipe his broad, perspiring face. And he stopped at sight of Cassidy's grizzled figure standing close to the booth.

Cassidy's Panama hat was pulled low in front. A half-smoked cigarette was in his fingers. And Cassidy stood staring for electric seconds of pregnant silence.

Mr. Maddox was jumpy. It took an effort to smile.

"Surprise, eh, Cassidy? I should have left the door open so you could hear easier."

Cassidy drew on the cigarette. His eyes were cold, thoughtful. "Who were you calling, Joe?"

"Oscar," Mr. Maddox said. "Anything else on your mind?"

"I hear Lonergan's out of the race tomorrow."

Mr. Maddox nodded and stopped smiling. "Tough on the boy. The race meant a lot to him. Already he'd had his share of bad luck in losing Larkspur."

"I hear you were watching when he was hurt," Cassidy said bleakly.

"That's right."

"Spent last night here in Goshen for the first time this season, didn't you, Joe?"

"That's right again," Mr. Maddox said. And now his broad face began to harden. "So what, Cassidy? What's that to you?"

"Where's your partner, Grasner?"

"My what?"

"Your buddy. Your roommate. The clerk tells me you and Grasner bunked together last night."

Cassidy stiffened as Mr. Maddox stepped close and jabbed a big finger at his chest.

"Don't blow off your mouth!" Mr. Maddox warned coldly. "The guy's not my partner. I took the only bed they had here. I didn't know that mug was around until I walked into the room."

In long years of knowing the big Masterton detective, Mr. Maddox had never seen Cassidy's mouth from such a steel-trap line.

"Don't hand me guff, Joe," Cassidy said coldly. "This last business about Tim Lonergan is too raw! I figured you were up to something when I caught you coming out of the Carlew, where Grasner had a room. But when I hear what happened to Lonergan and find you and Grasner holed up together last night, I know you've turned dirty crook, too."

Nothing as yet about Dandy Hoke. Mr. Maddox lighted the cigar.

"Be yourself, Cassidy," he said quietly. "I don't know Grasner—but I saw him with Roscoe Knerr last week. Last night Grasner told me he worked on the Chicago *Star*. I just put a call through to the *Star*. They didn't know anything about him. Ask the clerk. He'll have a record of the call. Why should I be checking on Grasner if I was thick with him?"

CASSIDY walked over to the desk and talked with the clerk. His face was a study when he came back.

"You made the call all right," Cassidy admitted.

"Who is Grasner? What's the idea of tailing him?"

"You wouldn't hand me a gag, Joe?"

"Tim Lonergan's my friend. Or would that mean anything to you?" Mr. Maddox said brusquely.

"If it's a gag, I'll nail you, so help me," Cassidy promised evenly. "Grasner's from Chicago. He works for that Loop bookie mob that took it on the chin when their wire services were cut off. They're making a dollar any way they can now."

Mr. Maddox nodded understandingly. "Scratching around for dough on the trotting circuit, are they?"

"Our Chicago office heard rumors about the Hambletonian," Cassidy said. "Larkspur was being talked up. Confidential stuff for the suckers who like an inside tip. I was told to look Goshen over for any of the Chicago mob. And Grasner was here giving everything the business like he was a Grand Circuit regular. If he ever bothered with a harness race before, I'll pay off in boxcars."

"You're safe," Mr. Maddox guessed.

"I saw him with Knerr," Cassidy said. "That made it a stinkaroo for sure. We've had Knerr down on the book ever since we were damn sure but couldn't prove that he planned that switch at Saratoga four years ago, when Ojibway ran as Claremont and paid off at $38.40."

Mr. Maddox scowled at the memory.

"So Knerr did that? I kissed better than eleven grand good-bye on that swindle before they found that the horse was Ojibway. Solly

Baines, the trainer, committed suicide before they could put him on the carpet."

"Baines died in his automobile with a bullet in his head and the gun in his hand," Cassidy corrected. "It looked like suicide and they wrapped it up that way. Nobody ever had any different evidence. But last year Baines's girl friend told me that Baines had been drunk and sore that night and said he wouldn't be a fall guy for anyone else. He drove away and was found dead. She kept quiet while the heat was on."

"Knerr used his Roscoe again, eh?"

"Nobody's ever proved it. But when I see Grasner here at Goshen with Knerr, it's enough."

"Tim Lonergan's out of the race."

"And what good does that do?" Cassidy countered impatiently. "The layers in Chicago are being tipped on Larkspur. Which means the mob don't think this Allison girl's horse will win. If Lonergan still owned Larkspur, I'd see some sense to what happened this morning."

"Cassidy," said Mr. Maddox, "sometimes you're dumb. Smart money in New York is coming out on Peter Kline."

"Larkspur's a better horse," Cassidy snapped. "I don't have to be clubbed to figure the racket. Larkspur gets it next—and Peter Kline has the race all his own way. The Chicago bunch keeps all the Larkspur money—and the wise guys collect on the dough they've laid on Peter Kline." Cassidy's jaw shoved out. "I'll put a guard on Larkspur until the race starts! And God help those crooks if they try anything!"

"Fast thinking," Mr. Maddox said. "Didn't I hear you say Grasner had a room at the Carlew?"

"You did." And some of Cassidy's suspicion returned. "It's mighty queer you showed up there too, Joe."

"Why should I lie about it? I hadn't the slightest idea Grasner had a room there. What was he doing?"

"You're too damned innocent," Cassidy muttered. "But I don't know where the catch is about you, Joe. And I don't know why Grasner was staying at that dump. He checked in there that morning, and he'd just gone out that evening. So I went up and frisked his room. I couldn't find a thing. But he wasn't there for his health. He still had a room at the Matador."

"That," said Mr. Maddox, "is funny. But you're keeping up with him, Cassidy." Mr. Maddox glanced at his wrist watch. "Going over to the track?"

"I've some telephone calls to make. And Joe—I just hope you're on the level with me."

Mr. Maddox chuckled. "We're practically pals. You can count on me for anything. I'll see you later."

Mr. Maddox was smiling when he walked out to the car. The smile faded, his face was bleak, grim as he drove fast to the track.

Cassidy evidently hadn't heard about Dandy Hoke's death in the Carlew. When he did hear, when he learned that Joe Maddox had been in touch with Dandy Hoke about the Hambletonian shortly before Hoke's murder, Cassidy would go into action. His testimony alone could put Joe Maddox under a murder charge.

Anne Allison and Terry Crown were talking outside Jonas Clearwater's barn when Mr. Maddox stopped.

"You drove up fast enough for something to be wrong," Terry Crown called genially as they came to the car.

"I'm in a hurry to get back to Tim Lonergan," Mr. Maddox said briefly. "I've a private message for Miss Allison, if you don't mind."

"Not at all—sorry." Crown walked back and left them alone.

Mr. Maddox spoke swiftly. "The police are tracing the telephone calls that Hoke made yesterday. Was he in his hotel room when he called you?"

CHAPTER NINE

BLIND MAN'S BUFF

ANNE CAUGHT her breath. "Why—why, I never thought. They'll know he called me!"

"They will if he used his room telephone."

"Wait—I remember hearing the operator ask for more money. I heard him put it in."

Mr. Maddox exhaled a breath of relief.

"Luck," he said. "Hoke was too smooth to leave a trace of that call. You're in the clear for a little. Don't do any talking at all."

"Won't the police be looking for you?"

"They are," said Mr. Maddox. "I'll do the best I can. Cassidy, of the Masterton Detective Agency, will put a guard on your horse until the race starts. He's right. Thank him for it. Don't let Cassidy pump you. He'll try. If anything serious comes up, go to Middleton or some place where you can talk privately, call this number and ask for Shorty. He'll get word to me if it's possible."

Mr. Maddox scrawled a Manhattan telephone number on a notebook and tore it out.

"Can't I do *anything?*" Anne begged.

"Keep your head up and your mouth closed, kid," Mr. Maddox said kindly. "I'll do the best I can."

There was no sign of Cassidy as Mr. Maddox drove left out of Goshen. But he did not relax until he crossed the New York highway and kept straight ahead toward Warwick, and Hamburg over in New Jersey.

This longer, roundabout way to New York was safer for Joe Maddox this morning. Through Newark, Jersey City and the Holland Tunnel, Mr. Maddox reached lower Manhattan. Near the Pennsylvania Station he put the car in a side street garage. At the corner he bought a paper and found Hoke's murder on the front page.

A maid had found the body. The police stated it was murder. Hoke had been registered as a Donald Murray. His real name had quickly been traced by laundry marks.

That was all that seemed to be known when the paper went to press. But by now the police might know much more. Cassidy, from Goshen, might have contributed his evidence over long-distance. A general pick-up might be out for Joe Maddox.

Circumstantial evidence was damning. In the long run a murder charge might not stick. But they could hold him for questioning. They could smear Joe Maddox in the headlines.

In a Pennsylvania Station telephone booth Mr. Maddox dialed the number of Shorty's place. Oscar should be there now unless the police had stopped him.

Shorty's place was called Chez Yvonne, after Shorty's plump French wife. Years back Shorty had been Wally Cartier, a coming jockey on the Big Apple tracks. A tangle of falling horses at Havre de Grace had left Wally crippled, broke, with no chance of marrying Yvonne. Mr. Maddox had loaned money to open Chez Yvonne. Now in all the country Joe Maddox had no more steadfast friends than Shorty and Yvonne.

Oscar was there. His voice was almost a groan of relief.

"I didn't know whether they'd get you or not, Joe! Have you seen the papers?"

"I have," said Mr. Maddox. "Did you get there without being spotted?"

"I made a Seventh Avenue subway just as the doors closed, Joe. No one else got on after me. I unloaded at the next stop and got across town fast." Oscar was jumpy, apprehensive. "Joe, the cops have got you fingered. An' it's murder!"

"It's worse than murder," said Mr. Maddox. "It's a squeeze on the Hambletonian. Has Louie Menzie laid any more dough on Peter Kline?"

"Not with us. Last night I heard of two grand more he's laid with other books."

"How about Knerr?"

"I couldn't hear anything about him."

"When that rat's quietest, he's working hardest. Is Larkspur getting a play?"

"Plenty," Oscar said. "The boys over in Jersey say it's coming in heavy from everywhere. The Allison girl's publicity is bringing out the small money. And her friends are putting up plenty."

"Lay off all the Larkspur money," Mr. Maddox directed. "Take every dollar you can get on Peter Kline. Telephone around town and over in Jersey and shake some of that Peter Kline money into our book."

"That Peter Kline money's hot!" Oscar warned. "It's wise money, Joe. Roscoe Knerr and his pals must be behind a lot of it. They seem sure Peter Kline will win tomorrow. It'll put you behind the eight-ball, Joe! If Peter Kline wins, you'll be cleaned."

"I'll take a chance," Mr. Maddox said. "I'm going to try a big bluff. If it works, we'll be sitting pretty. If it doesn't, I won't need the bank-roll anyway. Now listen closely."

"Joe, don't do anything foolish! You—"

"Shut up and listen!"

Oscar listened—and at the end he was almost apoplectic.

"You can't do this, Joe! It's murder sure as anything! You won't get away with it!"

"I'll try," Mr. Maddox said calmly.

"Joe, just once listen! I know what I'm talking—"

Mr. Maddox hung up. He was sober, thinking hard as he walked through the station to the taxi ramp.

LOUIE MENZIE'S Swiss Tavern was in that boiling, busy block of Seventh Avenue just above Times Square. Two white-clad sandwich chefs were busy in the neon-ringed window. A heavy luncheon crowd was noisy inside when Mr. Maddox entered. Not a seat was available. Mr. Maddox was blandly unconcerned as he walked back and found Menzie standing at the end of the bar.

Menzie took an ivory cigarette holder from his mouth. "Hello, Maddox. How's tricks?"

Menzie had been a hoofer when the Palace was in its prime. He still had the narrow-shouldered, wasp-waisted build of a hoofer. A black, hairline mustache gave a young-old look to his narrow, cynical face. Now Menzie was suddenly watchful, as if certain this meeting was something more than chance.

"Betting pretty heavy on the Hambletonian tomorrow, aren't you?" Mr. Maddox said genially.

"One bet," Menzie replied. "And I should get better odds. They tell me I'm giving you my money on Peter Kline."

"He's trained too fine," Mr. Maddox said. "Why not switch to Larkspur? It's O.K. by me."

"I never had any luck switching bets," Menzie declined.

"I'm looking for Grasner."

"He's not—I mean I don't know the guy."

"Too bad," Mr. Maddox said regretfully. "He's being fingered and don't know it. Roscoe Knerr wouldn't be around here either, would he?"

"I ain't seen him for weeks."

"Well, I'll be seeing you."

Mr. Maddox had taken the first departing step when Louie Menzie's hand caught his arm. "Wait a minute. I just happened to think of a guy named Grasner."

"From Chicago?"

Louie Menzie blinked with growing uneasiness.

"I don't know much about him. Maybe I can find him for you. What's his trouble?"

"It probably isn't the same man," said Mr. Maddox. "I had a room with him at Goshen last night. He's kind of meaty. Looks like a slob. Never mind. It's his worry, not ours."

"Wait!" Menzie said again. He moistened his lips. "Look, I ain't the one to pass up a guy who's in a jam. I'll make a call or two. Maybe I can find this fellow."

"Got a heart as big as a boiler, haven't you, Louie?" Mr. Maddox chuckled. "Tell him I'm on my way in about three minutes—and I hope he's still not staying at the Matador."

Menzie was suddenly jumpy. "It'll only take a minute, Maddox. Wait here for me."

Menzie hurried off so quickly he bumped a waitress and made her spill soup. And he was gone not much more than three minutes. In that short time his dapper assurance had vanished. He was perspiring when he returned.

"I found him. He remembers you. Look, he's sending a hack. He wants to talk to you. Will that be all right?"

"Why not?" Mr. Maddox asked cheerfully, and walked out front and placidly smoked a cigar as he waited for the taxi-cab Grasner was sending. Fifty cabs passed that he could have taken to any address— and if it bothered Mr. Maddox, his broad cheerful face gave no sign.

When a taxi finally stopped in front of the Swiss Tavern and sounded the horn, Mr. Maddox entered it. The driver held the door open a moment longer. Another passenger jumped inside.

"This cab's taken," Mr. Maddox protested as the taxi rolled on.

"I'm riding with you, Maddox," the wiry young stranger stated as he sat back hard and watchfully in the corner of the seat.

His smile had a cold edge. He looked out the back window as the taxi whipped past two slower cars and wheeled off Seventh Avenue at the next corner. His glance slid to Mr. Maddox's impassive face and out the back window again. "Just to make sure you ain't followed," he commented.

"Grasner thinks of everything," Mr. Maddox said mildly and relaxed while the taxi shuttled fast through the midtown streets, rolled up Fifth Avenue and turned into Central Park.

The driver called back: "How does it look?"

"I don't see anything behind. Let's deliver him." The young man tossed a pair of sun goggles on the seat. "Put 'em on."

"Son," said Mr. Maddox, "my eyes are all right."

"Who'n hell said they weren't? Put 'em on. Do I have to get tough about it?"

CHAPTER TEN

MASKS OFF

MR. MADDOX shrugged and put on the glasses. The side pieces closed snugly against his face. The lenses were black and opaque. A blindfold would not have cut off sight any better. And yet the glasses undoubtedly looked innocent.

Now and then the taxi was in heavy traffic. Sometimes not. After the first few turns it was impossible to tell which way they were going. Mr. Maddox had no idea where they were when the taxi rolled over a sidewalk ramp and entered a closed space. Someone closed doors behind the taxi. Mr. Maddox was taken out, guided through a doorway, up a short flight of steps, through a hall, into a room smelling of fresh cigarette smoke, and pushed into an overstuffed chair.

Mr. Maddox took off the glasses. A faint smile came on his face as he made out Grasner's pudgy figure several steps away. "This," Mr. Maddox said, looking around, "doesn't seem to be the Matador."

Grasner was scowling. The young man who had guided Mr. Maddox into the room stood watchfully near the doorway. A jerk of Grasner's head sent him out silently, closing the door behind him.

Window shades, curtains were drawn. By the furniture this was the living-room of a house. The bright afternoon sun against the lower windows placed it as facing west.

Grasner's demand was blunt. "How'd you know I was staying at the Matador?"

"How do I know a lot of things?" Mr. Maddox said. "What'll you take for those letters that Dandy Hoke had?"

Grasner's jaw sagged. Then his face began to get red. "What letters, damn you?"

Scalp nerves prickled under Mr. Maddox's hat. Planning a thing like this was easy. But when you blasted the truth into an ugly fear-mask on your man's face, the danger was suddenly coldly threatening.

"They won't get you anything now," Mr. Maddox stated coolly. "Hoke can't use them. Maybe I can. I'll take a chance. What are they worth?"

"Damn you!" Grasner said again. His voice was thicker. "What d'you know about this guy Hoke? And letters—"

"There's that business with Tim Lonergan this morning," Mr. Maddox mused. "And that eighth floor room you had at the Carlew...."

Grasner had a soft flabby look. Now back of that look he was ugly, dangerous. But before he could speak an answer came from the other side of the room.

"Letters ain't what you'll get!"

Roscoe Knerr had his gun out as he came into the room. He had the same elegant, pallid look. The soft grate of his voice was barely threatening.

Mr. Maddox sat straighter. "Better not, Roscoe. I'm not Solly Baines."

"Why you—" Knerr stopped as a man might who suddenly found himself on treacherous ground.

Grasner moistened his lips. "Who's Solly Baines?"

"He was a trainer at Saratoga," Mr. Maddox said. "Solly could have told things if he hadn't been found dead in his car. It won't work so well with me."

Knerr's gun was a thirty-two automatic, compact, lethal. The muzzle moved slightly as Knerr stood staring. Strained indecision showed around his mouth. The soft grate of his voice spoke to no one in particular.

"I should have fixed this guy before he ever came here. But if he gets out now with his squawk, it won't be any worse than if he's knocked off now. I might as well give it to him and take a chance."

GRASNER'S flabby face was moist. "I don't like it! He went to Menzie's place and started all this. He knows too much! He asked for trouble as soon as he got here. It ain't right."

Knerr looked at the Chicago man. "You sure he wasn't followed here?"

"The boys said not."

"Then what gives? Who knows if he's knocked off?"

"How do I know?" Grasner said. "Put up that damned gun until we're sure of it."

"Look—don't tell me what to do."

All of a sudden Grasner didn't seem so pudgy and flabby. "They wouldn't like it back home if you made trouble, Knerr. The boys don't like trouble."

Knerr thought that over and sulkily slipped the gun inside his coat. "All right. What about this guy?"

"Maybe he'll talk."

"Don't make me laugh. He didn't come here to talk. Ask along Broadway how much Joe Maddox talks."

"I've made dummies talk," Grasner said.

"Listen, you Halstead Street slob," Mr. Maddox said calmly, "talk about the letters. That's why I'm here."

"Look at him," Grasner said. "Giving orders. Don't tell me he ain't rigged something. O.K., Maddox—how's about five grand for those letters?"

"Maybe. Let's see them."

"Tomorrow."

"Today. And I want to see what I'm buying."

"You ain't buying anything yet."

"I'll give you time," Mr. Maddox said. "Three hours. And I want an answer in half an hour or I won't be responsible. Hoke was murdered. They burn guys up the river for murder."

Grasner swung quickly to Roscoe Knerr. "Hear him? See it that was followed. If you've put a monkey wrench in this business—"

"Cut it," Knerr warned. "He's got ears. Put him upstairs while we talk about this."

"Half an hour," Mr. Maddox warned.

Joe, the young gunman, took him upstairs to a bedroom. At least there was a small single bed against one wall, a table, water, bucket, tin basin and towels against the other wall. The air was close and stale when Joe closed the door. And almost instantly Mr. Maddox saw that the room had no windows and only the one door.

Mr. Maddox sat on the bed and eyed an ashtray heaped with old cigarette butts on the corner of the table. One overhead light was bright. The door was heavy. The room was a nice cell that had been used before.

Mr. Maddox whistled softly. He was close to the letters. Roscoe Knerr had tacitly admitted killing Hoke. So far they were bluffed, worried, uncertain. But now what?

Oscar should have been within sight of Louie Menzie's place.

Oscar should have tailed the taxi or gotten the license number. When ninety minutes passed without Mr. Maddox telephoning Shorty, at the Chez Yvonne, Oscar was to know there was trouble.

The half hour had passed. Mr. Maddox knocked on the door—and kept knocking until a voice answered.

"Open up. I've waited long enough," Mr. Maddox called.

"Take it easy. You've got a lot of waiting to do in there."

"What is this, a snatch?"

"You guess. An' don't waste time making a racket on the door."

Mr. Maddox lighted a cigar and stretched thoughtfully on the bed. He'd had to risk this. And now, locked up, held prisoner, he could bring charges against Grasner and Knerr. He had something to use against them.

The cigar left such rank smoke in the windowless room that Mr. Maddox did not light another. When the second half hour passed he hammered on the door again. And this time he was completely ignored.

They didn't know the police should now be looking for Joe Maddox. They didn't know Cassidy had been watching the Carlew. But they did know Joe Maddox had facts unhealthy for them. They should be smart enough to make a deal. Once the letters were in Anne Allison's hands, the matter of Dandy Hoke's murder and the running of the Hambletonian tomorrow could be taken up.

Time dragged. Mr. Maddox paced the room, now and then tried knocking on the door. But it was almost six p.m. when Grasner finally came in with the young gunman named Joe and a second man, narrow-faced, watchful.

"I warned you! Do you want trouble?" Mr. Maddox snapped.

"Shut up!" Grasner retorted. He took a gun from his coat pocket, closed the door and said: "You've had your three hours and more. And what happens?"

CHAPTER ELEVEN

MR. MADDOX TAKES IT

MR. MADDOX said nothing. Grasner sneered at him.

"The cops have been to the hack garage asking questions. They went away sure that they'd been kidded. You're on your own now, Maddox. Do you know where that leaves you?"

"You tell me," Mr. Maddox said slowly.

Grasner thumbed the safety off the gun. "Behind the eight-ball, Maddox. Now we'll see how you come around here blatting your mouth so much. What was on that paper you gave the Allison girl when you chased her press agent away from your car this morning?"

Mr. Maddox sat on the bed edge and bit off the end of his last cigar.

"So that guy talked to you crooks," Mr. Maddox said thoughtfully. "Miss Allison will be interested."

"Not her," Grasner sneered. "She's got other things on her mind. Her horse ain't winning the race tomorrow. She's through with Goshen and the headlines, sucker."

Mr. Maddox's big hand broke the unlighted cigar and let the pieces fall slowly through his fingers. He was stunned and looked stunned. He hadn't expected this. And yet looking back it had come like the pieces of a puzzle falling into place. It was all very neat and logical.

"You blackmailed her with those letters," Mr. Maddox guessed. "That's why you took 'em from Hoke. You must have known that Hoke was blackmailing her."

Grasner's smile was unpleasant. He looked well pleased with himself.

"How did you know about Hoke?" Mr. Maddox said and he was talking half to himself. "Crown! That's it! Her press agent! He knew Anne was paying blackmail. But he didn't know who the man was. Anne didn't tell him. So Crown and Hoke must have had contact. And then you crooks cut in to get the letters. But this Terry Crown wasn't worried at any time. So he was playing ball with you."

"Pretty smooth, if I do say so," Grasner admitted readily. "I like set-ups like that. There's no trouble. Lonergan's out of the race. The Allison horse won't win. Peter Kline will get it."

"And in Chicago they're betting heavily on Larkspur," said Mr. Maddox. "Your mob keeps that money. And here in New York you and Knerr are laying out big dough on Peter Kline—and those bets will win."

"You're smart too late," Grasner said. "We've bet ten grand more with your book. And it'll be paid—because we'll have you to order it paid."

That meant Joe Maddox wouldn't be knocked off tonight. And it meant too that Oscar was still on the job, taking Peter Kline money as ordered. And Peter Kline was framed to win. Here went Joe Maddox's bankroll and reputation. There wouldn't be enough money to pay off.

"You lousy rats!" Mr. Maddox said quietly. "This'll backfire on you some way. You can't monkey with a good horse like Larkspur. Goshen's not a flat-race track. Those trotting men will know if Miss Allison orders her horse pulled."

"That," said Grasner, "is up to her. If there's a slug afterwards she can explain it away—or else. Now where'd you get your dope about us? Who else knows it? And tell it straight if you want to stay healthy."

"Who said I wanted to stay healthy?" Mr. Maddox growled at the Chicago man.

"Clip him, Joe," Grasner said.

Joe had been standing close with drawn gun. Mr. Maddox saw the blow start. He parried with an arm as he ducked forward. Arm met arm. The blow deflected. Mr. Maddox's big hand gripped Joe's arm and twisted as he lunged up.

Both his hands were on the gun arm an instant later. His right hand clamped down over the gun. He swung Joe around—and never finished the move....

A GUN fired close behind him. Strength went out of his left arm. Numbness struck up into the shoulder. And an instant later he was slugged with a gun barrel. Joe wrenched away. All three men jumped Mr. Maddox. He was groggy as they threw him back on the bed.

Grasner was swearing.

"Take a look at his arm! We may need him tomorrow!" Grasner panted. "I thought he had Joe's gun!"

They got the coat off, the sleeve up. Dully Mr. Maddox saw the bullet-hole, the red blood. His head felt balloon-size, whirling.

Joe hurried out and returned with a small first-aid kit. Iodine bit and burned in the wound. Layers of bandage stained red before the bleeding seemed to slacken. Then Grasner said: "All right, Maddox—start talking!"

"Go to hell!" Mr. Maddox said thickly.

Grasner hit him in the face. Curly and Joe held him.

"How'd you know I was staying at the Matador?" Grasner asked.

"Give a guess, you cheap crook!"

Grasner hit him again. It was brutal. There seemed to be no end to it. Mr. Maddox's face was cut. He stayed groggy. Matches burned him, fingers were twisted to the point of breaking. Finally Grasner gave it up in a flurry of oaths.

"He's a damn clam like Knerr said! Leave him here! I want him alive tomorrow!"

Mr. Maddox lay motionless until they were gone. His body was one great ache and pain. And under that, anger was like nothing he had ever known.

They had forgotten the small first-aid kit. Mr. Maddox carried it to the wash table and grimaced painfully at his reflection in the mirror. A wet towel cleaned his face. Adhesive closed the cuts. He decided to let the arm alone. By ignoring the pain he could use it.

Back on the bed again he relaxed and tried to think. Joe Maddox's number was up. He knew too much. He didn't have a chance. Anne Allison had yielded to blackmail. The Hambletonian was going to be run crooked for the first time. Everybody would lose.

Hundreds, thousands of small horse players in Chicago, Tim Lonergan, Anne Allison, Joe Maddox, all would lose. And Joe Maddox would lose most of all because they would kill Joe Maddox after the book paid off.

No one returned to the room. Only by his watch could Mr. Maddox tell that it was night. Hours later he slept fitfully in his clothes.

He awoke, stiff, sore, feverish, head aching badly from lack of air. Out at Goshen it was Hambletonian day. The sun was bright on banners and flags. Trotters and pacers would be out on the track. Already the first trickle of the great afternoon crowd would be on hand, little thinking that mid-western crooks had already decided the result of the Hambletonian.

In the mirror Mr. Maddox looked at a broad haggard face patched grotesquely with white adhesive. His suit was baggy and wrinkled. He looked as bad as he felt. Washing did not help.

Mr. Maddox kicked the door. No one came. He was growling with impotent rage as he rolled the bedcovers into a bundle and tossed them beside the door. He placed the one chair in the room next to the bundle and sat down.

It was nineteen minutes to eight. Thereafter the long minutes stretched into hours. Mr. Maddox sat quietly with a vast, expressionless patience few men could have achieved. It was late noon when a key grated in the lock.

Mr. Maddox had the bundle of bedclothes in his arms and was waiting silently when the door opened. Joe's voice said: "Are you still around—"

Joe was in the doorway when the bundled sheets, bedspread and pillow struck his face and chest. He yelled an oath. The gun he carried crashed loudly.

But the bedclothes were coming down over the gun and Joe hadn't yet seen his target. He was just clawing his face free when a big infuriated bear of a man was on him silently.

CHAPTER TWELVE

MR. MADDOX DISHES IT OUT

JOE YELLED again when he saw the patched gargoyle of a face. His gun jumped two futile shots into the mass of bedclothes dragging his hand down. Mr. Maddox never knew where the bullets went. He slugged a big fist into Joe's contorted face with all the fury built up through the night and morning.

Joe reeled back. Maddox grabbed the gun arm once more. This time they were alone. Joe yelled with pain as Mr. Maddox gave the arm a mighty wrench. The gun dropped.

Mr. Maddox threw him against the wall, hit him again as he reeled away. This time Joe went down and stayed.

A man was running upstairs. His yell of warning preceded him. *"Don't kill him, Joe!"*

He burst into the upper hall an instant after Joe fell. It was Curly, gun in hand and ludicrous surprise showing at sight of Mr. Maddox snatching Joe's automatic off the floor.

Curly fired one shot as Mr. Maddox got the gun. Then bolted back down the stairs. Mr. Maddox lunged after him. In the hallway downstairs Curly fired a shot back.

The bullet chipped plaster down on Mr. Maddox's face. But his plunging rush down the stairs did not stop. Curly bolted into the adjoining room. But he lost time.

It was the living-room. Curly's foot slipped on the rug. He caromed off a chair and tried to turn. And the flying bulk of Mr. Maddox drove into him. The automatic Mr. Maddox carried buried half its length in Curly's side.

"Drop it!" Mr. Maddox rasped.

Curly dropped his gun as he brought up hard against the wall. "Don't do it! For God's sake, Maddox! Don't shoot!"

"Who else is in the house?" Mr. Maddox demanded.

"No one!"

The feverish, swollen left arm hurt badly as Mr. Maddox man-handled the young gunman away from the wall. He paused long enough to get the second automatic off the floor. Then, gun in Curly's back, Mr. Maddox grated: "Where's Grasner?"

"I don't know!"

"Don't lie to me!"

"Him and Roscoe Knerr's been gone all night! I don't know where they are! This is just a place Knerr comes now and then! My wife and I live here!"

"Where is this house?"

They were in New Rochelle. The thin-faced threat had gone out of Curly. He was shaking, looked like he was telling the truth.

"What about those letters?" Mr. Maddox demanded.

Curly shook his head. "I never seen them."

"Get upstairs."

Joe was stirring weakly on the floor. "Drag him in the room," Mr. Maddox ordered.

Curly obeyed, grunting with the effort. Mr. Maddox locked the door, went downstairs and telephoned the Vardon Hotel, without much hope of finding Oscar. But Oscar was there.

"Joe! I thought you were a goner! Where are you? What happened?"

"No thanks to you!" Mr. Maddox said scathingly. "Did you think I was out picking violets?"

"Joe, I saw you get in that taxi. I got the license number. The cops checked on it when I called them. The taxi with that license number had been in the shop two days for repairs. The tags were on it. They hadn't been out of the garage. Somebody had duplicate tags. The cops thought I was pulling a phoney. They almost pinched me."

"Maybe they should have," Mr. Maddox said sourly. "What about Hoke's murder?"

"Nothing new about it by today's paper."

"How much money have you taken on Peter Kline?"

"A hundred and twenty-three grand. I got all I could like you told me, Joe. I figured you knew something."

MR. MADDOX snapped: "I still know something. Peter Kline's due to win. We're sunk. Don't take any more money. Close the book."

Oscar's stricken silence spoke for itself.

"If you get track of Roscoe Knerr call the cops," Mr. Maddox said. "They'll want him. I'll see you later."

"What are you going to do, Joe? Miss Allison telephoned half of last night."

"What do you think? Stop that crooked race!" Mr. Maddox snapped, and hung up and then called Anne Allison, at Goshen. The Tavern clerk reported Miss Allison out. Swearing, Mr. Maddox looked at his watch. Time was short. He called the New York City Police, asked to be connected with Homicide, and spoke to a Lieutenant Jefferson.

Mr. Maddox spoke distinctly, calmly. "Take this address please.... This is Joseph Maddox. I'm staying at the Vardon Hotel. I've been locked up here all night by men responsible for killing Dandy Hoke at the Carlew Hotel. I've locked two of them in an upstairs room. They're taking orders from Roscoe Knerr and a man named Grasner, from Chicago. The Masterton Detective Agency will tell you about them."

"Anything more?"

"The guns these two men had will be under the telephone stand here. The key to the room they're in is under the telephone. I'm stepping out where I'll be safer, Lieutenant."

Mr. Maddox guessed he had several minutes start. He was lucky. Two blocks away he met an empty taxi and stopped it.

"Goshen," Mr. Maddox told the driver.

"Where?"

"The racetrack at Goshen. Go over the Bear Mountain Bridge. And I'm in the devil of a hurry."

It was a wild ride with Mr. Maddox urging the driver faster and faster, while the watch hands seemed to race. And Mr. Maddox was sweating with anxiety when the track flags and banners came into sight to the right of the highway.

"Hurry up!" Mr. Maddox said hoarsely.

Late as it was, automobiles were still arriving. Parking space was far from the grandstand. Mr. Maddox overpaid the driver ten dollars and left the taxi with an eighth of a mile to cover on foot.

He was sweating when he burst into the grounds. And he had not taken a dozen steps when a heavy hand fell on his arm and he was jerked around.

"I wondered if you'd have nerve enough to try a sneak in here this afternoon," Cassidy said with sarcastic satisfaction. "You're pinched and don't give me any guff about it!"

CHAPTER THIRTEEN

THE RACE TO THE SWIFT

I **I** *WOULD* have to run into you!" Mr. Maddox snarled. "Listen, you dumb flatfoot—this is serious! I'm in a hurry! Make your pinch later!"

Cassidy's jaw pushed out stubbornly. "Don't waste your breath! What a sucker you made of me yesterday! I hope they throw the book at you!"

"Are they running the Hambletonian?"

"First heat coming up."

"I've got to see about it!"

"Don't make me laugh, Joe. I didn't turn you in to New York Homicide because I wanted to grab you myself. Here—ain't this blood on your sleeve?"

"I've got a bullet hole there that hurts like hell when you paw it! But I've got no time to talk about it now! I've got to see Miss Allison before the race starts!"

Cassidy's angular face was a study—and then Cassidy shrugged and growled: "Come along. She's got a box. But no tricks, Joe!"

The murmuring excitement of the was like surf on a long beach. The mounting suspension could be felt like an electric charge in the air as they pushed to the front of the grandstand.

"Here we are," Cassidy said. "Make it snappy."

The Allison party filled the box in front of the grandstand. Buzz McAllister was there, and Crown, the pink-faced young press agent, and Loretta Rolande, the Broadway actress, and several older people Mr. Maddox did not know.

And Buck Allison was there and saw Mr. Maddox first. "Hello, Maddox. Sorry there's not a seat for you."

Anne heard, looked quickly and got up and came out of the box. The field was turning at the upper end of the track. The long breathless count of fourteen would be starting as the horses came back to meet the barrier.

"I tried and tried to get you," Anne said. "What happened?"

"You can't do it, kid," Mr. Maddox said under his breath. "You've got to win this race if you can."

"Oh! You know about it?"

"I know who's got the letters—but I couldn't get them in time. Your horse has got to win if he can—those letters will have to hit the headlines if it breaks that way," Mr. Maddox said grimly.

Anne's queer crooked little smile might have meant anything.

The eight horses in the race were almost to the barrier. The judges were tensely watching the count... twelve, thirteen, fourteen—the barrier shot up.

Larkspur was fourth from the rail, a bit slow on the start, half a head behind the leaders. But Larkspur's driver looked cool, unexcited as he gripped the reins and hunched almost lazily on the sulky.

Mr. Maddox turned speechlessly to watch the sulkies skimming through the dust haze into the turn.

"That looks like Tim Lonergan behind Larkspur!"

"Oh, watch him! Watch him come up!" Anne gasped. "Look at Tim drive! I knew he could do it!"

"Tim's got a broken leg!"

"It's in a cast," Anne said. "Tim insisted."

"Insisted?" said Mr. Maddox dazedly. "Tim Lonergan insisted on driving your Larkspur while his leg was broken?"

Along the backstretch and into the far turn those magnificent trotters flew. The crowd was coming to its feet. All eyes were on the horses and sulkies when Mr. Maddox jumped to the box entrance and grabbed Terry Crown, the press agent, who was unobtrusively leaving.

"Stick around, son!"

Terry Crown twisted violently, would have run had Mr. Maddox not yanked him stumbling back to Cassidy, who had forgotten everything but the race.

Cassidy looked around angrily at the rude interruption.

"Pinch him, Cassidy!" Mr. Maddox said. "He's working with Grasner and Roscoe Knerr. And here's where I win a hundred and twenty three grand!"

Mr. Maddox said it before he looked. And he just had time to look past Terry Crown and see Tim Lonergan driving Larkspur to the finish, half a length ahead of Peter Kline.

And Tim, up out of a hospital bed, with his broken leg stiff and straight in front of him, would take the second heat too, with that great horse Tim had raised from a colt. Sometimes you knew such things before they happened.

Mr. Maddox turned to Anne, who had tears in her eyes as she laughed up at him. "How did it happen?" he asked.

Anne's smile faded at the memory.

"A telephone call told me what I had to do. I said I would do it—and I couldn't. I couldn't do it to Larkspur. He had a right to win if he could. I went to the hospital and tried to give him back to Tim. He wouldn't take Larkspur back. So I told Tim what I'd promised to do and said I'd win anyway with Larkspur if I could, and it didn't matter who got hurt. I telephoned father right there and told him all the truth. And he said I was right."

"And what did Tim say?"

"Tim asked me to marry him," Anne said.

Cassidy's hand fell on Mr. Maddox's shoulder.

"Joe! This guy is talking already! Maybe I was a little hasty! Maybe your trouble can be smoothed out."

"Trouble?" Mr. Maddox said. "Who's got trouble after all the money I'm making today?"

Friends had surrounded Anne and were congratulating her. Mr. Maddox had to shout over their heads.

"Miss Allison—*what did you tell Tim?*"

"I told him I would!" Anne called. "What else could I tell that big noisy darling? He wouldn't have listened."

www.ingramcontent.com/pod-product-compliance
Lightning Source LLC
Chambersburg PA
CBHW061518020726
47502CB00006B/2135